The Missing Family

The Missing Family

TIM WEAVER

MICHAEL JOSEPH

MICHAEL JOSEPH

UK | USA | Canada | Ireland | Australia
India | New Zealand | South Africa

Michael Joseph is part of the Penguin Random House group of companies
whose addresses can be found at global.penguinrandomhouse.com.

First published 2024
001

Copyright © Tim Weaver, 2024

The moral right of the author has been asserted

Set in 13.5/16pt Garamond MT Std
Typeset by Jouve (UK), Milton Keynes
Printed and bound in Great Britain by Clays Ltd, Elcograf S.p.A.

The authorized representative in the EEA is Penguin Random House Ireland,
Morrison Chambers, 32 Nassau Street, Dublin D02 YH68

A CIP catalogue record for this book is available from the British Library

HARDBACK ISBN: 978–0–241–58691–4
TRADE PAPERBACK ISBN: 978–0–241–58692–1

www.greenpenguin.co.uk

In Memory of John Adams

PART ONE

00:00:42

POLICE: . . . and I work in the Major Crimes
Unit. The time is 9.17 p.m. For the tape,
could you please state your full name?

RAKER: David Raker.

POLICE: David, I need to inform you that
this interview is being both audio and
visually recorded and may be given in
evidence if a case is brought to
trial. Do you understand that?

RAKER: I do.

POLICE: Thank you. As I just mentioned,
my name is Detective Inspector
Phillips, but if it would make you
more comfortable, you can call me
Aiden. We've got a lot to get
through, but I'd like to start by
asking you how - and where - all of
this began.

RAKER: It began how it always does for me.

POLICE: And how's that?

RAKER: With a missing person.

One Year Ago

After they arrested him, they took the suspect down to the basement.

It was vast, a maze of nearly identical corridors and entrance-ways. Some of the doors had nameplates on but most didn't, and it would have been impossible for an outsider to memorize the layout. They could see that he was attempting to, could see that his eyes were going to the minimal signage that existed down here, trying to anchor himself to something – anything – a mental trail of breadcrumbs that would help him find a way back out again.

The two men either side of him knew exactly where they were going. Linkers and Ramis were long-time employees of the Skyline Casino and Resort and knew the layout of the base-ment intimately. Linkers had just celebrated his fourth year in the job; Ramis had been here since the Skyline opened in 2008 and was the most senior member of security. Before this, he'd done twenty-five years in the Met.

Ramis glanced at the suspect.

He hadn't been on shift when the guy had actually been arrested. Instead, he'd arrived fifty-five minutes later, after a 2 a.m. call from Linkers saying the suspect had returned to the casino and was now seated at one of the blackjack tables. Ramis had immediately told Linkers to arrest the man, get him away from the public and into a side room. Linkers had done as Ramis had asked.

It had taken Ramis almost an hour to get to the casino. At home, he'd had to pause at the edge of the bed, bones aching, head full of static, before hauling himself into the shower. It had been like this for a while. He was a week from retirement and knew, even if his mind was still fast, his body was calling time on the late nights, irregular hours and constant stress. As he'd dressed, his wife had told him gently that he didn't have to go in. But he said he had to be there.

'I need to be in when the cops arrive,' he explained. 'This is the guy.'

Lorna, his wife, didn't need to know more than that.

Ramis was still aching a little now, over an hour on, but he pushed it all down. They'd almost arrived at the holding cells, four consecutive rooms that looked exactly like cells in a police station: small spaces with a bench, and a reinforced glass panel – covered by a sliding steel plate – embedded in the door.

The cells were empty.

There had been no other incidents so far tonight.

Linkers opened the cell closest to them. As he did, Ramis glanced at the suspect again. He estimated the guy to be in his mid-twenties, although Ramis had never been great at ages. People aged differently based on the comforts they'd gone with or without, the kinds of lives they'd had. The suspect returned the look, and Ramis could see the man's eyes were a deep blue. The guy was handsome, he supposed.

'Can we get you a drink?' Ramis asked.

The man shook his head. 'No, thank you.' His voice was quiet. Ramis guided him into the windowless room, sitting him down on the padded bench. Everything smelled of disinfectant. Mostly, people ended up in here because they'd been caught trying to cheat the casino, or were drunk. Sometimes there were pickpockets, or small-time con artists working gullible patrons, or sex workers in the bars pretending they were hotel guests.

But they'd never had anyone like this guy.

Never a cold-blooded killer.

Linkers pushed the door shut and turned the handle ninety degrees to the left. Another clunk as a heavy-duty deadbolt locked into place.

Ramis and the man stared at each other through the glass panel, and then Linkers pulled down the steel plate. Ramis could no longer see the man but, softly, he thought he could hear him crying. He glanced at Linkers, whose expression seemed to echo his own. Somehow this felt different from what they'd expected. The man seemed smaller and more vulnerable than they'd imagined – a frightened animal trapped inside a six-by-seven room, with no window, an unbreakable steel plate, and a door that could withstand 250 pounds of pressure before it even shifted a centimetre.

This guy had butchered a man and stolen his money.

Now it was all over.

It seemed such a perfunctory ending.

There was a kitchen opposite, and Ramis started the coffee machine. In the meantime, he told Linkers to get back up to the casino floor and meet the two detectives from Thames Valley Police. As Ramis waited, he went to an app on his phone that his daughter had downloaded for him, which contained articles he'd saved from newspapers and websites. He loved current affairs, loved knowledge, and especially liked to be up to speed on the things young people were talking about, because that way he could seem more interesting to his children and grand-kids. He was midway through an article on an actress he knew his daughter loved when he heard a voice from the cell.

'Sir?'

Ramis decided to ignore the man.

The police would be here soon.

They could deal with him.

*

Ten minutes later, Linkers and the cops entered the corridor.

Linkers did the introductions.

Detective Inspector Bakhash. Detective Sergeant Clarkson.

Bakhash's eyes went to the holding cell. 'We appreciate what you've done here. If you two hadn't been on the ball, we might never have bagged him.'

'I was in bed,' Ramis said, 'so all the thanks should go to Neil.'

Linkers broke out into a smile. The younger man was chuffed with the praise from Ramis. He was a nice kid. Ramis nodded at him and gestured to the cell. Linkers grabbed the keys from his pocket and began to unlock the door.

The mechanisms clicked and released.

Bakhash stepped into the open doorway.

'What's going on?' he said.

To start with, Ramis thought he was talking to the suspect.

But then Bakhash glanced back across his shoulder at Ramis. 'I said, what's going on?'

The two security men moved closer; Ramis saw Linkers stiffen, heard him mutter, 'What the hell?'

And then Ramis stepped all the way inside the cell.

'I don't . . .' Ramis trailed off. 'I don't understand.'

The cell was empty.

The killer had vanished.

Now

I

The Empty Boat

I

I parked my car in the same spot the Fowlers had left theirs eight months ago.

It was May and the sun was out, but the temperature hadn't quite caught up: it still felt like early spring, a cold wind whipping in off the moors, a sea of yellow gorse close to the road shivering in the breeze.

The road I'd parked on ended twenty feet ahead of me at an old wooden gate. On the other side was the stone path that eventually led to the quarry. It was hard to see much of Dartmoor on my right because of a large, ragged tor, but on my left the moorland swept away from me in waves, a vast, undulating ocean of brown grass, grey crags and wind-battered trees.

I locked the car and headed to the gate.

It happens the September before.

It's a Sunday and the five of them have driven up early from their home in Totnes. The drive takes just over an hour. There's no parking close to the water, so they have to leave the car in a lay-by on the nearest road and walk the rest of the way, following a winding stone track half a mile up to the quarry. Marc and Kyle carry the boat between them, chairs loaded up inside, Clara has the towels, Sarah the cool box, and two-year-old Mable totters along behind them all.

It's a warm day, more like summer than autumn, the skies a pristine blue, and even on the elevated peaks of Dartmoor, there isn't a breath of wind. When the five of them finally arrive at the quarry, the lake is still in shadow, the ragged wall of granite on its eastern flank so high that the sun hasn't yet crested it. There's an almost identical sweep of speckled granite on the western edge, except this gently curves in an L-shape, creating a natural amphitheatre around the lake. The cliffs that encircle the former quarry are dramatic and beautiful, and that beauty is complemented by the tranquillity of the lake itself: once, Parson's Quarry had been a vast tin mine, crumbling miners' huts still scattered at its edges; now it's one of the best wild swimming spots on the moors.

That's exactly why the Fowlers have always loved it here.

It's why they're here today.

But, by sunset, three of them will have disappeared.

It took me just over twenty minutes to walk from the car to the mouth of the quarry, so it would have taken the Fowlers longer as the two men had been carrying the boat, and Sarah would have been constantly waiting for Mable to catch up.

After the initial dip into the ravine, the approach was almost all ascent, which would have added minutes too.

I looked around me on the way up, but there wasn't much to see: the climb had a hidden, secluded feel, views of the rest of Dartmoor obscured by steep hills and banks of trees and the skeletons of old miners' huts.

At the top, the quarry almost seemed to appear out of nowhere. The cloud-scudded sky was like a roof over it all, and as the trail faded under my feet and I moved on to the grass banks that fed down to the edge of the lake, it was as if I'd entered some secret chamber.

I understood straight away why the Fowlers had loved it here.

Other families begin arriving at the quarry an hour after the Fowlers have set up, but what Marc and Sarah have always adored about this place is how — even on the sunniest days — it's never packed. That's partly because a lot of people still have no idea it's a wild swimming spot. But it's mostly because there are only seven parking spaces in the lay-by, and the next nearest place to leave your car is over two miles away.

16

The sun crests the eastern flank of the quarry just after ten, and Sarah spends the rest of the day running around, applying lotion to Mable, who in turn immediately tries to wipe it off, gets it in her eyes, and then starts to cry because it stings. Sarah perches a chair at the edge of the water and she and Mable build mud-castles, throw a beachball around and paddle together, while the others repeatedly get out on the lake. Mable has arm-bands on, even though she's not keen on the water – but Sarah's not one for taking risks. At nineteen, she took a drunken risk with her then-boyfriend, and nine months later Kyle was born.

'Marc, you coming out again?'

Sarah looks up to see Kyle handing Marc an oar.

'I need to stay here with your mum, mate,' Marc says, glancing at Mable, who is fully into the clingy stage and throws a tantrum if Sarah isn't nearby. Sarah has been on toddler duty for almost eight hours, and Marc has prom-ised her that he's going to attempt to take the reins for a while to give her a few minutes to herself. 'Plus, we should probably start packing up in a bit,' Marc adds.

'Ah, come on,' Kyle responds, and throws the oar to Marc.

Marc has no choice but to catch it.

He looks at Sarah.

The other families that were here earlier have gone now, and much as Sarah likes it here, she's more than ready to go home.

'Please, Mum,' Kyle says, and gestures to Clara, at the sling she's sporting. 'My shipmate's injured, and the dinghy's so awkward without two of us rowing.'

Sarah wants to say no.

Instead, she says, 'Okay. But don't be long.'

'We'll just go to the middle and back,' Marc says.

'And make sure he doesn't drown,' Sarah tells Kyle, nodding at Marc.

Marc pretends to be offended, but Kyle and Clara both laugh. 'Bloody cheek,' Marc replies good-naturedly, and sits down in the boat.

Kyle and Marc grab an oar each and start to row the three of them out. The dinghy is just under fifteen feet long, but unlike many boats of its size, *it doesn't have a motor, making it easier to transport. Instead, Marc paid to have a clip-on roof put on to the back, so, if either he or Sarah take Mable out, she can sit in the shade. The roof also has roll-down sides that can be untied and dropped to provide further protection from the sun, and as the men continue to row out, Sarah can just make out Clara behind the yellow plastic. Her body is slightly favouring the left, some of the bandaging on her shoulder visible beneath her beach dress.*

Sarah checks her watch and collapses into her chair.

She's so tired.

Mable wanders over and climbs into her lap.

I went all the way down to the shore.

There was no one else here, just as there hadn't been at 6 p.m. on that Sunday in September. I was right in the middle of the shoreline – perfectly centred between the east and west sides of the quarry, which were about 200 metres apart – knowing that this was roughly where Sarah had been seated with Mable as the others had rowed out. North to south, the lake was slightly bigger – about 300 metres end to end – so when the dinghy finally came to a stop in the centre of the lake, it would have been a minimum of 100 metres away from land. I also knew that – exhausted from a day of running around after a two-year-old who wouldn't leave her side – Sarah had been unable to keep her eyes open and dozed off for less than a minute as Mable sat in her lap playing with some toys.

But less than a minute was all it took.

Sarah's eyes ping open.

Mable isn't on her lap any more. Her toys are scattered on the floor and she's hitting her spade against the arm of Sarah's chair, trying to get her mum's attention. Sarah sits bolt upright, squeezes her eyes shut and tries to wake herself.

She glances at her watch and feels a wave of relief. She dropped off for less than a minute. She's been aware of the sounds around her the whole time too — the water lapping at the shore, the birdcalls — but it doesn't bring her any comfort. Because when she looks at Mable — how small she is, at her nappy — Sarah realizes her daughter could have easily wandered off. She could have drowned, even with the armbands on.

She grabs Mable and brings her in for a hug. Mable tries to wriggle out of it, but Sarah holds on and it's as if the two-year-old realizes her mum may need this moment, because she settles, presses her head against Sarah's chest and goes quiet.

Sarah's gaze switches to the lake.

The dinghy is right in the middle now. It's come to a stop, the back of the boat facing her, Marc, Kyle and Clara obscured by the clip-on hood.

All around the boat, the lake is still, the surface like glass.

Sarah frowns, steps forward.

Something isn't right.

She moves down to the edge of the lake. One of the oars has become detached from the boat and is gently floating away. And as the oar drifts, as a throbbing at the back of Sarah's head tells her that something here is definitely wrong, the dinghy starts to turn, the point of the bow edging around in her direction.

That's when she sees that there's no one under the roof.

In fact, there's no one on the boat at all.

2

The Fowler house was a mile outside Totnes, built on the slope of a hill. The garage was at the top, just off a steep, narrow lane, and everything descended from there: the garage gave way to the back garden, and then the garden gave way to the house. There was another lawn at the very bottom, and then a gate. That had been the entrance I'd used the day before, when I'd first come to talk to Sarah – and, just as had been the case twenty-four hours earlier, in a private lay-by behind the gate, a BMW X5 and a trailer were parked up.

Sarah had left the garage open, so I pulled in next to a Mini and got out. The garage had the orderly chaos of a typical workshop, tools scattered everywhere, shelves full of nails, and – in a nod to Marc's career in engineering – unidentifiable machine parts. There was a bike against one wall and two air rifles in a rack on another. Wedged into the rack was a crinkled photograph of Marc and Kyle in a forest somewhere, holding their rifles. They were both wearing ill-fitting tweed suits. Kyle was smiling, looking down in apparent disbelief at what he'd been forced to wear; Marc was laughing hard, head back, eyes creased up, his arm around Kyle's shoulder. But none of that caught my eye as much as a calendar pinned above the workbench, a picture of the whole Fowler family on it.

It was still set to September 2022.

I headed down the slope to the house, knocking on the side door. As I waited, I looked at the BMW again. It was obvious that Sarah hadn't used it in the eight months since the disappearances at the lake. It wasn't just that the trailer remained attached to it. It was that the dinghy was still on the trailer.

Sarah opened up.

'Oh, hi, David,' she said, wiping her hands on an apron.

She gestured for me to follow her inside. She was in the middle of cleaning the kitchen. On the stove, some pasta was boiling. Off the kitchen was a playroom: I could hear a TV on in there, tuned to a children's show.

'Sorry about the mess. I'm trying to make Her Majesty's lunches for the next few days, as I'm going to an event tomorrow and Thursday and she's staying with my mum. Do you have kids?'

'One. A daughter.'

'So you remember the fussy stage?'

'Actually, no. I missed that part.'

She looked at me, clearly not sure how to respond.

'I didn't mean to pry.'

'You weren't,' I assured her. 'So Mable likes pasta?'

'It's pasta every time with her. She used to eat anything – you'd put it in front of her and she'd wolf it down. But since . . .' She paused. *Since September.* 'It's been . . .'

Her voice faded, her body shrinking a little.

'It's been different,' I said.

'Yeah. I mean, first week or so I pretended that her dad and brother were on holiday. But then, eventually, I told her the truth . . .' Again, she ground to a halt. 'After I told her that I didn't know where her dad and brother were, where Clara was – and she *loved* Clara – or when any of them were coming home, things slowly started to change. I don't know how much she understands – but she understands enough. She can see Marc and Kyle aren't here and I can tell it's unsettled her. She's started having tantrums, hitting me. That never happened before.'

21

She managed a smile so full of pain and grief it was like looking in a mirror. I'd been in moments like these when my wife died; I'd pushed out that same smile again and again, trying to reassure the people around me that I was fine, that I was coping. But it had all been a lie. After a while, you got better at hiding your wounds, and you didn't cry as often, but you were never the same – not when a scent, or a song on the radio, or driving through a place they used to love, could instantly reduce you to rubble.

Yet, hard as it was, as much as I missed my wife, it was still better than what Sarah was dealing with: her husband, her son and her son's girlfriend had been gone for eight months – and she still had no idea what had happened.

'Did you go and see it?' she asked.

'I drove up there this morning.'

'What do you think?'

'I can see why you liked it there so much.'

'But do you believe me?'

'I believed you from the start.'

'I know. I meant . . .'

She stopped.

She looked around the kitchen, her eyes lingering on a photograph of her and Kyle, framed and sitting on a shelf. The frame had a red wooden heart carved into it.

'What I mean is, can you see what I was talking about now?'

Sarah had spent most of the previous day reiterating the same thing to me over and over: how long she'd slept for at the side of the lake. She claimed it had been less than a minute, was adamant about it, said she'd checked the time as she'd sat down and her watch had read 18:17. When Mable woke her up by smacking her spade against Sarah's chair, it was 18:20. That was three minutes – but she hadn't fallen sleep immediately and reckoned two minutes must have passed before she did.

I was waiting for the missing persons report for Marc, Kyle and Clara, but from initial discussions I'd had with a source, it was fair to say the investigating team from Devon and Cornwall Police had doubts about Sarah's claims. After they arrived at the scene, they said Sarah was 'frantic, upset and in an elevated state of panic', and she hadn't mentioned the specific timings – 18:17 and 18:20 – until the next day in an interview room, even though she'd had the opportunity to tell them about it at the quarry. The inference was clear: they didn't necessarily think she was lying, they just thought she was mistaken. They kept coming back to the same thing: the lake was 75,000 square metres, so how could three people vanish from a boat in the middle in under sixty seconds?

Yet, despite that, I had meant it when I said I believed Sarah. Her grief was written into her skin, and that was powerful testimony. But so too was her strength, her resolve, the absolute certainty of what she was convinced she saw.

My watch said seventeen minutes past six. I'm not mistaken.

Her family didn't drown, something that police divers had confirmed in three separate extensive searches over the following four weeks. They definitely didn't swim to the sides either, because not only would there have been nowhere near enough time to do that in the minute Sarah said she had dozed off for, but Clara had been unable to swim that day anyway.

Two weeks before, she'd torn her rotator cuff.

She would have had to swim with one arm, slowing her down even more, or one of the men would have had to take her with them – and that would have slowed *them* down. It was 100 metres from the centre of the lake to the east and west flanks of the quarry, and the fastest time ever recorded for a professional, Olympic-standard swimmer doing that distance was forty-six seconds. There was no way they could have crossed the water inside the minute Sarah was out.

Yet, when Sarah woke up, her husband, her son and his girlfriend were gone. The boat was empty.

And now the question wasn't only how.

It was why.

3

We moved through to an extension, where the living room was.

It was stunning, like everything else in the house. I couldn't even guess how much it had cost to create a home that looked like this one, but it underlined how well Sarah and Marc had been doing. Except every room, every piece of furniture, the skylights and the expensive sofas, clearly meant nothing to Sarah any more. Money had no meaning without people to share it with. She simply passed through the rooms like a wraith.

We sat and I took out my notebook.

'You've got a beautiful home.'

'Thank you,' she said. 'We always loved it.'

Eight months of disrupted sleep and unanswered questions had taken its toll on her – her eyes were bloodshot and she looked exhausted.

'You and Marc had just celebrated your four-year anniversary, right?'

'Yes, two weeks before,' Sarah said. 'Well, wedding anniversary. We were together for almost seven years before we got married. It was eight or nine months after we got married that we bought this place.' She looked around her. 'It seemed like such a good idea at the time.'

'But not any more?'

'The mortgage is big . . .' She paused. 'After he vanished, Marc's company were good for the first three months. They agreed to pay his full wages. Then it went to fifty per cent. Now it's nothing. And I can't trigger our life insurance policy or his pension because Marc hasn't officially been declared dead.'

The word *dead* vibrated in her throat. 'I'm running out of money,' she said quietly, before realizing what that might make me think. 'Don't worry, I've got enough to pay you.'

This was where missing persons cases were unique, where they diverged from other tragedies: with no answers, there was no conclusion.

'Marc worked in aeronautics, is that right?'

'Yes. He was a director at an aerospace company.'

'That was here in Plymouth?'

'Yes. But he worked up in Bristol for years, at the MOD. His thing was guidance systems. That was what he specialized in. He was super smart. He was offered this huge university scholarship when he was eighteen. There was no way his parents could have afforded to send him to uni otherwise. But, obviously, by the time we started dating, that was all ancient history – he'd already moved back here to work for his old boss, who had set up a company in Plymouth. I'll be honest, a lot of what he did just . . .' She ran a flat hand across the top of her head, indicating that Marc's work was beyond her. 'It was like a foreign language. He loved it, though. He was happy, I was happy.'

Something lingered in her face, and I knew right away what it was: she wanted those moments back. She wanted Marc to sit here and tell her about his day, about all the things she didn't understand in his job.

'You've made a good career for yourself too,' I said.

'Yeah, I've been really lucky,' she replied, and then wavered.

Lucky. What was lucky about any of this?

'You've written five books?'

'Five *published* books, yes.' She smiled. 'I have another three manuscripts in a box up in the loft which will never see the light of day. Mainly because they're awful.'

'And you do it full-time?'

'Yes. I don't make mega-money, but I make a pretty good living. I don't earn as much as Marc did – but together we were all set.'

I'd already gone through the Fowlers' financials the previous day, but even a cursory glance told me there was nothing out of place. There were no unusual patterns, no big withdrawals in the run-up to the disappearances, no policy changes and no contact between the family and any of the banks or insurers that the Fowlers had used. The same was true for Kyle, whose finances were simplistic by comparison: he'd finished his A levels the previous June and was only a few weeks into a ranger apprenticeship with Dartmoor National Park. He had one bank account, no pension and no insurance policies. Clara's accounts were fairly unambiguous too: she was eking out a living as a freelance illustrator, like Kyle didn't yet have a pension or any insurance policies, and she was renting a small top-floor flat on the outskirts of Paignton. Not a lot was coming in, but not much was going out either. I'd look at it all again but I was pretty confident that, whatever had happened that day on the water, it was unlikely to have been anything to do with anyone's economic situation.

'You told me yesterday that Clara's parents are both dead?'

'Yes,' Sarah said. 'They died when she was eight.'

'In a car accident?'

'Yes. Their car came off the motorway, up near Exeter Racecourse somewhere.' Sarah's mouth flattened. 'Her dad fell asleep at the wheel. It sounded awful.'

'What happened to her after that?'

'She went into care. The home was down in Plymouth somewhere. She used to talk to Kyle about it, and he'd tell us things from time to time, but Marc and I never brought it up or tried to press her on it. From the bits and pieces Kyle would tell us, it sounds like she went on to live with a couple of foster-families, but I don't think she really clicked with them.'

'She was an illustrator, right?'

'Yes, and a graphic designer. She did stuff for local firms. You know, leaflets, posters, that sort of thing. To tell you the truth, I think she was scratching around a bit. I mean, there's not much work like that down here.' Sarah glanced around the extension and then seemed to wilt. *But money's not everything.* 'She said she was very happy, that she loved being her own boss. Before she met Kyle, she said she'd applied for jobs in London – but I think she decided she wasn't a big-city girl.'

'London's not for everyone.'

Sarah looked at me. 'I read that you were born near here.'

'I was. My parents had a farm in Start Bay.'

'So did you move to London for work?'

'For university.'

'But your daughter still lives down here?'

'Yes, always has done.'

I could see that she wanted to ask more about Annabel, about how I could have been in London since I was eighteen but have a daughter who had never left Devon. I'd shut her down earlier when we'd got on to the subject, but now I realized that she needed to know that I understood the bond between parent and child, even one that was grown up and living their own life – like Kyle had, like Annabel did. She needed to know this was more than just a job for me, more than a pay cheque to pick up when it was over. And even though I'd lived and breathed every single missing persons case I'd ever taken on, sometimes put my life on the line to try and find the truth, in this moment she just needed to hear that I loved my daughter.

'It's hard sometimes,' I said. 'Being so far away from her.'

'Are you staying with her at the moment?'

'Yes. With her and her half-sister.'

'Oh. Her half-sister isn't yours?'

'No. I told you it was a long story.' I smiled at her. 'Basically, I never even knew I was a dad until Annabel was in her late teens. I've had a lot of time to make up for.'

From her expression, it was obvious this wasn't what she'd been expecting.

I got us back on track. 'Just remind me how long Kyle and Clara were going out for?'

'Ten months.'

'And Clara was four years older than Kyle?'

'Yes. She was twenty-two. But Kyle was always a bit of an old soul. We used to joke that he and Clara were obviously meant to be together because they met in a club in Torquay, and Kyle hardly ever went out to nightclubs. He wasn't really into that sort of thing.'

'So what sort of stuff *was* Kyle into?'

Sarah smiled, her memories of her son warm. 'He loved his sport – he had trials at Southampton, and although that didn't work out, he still played football on a Saturday. He loved trail running, and biking. He did an Ironman up in Swansea last year and was due to do one in Weymouth towards the end of September. He just liked being outdoors, which is why he applied for the ranger apprenticeship. My Kyle, he was just . . .' She stopped, her voice soft now. 'I was so proud of him. I never had any problems with him. He never knew his dad, which could have created issues, but it never did. He was just a lovely boy.'

I spotted a box of tissues on the coffee table.

'Thank you,' she said as I handed them to her. 'I loved Marc so much as well. He was a great husband. He supported me, he treated me like a queen, he was brilliant with Kyle from day one, and when we had Mable, he was just such a natural. We didn't plan for her – I was thirty-six, he was almost fifty – but he never even batted an eyelid. I'd spent so much of my life on my own, bringing up Kyle, that I didn't know what it was like to have someone at your side, in the trenches with you, and what a difference it made. Marc was amazing, and I miss him *so* much, but Kyle . . .' She was trying hard not to cry again. 'It's different when it's your child. It's like a hole you can't fill in.'

'Kyle's dad never had any involvement in his life at all?'

'None.'

'What's his name?'

'Daryl Beaumont.'

'Is he from around here?'

'He was, yeah. He lived in Paignton, but I've got absolutely no idea where he is now. I don't even know if he's still alive. I told him I was pregnant when I was seven weeks, and that was pretty much the last time I saw him. But, you know, if we hadn't got together, I never would have had Kyle.'

She looked at me.

And I wouldn't have had to go through this heartache.

'You didn't notice anything different about Marc, Kyle or Clara before that day at the quarry? Anything that felt abnormal?'

'No, nothing.'

We stared at each other.

'I'm going to get you some answers,' I said.

I closed my notebook, pocketed it and thought about what I'd just told her. I really, genuinely believed that I would. But I'd left out something else, something equally as important – and much harder to admit.

Sometimes answers didn't bring relief.

Sometimes they were the things that hurt most of all.

4

I walked down to the boat.

The X5 and the trailer had both been here for eight months – all the way through the previous autumn and winter – and the evidence of that was everywhere: mulched, dead leaves lay in wet clumps on the bonnet and roof of the BMW, and the cover on the back part of the dinghy had come loose and now had four inches of rainwater in it.

Sarah had given me the keys to the BMW, so I opened it and went to the satnav, looking at the history in the run-up to 18 September. The last recorded trip was the Wednesday before the disappearances, to a postcode in Bristol. I googled the address. It was Abbey Wood, the MOD building in Filton. Searching the glovebox, and then the side pockets on the door, then the back seat and footwells, I found nothing.

I turned my attention to the boat.

The dinghy might have been the closest thing this entire case had to a crime scene. Marc, Kyle and Clara had gone out in it – and they'd never come back.

There was nothing in the central part of the boat, just rainwater and floating leaves. At the stern, there was a small bench, little more than a slab of solid plastic, where Clara had been sitting as the men rowed out. The clip-on roof was still fixed to metal cleats on either side of the dinghy, but the sides were rolled up and clipped into place. Otherwise, there was no lockbox, no other seats.

Behind me, Sarah emerged from the house.

I watched her set Mable down on the lawn, giving her

some coloured plastic boules to play with, and then wander over.

'I hate being down here,' she said. 'When I look at . . .' *When I look at this boat, all I see is that day.* For Sarah, it was quite literally a vessel for bad memories.

'Did the police ever take these away?'

Her gaze switched back to me. 'Sorry?'

'The boat. The trailer. The car.'

'You mean to examine them? No.'

'So they just looked them over, like I am?'

'Yeah, they came down here and searched the boat, got inside the car. I think they might have dusted both of them for fingerprints. But that was about it.'

'When was the last time you spoke to the police?'

'End of February.'

Over two months ago.

'And what did they say?'

'Nothing. It was just a courtesy call, really – an update to tell me, in so many words, that the search was going nowhere.'

'Do you remember the names of the cops you were dealing with?'

'PC Wiley. He was the one that came to the quarry. The next day, I went to Totnes station and Wiley was there for a bit, but it was another guy who interviewed me and then basically took on the case – PC Richardson. He was the one who did the two-second check of this.' She gestured to the boat, the bitterness evident in her voice.

'So when Wiley got to the quarry, what did he do?'

'It took them ages to even arrive and, by the time they did, it was getting dark, so we had to use torches. He brought a couple of other officers with him and they walked around some of the lake. At that stage, I guess they thought it might be a drowning. I mean, that was the most obvious explanation. When the dive teams searched the water the next day, and then during the two other searches after that, they didn't find anything – but, that first night, it made sense. I wondered if they'd drowned myself, even though I'm convinced I would have seen or heard something. You know, cries for help, or ripples on the water – something. Anyway, that night, Wiley called in the ranger service, and they came out an hour or so later. A few of them knew Kyle – he'd just started with them – so they took it seriously. They circled the lake properly, searched as much as they could – and they came out and searched the next day too.'

I'd be able to get a clearer idea of Wiley and Richardson's approach to the case once I got the missing persons report from my source, but it seemed to play into what I'd already suspected: the cops didn't believe Sarah had only dropped off for a minute; they thought she was mistaken, that it was much longer, and that within whatever period she was out for, Marc, Kyle and Clara had plenty of time to drown, or to get out of the boat and across to the sides of the quarry – whatever their reasons for doing so. But even if I understood the police's need to question Sarah, and their suspicions about her recollection, there seemed to be a lack of urgency in the case. Three people vanished in bizarre circumstances. It should have been enough to sustain the investigation way beyond the first days and weeks.

This whole thing felt under-investigated.

I needed to find out why.

5

Sarah returned to the house with Mable as I looked around the boat again, and then I put the cover back on and headed inside. Mable was sitting in her highchair, a plastic bowl full of pasta in front of her. She looked at me as I came in, her face stained red with tomato sauce, and started banging her spoon against the tabletop. I thought of the moments just before and after Sarah woke up at the lake, when Mable had been smashing her spade against the arm of her mum's chair.

'That's enough, Mabe,' Sarah said, re-entering the kitchen.

Mable didn't stop.

'*Mable.*'

Mable looked between us, her spoon paused in mid-air – and then she dropped it over the side of the highchair and went back to eating her pasta with her fingers.

I asked Sarah if I could look around upstairs.

'Of course,' she said.

I started with her and Marc's bedroom, going through wardrobes and drawers, pulling out boxes and sifting through them. When I found nothing, I moved on to Kyle's. Sarah must have tidied up in the eight months since her family had gone missing, because teenagers' bedrooms were rarely this well ordered. Her son's shirts and trousers were on hangers in the wardrobe, his T-shirts were folded, and his underwear was neatly segregated into boxer shorts and socks. There was something incredibly sad about it all, a forsaken bedroom that should have been cluttered and messy, full of youth and life and energy, reduced to little more than a museum exhibit.

On a desk in the corner was a laptop. I lifted the lid but nothing happened, so I put it on to charge and moved along the landing.

The next room was Mable's: it was so different from Kyle's, so lived in, toys everywhere, the chaotic story of a two-year-old.

The fourth bedroom was more sparsely furnished, but on the floor in boxes, and hanging in the wardrobes, I found Clara's things, including a laptop. Sarah had taken everything in after informing Clara's landlord what had happened. Like Kyle's, the laptop was dead, so I plugged it in and then started going through the wardrobes. They were mostly filled with equipment for her work: design books, folders full of project ideas, a laser printer. I returned to the laptop, which now had a little charge, and began going through her internet history and emails and found that Clara's life was quite small and unremarkable, most of it tied to her work and to Kyle. I wondered if some of that was a consequence of her childhood, of then finding a man she clearly adored, a family she'd been embraced by, and a career – modest as it was – that she seemed to love. The first part of her life had been traumatic and disrupted. After that, it had become secure and loved.

I headed to the study.

It was in a loft conversion – a beautiful space, skylights all the way down, the whole thing immaculately furnished. There were two desks either side of a divider, and two identical iMacs. On Marc's side were shelves full of box folders, files, engineering manuals and a whiteboard with Post-it notes and reminders all over it. I powered his Mac on – a picture of him, Sarah, Kyle and Mable stuck to the edge of it – then went to Sarah's side. It was quirkier, full of books, pot plants and trinkets. On the walls were movie posters for *When Harry Met Sally* and *Casablanca*, and another whiteboard. This one had a single line at the top: *Book #6 Ideas.*

The rest of the board was empty.

I powered Sarah's Mac on as well and then went back to Marc's and slid in at the desk. Sarah had given me the passwords for both computers, so I went through them in turn. Marc's was all reports, analyses and endless spreadsheets, while Sarah's Mac seemed to confirm how bad the last eight months had been for her. One document she'd saved as 'Book 6' had *Chapter 1* written in it and nothing else; a Word doc called 'New Ideas', which had been created at the end of August, had last been opened two days before the disappearances. I wondered if she'd even been up here since then.

I returned to Kyle's room.

When I lifted the lid of his laptop, it was still showing me a black screen with a red battery icon, so I took the whole thing – lead and all – downstairs.

I found Sarah in the living room. She'd opened the bifold doors to the garden and was sitting in the doorway, smoking a cigarette. Mable was back in the playroom watching TV.

'Sarah?'

She started, smiled, looked at the cigarette in her fingers. 'You caught me,' she said, and directed a flume of smoke out of the open door, turning briefly to watch it dissipate. 'Marc would be pissed off.'

'Why?'

'I told him I'd given up.' She watched the cigarette for a moment, tiny specks of ash flittering away from the end. 'His mum died of lung cancer when he was in his late twenties. She smoked like a chimney her whole life. Marc hated that I smoked.' She held up the cigarette. 'It's a disgusting habit – and I can't really afford it.'

I held up Kyle's laptop. 'Can I take this?'

'Of course. And anything else you need.'

'Did the cops ever take any of your computers away?'

36

'No. They just looked at them here.'

The lack of focus from the police continued to niggle at me, and I wondered again whether it was worth trying to get in touch with Richardson or Wiley to see if I could get some sort of conversation going with them. Dealing with local police stations – as opposed to ones in big cities – was often easier because their caseloads weren't as sprawling, so they had more time, and there were generally fewer egos. But not always. Sometimes they became more intransigent because they hated the idea of people rocking up on their doorstep, treating them like amateurs and calling into question their decisions.

I decided to wait until I'd been through the missing persons report.

Just then, my phone started ringing.

I glanced at the display – saw it was a London number I didn't recognize – and told Sarah to give me a second. 'David Raker.'

'David Raker,' a woman's voice echoed back.

I instantly knew who it was – even from the two-word response.

By then, she was already talking again: 'Well, this is a call I never thought I'd have to make . . .'

6

It had been seven years since I'd last spoken to Melanie Craw. Back then she'd been a senior police officer working for the Met, and we'd got close when she'd hired me to look for her father.

Close, but never quite close enough.

Something had always refused to click between us, a barrier that neither of us could ever get past. It could have been because, despite Derryn having been gone for five years by that point, a part of me had still been grieving for my wife, still unable to completely let go of the woman I'd loved beyond all others for a decade and a half of my life. But, more often, I wondered if it was to do with the fact that Craw was a cop and I was an investigator who picked up cases that cops failed to see through. That bred bitterness and suspicion in the police, and although I'd never got the sense that Craw had felt either of those things towards me, she'd never been able to bring herself to tell a single person she worked with that we were seeing each other. The longer it went on like that, the more frustrating it became, and then we both stopped trusting each other. The last conversation I had with her was when she called to tell me she was being promoted to superintendent and moving to Glasgow.

'Melanie Craw,' I said, stepping outside to continue the call.

'Seven years and you still remember my voice.'

'Your banshee wail is hard to forget.'

I heard her laugh. 'Cheeky twat.'

'How are you doing?'

'I'm doing all right. Sounds like you're keeping busy too. I've just been reading all about the testimony you gave at the Castle hearings last week.' The Castle was a member's club in central London that had been a key part of a case I'd worked five months before. I'd been called to give evidence at a public enquiry. 'You still look pretty good in a suit, Raker, I'll give you that.'

'A compliment. I'm honoured.'

A moment of silence. 'Look, Raker, I'm sorry about –'

'It's all right.'

'No, I should have called you at some point.'

'I could have called you too.' I felt around for something more profound, a line that might satisfy the both of us, but I wasn't exactly sure what that was, or if it even needed to be said. Our relationship – if it had ever been that – had never really got going. Some sparks went out and weren't meant to be rekindled.

'You got a couple of minutes?' she asked.

I looked through the skein of rain, drifting and swirling across the garden, to where Sarah was. 'I'm on a job,' I said. 'It might have to be quick.'

But Craw didn't continue.

'Craw?'

'Yeah.' She cleared her throat. 'Yeah, so you'll remember I moved north for that promotion. Well, I ended up spending five years up there, but then the girls left school and came down south again to university, and I started to miss them both a lot. I started to fall out of love with police work too. Not the investigation side, but all the bullshit. All the box-ticking and the paperwork. It's just admin, constantly – like being an accountant, not a cop.'

'You left the force?'

'I did. I live in Surrey now. I took some time off, but I'm fifty-three, not eighty-three. I got restless. I needed to be doing something. I needed that stimulation, and after a while, sitting around having coffee and doing yoga classes at the village hall . . .'

'It wasn't doing it for you.'

'No. Have you ever heard of the Skyline?'

'The casino?'

'*Resort* and casino, Raker.'

She was joking, but she was right: the Skyline wasn't just a casino – although that was a major part of it – it was a massive entertainment complex, with a hotel, a nightclub, a concert hall, an underground shopping mall and an indoor water park. Modelled after the theme hotels that lined the Las Vegas Boulevard, it was just north of Heathrow Airport, in a square of land off the M4. I'd only been once a couple of years back, when a friend of mine from my days as a journalist had got us tickets to see a band we'd both loved.

'What do you do there?' I asked.

'I run security.'

'For the whole place?'

'Yep. All 195,000 square feet of it. Been doing it for ten months now. It's different from police work – I mean, that goes without saying – but a lot is similar.'

I tried to work out where this was heading; even started to wonder if she was about to offer me a job.

'Anyway,' she said, finally, 'I'll cut to the chase. Last week, we had this new resort manager start. Previously, he worked for the Zinters – that's the brothers who own the Skyline – at their casino out in Macau, but now he's here looking for ways to make a good first impression. And one of the things he's got a bee in his bonnet about is this huge hit the casino took twelve months ago.'

'What kind of hit?'

'You ever heard of the Whaler?'

'No.'

'But you know what a whale is in gambling terms, right?'

'I do.'

In casino lingo, a *whale* was the term used to describe a high roller who gambled hundreds of thousands – sometimes even millions – in a single game.

'Long story short,' Craw continued, 'this Whaler befriended one of our biggest high rollers over the course of five months, slowly gained his trust, and then – as soon as he *got* that trust – made off into the sunset with four hundred grand of the high roller's money.'

'That's a lot of stolen cash.'

'It is, and we'd like it all back. But stealing a shitload of money wasn't the only thing the Whaler did.' A pause. 'He left something behind.'

'What?'

'A dead body.'

I frowned. 'He *murdered* the high roller?'

'In cold blood. In the Skyline's penthouse suite.'

I tried to cast my mind back, tried to think whether I'd read anything about a murder at the Skyline in the press. Maybe, vaguely, I had some distant recollection now that Craw had mentioned it, but I struggled to recall much else.

'Did the Met find the guy?'

'Thames Valley Police. The casino is just outside the M25, so it's their patch. And no, they didn't find him. In fact, they couldn't find anything at all. The Whaler, he's a total ghost. So, the police tell the security team at the Skyline to be on the look-out for him – which stinks of desperation because why would a murderer, a guy who'd stolen four hundred grand and got away with it, return to the scene of such a successful crime? But that's exactly what this guy *did* do one week later.'

'He came back?'

'Came back and sat at one of the blackjack tables, bold as brass. So the security team spot him, arrest him and call the cops.'

Even down the telephone line, I could feel it.

Something big.

'They lock the Whaler in one of the cells, then the cops turn up. Bear in mind, my predecessor says he was *right there* outside the cell the whole time.'

And that was when I understood why Craw had called me.

'The Whaler disappeared?'

'Yep.'

'From inside the cell?'

'From inside the cell,' Craw repeated.

'The cell was definitely locked?'

'Locked, deadbolted. No windows, no way out.'

'Then how the hell is that possible?'

'I don't know,' Craw said. 'That's what I want you to find out.'

7

I tried to process what Craw had just said. There was no point in pretending I wasn't hooked – I instantly needed to know how a man could vanish from a locked cell – but something had already started niggling at me.

'Why now?'

'What do you mean?' she replied.

'I mean, it's been twelve months. The Whaler's in the wind. And the four hundred grand he stole? If you're talking about trying to recover that, we both know that probably won't ever happen. If this guy had messed up somehow and left some sort of trail, the money would have been found already – and so would he. Why go after the Whaler now and not when all of this happened a year ago?'

'Like I say, there's a new resort manager. He's trying to impress.'

'That's not an answer, Craw.'

'This guy's a killer. We want to bring him to justice.'

'So suddenly everyone at the casino's got a conscience?'

'We just want to find him. That's all.'

Again, I got the same sense that something wasn't quite right here. 'And the four hundred grand?' I said. 'That doesn't even belong to the Skyline, it belongs to the high roller.'

'It's still money we'd like recovered,' Craw responded in the same neutral voice. 'And obviously we'd like you to try and find it for us – hence the call.'

'What do the police say?'

'It's a cold case. I mean, it's still open –'

'But they've stopped actively looking for the high roller and the stolen money?'

'Yes.' She paused for a moment. 'Look, part of the reason this has become a big focus for the higher-ups is because the high roller was a guy called Anthony Yanis. Have you ever heard of him?'

'No.'

'He was a billionaire. He put money into the Skyline when it was built.'

'So he's a business partner of the Zinter brothers?'

'More than that. He was a close friend of theirs.'

Now it was becoming clearer.

'So what you're telling me is that it's really the brothers who want this Whaler guy found, not your new resort manager?'

'The resort manager does too.'

'But his orders are coming down the line from the Zinters?'

'They're the bosses. That's how it works.'

'So, again, why have they waited twelve months?'

'What, a guy vanishing from a locked cell doesn't float your boat?'

'That's not the question I asked.'

'Look, I need someone on this, Raker. Are you —'

'Why wait a year?'

Silence this time.

'Why don't you come in?' she said finally. 'I'd rather talk about it here.'

'I'm not in London at the moment.'

'Where are you?'

'Devon.'

I heard her pause. When I'd tried to find her father, the search had started in her parents' place on Dartmoor. This area held a lot of bad memories for her.

'How long are you going to be down there for?'

I glanced over at Sarah again. She was watching me through the doors, drifting in and out of view as rain ran off the small wooden pagoda I'd sought cover under.

'I'm not sure,' I said.

'The Zinter brothers have more money than God –'

'It's not about my day rate, Craw.'

'They will double whatever you normally –'

'It's not about the money.'

'I need you on this, Raker.'

There was a hint of desperation to Craw's voice now – a minor tremor in her words – that made me wonder if there was something else she hadn't said. She was dancing around the reason why the casino had waited a year to go after the Whaler and the stolen money, and it had set off a low-level alarm. I couldn't deny I was tempted by the prospect of digging a little deeper; being able to charge twice what I normally did was attractive too: I'd just moved house, the house needed things doing to it, and tradesmen were expensive. But Sarah was my priority – and there was something I was already certain of in everything Craw was telling me.

This case isn't what it seems.

'I'll call you back later,' I said.

'Raker, I need someone I can trust on this.'

'Let's talk later.'

She was pissed off. It was like an electrical charge travelling down the line. But as we said goodbye, I thought I could hear something else embedded in her anger.

It sounded like fear.

Healy

London | *Now*

He saw them a long time before they saw him.

They were sitting in the window of a coffee shop near the Barbican, the three of them talking. They'd already got drinks, and Ciaran – his eldest son – was eating a sandwich. Healy stood there, watching them. Ciaran was thirty-four, engaged to be married, and worked in Canary Wharf for a US investment bank. He must have been on a late lunch: he was in a suit and tie, his red hair – the same colour as Healy's – slicked back. He looked smart and confident. He was saying something, miming someone smoking, and then – next to him – Liam suddenly burst out laughing, and so too did Liam's girlfriend in the seat beside him.

Healy didn't know much about her.

Not that he knew all that much about his sons either – or, at least, not this version of them. In the emails he'd received from the boys, they'd said her name was Alice-Leigh, and she was twenty-two, eight years younger than Liam.

She was also seven months pregnant.

Healy wasn't certain what Liam was doing for work now. In the last email he'd got, the one where they finally agreed to meet him, Liam had said he was being made redundant. Maybe he hadn't found anything new, because he was dressed in track-suit trousers, trainers and a hoody, so unless he'd got a job as a personal trainer – which wasn't beyond the realms of possibility given his build – it seemed unlikely he'd have come from an

46

office. If he really was out of work, Healy imagined that Liam and his girlfriend would be able to absorb the cost of that for a little while – Alice-Leigh was a solicitor – but probably not for too long. In eight weeks, maybe less, they'd be having a baby. Babies were expensive. London was expensive. Liam was physically big – much bigger than his older brother – but he still had the echo in his face of the boy Healy had left behind over eight years ago. As he watched him, Healy wondered how Liam would cope with being a father. Healy had no idea. All he knew was that, however Liam was feeling, whatever fears he held, he'd be absolutely convinced of one thing.

He'd be a better dad than Healy ever was.

Healy became aware that he was rubbing his finger and thumb together. It was a hangover from his years of being a smoker. He was nervous. He'd written emails to his boys after he'd got out of prison. He'd even had a couple of phone calls with Ciaran, both of which had been filled with awkward silences but had basically been cordial. He'd sent them photos of the place he'd started renting in Lewisham, and of his first day working security at a high-end block of flats in Greenwich. They'd sent photos of themselves back, though not many. There was still a hesitation there, as if they didn't want to share too much with Healy in case he disappeared on them like he'd done the last time. That was part of the reason Healy was so nervous: he wanted to say the right things; didn't want to see the disappointment in their faces as he talked.

But it wasn't the whole reason.

Mostly he was nervous because his sons weren't young men any more. Eight years ago, they'd still needed him for things – life advice, even financial support. But now there was nothing binding them to him at all. They'd survived and flourished without him. If things went badly this time, they'd just walk away. Healy needed them far more than they needed him.

Taking a long breath, he turned to look at himself in the window of a deli he'd stopped next to. He'd bought a new jacket for today and had dug out a shirt, but now wasn't sure if he looked smart or ridiculous. When he'd been a cop, he'd worn suits all the time. Then his daughter had died. After that, he'd got angry, and he'd got fired. That had been the start of his spiral. Being a cop was all he knew; not working cases was like having the floor collapse under him. He couldn't cope. Some time after that, a pariah at the Met, ostracized by his family, he'd become sick and then suicidal, and then had faked his own death because – at the time – it seemed like the only way he could ever hope to start again. In over seven years, moving between places using fake IDs – avoiding people, working jobs cash in hand – he hadn't put a suit on once. But then the police had eventually found him, had charged him, and he'd gone to prison.

He'd finally pulled on a jacket again for his first court appearance. Then the case against him had collapsed and he'd got out of prison and he'd dumped the jacket, never wanting to be reminded of his time behind bars. He'd let his shaved hair grow back, to something close to how it used to be. But, after he did, he looked in the mirror one day and saw the years-old ghost of the broken man he'd become after the Met, the man his boys had grown to distrust, so he'd taken the clippers to it all.

Now he looked old: every one of his fifty-seven years.

The nerves hit him again.

Ciaran was still pretending to smoke and the three of them were still laughing. And in that moment, Healy felt himself shrink. The spark of excitement he'd come here with, the words he'd practised in his head – all of it vanished.

What if they were making fun of Healy?

The version of him his boys had known had always been overweight; always unfit, perpetually out of breath, either smoking or in the middle of the latest attempt to give up. While he'd

48

been at the Met, he'd eaten too much and he'd definitely drunk too much. Looking back, he'd probably been a borderline alcoholic. There were times even before his daughter died, before he split from his ex-wife, Gemma, where he'd chosen to go to the pub after a late shift, rather than go home, because he didn't think he could handle his kids. He couldn't deal with the petty shite that orbited their lives without something to take the edge off. He'd walk in sometimes and Ciaran or Liam would be arguing with Gemma about meaningless crap like homework, and all Healy could think was: *What was the point?*

He'd spent the day looking at dead bodies.

Who cared if one of the kids hadn't written some essay?

His gaze went back to the window of the coffee shop. They were all just talking now. No more gesturing, no more laughter. Maybe they hadn't been making fun of him. Maybe it was just the guilt talking, his doubts making him paranoid.

He headed towards the coffee shop.

Or maybe they're just lying in wait for me.

Maybe this whole thing is about to implode.

8

'Sorry about that,' I said to Sarah as I entered the house again.

'It's okay.' She looked sad, beaten down.

'Is everything all right?'

Her eyes began to well. 'It's silly.'

'What is?'

She glanced at me again, and then her attention switched outside, to the pagoda I'd sought cover under. 'I don't know,' she said. 'I wasn't listening in to what you were saying, I promise. I just . . .' She wiped at an eye. 'I just need you to find my family.'

'That's what I'm going to do.' I pulled one of the chairs out and sat down next to her. On the table, Sarah had gathered a pile of photographs for me to take away. I glanced at them, then at her. 'Sarah, your family are my number-one priority. I mean that. Finding out what happened to them is the only thing that matters to me. I have many faults, believe me, but not being invested enough definitely isn't one of them.'

She smiled at me. 'Okay.'

I looked at the photographs again and started going through them, seeing how eloquently they spoke of who her son, his girlfriend and her husband had been – not just faces in a file or a news report, but living, breathing, three-dimensional people. There were fewer portraits of Clara, understandably, because she'd only been in the Fowlers' lives for ten months, but Kyle had mounted a board in his bedroom and filled it with selfies of the two of them, so Sarah had grabbed all of those for me as well. Ultimately, all photos were staged to some degree or another – but some pictures were more honest than others. And I kept coming back to one in particular.

It was of the three of them in the minutes before they took the boat out on the lake that final time: Clara had been caught mid-laugh, her eyes alight as Kyle tugged up the band of his stepdad's swimming shorts so that it looked like Marc was wearing them above his belly button; Marc was laughing too, half swatting Kyle away, half trying to pull his trunks back down. It was a lovely shot, spontaneous and genuine, and – when Sarah saw me holding it – her eyes lingered on the image. This picture was the last she'd ever taken of the family she adored, captured in the final moments they'd spent together.

I took out my notebook and opened it to the last page I'd been working from. 'You said that some of the rangers Kyle worked with were at the quarry that night. Could you give me the name of someone to talk to there?'

'Barney Cowdrey. He was Kyle's boss.'

I wrote down the contact details Sarah had for Cowdrey. He would be a good first port of call. There were others on my list – friends of Kyle and Clara, work colleagues of Marc's – who may just have been boxes to tick but who would need running down as well. And then, at the bottom, was another name.

Daryl Beaumont.

Sarah's ex-boyfriend and Kyle's father.

Most likely, given that he hadn't ever been in Kyle's life, he was a dead end as far as the disappearances were concerned. But I needed to make sure.

'When I came to the house yesterday, you told me that Marc, Kyle and Clara all left their phones with you when they rowed the boat out?'

'Yes.'

'I'm going to take those phones now if that's okay.'

She got up from the table, went to a sideboard in the extension. From the top drawer, she took out three mobile phones and two wallets.

'You also said yesterday that the police looked at these?'

'Yes, they took them away for a few days.'

'Did they look at yours too?'

'Yes.'

So unlike the boat and the laptops, the police had actually done something with the phones – removed them, pulled off the data. Given that all of them had been returned to Sarah, it was probably safe to assume they were another blind alley. That was likely to be true of the ATM cards too: normally the police set up an alert on the bank accounts, so if the cards were used they'd be able to zero in on where.

I set all three phones down on the table.

Clara's was in a flip-open case with credit card slots on the left. Her bank cards were poking out, half of her photo visible on her driving licence too. The men's wallets were similar, full of cards and receipts.

I tried powering on the phones.

All three of them were dead.

I hoped it wasn't some kind of omen.

9

My daughter, Annabel, lived just outside Newton Abbot.

It was three o'clock by the time I got back and the house was empty, as I'd expected it to be: Annabel was a dance and drama teacher and normally didn't get home until at least seven, while her half-sister, Olivia, was in her second year of college, studying fashion and textiles in Exeter. According to Annabel, Liv had recently started coming home a couple of hours later than usual, claiming she was staying on for extra study sessions, but Annabel suspected she had a new boyfriend – and if it was one she wasn't being open about, it was one she knew Annabel wouldn't like. Annabel was turning thirty-five this year, and – ever since the death of the couple she'd thought were her parents – had taken on a more maternal role. In response, Liv saw Annabel more like a nagging mother than a big sister.

When I let myself in, there was a brown A4 envelope on the floor addressed to me. It was the missing persons report I was waiting for, sent to me overnight from a contact of mine in the police, Ewan Tasker. Task and I had been friends since my days as a journalist, when he'd become a source.

Scooping up the envelope, I put on some coffee.

It was mid-afternoon now, the sun out again, so I set up in the conservatory, with the warmth at my shoulders, and went back through what I'd already gathered on the Fowler family in the run-up to today, just to remind myself. It wasn't very much. The news reports played up the strangeness of the disappearances, but it was obvious that solid details were scant and the police weren't playing ball on theories. That was because, at the time, the police basically didn't have any: divers hadn't found bodies; Marc, Kyle and Clara had nothing in their backgrounds that would suggest they'd planned a disappearance, or if they had, what their reason might be for doing so; and they still doubted Sarah's recall when it came to timings. In press reports, the cops gave the media a bland, catch-all statement to assure them that they were working 'all angles', but I imagined it was more to give themselves some breathing room. They wanted to avoid a feeding frenzy in the press, because if the investigation caught light in the media, it created extra pressure. Sarah's version of events was an unexplainable mystery, the kind of story that big, ravenous coverage was built on; the police's statements underplayed it all, giving them the space they needed to dig deeper. In principle, that was smart. In reality, this investigation had never really got going.

I opened the missing persons report.

It was only thirteen pages, which communicated instantly how little progress had been made. I started on the background the cops had done on Marc, Kyle and Clara. I knew most of it already, but what they had was useful where Clara was concerned, as it listed the children's home she'd grown up in and confirmed the date of her parents' death, neither of which Sarah had been certain of. On the next two pages was some additional background on the three of them, but it was a repeat of what Sarah had told me earlier: what Marc did for work, the ranger programme Kyle had just started, confirmation that Clara had been self-employed as an illustrator and graphic designer, as well as the address of her rented flat in Paignton.

Next were Sarah's statements.

The first was brief, taken at the scene the night of the disappearances. She was adamant that she'd dropped off 'only for a very short time', though nothing was said here about her having checked her watch or that the 'very short time' was around a minute. I wasn't necessarily worried about that: she was in a heightened state of panic and angered by how long it had taken police to respond to her call. She had Mable to worry about as well, and at that time of night, her daughter would have been fractious.

Even so, as I read the statement through a second time, a part of me began to understand why the cops might have found it strange, perhaps even suspicious, that Sarah *didn't* mention the precise timings until the next day. Despite how disordered she must have felt at the quarry, her statement from the scene appeared surprisingly clear-headed, so why only mention the timings the following morning?

I turned the page to another statement, this one led, not by the cop, Wiley, who'd gone to the quarry, but by the second cop, Richardson, at the station in Totnes the next morning.

SARAH FOWLER: When they started rowing out,
    I remember looking at my watch.
PC RICHARDSON: Wait, you checked your
    watch?
SARAH FOWLER: Yes.
PC RICHARDSON: What time did it say?
SARAH FOWLER: 6:17.
PC RICHARDSON: And the next time you looked
    at your watch, after you woke up,
    it was what time?
SARAH FOWLER: 6:20.
PC RICHARDSON: Did you mention this last
    night to PC Wiley in the statement
    you gave him?
SARAH FOWLER: I don't know.

PC RICHARDSON: I don't think you did.

SARAH FOWLER: Well, I'm mentioning it now. What difference does it make?

PC RICHARDSON: It makes a difference because it's new, potentially important information.

SARAH FOWLER: Good. Then you can use it.

PC RICHARDSON: It's not as simple as that, Sarah. You're changing your account of what happened.

SARAH FOWLER: I'm not changing my account.

PC RICHARDSON: These are new details.

SARAH FOWLER: Look, those were the times I saw, okay? I don't know if I mentioned them to your colleague or not. Maybe I would have done if he hadn't been so bloody slow getting there.

PC RICHARDSON: Calm down, Sarah.

SARAH FOWLER: Don't patronize me.

PC RICHARDSON: I'm not patronizing y-

SARAH FOWLER: I know what I saw. Marc, Kyle and Clara were there - and then they weren't. I can't explain it to you, but I'm telling you that's what happened. So instead of treating me with suspicion, why don't you do your fucking job and find my family?

Afterwards, Richardson retreated to simpler questions to get her back onside before coming back to the moments around the disappearances. He stopped short of saying, *But how is any of this possible?*, even though it was there, implied by his words, but by the end it was obvious Sarah had failed to turn the tide. Introducing the timings the next day, and not at the quarry, clearly bothered Richardson a lot. It was impossible for three people to go up in a puff of smoke in under a minute, and in his search for answers, Sarah's sudden, out-of-the-blue recall of potentially important details felt anomalous – especially as, the night before, in the statement she'd given Wiley, she'd remembered the moments that followed her family going missing with such lucidity.

There was also a second passage later on in the interview that caught my eye. This time, though, Richardson's angle was less certain.

PC RICHARDSON: Is there any reason you
    might have misremembered certain
    details about yesterday?
SARAH FOWLER: What?
PC RICHARDSON: Is there any reason you can
    think of that you might have recalled
    certain details incorrectly with
    regard to what happened?
SARAH FOWLER: No. No, absolutely not.

It felt like a loaded question, but I couldn't figure out what was behind it. If he had evidence that might diminish Sarah's credibility as a witness, especially in terms of the timings, why not just come out with it? And if that was the case, why wasn't the evidence somewhere in the paperwork? I reread the same passage again, then went back through the pages of the file, but I was still in the dark by the end of it. After a while, I started to wonder if I was reading too much into it.

Except I couldn't quite let it go.

I underlined the whole section and stuck a Post-it at the top of the page, then moved to the last part of the casework. It was a breakdown of the investigation – such as it was – including a chronological list of updates. The updates had ceased at exactly the time Sarah had told me the police last called her – late February. Even before that, though, activity was increasingly sporadic. In late September and October, Richardson went to the Fowlers' home, to Clara's flat, he sent divers to the lake for a second and third time, talked to friends and family, and requested financial details. He'd instigated a forensic search of all the phones as well. The friends and work colleagues were presumably a dead end, as no potential leads were noted from any of those visits. The financial backgrounds received a three-word summation from Richardson – *No unusual activity* – which just left the phones. On those, the forensic analysis didn't drop into Richardson's inbox until mid-November, but when it did Richardson once again entered: *No unusual activity*.

I'd told Ewan Tasker not to worry about sending the phone analysis through as I was getting them sourced in more detail from another contact of mine, but once the phones proved a dead end in the investigation, you could almost see the slow decay of the case, the last of the momentum dying out as a smoking gun failed to surface. It still bothered me that Richardson didn't work the disappearances harder, though. Why didn't he care more? Even if he thought Sarah's recollection was skewed – or she might be holding back, or even outright lying – his instincts as a cop should have made him want answers.

Grabbing my laptop, I went to the Devon and Cornwall Police website, then put *Totnes* into the 'Your Area' tab. Hitting Return, it took me to a 'Your Local Team' page. I scrolled down to a bank of portraits. There were nine people working in Totnes.

Richardson wasn't one of them.

I stared at the screen. Where was he? Had he moved stations? Was that why Sarah had received so few updates since February?

Switching to Google, I typed in *Richardson Totnes Police Constable*, hit Return, and only three pages of results loaded.

But the first one told me everything I needed to know.

Richardson was dead.

10

The only story about his death had run in a local newspaper – and now it was obvious why the cops hadn't contacted Sarah since February: the one person still actively trying to find her family had died a week after his last call to her.

It had been sudden: he was fifty-one, in pretty good shape, although his wife told the reporter he'd been feeling off for a few months. She said he'd had headaches and had felt constantly tired, which may have explained why the case felt so under-worked and why he'd cut corners on things like having the boat examined more closely. On Friday 1 March, after getting home from a long shift, Richardson had suffered a massive heart attack.

Wiley – the first officer on the scene at the quarry – had ceded control of the case to Richardson, apparently in its entirety. I didn't see a single other mention of his name aside from in the initial interview. That meant that when Richardson died, the case died too. It might have been passed on to someone else – but if it had, there was no evidence it had been worked in any meaningful way.

I pushed the file aside and reached for the three phones. As they fired up, I went to my emails to see if the phone records for Marc, Kyle and Clara had arrived. They had. My source, a former hacker I'd used since my newspaper days, had come through for me. First, though, I concentrated on the handsets: they'd all had passcodes, but those had been disabled by the police.

Marc's phone was paid for by his employer, which meant

most of what was on it was related to his job. I took some time with his texts and emails, writing down the names of people who contacted him, working out who were work colleagues and who were friends. I knew the phone records I'd been sent would list the names and addresses associated with every number that Marc, Kyle and Clara had been in touch with, so I could easily cross-reference everything and remove anyone I didn't think was of interest. But it was slow, tedious work and that sense of inevitability – that certainty this was going nowhere – kicked in well before the end.

I finished with his photos.

There were over a thousand, some repeats of ones that Sarah had already given me. I looked through them for a while, then played one of the videos.

It was taken at a barbecue in the Fowlers' back garden the July before the disappearances. Marc was at the grill, filming himself, showing the camera an apron he was wearing with *I'm All Cook Up* written on it. When he swivelled the camera around, Kyle, Clara and Sarah were at a table nearby, Mable playing on the grass behind them, all of them watching as Marc started singing the words on the apron in the style of Elvis.

'I'm so sorry you have to see this, sweetheart,' Sarah joked to Clara.

Clara smiled. 'It's a pretty good impression, actually.'

'Thank you, thank you very much,' Marc responded, and gave Clara a small bow. 'Sarah and Kyle think impressions are my big strength.'

Sarah and Kyle burst out laughing.

'You should do your Arnie,' Kyle said. Sarah rolled her eyes playfully, and then Kyle turned to Clara to explain: 'We did laser tag last year and Marc nicknamed himself "the Terminator" because he got the highest score.'

'That's not true about the nickname, Clara,' deadpanned Marc.

'I'd forgotten about that,' Sarah chuckled.

'After the guy told him he finished first, Marc said "I'll be back –"' Kyle did a passable Arnold Schwarzenegger impression '"– next year."'

They all started laughing again.

'Get to the chopper!' Marc and Kyle quoted in unison, and then Marc started laughing so much, the phone jiggling so hard in his hand, the picture became a blur.

The video ended.

As I stared at the last, paused frame – Sarah and Kyle laughing, Kyle in the middle of saying something to Marc, all their faces, including Clara's, painted with joy – I felt a deep swell of sadness for Sarah. She'd told me the day before that she'd transferred the videos on to her own phone so they didn't go missing. They must have been so painful to watch.

I set Marc's handset aside and went through Kyle and Clara's phones. They hadn't emailed, texted or called anywhere close to as much as Marc had. Clara had utilized hers more than Kyle, her Sent folder full of messages pitching for work, but from the lack of replies it didn't seem as if she'd been very successful.

I played one of the videos on Kyle's phone.

He and Clara were somewhere on Dartmoor, sitting next to a pretty stream running under a picturesque grey stone bridge. Kyle was setting up his camera so it would record both of them, and then – once the phone was in position – he went back to Clara, snuggled in next to her and kissed her on the cheek.

'Happy six-month anniversary,' he said to her.

Clara pushed her head in against him contentedly. 'Aw, thank you, baby. Happy six-month anniversary to you too.'

And then Kyle went to his backpack and pulled out a bottle of champagne that Clara obviously had no idea he'd brought along. Her face lit up and she threw both of her arms around him. 'I don't know if this is the type you like,' he said as she hugged him hard. 'I don't know anything about champagne.'

'This is perfect,' she said. '*You're* perfect. Thank you so much.'

Kyle popped the cork, poured some of the champagne into white plastic cups, then came over and grabbed his phone.

The video ended.

Texts between the two of them were frequent, but texts to other people – friends and colleagues – were fewer. There was nothing in the messages that raised any immediate alarms with me – nothing in their photos or in the videos – but being in each other's pockets the whole time wasn't always a positive thing. It was sometimes where control and obsession were born. There was no suggestion that was the case here, but it seemed like they rarely spent time with anyone else and, if I was looking for angles, perhaps this was one.

Setting the mobiles aside, I returned to the phone statements. The PDF was thirty-two pages long, and most of the calls were from Marc: his activity took up twenty-six pages. Using the information I'd already gleaned from the emails, texts and apps – as well as a list of friends and colleagues Sarah had provided me with – I started going through the logs, looking for anything that didn't fit or looked wrong. It was dead end after dead end, everything fitting with what I'd seen already, every name on every call matching names I'd got from Sarah or had found information on as I'd gone through the emails and texts. After Marc, I moved on to Kyle, then on to Clara. An hour later, I realized Richardson was right. *No unusual activity.*

He'd only looked at four weeks, I'd looked at twelve, but the outcome was the same. I leaned back, frustrated, the conservatory darkening as the sun disappeared.

That just left Kyle's laptop.

It was charging in the other room, so I went and retrieved it, making myself a coffee on the way past.

I started going through the hard drive, through folders, every document on the desktop. Kyle's activity on the PC had dropped off dramatically after the end of his A level exams the previous June. Most of what remained on the desktop was revision for those – Geography essays, Biology and Physics test papers, files from school full of graphs, charts and science equations.

I went to his browser history.

Sarah had talked about her son loving trail running, being outdoors, and sport in general, and all those things were evident in the websites he visited. I kept going, scrolling further, back through July, and then June, through May and then April.

And then I stopped.

At the start of April, he'd spent almost an entire week returning to the same website every day. He'd done it with other websites too, but those were of a certain type, covering the things – the sports, the hobbies – he loved doing in his downtime.

This wasn't.

This was like nothing else he'd ever looked at before or after.

It was a true crime website.

Healy

London | *Now*

They didn't see him until he was almost at the table, and then Liam happened to look up and lock eyes with Healy. Healy smiled; Liam took a moment, as if he wasn't sure if this really was his father – this slimmer, shaven-headed version of the man who'd drifted like a spectre through their teenage years – and then, finally, he smiled too and tapped his older brother on the thigh.

Ciaran turned and briefly nodded – a minor tilt-up, a hello. The only one of the three who looked genuinely pleased to see Healy – even if she was only doing so for his benefit – was the only one Healy had never met.

'Hi, boys.' He looked at the girlfriend. 'Hi, Alice.'

'Hi,' Alice said in response. She clambered to her feet, and then came over and offered Healy her hand. 'It's so nice to meet you. Liam has told me all about you.'

'Oh dear,' Healy joked.

Alice smiled. The boys didn't.

'Can I get anyone a drink?'

'I'm fine, thank you,' Alice said.

The boys just shook their heads.

Healy went to the counter and ordered a black coffee. As he stood in the queue, he could feel their eyes on him, could see their reflections in the glass case, where the cakes were. Liam had clasped Alice's hand, a gesture that looked almost defensive to Healy, as if his son were saying to his girlfriend, *You're with us, not him*; on the other side of the table, Ciaran had half turned towards Healy, as if he too was trying to keep something of himself back. When they were younger, when Healy had still been around, most of the conflict in the house had been between him and Leanne. Ciaran was eighteen months older than Leanne, but, before she died, it was always Leanne who was the tip of the spear: she went into battle for the three of them, she stood her ground against Healy, she told him plainly how much they hated him. Healy would have done anything to have those moments again, to say the things he should have done, to hold his tongue on the parts that didn't matter. Back then, everything had been a fight, every decision a war. The very last conversation he ever had with Leanne was a screaming match about something he could barely remember.

Finally, one of the baristas put his coffee down at the end of the counter, so he scooped it up, took a sip – searching for the caffeine kick – and then headed back to the table. 'Thank you for agreeing to meet me,' he said, sitting down. 'I know you will have a lot of questions –'

'Are you going to tell us why you did it?'

Healy watched as Liam glanced at Ciaran, an expression on his face that said, *Calm down*. But Ciaran kept his gaze fixed on Healy. They'd clearly discussed what they were going to say, but Ciaran had taken a wrecking ball to that inside the first ten seconds.

'I know you're angry,' Healy said. 'I know you both have a lot of questions. I tried to answer them in the emails, but I know it's not the same as hearing it from the horse's mouth.' Healy stopped. He had practised this moment, but now – with their eyes on him – he started to lose his train of thought. 'Eleven years ago, when I got fired from the Met . . .' He paused again. 'I don't know. Being a cop was all I knew. When I got fired, I felt . . . directionless.'

66

'That was all you knew?' Ciaran repeated back to him.

'I mean, professionally, not –'

'You still had us.' Liam this time.

Healy turned to him. 'I know I did, son. I know I did. I loved you boys –'

'If you loved us, you wouldn't have done what you did,' Ciaran said, instantly cutting him off, fired up. 'You cared more about being a cop than you did about us.'

'I didn't.'

'You did. You got sacked, and instead of getting closer to Liam and me, you grew more distant. You didn't have your precious job and it was like you suddenly didn't have *anything*. We remember. After Leanne died, we *needed* you. *Mum* needed you. But you were never there. You were never there for us when you were with the police; you sure as shit weren't there after. In fact, when we were told you'd died, there was a weird part of me that actually felt relieved.'

'Ciaran,' Liam said, cutting across him.

It was taking everything Healy had to stay silent. They needed to say what they needed to say – he knew that; it was what had to happen before they could move on. And some of what they were saying was pretty close to the truth: sometimes it *had* felt like he knew more about being a cop than he did about being a father; sometimes he'd looked at his sons, or at Leanne before she died, and had seen strangers staring back at him. He hadn't known how to handle them as they got older. He'd told them often he loved them, but telling them and making them *feel* it weren't the same thing.

Ciaran was still ranting, years and years of frustration pouring out of him. 'You could have done literally *anything* except what you did,' he was saying. The people on the neighbouring tables glanced across. 'You made us believe you were dead for nearly eight years. I mean, they found that body that was supposed to be you. We went to your *funeral*. But do you know what's even worse? The first time we found out you *weren't* dead was when the police called us last year to say you were in prison.'

Healy nodded. 'I know. It's a lot.'

'You think?'

Healy gave himself a moment. 'I understand you're both very angry. I do. And I'm so sorry. But if you can just let me explain to you why I did what I did, maybe I –'

'Nothing you say will make it better.'

'Ciaran,' Liam said, looking at his brother.

'What, you're falling for this shit?' Ciaran stared at his younger brother. And then, finally, he relented, looked at Alice, at the people at the tables around them, and seemed to realize he'd lost control. 'Fine. Whatever.'

'Thank you,' Healy said.

He reached for his coffee, took another long sip.

This is it. This is your chance.

Don't screw it up.

'When your sister died,' he said, and stopped. His voice was wavering already. Images of Leanne flashed in his head: as a toddler, as a teenager – and then when he'd finally found her, hidden in the darkness where she was never meant to be found.

My baby.

He blinked, trying to rid his head of the last memory.

'It just messed me up,' he said. 'I didn't know how to deal with it. I was already angry all the time, and losing her the way we did . . .' A hitch in his voice.

Ciaran just stared at him unmoved.

But Liam was different – and so was Alice. He must have told her all about Leanne; about how his sister had been abducted by a monster – imprisoned, murdered. Alice squeezed Liam's hand; Liam blinked, eyes wet. The thing was, Liam didn't even know the half of it. None of them did. They knew she'd

68

been killed, and who had wielded the knife, but they hadn't been there in that place, like Healy had been.

If they had, they'd understand.

They'd understand why I never got over it.

'I was just angry. I was hurting. I couldn't deal with the grief. And then, a couple of years after Leanne died, when I got fired from the Met, it was like another pillar had crumbled. I felt completely unbalanced. And the man I was then, he didn't know how to handle it. I let you guys drift away from me – I lost you, I lost your mum, lost my home after she and I split. I lived on the streets, but even that wasn't the bottom. I . . .' He ground to a halt. 'Five years after Leanne was killed, I was *still* lost. And, one day, I just thought, "What difference would it make right now if I was dead?" '

'We all loved Leanne,' Ciaran said.

'I know, son,' Healy replied. 'I know.'

'Not just you.'

Healy wanted to say, *But you weren't there when I found her. You weren't her father. You don't have the first idea what it's like for a parent to bury their child.* But that would have been the old Healy, the one who had put him in this position in the first place. Sometimes he would see that version of himself flicker into existence in a mirror or feel the echoes of that man in moments like this, but he'd become better at controlling it. He could push the old Healy all the way down. So he said, 'I know, son. You boys were brilliant brothers. She was very lucky.'

'So you're working as a security guard?'

Alice now, clearly uncomfortable with the tension. Healy looked at her. She was a tall, pretty brunette with very green eyes.

'Yes,' he replied. 'At some flats in Greenwich.'

'How do you find it?'

'Oh, it's very glamorous.' He smiled at her, and she returned it. 'It's fine. It pays the rent. And I can get my steps in.' He held up his smartwatch. 'Got to get in your ten thousand a day. I mean, this body won't pay for itself.'

Another smile.

And the hint of one from Liam too.

Maybe I'm starting to make some progress.

'Would you mind if I asked you something?' Alice said.

'No, of course not.'

She shuffled forward on her seat.

Healy waited, wondering what was coming.

'I'm just curious,' she said. 'What's David Raker like?'

11

The true crime website Kyle had been looking at was called *Evidence Bag*.

Most of the time he'd spent on the site had been in the afternoons of that first week of April, between about 1 p.m. and 5 p.m. He was still at school then, but would have been on Easter holidays, and on his desktop I could see a revision timetable for the two-week break, with his A levels only a couple of months away. Except, instead of studying, he went to *Evidence Bag*. Why?

Aside from serial killer biographies and videos that ran on the TrueCrimeUK TV channel, which *Evidence Bag* had a tie-in with, mostly he'd returned to a section marked 'Top 5s', which included lists like 'Top 5 Most Lethal Serial Killers', 'Top 5 Deadly Females', 'Top 5 Weirdest Disappearances', and 'Top 5 Unsolved Murders'. Among these, there was a single, small area of repetition in his browsing: on each of the six days, Kyle had visited and revisited one page in particular: 'Top 5 Unsolved Murders You've Never Heard Of'.

I read the first entry.

#1 BELLA IN THE WYCH ELM
In April 1943, four Worcestershire boys discover a woman's body in the hollow of a wych elm tree.

The title of the entry had got one part right: Bella in the Wych Elm *was* still an unsolved murder. But to call the case 'unheard of' was a stretch: Bella was, in fact, one of the UK's longest-standing mysteries.

I moved to the next entry.

#2 THE SMILEY FACE MURDERS
Between 1990 and 2010, forty-five men in the US Midwest 'accidentally' drowned in bodies of water. Were they the victims of a serial killer?

I knew about this one too. The smiley-face murder theory had originally been put forward by two NYPD detectives and a criminal justice professor and apportioned the blame for forty-five deaths of young men in bodies of water, not to inebriation, but to the work of a serial killer, or killers. At a few of the 'crime' scenes, similar smiley-face graffiti was found painted on to walls nearby.

I'd never heard of the other three cases, though.

#3 THE WOMAN IN THE DESERT
In 2020, the skeletal remains of a woman were found in the Mojave. The detective who worked the case nicknamed her the 'Desert Angel' . . .

#4 THE ICE CREAM SHOP MURDERS
Firefighters responding to a blaze at an ice cream shop in Cape Town in 1997 discover four teenagers inside. They've all been stabbed to death.

#5 THE HANGING OF PIERRE DECROIX
Promising young French artist Pierre Decroix was found hanging from a tree in an apple orchard near Buckfastleigh in 2012. Who was responsible?

Buckfastleigh.
That was only fifteen minutes from Totnes, where Sarah

was living, and about forty from Parson's Quarry. I clicked on the link.

Pierre Decroix, 21, was in his third year at Exeter University studying Art. Originally from Paris, Pierre had moved to the UK with his family when he was fourteen. His friends described him as 'happy, creative and relaxed' in the days leading up to his death, and yet – on Tuesday 10 April 2012 – he was found hanging from an apple tree in an orchard near Buckfastleigh, Devon, in south-west England. Police determined that it wasn't a suicide, not only because Pierre showed no indications or history of suicidal thoughts or behaviour, but because the crime scene, the tree, the noose and the way Pierre died made it unlikely he could have carried it out himself. So who killed Pierre Decroix?

Aside from the death having occurred in Devon, I couldn't see any other links to the Fowlers' case. I reread all the other entries in full, just to be sure I hadn't missed something, but one of them had happened back in the 1940s, and the other three had taken place thousands of miles away.

So why was Kyle looking at these pages?

And why did he stop after only six days?

I grabbed my phone and dialled Sarah's number. When she answered, I could hear she was in the car. The radio was playing, Mable gabbling in the background.

'I'm just taking her to toddler gym,' Sarah explained.

'It's okay, this won't take long.' I glanced at the laptop. 'Weird question, but did Kyle ever express any interest in true crime? Cold cases, murders, that sort of thing?'

A confused silence. 'No. No, I don't think so. Why?'

'I'm just going through his laptop and he spent a little time looking at – and returning to – a true crime website called *Evidence Bag*. I'm trying to figure out why.'

And if it matters.

I glanced at the window that Kyle's history was open in.

It must have mattered.

'Did you ever watch crime documentaries or shows of that type with him?'

'No. I mean, he may have watched them on his own, I guess.'

'But he didn't ever talk about having an interest in that sort of thing?'

'No, never. Not even once.'

As I stared at the screen, a part of me started trying to talk myself back. *Don't get hung up on this. He was a teenager – there were probably tons of things he didn't tell his mum about. You could chase your tail for days.* But none of those thoughts took hold – because I knew, instinctively, this was important.

It was a lead, however small.

I just had to work out where it went.

Olivia arrived home at half past six.

I wondered for a moment how much – if anything – I should tell Annabel. Liv was over three hours later than she should have been if she'd left college when her last lesson ended, but she was also a few months short of turning eighteen and, within reason, could come and go as she liked.

'Hey, Liv.'

She started as she came into the living room. I'd been so engrossed in Kyle's laptop that I'd forgotten to put on any lights – and now I realized the house was gloomy, rain spattering against the roof of the conservatory.

'I keep forgetting you're here,' Liv muttered.

'Don't worry, it'll only be for a few more days.'

'No, I didn't mean that.'

'It's okay. It's a pain having people to stay. I get it.'

'It's fine.' Her tone was neutral.

'How was your day?'

'Boring.'

'That's good.' I smiled. 'It wouldn't be school if it was interesting.'

She just looked at me. She was a beautiful girl – dark eyes, jet-black hair, a tall, slim physique that had made her look awkward when she was younger but which she'd fully grown into now. She had a lovely smile too, but I hadn't seen much of that in the time I'd been here. Since I'd last visited them both, she'd cut her hair incredibly short – mostly, I imagined, to bait her sister, who had loved her long hair. I'd always tried to treat Liv exactly the same as I treated Annabel, but that hadn't stopped an unspoken disconnect developing between us. It hadn't been there when she was young, but the older she got, the easier it was for me to see.

It said, *You're not my father.*

And I'm not your daughter.

'I have some homework to do,' she said.

As she was walking away, my phone buzzed.

So are you going to find me the Whaler?

I'd almost forgotten about the conversation with Melanie Craw earlier on. For now, though, I didn't want to get distracted by another disappearance in another place, so I went back to the names of friends and family that Sarah had given me and began to ring around. It was nothing more than a fishing exercise. Most of them I'd already crossed off my list. But I liked to speak to people, because it was harder to hide things in a conversation than it was in an email or text.

'We absolutely loved him here,' Marc's boss told me. 'Just a great guy: brilliant at his job, really fun to be around, and he absolutely adored Sarah and the kids. We used to organize a summer party every year, where all the families got to come along, and you saw how much Sarah, Kyle and Mable meant to him.'

'He was coping okay with his workload?'

'Never had a problem with Marc on that front. He was so organized.'

'Any difficult customers? Anyone he didn't like?'

'Again, no. In our area of specialism, he's one of the best in the country, and our customers love that about him. I felt lucky to have him, to be honest.'

I rang off and then talked to someone called Francesca, who had become a friend of Clara's after they met in a book group:

'Oh, she was so sweet. She was quiet – to start with, anyway – but after a while you realized she had a brilliant sense of humour. She was really good at impressions, actually.'

'She was?'

'Have you ever seen the film *Fargo*?'

'Yeah, a few times.'

'She did an *amazing* impression of the character Frances McDormand plays in that. Uh . . . the detective. Oh, what's her name?'

'Marge Gunderson.'

'Right! Honestly, the accent was spot on. "Oh yah."' Francesca started chuckling to herself. '"There's a high-speed pursuit, ends here, and then this execution-type deal."' She started laughing again. 'You should have heard it.'

The detail about the impressions surprised me. I was finding out more about Marc, Kyle and Clara all the time, but most of it so far had broadly been similar: they were a tight-knit family who had brought Clara into the fold like she was one of their own. Marc was gregarious, dedicated and highly respected at work, caring and supportive at home; Kyle was active, always on the move, always looking for a challenge, but deep down an easy-going and sensitive soul; Clara was quiet, studious in her work, and was constantly described as either *sweet* or *kind*, or both. Maybe that was why her gift for impressions was so surprising – it suggested a confidence I didn't expect her to have.

At seven thirty, Annabel finally got home.

'Hey, sweetheart.'

'Hey,' she said, dumping her bag in the hallway.

'That was a long day.'

'I felt every minute of it.' She came over and gave me a hug. 'How was yours?'

'A lot of chasing my tail.'

'Ah, I'm sorry.'

'It happens. I'll make us some dinner.'

She smiled. 'Thank you.'

I studied her: she seemed tired, ground down. Physically, she was so different from Olivia – a little shorter, a little curvier, lighter skin, lighter hair – but her face had always carried a warmth which I loved. Even now, even exhausted and stressed, it lit her gaze like a flame. She was my daughter – so she would have been beautiful to me regardless – but I'd always thought there was something very special about her eyes.

'I think I'm going to run a bath,' she said. 'Is Liv home?'

'Yeah, she's upstairs doing her homework.'

'Okay,' she said. 'We'll catch up after I've decontaminated.'

As she disappeared upstairs, my phone started ringing. It was one of the numbers I'd just been calling: Kyle's friend, Jacob Miller. I'd left a message with him.

I picked up and reintroduced myself. The two boys had done A levels at the same school, and now Jacob was doing a marketing degree at Plymouth.

'Thank you for calling me back,' I said.

He sounded nervous, which I didn't read anything into. He was eighteen, just a kid – and this probably felt something close to being dragged into a police interview.

'Is this about the arguments?'

I frowned. 'I'm sorry?'

'Is that what you're calling about?'

'The arguments? Who was arguing?'

'Kyle's parents.'

'Sarah and Marc?'

'Yeah.'

I glanced at a photograph Sarah had given me, of her and Marc sitting next to each other on a park bench, eating ice cream in the sun, beaming.

'I didn't know they were arguing,' I said.

'Oh.' A beat. 'Well, they were.'

'Kyle told you that?'

'Yes,' Jacob replied. 'He said they were arguing all the time.'

13

I glanced at the photograph again.

Sarah and Marc stared back – happy, smiling.

I remembered the thought I had earlier: *all photos are staged to some degree*. Was that what this one was? Was that what all the photos of the two of them were?

'When did Kyle tell you his mum and stepdad were arguing?'

'I don't know exactly,' Jacob said. 'Just before he disappeared.'

'A few days? A few weeks?'

'I'm not sure.'

'Did he say what the arguments were about?'

'No.'

'He didn't want to tell you?'

'It wasn't that. I don't think he could hear very clearly. He said he would just hear raised voices at night. His room was across from theirs.'

'Did he ever ask his mum about it?'

'He did. She kept saying that it was nothing, just money issues.'

Sarah had told me earlier that she was going to be struggling financially before long – but *before* the disappearances she said everything had been fine. So why would they have been arguing about money? Had Sarah lied to her son about what they were arguing about?

Or had she lied to me?

'Did the police speak to you when Kyle, Marc and Clara vanished?'

'No.'

'Have you told anyone else about this?'

'No. Well, only my mum.'

I glanced at Kyle's laptop, trying to put my thoughts into some sort of order. 'Did Kyle ever talk to you about an interest he might have had in true crime?'

A confused pause. 'What?'

'True crime. You know, real-life murders, serial killers, that sort of thing.'

'*Serial killers?*' He sounded completely thrown. 'No. Why?'

I'd asked the same question of all of Kyle's friends, and the answer had been the same throughout. Kyle had never shown any interest in true crime, either talking about it, watching it or reading it.

My thoughts returned to Sarah and Marc.

Would Sarah lie to me? What would she achieve by hiring me and then doing so? I thought of the missing persons reports I'd read and the interviews she'd done with both Richardson and Wiley. And I thought of the suspicions they'd had about her recollection, and – threaded throughout their questions – the sense they obviously had that something was off, even if they couldn't quite put their finger on what.

An instinct for what was out of kilter never helped a case get to court – but it didn't mean that intuition wasn't valid. Maybe I hadn't given Wiley and Richardson enough credit. Or maybe I'd given Sarah too much.

I'd believed her.

I'd trusted her.

What if I was wrong to?

14

At dinner, I listened to Annabel and Olivia discussing a project Liv had, which required her to design a gown for a summer ball. There was a stilted quality to their conversation – Annabel was exhausted and wanted to avoid a fight, so was on eggshells; Liv was gruff, as if her defences were permanently up – but it was better than what I'd seen the previous night.

Afterwards, I took the plates through to wash up, and as I did, their voices began to drift and my thoughts returned to Sarah again.

I was conflicted.

Half of me wanted to video-call her and ask her directly if she'd lied to me about her finances and her relationship with Marc. I wanted to hear the timbre of her voice and watch the movement in her face. I wanted to see her eyes as she replied, because so often that was where deceit crumbled first.

The other half didn't want to tell her anything.

If she really *had* lied to me, I wanted to know why, and often that was easier to do when the person wasn't aware that you were circling them.

'Thanks for doing this.' Annabel brought some glasses in from the table and, behind her, I saw Olivia heading off to her bedroom again, her face illuminated by her phone.

'No worries,' I said.

'We haven't really talked much about your day.'

Just over a decade ago, it was one of my cases that had brought us into each other's lives for the first time, so she'd seen my work from the inside as a missing person herself. Even so, I kept a lot back from her, not because I didn't think she'd understand, but because I knew she would – and then she'd just worry about me.

'I was reading about the Fowlers today,' she said.

'You were? What do you think?'

'I don't know. There's not much about it online considering how crazy it is, is there? The way you'd described it and the way it was reported seem very . . . different.'

I smiled.

'What?' She smiled too.

'No, nothing. You've got good instincts, that's all. Basically, I think the police stopped short of giving the media anything too exciting.'

She remained quiet but her eyes stayed on me.

'Something on your mind, Detective?'

She broke out into another smile. 'I wasn't peeking, I promise.'

I glanced across at Kyle's laptop, the missing persons report and the phone statements. They were all still laid out on the table in the conservatory. My notebook was next to them, its pages open.

'I just saw that you'd written down *Melanie Craw*,' she said.

'Ah.'

I'd forgotten Annabel had met Craw. 'Are you two' – Annabel winked at me – 'y'know, back in touch?'

'Not like that, no. She offered me some work.'

'Oh.' A frown. 'After all this time?'

'After all this time.'

'So, all of a sudden, the police want your help?'

'That's the thing, she's not a cop any more. You ever heard of the Skyline?'

'That big casino up in London?'

'She's head of security there.'

'Wow. And what does she want you to do?'

I glanced at the notebook in the conservatory.

'Find someone,' I said. 'And locate some money.'

'Are you going to do it?'

'I have the Fowler case. I can't really commit to it now.'

'So you're *not* going to do it?'

I glanced at my daughter. 'Are you making fun of me?'

'No.' She chuckled. 'But I've seen that look before.'

'And what look is that?'

'The one that says, whatever Craw has asked you to do, and however much you delay taking it on, it's too late.' She shrugged. 'It's already got its hooks into you.'

15

After Annabel headed up to bed, I went back to the Fowler disappearance.

First thing in the morning, I was meeting Barney Cowdrey, Kyle's former boss, at the quarry, because he was working close by, and then I'd head into Paignton, to Clara's flat. I'd called her former landlord and asked him if I could look around. He'd let the flat to someone else for six months in the intervening period, but they'd just moved out and it was now lying empty until the end of May. I didn't expect to find much of worth there, I just wanted to see the place that Clara had lived in. Homes helped me visualize people as more than just a name on a report, or a face – frozen forever – in a photograph.

I had one other piece of business in Paignton as well.

It was where Kyle's dad, Daryl Beaumont, still lived.

I'd tracked him down to the middle house in a row of terraces just south of the town centre. According to what I'd been able to find out, he was thirty-nine, unmarried, had no other kids, and worked for a builders' yard on the outskirts of Brixham. At the moment, he was an unanswered question and no one, especially Sarah, could help me colour him in.

Next to me, my phone burst into life.

'Evening,' Colm Healy said after I'd picked up.

'Evening. You okay?'

'Yeah, not bad. Been at work for three hours already and have read most of the book I brought with me – so now I've got to spend the rest of the night eking out the final fifty pages.' Healy paused. He hated his job as a security guard. When he first got out of prison, I'd offered to pass some work his way, but the cost-of-living crisis had already hit – and hit hard – and there just wasn't enough money coming in to sustain us both. So he'd applied for a job as a night guard at a block of flats in Greenwich.

'How did it go with the boys today?' I asked.

'All right. Ish. Ciaran went off like a rocket – but he settled down into a moody silence. Liam was okay. He didn't say much, but he was more . . . I don't know . . .' I heard him take a long breath. 'It seemed like he was more willing to hear me out, so maybe he's more open to the possibility of us starting over.'

'You don't think that's the case with Ciaran?'

'I don't know,' Healy said again. 'I don't really know them any more. I left them when they were basically still kids, and now they're fully grown men.' He stopped again, and in the silence I thought about the seven years Healy had spent moving from place to place, pretending he was dead. I'd aided him – had helped with money and fake IDs – and I'd done it because I'd recognized his pain. He was grieving for his daughter, Leanne, I'd been grieving for my wife, Derryn: much of that grief was what had brought us together in the first place; it was the accelerant that had kick-started our partnership, and the fuel that had kept us going. Faking his death had become an anchor to us – and while we were both relieved we didn't have to lie any more, neither of us looked back on those seven years with any great regrets. There were moments when it had felt like a burden, but the stillness of anonymity had allowed Healy to breathe, to take stock, even to change as a person – to become less angry and combative – and to realize what he had done wrong and what he needed to put right.

Ciaran and Liam were the first thing.

'To be honest,' he said, 'I think it's going to take a lot for

86

Ciaran to come all the way back. He hasn't got over Leanne's death; hasn't allowed himself time to do that. I mean, I get it. When I think about her . . .' I knew him so well now, I could guess what image was in his head. I'd been there alongside him when he'd found Leanne, and I knew, even almost thirteen years on, that image still kept him awake at night. 'Being alone for so long, I've spent a lot of time with my own thoughts. I've dealt with it as best I can. He hasn't dealt with it at all. He sat there today and I saw the anger in him. He's looking to hit out, and I'm a good place to start.'

'Maybe he just needs to get it out of his system.'

'Maybe,' Healy agreed. 'Anyway, Liam was basically all right, which is a start. And his girlfriend seemed like a sweet kid.'

'Can't be long for them now, can it?'

'Eight weeks until her due date.'

'Big moment.'

'Yeah. Actually, I wanted to ask you about her.'

'What do you mean?'

'Her name's Alice-Leigh. I think her surname's Reddy. You ever heard of her?'

'No.' I frowned. 'Should I have?'

'No, probably not. She just seemed to be a fan of yours.'

'Did she?'

'Yeah. She was asking me about you.'

I pulled my laptop towards me. 'Asking you what?'

'Just what you were like.'

'Why would she want to know that?'

'She's a solicitor, works for some company in the city. I think they're handling all the paperwork for the Castle hearings. You gave testimony last week, didn't you?'

'I did, yeah.'

'She said she was in court when you did.'

I knew the name of the law firm, so I googled that and then

went to the 'About Us' section of their website. Her photo-graph was at the foot of the page.

I'd never met her.

'She must have been impressed by you, I guess,' Healy said.

'Well, I wore a new suit.'

'That'll be it. So what's new with you?'

I closed Chrome. On-screen now were all my text messages, including the one I'd got from Melanie Craw I hadn't replied to yet:

So are you going to find me the Whaler?

'Don't you work seven nights on, three off?' I asked.

'Yeah.'

'You got plans for your days off?'

'Not really. Why?'

'I wondered if you wanted to look into something for me.'

1993

Los Angeles, California

It's a cold day in early March.

Detective Pete Tomer arrives at Crescenta Valley station just before 8 a.m. This is his second-to-last month at the Los Angeles County Sheriff's Department, although he doesn't realize that now. In five days' time, a guy he knows at Glendale PD will pick up the phone and offer him a job with more money and better terms and Tomer will finally call time on fifteen years at the LASD. But for now, he's still a sheriff's detective, still the same cop who everyone used to rave about when he arrested the Flintside Strangler at a motel in North Hollywood.

Not that anyone remembers him as that cop any more.

That was a decade ago.

These days, Pete Tomer is just background noise.

Intermittently, he wonders if he ruined his career by moving to Crescenta Valley two years ago, by taking what might be seen as a step back from Compton, where he was before. Crescenta Valley is quieter, safer and very definitely easier, so maybe he has. But Tomer tries not to linger on it too long, tries to concentrate on the reasons why he opted for a transfer here in the first place: it gives him more time with his son. He needs that for two reasons: one is that Billy has just turned seven, and it feels like he's growing up at double speed already; the other is that it's now two years since Georgia, Tomer's wife, died in a car accident on the 210. So, on this damp day in March, as he gets out of his car, he thinks this is all his job is and ever will be – and if this is all it's going to be, better it's built around his son.

He's barely crossed the lot before he sees Darnell Savage coming out of the doors at the front of the station, making a beeline for him. Sometimes he forgets how big Darnell is, how tall, how wide, because they spend so much of their time sitting at their desks or riding around in cars. Tomer is slight and lean, five-ten and about 165 pounds; Darnell is a giant, six-four and 230. Darnell's in good shape, but it's impossible for him to move quickly, even when he's running – so when Tomer stops, and waits, it's still a while before Darnell reaches him.

'Morning,' Darnell says.

'Morning.'

Tomer, his pack still on his shoulder, goes straight to the unmarked Ford Crown that Darnell's signed out. He gets in the driver's side, and after Darnell hoists the passenger seat all the way back, he hands the keys to Tomer.

A minute later, they're on Foothill Boulevard.

Darnell begins filling him in: 'White female, late teens, early twenties. Her body's been dumped off the side of the Two – half a mile from the turn-off for the Switzer Falls picnic area.'

The Angeles Crest Highway is part of State Route 2, starting in La Cañada Flintridge and snaking up through the San Gabriel Mountains and the Angeles National Forest for sixty-six miles to the San Bernardino County line. They wouldn't have to go that far, but it's still going to be a thirty-minute drive and over 4,000 feet of elevation before they get to the scene. And if the weather is cool and damp down here, it's going to be even worse up there: fog has been skirting the mountains for days and the ski resorts out east have had record snowfall.

'Who was she found by?' Tomer asks.

'Some hikers. They were going to head up from Colby Canyon to Strawberry Peak, so got there early and left their car at the trailhead. They saw her in a ravine on the left-hand side of the parking lot as they were getting out of their vehicle. I don't know if you've been there, but it's just an unpaved lot. Basically dirt, a lot of scrub all around – it's small, only space for, like, ten or eleven cars. There's a roadside barrier on the left side because it's on a bend. She was dumped over the barrier.'

'And – what? – she tumbled into the ravine?'

'Yeah.'

'What else do we know?'

'Not a lot. Two deputies called it in. They're still up there. Forensics should be on their way, and I put in a call to the coroner. Just got to hope this weather doesn't screw things up too much.' Darnell glances out of the window, ducking his head so he can see the approaching mountains. Tomer looks too.

Mist hides most of it from view.

They don't talk much after that, both of them quiet as they prepare for what's coming. The drive up takes longer than thirty minutes, the mist dense, sitting like a shelf across the peaks, the drizzle they left in the city soon replaced by swirling flurries of snow. Tomer has to take it steady, turns in the road disguised, bends suddenly upon him. But then, up ahead, they see flashing lights and he pulls the Crown to a stop.

Ahead of them is the unpaved lot that Darnell described on the way up, the pitches and cants of the mountains surrounding it, with two cars and a van parked up. One car belongs to the couple who found the body. The other is an LASD patrol vehicle. The van has been driven here by a forensic team, who've arrived before the coroner.

They get out and head towards the scene, and Tomer spots the two officers almost immediately. One is talking to the couple who found the body. He's on his haunches next to their car, the man and the woman in the front seats. He has a notebook out, a pen poised above the page, and is asking them questions.

The other officer is in the ravine with the forensic tech.

Tomer can't actually see them, only their breath. It's starting to sleet now, the air bitterly cold. The officer comes into view as Tomer and Darnell climb over the barrier and clamber down to the girl's body. There's snow on the ground, and the girl is in a blanket of it, on her back, eyes staring up at the heavens.

Later, they will find out her name is Wilma Steski.

She's a stunning biracial girl of nineteen. The photograph the LA Sheriff's Department uses in the press is of Wilma smiling, a mouth full of clean white teeth, her hair braided, a scattering of freckles under her eyes and across the bridge of her nose. Wilma is a first-year student at the California Institute of Technology, bright, driven, and – in being female and choosing to study Applied Physics – a rarity on an undergraduate course that's entirely male, except for her. The men Wilma knew are where Tomer and Darnell start after finding the body – the other students on her course, the boys that she hung out with in the classroom and at parties – but the interviews, the leads, the theories, all get them nowhere.

Wilma Steski is just one long dead end.

But all of that will come in the days ahead.

For now, Tomer crouches down next to her body.

Wilma has an exit wound in the front of her face. It's a through-and-through, the cavity just above her left eye. By the way the blood has frozen, by the condition of the body, Tomer can see that Wilma's been out here a couple of days.

He can also see both arms are tucked under her spine.

He looks at the forensic tech. 'Are her wrists tied?'

'Seems that way,' the tech says.

Still keeping his distance from the body, Tomer gets down on to his knees and lowers the side of his face to the hard, compacted ground, to the snow, trying to see what's going on with the wrists.

They've been tied.

Thick rope. Knotted.

Getting back on to his feet, he glances at Darnell, who's on the other side of the girl's body, looking at her legs. Her pants have torn below the knees, and what's left of them have ridden up to reveal her shins and the slender curve of her calves.

There are marks on her exposed legs.

'Are they scratches?' Tomer asks.

'Yeah,' Darnell answers. He leans across the girl. 'All over, actually.'

Darnell removes a pen from his jacket and points in the direction of the cuts on the girl's legs, at the bruises – yellow-purple – on her shins and below her knees.

Tomer comes around and takes a closer look.

And as he does, as he looks from the cuts and bruises on the legs, to the torn clothes, to the arms bound under the girl, to the bullet wound, his stomach curdles.

'Tomer?'

Darnell knows something is up.

'How do you think she got those?' Tomer asks, pointing to the girl's legs.

Darnell's clicking his pen, thinking, not looking at the body now. Tomer can tell he's affected by the sight of the girl, by what's been done to her, by this beautiful, vibrant life cut short in the most heinous way possible. Darnell doesn't have kids yet, but he comes from a big family. He has three sisters – including one around the same age as Wilma is. He has a girlfriend he dotes on. One of the many reasons Tomer gets on with Darnell is because he feels something.

Maybe, like Tomer, a little too much at times.

Darnell's eyes go off to the mountains. He looks at their

snow-painted hollows, at the trees that blanket every single inch of the valley they're in, and then finally he says, 'Maybe she made a run for it.'

'Maybe.'

'You don't think so?'

Tomer stares at the girl. 'It looks more like she was hunted.'

2
The Driver

16

A Land Rover pulled into the lay-by just after 8 a.m.

It was drizzling, Dartmoor covered in a low-lying shelf of cloud that cut across the moorland and sliced off the top of the tors. I watched for a moment in my rear-view mirror as Barney Cowdrey got out of the car and zipped up a big green anorak, and then I pulled up my hood and went over to introduce myself. He was a large man in his late forties, with shaved black hair and a patchy beard.

'Thanks for meeting me,' I said.

'It's no problem,' he replied in a thick Devon accent.

'Where's the sunshine?'

He smiled. 'Welcome to Dartmoor.'

I let Cowdrey lead the way, even though I knew the route, and as we walked to the quarry – the sound of rain tap-tapping on the stone path ahead of us – I asked Cowdrey for his memories of Kyle in the weeks before the disappearances.

'Everything seemed fine with him,' he said, his voice sincere. 'I never got the sense there were any problems. Kyle was a lovely kid. He'd only been working for us – officially – for a few weeks, but he'd done work experience before that, so when he started in September, we already knew him pretty well. It never felt like he was new.'

'So everyone got on with him?'

'Oh yeah. He just seemed a happy kid.'

We passed the broken miners' huts on the way up and then followed the trail down to the quarry itself. It looked different today, the rain and mist obscuring the back half of the lake from view, the sweeping granite walls disappearing into the low-hanging fog. Cowdrey led me to the edge of the lake and out to the right, following a well-trodden path along the fringes of the water. We were heading away from the shoreline where Sarah and the family had set up, out to the edges of the quarry. Walking in silence, the rain getting heavier, I watched as, ahead of me, the trail dropped away sharply into a small dip full of overgrown ferns and bright yellow gorse – and, once Cowdrey had arrived there, he stopped and waited for me.

'This is the lowest point,' he said, gesturing to the water, which was very gently lapping at the path and occasionally washing over it entirely. 'It probably gives you the clearest view of the whole lake. That's where the boat was.'

He was pointing to an area in the centre. The rain was disturbing the surface of the lake, and the greyness of the day seemed to have been absorbed into the water, but I didn't need the sun to be shining to confirm what I already knew: there was no way that Marc, Kyle and Clara had got to either this end, or the other, inside the minute Sarah had told the cops she'd been out.

Which meant what?

That Sarah had been mistaken about how long she'd been out? Or that – whatever her reasons would be for doing so – she'd lied?

'Sarah said the cops called you and your team in that night?' I asked.

'Yeah. We got here about 10 p.m.'

'Where did you search?'

'There were four of us. Two on that side' – he jabbed a finger across the lake to the far shore – 'and two along this one. Basically, we covered the whole circumference of the lake between us.'

'And you found nothing?'

'No.'

But something remained in his face.

'You did a search the next morning too, didn't you?'

'We did.'

'Did you find anything then?'

'Nothing conclusive.'

'But you found something?'

He eyed me for a second and then looked ahead of us, up and out of the dip and along the rest of the path. 'It's probably better if I show you.'

17

Further down the path, there was a sloped bank on the left. It was a natural slipway of loose stone and wet mud that ascended out of the water, up across the path and on to a small, grassed area to the right of me. At the back of the grassed area was a long-abandoned vehicle track that wound its way up the granite wall, through a series of sharp switchbacks, towards the apex of the quarry on this side. It had probably been created originally to bring horses and carts down to the mine.

'There was a tyre track,' Cowdrey said.

I looked at him. 'Where?'

'There.'

He pointed to the grassed area.

'You found it on the night of the search?'

'No, the next morning.'

So why hadn't it been mentioned in the police report?

I looked upwards. 'What's at the top?'

'There are ranger routes on the moors which are off-limits to the public. A lot of them are just old army trails, because they do live firing not too far from here. The track that winds up the side of the quarry here connects with one of those.'

'The cops never mentioned there being a tyre track down here.'

'No. That's because they thought we made it.'

'What do you mean?'

He gestured from the slipway to the grassed area and then to the trail on the side of the quarry. 'The foundations here aren't as strong as they look. All the digging and drilling that went on back in the day, it's led to a ton of erosion. So we keep an eye on it, especially in prolonged spells of warm weather, which was what we had last September. That meant I was down here most mornings, including the day they disappeared. I remember the ground was rock solid because we hadn't had any rain for a couple of weeks, so existing tyre tracks had already hardened and any new ones had barely formed due to it being so dry.'

'So what are you saying?'

'I'm saying, the following morning, the morning we did the second search, one of my boys thought he saw a tyre track just here.' He pointed to the grassed area. 'He calls me over, and I look at it myself. The track is incomplete. There's, like, one half of a tyre tread imprinted in the grass.'

'And – what? – the police thought it came from one of your Land Rovers?'

'It could have.'

I eyed him. 'But you don't think so?'

'We all have the same tyres on our vehicles.'

'And that wasn't the half-tread you saw imprinted in the grass?'

'It didn't look the same to me, no.' Cowdrey glanced at me from beneath his hood, a faint hint of breath gathering in front of his face. 'I could be wrong.'

But it didn't look like he believed he was.

'Do you remember which cop you told about the tyre track?'

'The guy who came up from Newton Abbot.'

'Wiley?'

'Yeah, that's him. He didn't come out for the daylight search, he just said to call him if we found anything. So I sent him a picture of the tyre track, and then he asked me how often we were down here, and I told him exactly what I just told you – all the time in the summer. And he said he'd pass it on to a colleague in Totnes.'

Richardson.

'The Totnes guy called me up, said he'd seen the picture, but he didn't seem worried about it. In fairness, it was half a tread – pretty far from being definitive – and I couldn't say with absolute certainty that it *wasn't* one of ours.'

I understood Cowdrey giving Richardson the benefit of the doubt, but to me it was just another example of sloppy police work. So often these were the reasons that cases went cold: something wasn't investigated properly, not followed up on, or some corner was cut; or a police officer became entrenched in a theory about a case, about a suspect, that blinded them to other equally important things.

I looked out at the quarry.

If Cowdrey's instincts were right, a vehicle had been down here some time just before or after Marc, Kyle and Clara vanished – and it wasn't one of the rangers.

'Who else uses this route?'

I pointed to the track leading up the granite wall.

'No one.'

'Not the army?'

'No. They're a few miles over.'

'The public?'

'No,' Cowdrey said again. 'It's clearly marked from the main roads what tracks are private, and most of the ranger routes are blocked at their entrances by wooden gates. I guess you could open them, but we've honestly never had an issue with that.'

Yet someone had come down.

The Fowlers would never have seen a vehicle descending the track from where they'd set up for the day, because of the angle of their position. But Marc, Kyle and Clara would have seen it once they'd rowed out to the centre of the lake. So what happened after that? Did someone lure them into shore while

Sarah slept? Or was it all part of some escape plan the three of them had set up? Whichever it was, it would have taken time.

Five minutes.

Ten.

Probably even longer.

Certainly not the one minute Sarah had claimed.

18

On the way back down to Clara's former flat in Paignton, I stopped at an orchard on the outskirts of Buckfastleigh. It was where the body of Pierre Decroix, the French student from Exeter University, had been found hanging. I got out and walked around, more out of hope than expectation, searching for a reason – any reason – why Kyle might have been interested in what had happened here eleven years ago.

I returned to the car, none the wiser.

Thirty minutes later, I pulled up outside Clara's flat.

It was on the top floor of a two-storey house, one road back from the seafront, the gaps between the houses opposite showing glimpses of pastel-coloured terraced homes on the promenade. The weather had got worse, so the beach was completely empty except for a solitary dog-walker, mummified in a soaked anorak.

Behind me, a gold Lexus pulled into a parking space. A man in his sixties with a wash of white hair got out, a set of keys in his hand. He introduced himself as Barry, then I followed him from where I was parked to the mid-terrace a couple of doors down.

We entered a downstairs hallway, carpeted in neutral beige, the walls cream. Ahead were the doors to two ground-floor flats, and a staircase to the right.

'Was Clara a good tenant?' I asked as we headed up.

'Never had a problem with her,' Barry said, 'and, in my book, that makes her a *very* good tenant.'

There were three doors up here; he started to unlock 2C.

'What are you hoping to find?' he asked as he pushed the door open.

'Probably nothing.'

I moved past him, into the empty flat. As I took it in, I could see a kitchenette to the left and then a bedroom and bathroom ahead of me. A sofa, a few years past its sell-by date, remained in the living room along with a bookcase, as did a single bed in the bedroom, the mattress gone and wooden slats exposed.

I wandered from room to room, already knowing this was a waste of time in terms of evidence gathering, as I always suspected it would be. Through one of the windows, there was a partial view of the sea and I saw an imprint in the carpet where a desk had been. I wondered if this was where Clara had worked, illustrating, laying out pages, firing off emails to prospective clients.

'Do you remember how long Clara was here?' I asked.

'Six months.'

'And you said you didn't hear much from her in that time?'

'Not really. You know, a few minor things; just the usual stuff with tenants. I remember the shower door started leaking shortly after she got here, and the oven packed up once. A couple of times we had complaints about the people down in 1B – not from Clara, but from the others up here – so obviously I spoke to her then. Apart from that . . .' He paused, brow furrowed, trying to think. 'I maybe saw her two or three times in the entire period she was renting from us. She was a nice girl, though. Very polite and chatty. Good manners.'

'When did you hear about what happened to her?'

'Oh, I think it was a couple of weeks after she disappeared. Someone called to tell me.' He paused again, his brain ticking over.

'Sarah Fowler?'

'Yes. Sarah, that was her. Clara's boyfriend's mum. She called me to tell me what had happened, and obviously that she had no idea when – or if – Clara was going to return. So I did what I felt was the decent thing and put the last month of rent back into Clara's account. I didn't want to be taking money from her.'

'That was good of you.'

'You do what you can.' He opened out his hands. 'Sarah was very upset. I mean, understandably. It must be so hard losing your whole family like that.'

Maybe it was all an act on Sarah's part, but if it was, it was a good one because this guy had obviously reacted the same way to her as I had, and every second of who'd she'd been at the house had felt real to me. Yet there was still the question of the arguments between her and Marc. So could *all* of it have been real? Could the devastation Sarah felt, a potential lie about her financial situation, and her arguments with Marc *all* have happened?

'How is everyone doing?' Barry asked.

'Not great.'

'I guess that's why they've asked for your help.' He flattened his lips. 'Well, not that she'll remember me, but please give Sarah my best.'

'I will.'

'And Clara's friend too, if you see her.'

I frowned. 'Her friend?'

'Yeah, her best friend. Was it Tori? Or Toni?'

I grabbed my notebook. 'You met this friend?'

'Yes. She was here that time I fixed the oven for Clara.'

I flipped to the list of names I'd compiled in my notes.

'Is everything okay?' Barry asked.

'You're sure Clara introduced this woman as her "best friend"?'

'Yes, I'm positive.'

'How many times did you meet her?'

'Only that once. I came around and fixed the oven, and I saw an inflatable mattress had been set up in the room here – a bed, pillows. Clara joked with me and promised that she wasn't subletting; that her friend was just staying for the night.'

'And you said this friend's name was Tori or Toni?'

'Yes, one or the other.'

I looked at my notes.

No Tori. No Toni.

Clara had a best friend I knew nothing about.

Healy

The Skyline | *Now*

It took him an hour and fifteen minutes to get from Lewisham all the way out to West Drayton and then another fifteen minutes on a shuttle bus. As the bus rattled along the M4, Healy knew it would have taken him just as long in a car, if he'd had one. But at least if he'd owned a car, he wouldn't have spent the first half of his journey in the armpits of commuters, and the second in the company of overexcited tourists and full-time gamblers. Or maybe *addicts* was more apt, because every single one of them looked fried, as if they weren't going *to* the casino but had already spent the night there.

The bus took the turn-off to the M25 and then, before it had even gone a mile, was leaving the motorway entirely, following the signs for the Skyline. Almost right from the slip road, Healy could see it. A sprawl of conjoined buildings, it was gigantic, even from a distance, its mammoth edifice an imitation of a cityscape, skyscrapers of different sizes and shapes all reaching for the morning sky; behind that, the rest of it unfurled like a splayed gown.

The bus pulled into the drop-off area under a huge, intricate iron awning. Thousands of white lightbulbs – dazzlingly bright – were embedded in the underside, and music was being pumped out of speakers at ear-splitting volume. It was a Sinatra classic, the Skyline obviously trying to play heavily on the fact that this was a Vegas-style resort. *Just without the Vegas-style weather*, Healy thought, as he stepped off the bus and the rain hit his face.

He went through one of the doors.

The interior had been done up like the lobby of an art deco hotel, all the windows not in fact windows at all but video screens – some huge – offering views of a skyscraper-filled city, as if the foyer were on the ninetieth floor of a tower in Manhattan or Hong Kong. Reception desks for the hotel were off to the left, signs for the concert hall to the right of that, and then more signs, this time for the casinos – plural – indoor water park, nightclub and underground shopping mall. Between the entrance to the first casino and here was a long, semicircular walkway made of glass with an aquarium built around it. As people left the lobby and headed in that direction, fish, eels, rays, even reef sharks, glided overhead and to the sides, the huge glass panels of the tank finished in gold-leaf edging.

Everywhere was noise, and lights, and faux opulence.

Healy reached into his pocket and took out a notebook. It was completely empty except for the information that Raker had given him: *Empire State, Entrance 4D, 11 a.m.* He'd studied floorplans of the resort the night before and knew that there were four gaming areas, and each was named after an iconic skyscraper: the Burj Khalifa, the Shard and the Chrysler were the smaller ones. Empire State was the largest and the one he needed.

He headed through the aquarium.

Halfway down he passed a couple with a girl of about four, the dad down on one knee next to her, his finger pressed to the glass as a school of clownfish swam past. Healy listened to the girl squealing excitedly, 'There's Nemo, there's Nemo!' and – as he did every day – he thought of Leanne. He tried to remember her at that age, tried to remember things they'd done as a family, and – when it wouldn't pull into focus – he pictured her when she was older instead, a teenager, prickly and temperamental, and eventually ended up where he always did: the last conversation he ever had with her.

It wasn't a conversation, it was a fight.

The worst thing was, he couldn't even remember what the fight was about; it was just a series of images, moments cast in bronze and seared into his mind forever.

The smell of alcohol from a nearby bar brought Healy back into the moment – the whiff of JD and Coke passing him on the tray one of the waiters was carrying – and, for the first time in a long time, he craved a drink. He looked around the casino floor, searching for a clock, wondering if it was eleven yet, but didn't see any and remembered that this was what they did in Las Vegas too: never showed punters the time, so it was just one, perpetual day when it was okay to get on the booze before breakfast and spend whole nights at the tables.

He'd left his watch at home, the battery dead, so he got his mobile phone out and checked the display. It was five to eleven. He glanced at the bar a second time, at the rows of spirits lined up, and then he forced himself forward, following the signs for the other casinos. It was even louder here than it had been in the lobby – the incessant *ding, ding, ding* of slot machines, the music being pumped through speakers, conversation, laughter – but after almost ten minutes of walking, he reached the centre of the Empire State casino and a grey door marked 4D. It was right in the corner – away from customers, away from the tables, hidden behind a bank of slot machines and next to doors for male and female toilets.

Beside the door was a card reader with an intercom.

Healy took a breath, and then thought of what Raker had said to him on the phone: *I wondered if you wanted to look into something for me.*

He'd also told Healy afterwards that he might not like it.

Healy pushed the buzzer.

Raker was right: Healy didn't like it. He already knew he didn't. Or, rather, he didn't like who he was about to meet. But it was hard to resist the work Raker was offering him. It felt a hell of a lot more worthwhile than guarding a block of flats and spending his nights walking empty hallways like a zombie.

'Yes?' A male voice from the intercom.

'My name's Colm Healy. I'm here to see Melanie Craw.'

He stepped back from the door. His heart had started beating faster now. It wasn't the pressure to do right by Raker. It wasn't even that it had been so long since he'd done this kind of work. It was the thought of seeing Melanie Craw again.

The door buzzed.

He waited as it opened towards him, and then watched as Craw came out. It had been eleven years since they'd last seen each other, and both of them had changed. Craw had never seen Healy this slim or this bald. He'd never seen Craw with long hair or as muscular. Before, her hair had always been short, clipped, and she'd been thin.

'Colm Healy,' she said, smiling. 'It's been a while.'

'It has.'

They didn't shake hands.

'When Raker called me to say he was sending you over this morning, I wasn't sure if you'd actually come. I didn't know if you were still doing . . .' She paused. 'This.'

'Do you mean, you didn't know if I was still capable of it?'

'No, that's not what I meant.'

'It's okay,' he said. 'It's a legitimate concern.'

'I'm not going to lie, I'd prefer Raker to be here.'

'I'm sure.'

'But I trust his judgement.'

'Anything we talk about today will be fed straight back to

him, so he will know what's going on. But he wouldn't send me if he didn't think I was up to it.'

'I know.'

They stared at each other for a moment.

Eventually, Craw said, 'I'm trying to think of the last time I saw you.'

'Are you?'

A hint of a smile. 'Right. I'm guessing it must have been . . .'

But she didn't finish, and they both knew why.

Healy nodded. *That's right. That was the last time.*

'I'm sorry it had to come to that, Colm.'

'You did what you thought was right.'

'I would do the same thing now.'

He just shrugged.

'Is there going to be a problem here?' Craw asked.

'No,' Healy said. 'There's no problem.'

But that wasn't the truth. He was lying to Craw now, like he lied to Raker last night when he told him – *promised* him – that he could do this, that he could deal with Craw and set the past aside. Healy had genuinely thought he could on the phone. He thought he could on the way here this morning. Eleven years was a long time and so much water had passed under the bridge. But seeing Craw, realizing how unapologetic she was – how she hadn't changed one iota – had immediately got his blood up.

He followed her inside.

She'd started talking politely, but he wasn't listening. He'd already tuned her out. All he could think about was his last day as a cop, those final moments in her office. And as he looked at the back of her head, he thought, *You fired me.*

You took away the only thing that made sense to me.

My entire life imploded because of you.

And now I want revenge.

19

The builders' yard was halfway along the main road between Paignton and Brixham. I found the turn-off easily and followed it down to an ugly corrugated iron warehouse.

There were a few men dotted around – lifting things off pallets or operating machinery – but most of them were in their late teens and early twenties, which put them well below the age of Daryl Beaumont.

A tatty reception was on one side of the warehouse, so I locked the car and headed in. Sitting at the counter, stabbing at the Tab button on a keyboard, was a man in his late sixties.

'Morning,' the man said, not taking his eyes off the screen.

'Morning. Is Daryl around?'

He ripped his gaze away from the monitor and removed his glasses. 'Is there something I can help with?'

I took out a business card and put it down on the counter.

'I'm just looking for Daryl.'

'Missing persons,' the man muttered as he picked up the card. He shook his head. 'Daryl's gone to Bovey Tracey for a delivery, so he could be a while. Is he in some kind of trouble again?'

'"Again"?'

He eyed me for a moment. 'Why do you want to speak to him?'

'I wanted to ask him about his son.'

'His *son*? Daryl's got a son?'

I stepped closer. 'What's your name?'

'Phil.'

'What kind of trouble has Daryl been in, Phil?'

He still had my card in his hand, pinched between the dirty nails of his thumb and finger. 'I don't want to talk out of turn,' he said, but I got the sense that wasn't going to stop him. I'd already got a pretty good read on Phil, even from the little we'd talked, and I was willing to bet he liked knowing things. 'Daryl's been in trouble with the law before.'

'But he hasn't got a record,' I said. 'I checked.'

'No. He's been a lucky boy. A couple of times he's got away with some things that he really probably shouldn't have.' Phil made me wait. 'Five, six years back, he got pissed on a night out in town and tried to crack on to some girl who already had a boyfriend. There was this massive punch-up and Daryl ended up pushing this girl through a glass door. Anyway, the police were all over him – but the girl didn't press charges. I heard it was because she and her bloke had all these cannabis plants in their flat and didn't want the cops sniffing around.'

'You said there were other times too?'

'He's been in a few fights, put one kid – who was supposed to be a friend of his – in a neck brace for eight weeks. I always joke he's made of Teflon.'

Beaumont sounded like an arsehole, but that didn't make him relevant to the family's disappearance. Except, if Kyle's friend was right, Sarah and Marc had been arguing about *something*. What if it was him?

'Then there was the thing last summer at the yard here.'

I glanced at Phil. 'The thing?'

'Daryl and this guy had a big screaming match.'

'About what?'

'This guy came to see him and told Daryl to – excuse my French – stay the fuck away from something or other.' Phil gave me a *Can you believe that?* look.

'Did you hear anything else that was said?'

'No. The yard was too busy.'

'What did Daryl say about it after?'

'He didn't, which wasn't like him. Normally he acknowledges what an idiot he can be, how the booze trips a fuse.' Phil seemed to genuinely like Beaumont – or, at least, the sober version of him. 'But that thing in the yard? He's never talked about it.'

Phil started trying to find something under the counter.

'You said that Daryl has never mentioned having a son?'

'Not once. And we had some good, long chats.' He reached for his glasses and put them on again. I heard a pen pot topple. Phil was distracted now.

'When Daryl gets back, get him to call me.' I tapped the business card. 'Tell him it's important we speak.'

Phil didn't respond.

'Phil? Did you hear what I said?'

'Here it is,' he responded. In his hands, he was holding a scrap of paper. 'I knew I'd left it here somewhere, I just couldn't remember where I put it.'

'What's that?' I said, looking at the paper.

'It's the reg number.'

'For what?'

'For that guy who came to the yard. The guy Daryl had the ding-dong with. I wrote down his reg because I didn't know if I was going to have to call the cops.'

Phil handed me the note.

I unfolded the paper and looked at the registration number. It took me a second to realize I knew the plate – and a second longer to realize where from.

It was Marc Fowler's BMW.

20

I headed back into Paignton and parked outside Daryl Beaumont's house.

I could have stayed at the yard and spoken to him there, but I didn't want Phil listening in, or for Beaumont to feel publicly interrogated. Being in his own space at home would hopefully make him more relaxed. If he was relaxed, his guard would be down. And that was what I needed him to be, because last year Marc had driven down to the yard to confront Beaumont and I had to get to the reason why. Until now, I hadn't heard a single negative thing about Marc. He was a loving husband and stepdad. He was respected at work. He was organized, calm, kind.

Now, suddenly, he was angry and potentially violent.

Knowing Beaumont would be at least another couple of hours, I wandered into town, along the seafront, past the arcades and into the shopping area. It was pretty much deserted, the dreary weather keeping people away.

After finding a café, I took a seat in the corner and thought again about Clara having a best friend no one knew anything about. The name Tori or Toni wasn't on the list of contacts Sarah had passed on to me, and it had never come up in the work on Clara that I'd done myself.

Which means what?

I stopped and looked up, my thoughts racing.

It's just another thing Sarah might not be telling the truth about?

I made a series of calls to friends of Clara's that I'd already been in touch with the day before, to ask them if there was anyone named Tori or Toni among their group – or if any of them had ever heard Clara talk about someone with that name.

Every single one of them said no.

I'd downloaded the photos Marc, Kyle and Clara had on their phones on to my laptop, and now I went through them all again, looking for something I'd missed, especially in the photos of Clara: a face, a woman somewhere, that I'd flicked past, or overlooked as an irrelevant background detail the first time. A part of me worried that the friend might be a cul-de-sac I'd spend days on, something that ultimately took me nowhere. But even if the landlord hadn't remembered every detail correctly, he had seen a woman staying over in the flat with Clara, and I didn't know who she was.

It had been ninety minutes since I'd parked at the house, so I headed back, immediately hitting a wall of rain. It really was miserable for May, the wind stirring now too, whipping in off a grey, tormented sea.

Beaumont's house was another mid-terrace, just like the one Clara had lived in for a time, but this road was more run-down, the cream paint on the front of his place discoloured and marked. A car had pulled into a parking space just in front of mine -- a battered Citroën I recognized from the yard – so I knocked on the front door.

When Beaumont answered, he was midway through a conversation on the phone: '. . . told him already we were meeting at six.' He paused, looked me up and down. I knew he was thirty-nine, but he looked older, his face weathered. 'Give me a sec,' he said to the caller and then glanced at me dismissively. 'Yeah?'

'Daryl, my name's David Raker.'

A spark of recognition. Phil had obviously mentioned my visit. From his pocket, Beaumont removed the card I'd left. 'You came to the yard earlier,' he said.

'I did, yeah. Have you got a minute?'

'Not really.'

'Why don't you make a minute?'

He smirked. 'And why the hell would I do that?'

'Because I want to talk to you about your son.'

The aggression instantly dropped from his face.

'Kyle?'

The way he said Kyle's name immediately hooked me. It wasn't the way a man sounded when he knew nothing about his child at all. Sarah said Beaumont had never had anything to do with Kyle, at any stage of his life – but Kyle definitely wasn't a complete mystery to him. At the very least, Beaumont knew his child's name.

He glanced at my card. 'Wait, is Kyle missing?'

'Yes. He's been missing eight months. You didn't see it in the press?'

'I don't read the papers,' he muttered.

'I also wanted to talk to you about Marc Fowler.'

He just stared at me.

'You and he had that argument at the yard.'

'Oh.'

'What do you remember about that day?'

There was no bravura in Beaumont any more – none of the aggression, or the confidence; nothing of the man I'd been told about, who got drunk and hit out.

He was solemn and pale.

Maybe even a little unnerved.

'Not much,' he said finally. 'I just remember he was a total psycho.'

21

I followed him into the house.

It was narrow but went a way back, the rooms sparsely fur-nished, as if Daryl Beaumont was perpetually on the point of moving in or moving out. We reached a kitchen, where the back door was ajar, and on a table outside, atop a patio awash in weeds, I saw half a cigarette smoking in an ashtray. He went straight out to it, took a drag and then stood next to the table, under an overhanging roof, out of the drizzle.

'The kid has really been missing eight months?' he asked.

The kid.

He clearly didn't want to show me any more emotion than he already had.

'Since last September, yeah.'

'And – what? – she's asked you to find him?'

Again, *she.*

'If you mean Sarah, then yes.'

He took another drag.

'Why did Marc Fowler come to the yard, Daryl?'

He didn't respond. I got the sense it was some kind of power play, a pointless attempt to tilt the conversation back so that I was no longer dictating the tempo. He was a big man, used to being the alpha in the room.

'Daryl, unless it's directly related to my search for Kyle, I don't give a shit who you are, or who you want me to *think* you are. All I care about is finding that family.'

A frown. He'd picked up on the *that family* part.

'It's not just Kyle that's missing. It's Marc too. It's Kyle's girlfriend. I've been in a lot of rooms with a lot of dangerous people and this' – I waved a hand at him – 'you don't need to bother on my account. You don't intimidate me. This tough-guy act just makes it harder for me to find out what happened to Kyle. So if there's any part of you that cares about your son – and I get the impression there is – why don't you tell me what I need to know?'

A brief flash of anger – and then I could see him relent.

'Have you ever met Kyle?'

He shook his head. 'No.'

'But you obviously knew about him?'

'We were just kids.' He took another long drag. 'When she told me she was pregnant, I don't know . . .' *I couldn't handle it. I didn't want to face it. So I walked away.* He'd never spent even as much as a single second in Kyle's life. Even for a man like Beaumont, a decision like that would eventually start to corrode you. 'A few years back, I just felt like I wanted to meet him.'

This was where I thought it might have been going. Phil at the yard had heard Marc telling Beaumont to 'stay the fuck away' from something.

That something was Kyle.

'So you spoke with Sarah?'

'No,' he said, which at least meant Sarah hadn't lied to me about having had no contact with Beaumont in eighteen years. 'I just chewed on it for a long time. And then I did some asking around – there are still some people from back in the day that know both of us – and I found out she was living in Totnes. So last June I called her – but it wasn't Sarah who picked up the phone, it was . . .' A long, leaden pause. 'It was him.'

'Marc?'

'Yeah. I told him who I was and that I wanted to speak to Sarah about maybe, you know, meeting Kyle or whatever. He seemed all right on the phone. I gave him all my info – my phone, my email – and he said he'd get Sarah to call me back.'

'Did she?'

'No. And a few days after that he turns up at the yard.' He stubbed out the cigarette, watching as the drifting smoke vanished into the rain. 'He went mental. He basically just kept repeating the same shit over and over again. "Don't call the house. Don't ever speak to Sarah. Don't ever speak to Kyle. Just stay the fuck away from my family." *His* family. Can you believe that shit? It was *my* bloody boy.'

I didn't bother arguing the point that Beaumont had given up any right to Kyle the second he left Sarah alone to carry, give birth to and bring up their son entirely on her own. Plus, from everything I'd seen and heard so far, Marc had been a very loving stepfather to Kyle, to the point where, when Sarah married Marc, Kyle had been comfortable enough taking Marc's surname. So was that where all Marc's anger had come from? Had he been worried Beaumont would enter their lives and drive a wedge between them all? Marc's reaction seemed out of character, but even if he'd gone too far at the yard, his motivation felt a good deal less opaque. He loved his family.

'It wasn't just his words,' Beaumont muttered softly. 'It was more . . .' He stopped. I waited for his gaze to come back to me. 'It's hard to explain.'

Again, I waited.

'It was more like . . .' He twirled a finger around, trying to come up with the right phrase. 'It was his manner. I could see how much he loved Sarah, how much he loved Kyle, loved their family.' Beaumont swallowed. 'And I could see how far he would go to protect them.'

Healy

The Skyline | *Now*

Melanie Craw led Healy down into the bowels of the Skyline.

Eventually, they reached a door with Craw's name printed on it and HEAD OF SECURITY under that. There was a reader on the wall, which she used a card on, then she pushed open the door and invited him to go in first. The overhead lights had been on energy-saving mode, but now panels in the roof sparked into life as he entered. Craw went around her desk and sat, waking a desktop PC from its slumber.

He looked around. There were no windows because they must have been forty feet under the earth, so in order for it not to feel like a dungeon, a large digital picture frame had been hung on the wall. It showed a live, widescreen feed from one of the casino floors – people at tables, at slots, gathered at the bar – giving the impression all of it was just next door.

'How are the family?' Craw asked.

'They're fine.'

'Your boys doing all right?'

'They're doing fine,' Healy said, getting out his notebook.

'I see conversation's still not your strong point.'

He took a pen from his jacket and clicked it on. 'Look, Craw, you don't like me, I don't like you, so let's not pretend that we're interested in each other's lives.'

'Fair enough,' she said, her voice neutral. 'So where do you want to start?'

'Let's start with a bit of background on your bosses.'

She opened out her hands. 'The Zinters brothers – Asha and Caleb. Everyone thinks they're twins, because they're the same age and look similar, but they're not. They were born within eleven months of each other – Asha first, Caleb second. Their old man, Paul, set up Zinter Entertainment at the end of the sixties, and ran it up until the early 2000s.'

'Paul Zinter died in 2004, is that correct?'

'You've done your research.'

'It's all on Wikipedia.'

'And what else does it say on Wikipedia?'

'It says the brothers run this place, the Afrique in Vegas and the Red Phoenix over in Macau.'

'Then Wikipedia is correct. The Skyline is the biggest casino in Europe, the Red Phoenix is the biggest casino in Asia, and the Afrique is the biggest casino in the world. The one thing I'll say about the Zinter brothers is they're not fans of small.' She sat back, eyed Healy. 'I mean, I'm not sure how deep you want to go here. They're Sagittarians. I'm sure they love long walks on the beach. Do you care that they're both divorced? Do you care that Caleb has never had kids and that Asha had two before his son died just before Christmas three years back?'

'How did he die?'

'Speedboat accident.' Craw tapped a glass next to her. *He was drunk*. 'Never should have got behind the wheel of that thing, but that's kids, right? They break our hearts.'

Healy thought of Ciaran, Liam and especially Leanne.

'So how does Anthony Yanis fit into all of this?' he said.

'He, Asha and Caleb were all at university together. The two brothers went off and worked for Daddy, who already owned four casinos in Las Vegas, and Yanis went out and made a fortune in the technology sector. He was one of the first investors in Retrigram.' That had been a smart move. Retrigram was the world's biggest social media platform. 'Yanis married an English girl and then moved to the UK in the late nineties. A few years after that, Paul Zinter realized mega resorts were the future in Vegas, not gaming-only spaces, so he sold all four of his casinos and pumped the profits into opening the Afrique there, then the Red Phoenix in Macau a few years after that. Asha ran one, Caleb ran the other. Then, in 2006, a couple of years after the old man died, the brothers bought the land here, and started construction on the Skyline, only for the financial crash to hit less than a year later. That's when their old pal Anthony Yanis rocked up to the party with his wallet out and offered to put in thirty per cent of the money. From what I've been told by people – and, in fairness, by the Zinters themselves – the brothers always treated him like a king, and he had the run of this place, because, basically, without him sticking in that thirty per cent, their entire business would have gone down the pan.'

'Yanis lived up in Yorkshire, didn't he?'

'I believe so, yes.'

'So he used to come down here for weekends?'

'Three weekends a month.'

'And he always stayed in the penthouse suite?'

'Always. He was a big gambler, even before the Skyline opened, and from the stories I've heard, he had a few paydays on his visits here. But the Zinters said they never used to mind too much because, at the end of the day, the house always wins.'

'They made plenty of money out of Yanis?'

'They make plenty of money out of *everyone*. The minute you enter the doors of this place, you're asking to have your pockets emptied. It's the nature of casinos. Anyone who thinks they're beating the house is living in cloud cuckoo land. So, like I say, Yanis was a big gambler. He knew the deal. He just liked coming down, being put up in the best suite, sitting at the tables, getting treated like The Man. I mean, who wouldn't?'

'So when did he meet this Whaler guy?'

Craw swivelled in her chair to face her PC and used the mouse to click on a couple of things. 'I've had my guys go through the security footage. We've got over three thousand cameras at the resort, we've got a twenty-four-hour team watching seventy-five monitors, we've got access to facial recognition tech, and everything we see here gets downloaded on to six hundred different devices. This stuff is state of the art.' She clicked something else and a printer sprang to life behind her. 'You're free to access all the footage – we have a room you can use here; you can stay there as long as you like, we just can't let any of the footage off-site – but we've been through every minute of video as a team, multiple times, so let's call this next part a shortcut.' She turned in her seat and took the printout from the tray. It was a full colour CCTV shot from one of the blackjack tables. Handing it across, Craw said, 'This is the first time the Whaler visited us – Saturday 11th of December 2021.'

Five months before Yanis was murdered.

'That's Yanis,' Craw said, pointing to a large man in his early fifties, dressed in a floral shirt and a pastel-blue jacket. The quality of the shot was excellent, allowing a clear view of Yanis's features: he was bloated, a second chin under his first, his skin tone a little flushed. He had a mane of thick, grey hair, which he'd combed back and styled with oil. He was seated in the middle of the blackjack table, the central figure in a line-up of four men and one woman. 'And that's the guy who killed him,' Craw added, putting her finger to a face at the end of the table, two people down from where Anthony Yanis was sitting.

'Is this the best shot you have of the Whaler?' Healy asked.

'We have others where he's closer to a camera, but they're not as clear, or he's facing away. This is definitely the most detailed shot of him; certainly the best shot of his face.' She paused, her eyes on the CCTV still. 'Maybe I'm wrong, but since I got asked to look into this, we've been through a *shitload* of video – hundreds of hours – and I'm starting to think all of it might have been deliberate.'

'All of what?'

'The Whaler never *quite* being caught on camera after this first night.'

'What, you think he memorized the layout of the cameras?' She shrugged.

'You said you've got over three thousand cameras here.'

'I know how it sounds,' she said.

Healy traced the details of the Whaler's face. He was looking directly into the lens. And Craw was right: there was something in his expression, an overt moment of realization – in his eyes, in his mouth – that he was being captured on tape. Was this why he made sure it never happened again?

'Every time he came to the casino after this,' Craw said, 'he was wearing a cap. Every time.'

But not that first time.

Healy drew the printout closer. The Whaler looked like he was in his mid-twenties, with short black hair, dark eyes and light, smooth skin. Even seated, it was clear he was tall and slim – quite literally half the width of Yanis – and he was wearing a pale shirt with pockets on the front, the sleeves rolled up. Healy remembered a section he'd read in a newspaper story he'd found the previous night.

One of the police officers who worked the original case referred to the Whaler as 'very good-looking', and some of Yanis's friends who saw them together in the weeks leading up to the murder also said the suspect was 'handsome'. When Yanis introduced the Whaler to his friends, he introduced him as Morgan Annerson.

'The name Morgan Annerson is a dead end, is that right?' Craw nodded. 'Correct.'

Healy looked at the Whaler again. If that *wasn't* his name, why choose it? Was there some significance to the use of Morgan? In Healy's experience, aliases – particularly first names – were rarely chosen at random.

'So the 11th of December 2021 was the first night he got talking to Yanis, and over the next five months they got closer?'

'Yes.'

'Was there anything physical between them?'

'Not that anyone saw. It was an open secret that Yanis cheated, but while he wasn't a big believer in marriage vows, everyone says he was straight.'

'Could everyone be wrong?'

'There's always the possibility. Mostly, though, people have said the same thing – he liked beautiful women, and he liked them young. Not illegal, but definitely much younger than him. Which means, in all likelihood, he and the Whaler were just platonic – two men who got close. Or, at least, that was what Yanis thought.'

Healy gathered his thoughts. 'So, if Yanis liked to cheat, do you think the Whaler could be the husband or boyfriend of someone Yanis shagged?'

'He could be. It was something Thames Valley looked into as well. The reason that theory niggles at me, though, is why spend five months carefully gaining Yanis's trust? Why not just go in all guns blazing? A jilted husband out to get even with the man who shagged his wife is very unlikely to play the long game. No offence, but most men – particularly angry, jealous men – aren't that complex.'

'So why let the Whaler get close to him at all? Yanis was a billionaire jetting anywhere he wanted, banging anything that moves, living the playboy life, but it was this guy he decided to let all the way into his life.'

'Maybe Yanis just needed an *actual* friend.'

'As opposed to?'

'Having lots of money doesn't mean having lots of friends. You get suspicious of people, and you don't let them get too close, because you know all they're doing is leeching off your wealth. But then out of the blue you meet someone, you click, and without realizing, you've opened yourself up to them because this one feels different from all the other so-called friendships you've had. I'm not saying that's how it went, but I've seen it up close on repeat since I began working here: rich people are lonely.'

Healy took a breath.

There was a lot to process here.

'What about Yanis's widow?' he said. 'Is she still around?'

Craw leaned back in her chair. 'I know you're going to ask me, because Raker asked me too: it's been a year since Yanis was murdered – why did the Zinters wait that long? Why go looking for the Whaler now? Well, Yanis's wife is one of the major reasons. She died about eight weeks ago – liver failure. So the Zinters are pissed off that she never found out who murdered her husband.'

'Did she care?'

'She was his wife.'

'A wife he repeatedly cheated on.'

'Unanswered questions tend to eat at you, so, in the months before she died, she *really* started wanting to know, even though their marriage had never been what you might call normal. After Yanis was murdered, she became the Zinters' business partner, someone they trusted and liked, so, as I say, the Zinters are pissed off about her never getting the answers she sought. They're pissed off because Yanis was their friend, she was their friend, and Thames Valley Police have got absolutely nowhere since last year. And they're *also* pissed off at the security team who were here the night the Whaler, or Morgan, or whatever the hell his name is, went up in a puff of smoke. Basically, right now, you've got two very rich, very pissed-off brothers.'

'So, let me make sure I've got this right,' Healy said, going back over his notes. 'The Whaler first turns up here on the 11th of December 2021. Over the next five months, he befriends Yanis. On the 14th of May last year, he murders him, and then a week later he comes back to the Skyline and is arrested, locked in that cell and escapes?'

'That's pretty much it, yeah.'

'Do any of the original security team still work here?'

'No. The guy who was doing my job back then retired shortly after. That was always the plan, I think, but he would have been shoved if he hadn't leaped. The other guy who was here that night got demoted, and shortly after that he resigned.'

'Do you know their names?'

'Gordon Ramis was the head of security. I can give you his contact details. And the other guy was Neil Linkers. I did some asking around out on the floor, and some of the people who are still in contact with him say he's working on the doors for a bank in Canary Wharf.'

A basic security job.

I know how he feels, thought Healy.

'And you don't have cameras in the cells?'

'No.'

'What about outside them?'

'Yes. There's one out in the corridor, directly facing the cell doors, but something went wrong with it when they brought the Whaler down.'

' "Went wrong"?'

'Ramis and Linkers missed something. It's one of the main reasons the Zinters went scorched earth on them.' She pointed to the picture of the Whaler that Healy had hold of. 'He had an EMI transmitter concealed on him.'

'"EMI"?'

'Electromagnetic interference. It was probably inside his boxers. Basically, if you watch the footage, it starts to crackle and break up as soon as he nears the cells, and only comes back on again nine minutes later, once he's gone. The whole time in between, the video is just static.'

'That's clever.'

'Very.'

'Any video of the Whaler exiting the wider resort the night he escaped?'

'No.'

'What, none at all?'

'No. Nothing. We've spent hours trying to find him, because he left the casino somehow that night.' Craw leaned forward. 'So far, nothing.'

'So not only did he vanish from the cell, but he vanished from the whole casino?'

'Yes.'

Craw went to the top drawer of her desk, removed a file and passed it over to Healy. It was a photocopy of the investigation into the murder of Anthony Yanis.

'I called in a couple of favours,' Craw said, 'because I thought you'd probably want to take a look. There's not much to get your teeth into, though. The Whaler's a ghost. They went back through Yanis's life trying to find this guy – Yanis's finances, his emails, his internet, his phone – and this Whaler-stroke-Morgan *was* in there. He emailed Yanis, texted him, called him – but he'd used a VPN to mask his IP address, and all the texts came from a burner.'

Healy tapped his pen against his notebook. 'I don't get why he came back. The Whaler murders Yanis on the 14th of May, then *returns* to the casino a week later on the 21st. And not only that, when he does, he just sits there at a blackjack table and does . . . nothing.' In news reports Healy had read, it said it was as if he was waiting to be spotted. And, as Healy leafed through the police report, he could see that was exactly right: witness statements from Ramis and Linkers seemed to confirm it. 'Why the hell would he come back?' Healy said again.

'I don't know.'

'Is there any video of him cashing in the chips the night of the murder?'

'Yes, we can provide that footage to you, but you can't see his face. He's wearing a cap; keeps his head down the whole time.'

'Did he cash in before or after murdering Yanis?'

'After.'

'That's cold.'

'Ice cold.' A beat. 'There's one other thing you'll see in that file. This didn't get released to the public. Do you know how Yanis died?'

'I read that he was stabbed.'

'Twenty-seven times. When the cops got up to the penthouse suite and found Yanis's body . . .' Craw stopped; glanced at the file. 'They found a message.'

'A message?'

'On the walls of the suite. It was written in Yanis's blood.'

'*What?* Are you serious?'

Craw nodded. '*Ephesians 5:13.*'

'That's what the message said?'

'Yes.'

'It's been a while since I went to Sunday school.'

'Me too. Luckily, Thames Valley did the hard work for us.' Craw gestured to the file. '"All things become visible when exposed by the light . . ."'

22

Outside Daryl Beaumont's house, I sat in the car and tried to get my thoughts into some sort of order. Things were piling up now. Kyle looking at the true crime website. Clara having a best friend I knew nothing about. Sarah and Marc arguing about their financial situation. Marc going to the builders' yard to confront Beaumont. The tyre track at the quarry. And still there was the biggest question of all: how the hell did three people vanish from the middle of a huge lake in under sixty seconds?

I fired up the engine, still turning it all over in my head.

That was when I spotted the green Mondeo.

It was squeezed into a narrow parking space at the end of Beaumont's road, partially hidden by a white van. Someone was at the wheel, a shadow inside, and as I glanced at my rear-view mirror, they moved to their left, leaning across the space between the front seats, as if reaching for the glovebox. Now I couldn't see anything of them at all.

I buzzed down the passenger-side window.

The car was idling.

I waited, listened. The person inside continued to lean over, still below the line of the dashboard, although I could see the dome of their head moving slightly up and down, as if they really were going through the contents of the glovebox.

Don't get paranoid.

I started to pull out but then stopped again. In my rear-view mirror, I couldn't see all of the car's registration plate – the second half of it was hidden by the white van – but, just in case, I wrote down what I could read, then headed to the end of Beaumont's road.

I wanted to see whether the driver followed me out.

They didn't.

The Mondeo stayed exactly where it was, the person inside still below the dashboard. I turned right into Totnes Road, my gaze constantly returning to my mirrors. But there was no sign of the car, and then – before long – I was leaving Paignton entirely and heading out into the countryside. It would have been easy to spot someone following me.

I dismissed the whole thing again.

You're searching for things that aren't there.

But then, a few miles on, still unable to quite shake the idea that something wasn't right, I called Ewan Tasker, the source who'd sent me the missing persons report for the Fowlers. Even though Tasker was well into his seventies now, he still did consultation work at Scotland Yard three days a week. I knew there was a good chance he'd be in the office, which meant he'd have access to the Police National Computer.

'Raker,' he said when he answered.

'How you doing, Task?'

'Pretty good. Did you get the file?'

'I did. I appreciate it, old man.'

'So, to what do I owe the pleasure?'

'I've got a partial plate. Could you run it for me?'

'I can try. Hold on a sec.'

I heard him moving, a door closing, the low hum of conversation immediately dropping away. A couple of taps of a keyboard, and then: 'Okay, what have you got?'

'SN65.'

'That's it?'

'That's it?'

'Make? Model?'

'A green Ford Mondeo.'

More keyboard taps.

'There's seventy-five nationwide.'

'Any registered to addresses in south Devon?'

'Hold on,' Tasker said.

I glanced in my rear-view mirror again.

No Mondeo. No tail.

'No,' Task said, 'no addresses in Devon.'

I tried to think whether this was worth spending any more time on and cursed myself for not just getting out of my car, walking over and checking who was inside.

'Can you send the list over to me anyway?' I asked.

'Sure. I'll shoot it over.'

'Thanks, Task.'

We chatted for a little longer, mostly about his wife, who hadn't been well for a while, and then I hung up. I was approaching the outskirts of Totnes, the road sloping down into the dent in the valley that the town was in. I called Sarah.

'David,' she said as she answered, 'hi.'

'Hey, Sarah. Are you home?'

'Yes.'

'Can I pop in?'

'Of course. What sort of time?'

'I've just got to Totnes.'

'Ah, right. Well, I'll put the kettle on, then.'

She didn't sound concerned that I was coming.

'I've got some new information I need to speak to you about,' I said, testing the water – and this time she went quiet. 'I'll be there in ten minutes.'

23

Sarah answered the door in a dressing gown, her hair in curlers.

'Excuse my appearance,' she said. 'I've got that event tonight.'

I remembered her mentioning it the day before: she was leaving Mable with her mum overnight. I watched her as I entered, tried to see if there was anything in her face, any echo of the silence that had greeted me on the phone a few minutes before, and whether – in that silence – there was something suspicious.

But she seemed back to her usual self now.

As I followed her inside, I said, 'Where's the event?'

'It's a literary festival in Cardiff. I'm not looking forward to it, to be honest.' In the kitchen, the kettle had just finished boiling. 'When you go to these things, people either dance around what happened and pretend they don't know, or they look at you with pity and tell you they're sorry. More people know me and my books than they ever did before – but I'd trade it all to have my family home.'

Everything was consistent: a slight tremor in her voice whenever she mentioned her family; the way she'd occasionally falter and look around the house, as if suddenly aware of its scale. As I listened, I had the same thought as every other time we'd met.

This feels completely genuine.

So why would Kyle tell his friend that he'd repeatedly heard Marc and Sarah arguing before the disappearances? And had Sarah deliberately not mentioned it?

From the den, Mable tottered through, a threadbare teddy in

one hand. She looked up at me, a frown on her face that said, *Who are you again?*

'Hey, Mable,' I said, gently.

She wandered across to Sarah.

'Sorry,' Sarah said, picking Mable up, 'someone's tired. I might try and put her down for a short nap. She didn't want to go earlier but she's absolutely knackered. If she doesn't sleep a little she's going to be a nightmare for my mum tonight.'

Sarah took Mable upstairs.

A few minutes later she returned, and as she re-entered the kitchen she said, 'So you mentioned on the phone that you had some new information?'

'I do.' I'd decided in the car I'd get to the arguments with Marc last, so I set down my laptop and spun it around for her to see. 'Kyle seemed to be interested in this website.'

Sarah leaned in. '*Evidence Bag.*'

'It's the true crime website I told you he'd been visiting.' I paused, watching Sarah. 'I just wanted to confirm: you never saw him looking at this?'

'Never.'

I glanced at my notebook. 'What about the name Pierre Decroix?'

'Who?'

'He was an Exeter University student.' *And he was murdered in Buckfastleigh, fifteen minutes from here, his body found hanging in an apple orchard.*

I watched her again.

'No,' she said. 'No, I've never heard of him. Who is he?'

'I'm juggling a lot of names here and trying to figure out who is relevant and who isn't.' I moved on. 'Did you ever meet Clara's friends?'

'No. No, I don't think so. Why?'

'Ever hear her mention the name Tori or Toni?'

136

Another shake of the head. 'No.'

'Did Kyle ever talk to you about her friendship group?'

'Clara's? Not that I specifically remember, although obviously they went out with her friends from time to time, as she did with his. Why, is something wrong?'

Closing the lid of my laptop, I moved my notebook from my pocket to the table. Sarah watched me, clearly realizing there was more to come.

'I need to ask you about something,' I said. 'It's about the weeks leading up to the day at the quarry. You told me you and Marc were financially secure back then.'

She frowned. 'We were. Why?'

'One of Kyle's friends said Kyle heard you and Marc arguing.'

'Arguing?'

'Apparently. More than once.'

Another, even deeper frown. 'Really?'

'Kyle said he asked you about it and you said it was about money issues.'

Sarah leaned back in her seat, her eyes still on mine.

And then a twitch in her expression.

Something had snapped into place.

'Oh,' she said. 'Oh, I know why I told Kyle that.'

'Why?'

'I didn't really think it was relevant until now, but . . .' She took a long breath. 'There's something you should know about me, David . . .'

Healy

The Skyline | *Now*

Craw led Healy to the cells. There were four of them in a row on the right, and on the left was a kitchen with a long window looking directly out.

'Ramis was sitting in here,' Craw said, indicating the kitchen.

'The whole time?'

'Yep.'

With a clear, uninterrupted view of the cells.

'Which cell was the Whaler in?'

Craw pointed to the first one on the right.

Healy stepped towards it and slid aside a reinforced panel in the door so he could see into the cell – a bench, a strip light and a toilet bowl.

'Can you open it up?' he asked.

There were card readers on the wall next to each cell but, even after Craw held her pass to the reader, she still had to use a physical key to unlock the door and then rotate a handle to spring the deadbolt.

'Has the security changed since last year?' Healy asked. 'I don't remember seeing anything about there being card readers the night he escaped?'

'It got updated about six weeks after.'

'So the previous locks weren't up to it?'

'No, it wasn't that. The locks they had in here before were as secure as it gets. We didn't even used to have security that good in police stations. They were changed because the Zinters wanted the whole thing wired into the network, so that, if a door ever opened without one of us unlocking it, it would send out an immediate warning.' Craw held up her phone. 'Now we get buzzed if any of these doors open. Back then, it was all analogue.' She hauled open the door. 'But it was secure, believe me. Once the deadbolt hits home, it's like Fort Knox.'

Craw backed away.

Healy stepped past her, into the doorway of the cell.

There was hearing about it, and then there was seeing it: the whole journey down – the entire time since talking to Raker the night before – Healy had been thinking about how someone could have vanished from the inside of a locked cell. He'd imagined himself inside the old police cells they used to have and then inside the Pentonville cell he'd spent four months in the previous year, before the charges against him were dropped. He'd tried to consider potential weak points. He'd been adamant there would be *something* in the cells here – maybe a lock that didn't quite turn, or a grille plate on the wall that might have been big enough for the Whaler to squeeze through.

But now, as he stood in the middle of the cell, looking for answers that weren't here, he finally understood the depth of this mystery. The cells didn't have windows. They didn't have grille plates to remove. And the locks, even twelve months ago, were just about as good as you could hope for.

Yet a man had vanished from inside.

And not just any man. A man who, a week before that, had stabbed someone twenty-seven times, then gone on to calmly cash in £400,000 of stolen chips, and – in between doing both of those things – scrawled a Bible verse on to the wall of a hotel room using his victim's blood.

All things become visible when exposed by the light.

'What do you think?' Craw asked.

He looked at her. She held his eye for a moment, then turned away, back towards the open door of the empty cell. As Healy watched her, he said, 'Was there anything else you needed to tell me?'

'No,' she said, glancing at him – but as soon as she responded, she turned away again and continued staring at the cell.

Was there something up with her?

Or was it just that he didn't know her any more?

His instincts were firing, the bitterness he felt towards Craw replaced – at least for now – by a buzz he'd been craving for so long. It flooded his system and took him all the way back to his days at the Met, when he'd been standing at the threshold of a case. Back then, he'd always get a sense for how deep an investigation might go.

And he was getting that same sense now.

This went deep.

And none of it was going to be good.

24

'I have a brain tumour.'

I stared at Sarah, stunned. She moved her mug on the table, the dregs of her tea sloshing around. Her eyes lingered on it, as if searching for the words inside.

'Sarah, I'm so sorry.'

'It's okay. It's benign. But it's in a bit of a tricky area.' She tilted her head and tapped the back of her skull. 'It's Grade two, so it's not growing fast, but it's growing. The longer it's there, the riskier things get. I've had three seizures since I was diagnosed. They weren't bad, but they were bad enough.' She pushed out a weak smile. 'It's scary, you know? Being here on my own. When Marc was here, when Kyle was around, I was worried, but I always had the reassurance that they were close by. I don't want to have a seizure when it's just me and Mabe here.'

She looked at the rain hitting the kitchen window.

'Because of where it is, there's only a couple of options. One is this thing called Gamma Knife stereotactic radiosurgery, which is basically just a posh way of saying they blast your brain cells with these beams to try and shrink the tumour. I'm on the waiting list.' She shrugged. 'I've been on it for ten months now.'

'Do they think it'll work?'

'You know what they're like: they don't really commit. But I think, from what they've said, it may. Even if it does, though, there's a chance the tumour will return – perhaps even quite quickly.'

'And the other option?'

'The other option is this brand-new treatment. Um, proton, uh . . .' She paused. 'Proton, uh . . .' She squeezed her eyes shut. 'Bloody hell, what's its bloody name?' When the name of the treatment wouldn't come to her, she glanced at me. 'This is when I start to feel scared. I keep forgetting things. I don't want to forget.'

I don't want to forget them.

I don't want to forget my family.

As I watched the panic flicker in her face, I thought of the timings at the lake, and how she'd been adamant she'd only dozed off for less than a minute. Could the tumour have skewed her perspective? Could it have made her confused? Could she have forgotten important details like she'd forgotten the name of the treatment?

I thought of something else too: the section in the police interview transcript I'd read the day before where Richardson had posed what felt like a loaded question.

PC RICHARDSON: Is there any reason you can think of that you might have recalled certain details incorrectly with regard to what happened?

SARAH FOWLER: No. No, absolutely not.

'I'm not wrong about the lake,' she said.

I tuned back in. Was I that easy to read? Or did she expect my thoughts to go there? 'I never thought you were,' I lied, because it was what she needed to hear. 'Did you tell Richardson about the tumour?'

'No. The day he interviewed me, I was struggling a bit physically. The stress of it all wasn't helping, obviously, but I was feeling light-headed. I was worried I might have a seizure right there in the police station. Richardson noticed I wasn't looking great, so I just told him it was an ear problem. I didn't need him to disbelieve me any more than he clearly already did, and if I told him the truth . . .'

She stopped.

Suddenly, things started to make more sense.

Richardson had already been suspicious about the timings; it was the reason he'd been circling Sarah the whole time, trying to catch inconsistencies in her story. If he'd thought she was ill, if he'd thought an illness – however minor – could have disrupted her recall or perspective, it would only have bolstered his doubts about her. And perhaps those doubts, as well as his own health issues in the run-up to his heart attack, had contributed to him not working the case as hard as he could have done.

'Anyway,' Sarah was saying, 'this other treatment's the same kind of deal: they blast you with energy waves and try to target the specific cells. But to be honest . . .' She swallowed. 'I kind of stopped reading up about it after Marc vanished.'

'Why?'

'Because it's not even available on the NHS.'

'So you'd have to go private?'

'It's not available anywhere in the UK yet. We'd have to go to Singapore.'

'And how much would that cost?'

'About two hundred and fifty thousand.'

Now I was starting to understand.

'So this was what Kyle overheard you and Marc arguing about?'

'It must have been. This treatment, it's still at the trial stage, but the outcomes have all been really positive, and it's especially good with tumours like mine. It's probably the best option I've got to shrink this bloody thing for good.'

'And – what? – Marc wanted you to go to Singapore?'

'Yes. But we didn't just have two hundred and fifty thousand lying around down the back of the sofa. I kept telling him that, but he said we would come up with the money somehow. He was *desperate* for me to do it. I kept telling him it was an obscene amount of money, that even if we *were* doing okay financially – which we were – we couldn't just magic up two hundred and fifty grand. But he said . . .' Tears welled in her eyes. 'He said he would sell everything we owned – every single thing: the house, everything – if it meant I got better.'

'When did you find out about the tumour?'

'A year ago.'

'Last May?'

'Yes.'

'And did Kyle know about it?'

She shook her head. 'No. He was slap bang in the middle of his A levels. I literally went in to see the neurologist four or five days before Kyle had his first exam. He'd worked so hard, had revised so hard – I knew if I told him, it would just mess with his head.'

'But you never told him after his exams were over either?'

'No.'

'Why not?'

She dropped her head. 'I don't know. He was just so happy. All his exams were done, he and Clara were so loved up, he was relaxed, he'd just got the apprenticeship offer and was *so* excited about it. I know I should have told him.' She started sobbing again. Gently, I touched a hand to her arm, conscious of making her uncomfortable – of overstepping – but feeling I needed to do something.

So Kyle had heard them arguing about money, but it was an argument born out of desperation, out of love, out of Marc's desire to do anything to get Sarah to Singapore for an op that could cure her.

Another puzzle piece had clicked into place too: why Marc

had been so angry that day at the builders' yard, his outburst so out of character. Because Beaumont had called the house in June – just a few weeks after Sarah had found out about the tumour; at the time she and Marc were trying to process it and figure it all out. It was the worst possible timing from a man who had spent eighteen years not giving a shit about his son, or the woman he got pregnant. Marc's reaction – while over the top – was understandable. He'd been the father Kyle had deserved. The husband Sarah had needed. He knew Beaumont was a bomb he needed to defuse.

I gave Sarah a little time to gather herself and headed upstairs to Kyle's room again. Two questions had been answered – whether Sarah had lied to me about her financial situation; and why Marc had confronted Daryl Beaumont – but there were others that hadn't.

One was Kyle's interest in *Evidence Bag*.

I went through his cupboards again, even more forensically than I had the first time, taking every item of clothing out, emptying boxes, tins, flicking through folders.

And then, in my pocket, my phone buzzed.

I took it out, saw it was an email and suspected – even though it had been sent from an anonymous account – that it was Ewan Tasker, following through on the favour I'd asked: a list of green Mondeo drivers, nationwide.

I opened the list on my phone and scrolled down.

Name after name, and none of them I knew. I looked for addresses that might ring a bell with me, in places that might be related to this case – but three-quarters of the way down the list, this whole line of enquiry started to feel way off-base.

Then I got to a name three from the bottom.

It was the owner of a green Mondeo – originally registered in October 2015, but bought by them second-hand ten months ago – who lived in a flat in the Angel area of north London. But it wasn't the address that caught my attention.

I went back downstairs and asked Sarah to go through the list to see if she recognized anyone on it. It didn't take her long.

'No, none of those people seem familiar,' she said, handing me the phone.

Clara had a best friend I hadn't been able to find any evidence of.

Until now.

The driver I'd seen on the list had the surname Wolton.

Her first name was Tori.

2008

Los Angeles, California

Detective Calvin Sanders is in a Starbucks when his cellphone rings.

It's 5.30 a.m. and the call's coming from Parker Center.

Sanders grabs the coffee from the end of the counter and then – as he heads out to the parking lot, where his Taurus is the only car here this early – he picks up.

'Sanders.'

'You on your way in?' comes the curt response.

It's Hessian, Sanders's lieutenant in Robbery-Homicide. He's an abrasive, often monosyllabic LAPD veteran who has a hard-on for timekeeping.

'I'll be there in thirty, LT,' he says to Hessian.

'Don't bother. I got one right on your doorstep.'

Sanders comes to a stop beside his car. 'In Sunland?'

'Haines Canyon.'

Sanders lives in Sunland-Tujunga with his wife and daughter, which along with Haines Canyon is a neighbourhood in the eastern corner of the San Fernando Valley.

'Uniforms are already at the scene,' Hessian says, 'and forensics are on their way. You know where Haines Canyon Debris Basin is?'

Sanders does.

As its name suggests, the basin is where debris washed out of the canyon by storms is collected – gravel, sediment, vegetation – and is designed to protect communities like the one Sanders lives in from getting flooded. When his daughter, Amy, was younger, Sanders and his wife sometimes used to take her past the basin and on to the Graveyard Truck Trail, which winds past the house made famous in *E.T.* and ends up at a lookout with sweeping views of the valley. But the last time Amy joined them on a walk was years back. She's seventeen now and hiking with her parents, rather than going to the mall with friends, isn't even an option – so Sanders can't recall when he was last at the basin.

Sanders gets into his car. 'What will I find up there, LT?'

'Bodies,' Hessian says matter-of-factly. 'Three of them.'

Sanders arrives at the Haines Canyon Debris Basin less than ten minutes after Lieutenant Hessian's call. He has to park on Haines Canyon Avenue and walk the rest of the way, because once the houses stop, the street turns into a dusty, single-track road, fringed by the steep foothills of the Verdugos.

As he rounds a corner on foot, he sees a lightbar flashing on a patrol car out front. It sends colour down into the debris basin in a series of dramatic red and blue pulses, and as Sanders gets nearer, he can see white-suited forensic techs making their way down the sloping concrete sides of the basin to the water's edge.

Passing an open boom gate, which Parks and Rec normally keep locked between sunset and sunrise, Sanders flashes his badge at the cordon. As he ducks under the tape, he looks ahead and up, to see where the sun is: it's just cresting the peaks now, its molten orange glow bleeding out along the ridges. Sanders wants it to hit the basin as soon as possible. He can see enough in the grey twilight of early morning, but not everything, and he's worried about missing something important.

Looking down from the southern end of the basin, and despite it having been dry in the city for almost a month, there's still some rainwater in it. It's a murky grey-blue. A large branch is floating on the surface and a member of the Parks and Rec team is trying to fish it out with a net, but her angle is all wrong. She's trying to keep what's at the other end of the basin out of her sightline.

As he clambers down to the edge of the basin, Sanders spots another Parks and Rec officer, this one older, answering questions from a first responder.

The man has a look in his eyes.

Sanders has seen it hundreds of times.

He's the one who found the bodies.

Sanders passes them both and heads around to the northern end of the basin, then shuffles his way down the steep concrete to the edge of the water. The ME isn't here yet, just a crime-scene photographer, a bearded guy in his twenties who is moving in a slow circle around the body of what appears to be a Hispanic female.

Sanders doesn't know her name – at least, not officially.

But he's almost certain this is Florida Jones. On the way over here, someone from RHD fired over a missing persons report for three friends – two women from Reseda, and one male from North Hills – which was filed three days before by Michael and Selina Jones, and Trish Ling, the parents of 21-year-olds Florida Jones and Ryan Ling. As Sanders brings the report up on his phone and moves to the photograph of Florida, he can instantly see the likeness to the young woman lying at the edge of the water now. The friends were on a five-day trip out of state and none of them returned.

Until now.

Florida is on her back, everything up to her knees submerged in water, one arm caught underneath her and bent at an unnatural angle. Sanders looks up the slope. He can already tell from the absence of livor mortis – of blood pooling at the lowest part of the body – that this isn't where she was killed. She's been moved. She's still fully clothed, which may or may not mean anything, but her T-shirt has ridden up, revealing a swathe of skin. The skin has a sheen on it where blisters have started to form, and although Sanders will have to wait for the ME to get here, there's no sign of bloating, so that means she's probably been dead under four days.

'So were you killed up there?' he says quietly, looking up, into the scrub on the other side of the fence at the northern end. The sun has come up over the mountains now and he can see two forensic techs, all in white, drifting like spectres behind the dense willow trees.

The crime-scene photographer glances at him, says nothing, and then goes back to taking pictures. As the camera flash blinks, Sanders notices there's some rope around Florida's left wrist and some rope burns on the right. He shuffles in closer to the area at the side of Florida's head, where there's a bullet hole just above her ear.

As the crime-scene photographer finishes, the uniform who was interviewing the officer from Parks and Rec makes his way over.

'Detective Sanders?'

Sanders stands and glances at the officer's badge.

Lapier.

'Was that who found the body?' Sanders says, gesturing to the Parks and Rec officer, who is now standing alone, on the other side of the gate.

'Yes, sir.'

'He found the other two as well?'

Lapier looks beyond the basin, into the scrub and the trees.

'Yes,' Lapier says. 'There's one white female and one Asian male up there.'

Ryan Ling, Sanders thinks, *and the third friend, Casey Ryker.*

It has to be them.

'Have they got similar injuries to this?' Sanders asks.

'Yes,' Lapier says. 'They've all been shot in the head.'

'Wrists tied?'

'Yes.'

Sanders glances at the bullet wound again, and then Lapier says, 'Why would one body be here and the other two up there?'

'We're not going to get lost in speculation yet,' Sanders responds, shutting Lapier down, although Sanders has been pondering the same question himself.

Maybe the killer was disturbed.

Or maybe he was panicking.

He looks at Lapier again, who is still staring back up towards the willow trees, their leaves stirred by the wind, the two forensic techs flickering in and out of view.

'Lots of people get shot in this city, son,' he says to the young officer. 'If you're gonna be a cop, you better get used to it.'

Lapier doesn't seem to have heard him.

'I said, you better get used to it if you want to be a cop in Los Angel–'

'Their wrists have been tied and they've been shot in the head,' Lapier says, repeating what they've already established.

But Sanders can feel it.

Something is coming.

'The techs have found a bullet,' Lapier says.

'And?'

'And they think it might be a .270 Winchester.'

This time, Sanders doesn't respond.

Because now, finally, he understands why Lapier is spooked.

The .270 Winchester is a hunting round.

3
The Friend

25

I was home just before 11 p.m.

I'd had an early dinner with Annabel and Olivia and then packed up my things and got on the motorway. The journey back to London took almost four hours but it gave me time to think. It also gave me time to make a few calls and try to build some sort of background on Tori Wolton. Not that there was much to build from. As I'd left Devon, all I'd really known about her was her address and the fact that she drove a 2015 green Mondeo. By the time I pulled on to my driveway in Kew, I'd found out she was twenty-six, born in east London, and apparently had no employment history at all.

There could have been legitimate reasons for that. Either she'd genuinely never been in work, or she'd been in permanent, full-time education all the way into her late twenties – both of which felt like a stretch. Even if that *was* the case, how did she afford to pay the rent on a flat in north London? And if she was in higher education, studying for a Master's or a PhD – or she was unemployed and claiming benefits – why couldn't any of my sources find a single shred of evidence?

She wasn't running a business either – at least, not under the name associated with the Mondeo. I'd failed to find her in a Companies House search under 'Wolton', 'Tori' or 'Victoria', *or* when I'd used the address of the flat. Which meant, if she was bringing money in – which she had to be to afford the flat, unless someone else was paying for it – she was doing it under the radar, not declaring any of her earnings.

Or there was one other possibility.

The name Tori Wolton was simply a shell. It was an identity someone else had assimilated, a mask they'd pulled on. And after a long time working missing persons cases – of trailing ghosts like Tori Wolton into the shadows – I knew there was usually only one reason for that: she was involved in something she shouldn't have been. The big question was whether whatever Tori Wolton may have been involved in had anything to do with the disappearance of the Fowlers.

Could she have been at the quarry that day?

Was it her tyre track at the lake?

I got out of the car, thinking about those questions – and whether, if Wolton was involved, it was conceivable Clara might have been working alongside her.

So far, I hadn't found anything to suggest as much.

When I'd dug down into Clara's history, there were no red flags, nothing to alarm me. I'd noticed early on how small her group of friends was and how the friends she *did* have seemed to have mostly been made through her graphic-design work, rather than through other, older social channels like school, or clubs, or the homes she'd grown up in. The book club she'd attended for six months before she vanished was, in truth, something of an outlier in that respect. Not that there was anything suspicious or wrong about any of that – and the friends she did have spoke highly of her – but it made me wonder whether Clara may have just been an easy target. For whatever reason, she'd clearly never found a best friend – besides Kyle – so, when Tori Wolton entered her life, perhaps Clara finally thought she'd found a companionship that was more profound and connected. The question was, was that relationship genuine to Tori Wolton too – or was it transactional? Was Clara simply a bridge for Wolton to get to the Fowlers? And if that was the case, why did Wolton target the family in the first place?

The security light snapped into life as I approached the front door, and I thought again – as I always did – about how strange it felt coming home to this place. For two decades, I'd lived in the bungalow I'd bought with my wife, Derryn, in Ealing, which in the end just had too many memories written into its walls. I'd loved my wife with everything I had, but eventually I couldn't breathe in the house we'd shared. Yet, almost five months on, coming here still felt like visiting another person's home.

It wasn't as big as my old place, but it was in a nice spot, at the end of a quiet, leafy street. From my bedroom window upstairs, I could see out across Kew Gardens to the west and the Thames to the north.

I switched off the alarm and went up to shower and change, and as I stepped out of the shower, my phone buzzed.

It was Ewan Tasker.

He'd emailed me Tori Wolton's driving licence.

I opened the attachment and Tori Wolton – or the woman using that name – stared back at me for the first time. She had blonde hair that was loose in the picture, the two sides of it framing a very attractive face. High cheekbones. Blue eyes. A slim button nose.

Pretty soon, my phone started buzzing again: a call this time.

It was Healy.

'I was just about to go to bed,' I said, after answering.

'It's early for you, Raker.'

'I'm an old man now, what can I say?'

'Do you want me to call back?'

'No, it's fine. How did it go at the casino today?'

'It went okay.'

'But?'

'But this thing you've got me looking into . . .' A long pause on the line. 'I've just got a bad feeling about it.'

26

'Ephesians 5:13?'

'Yeah,' Healy said. '"All things become visible when exposed by the light".'

He'd just run through his visit to the Skyline, and I could feel a familiar charge in my blood: the instinctive sense that something big was buried behind that message, that this was a rabbit hole we were only at the very top of. As I googled Anthony Yanis's killing again, I said, 'So is the Bible quote what you've got a bad feeling about?'

'No, it's Craw,' he said. 'You know what she's like. She sits there with her poker face as standard, so it's difficult to know *what* she thinks. But I don't know . . .' Healy paused. 'She's the part I don't like in all this.'

'What do you mean?'

'There's something she's not telling us.'

My gaze went back to my laptop, to a tabloid story I'd clicked on: BILLIONAIRE BUTCHERED AT LONDON SUPERCASINO. To the right of the headline was a photo of Yanis: he was fifty at the time, tanned, probably three or four stone overweight, a thick sweep of grey hair combed back from his face.

'You think she's holding something back?'

'I don't know for sure, but . . .' A breath. 'Let me just run through the rest of what I found out, and then you can decide what you want to do about it.' I heard him turn some pages. 'So I spent the whole afternoon looking at their CCTV footage, and what we've got on this guy – the Whaler – basically amounts to one decent shot from the very first night he popped on to the radar. In all the other footage of him, he's either turned this way or that way, or the peak of his cap is obscuring his face. Craw's theory is that he memorized floor layouts and knew where the cameras were.'

'Which would mean he would have to have —'

'Done some reconnaissance *before* the first night he met Yanis. Right. So I started going back through video of the weeks before, using the facial recognition tech that Craw gave me access to — and it's a dead end. He doesn't appear to have come to the casino at all in the weeks leading up to his first meeting with Yanis. And the night of the murder, the best shot of him we've got is when he catches an elevator down from the top floor after he offed Yanis in the hotel suite. His head is down and he's wearing his peaked cap. Then we've got some footage of him crossing the floor to the chip cage, where he cashes in the four hundred grand that he swiped from Yanis.'

'Anything from the cage?'

'Nothing usable.'

'How the hell do you memorize the positions of the cameras if you've never come to the casino before?'

'That's the big question.'

'Could he have had blueprints for the Skyline?'

'It's possible, but at this stage it's hard to say for sure.'

'What about a week later, when he came back?'

'Same story. He knows where the cameras are. He slides in at a blackjack table and looks up twice — both times very quickly — into the camera closest to him. Craw reckons he *wanted* the facial recognition tech to do its thing.'

I looked at the news report about the murder again. Why come back to the casino a week after slaughtering someone? Why actively try to get yourself arrested?

'Any footage from the cells?'

'He was using an EMI jammer. How he got out of that

basement is another mystery, though – it's like a rabbit warren down there.'

'So, basically, this guy went up in smoke?'

'It appears that way.'

'What about the money that he stole from Yanis?'

'No sign of it. The cops hired a forensic accountant to follow the money trail, but it went nowhere. The money from the chips automatically transferred back into Yanis's account, then an hour later – at which point Yanis was dead, so we are assuming it was the Whaler – it was wired to an account under the name Morgan Annerson.'

'Forensics couldn't follow the money from there?'

'No, because guess where the Morgan Annerson account is located?'

I knew the answer, just from the way he'd phrased the question. 'The Empress Islands.'

The Empress Islands was a tax haven. Six years ago, I'd worked a case where I'd followed a similar sort of money trail – and, once I got to the islands, the trail stopped dead. It wasn't impossible to unearth the identities and details of people behind accounts there, but it needed the sort of international, cross-jurisdictional cooperation that almost never happened, and certainly not at the request of civilians like Healy and me.

'Did the cops look into Annerson at this end?'

'Yeah. Thames Valley ran down his details. His home address – the address he used to apply for a passport and driving licence – is unoccupied. It's part of some sink estate in south London with black mould problems. It was all over the news a couple of years ago. The thinking is, this guy – the Whaler, Morgan Annerson, whatever his real name is – used the house to receive his mail – the passport, the driving licence. And he chose it because the previous occupant died from a heart attack a few months before the houses were condemned. Guess what the dead guy's name was?'

'Morgan Annerson.'

'Correct. So the Whaler didn't just steal a postbox – he stole an ID.'

He'd ghosted someone's life.

'So what exactly do you think Craw's holding back?'

'It's just a gut feeling,' Healy said, 'but you told me she wanted you to find that four hundred grand as well as the Whaler, right?'

'Yeah,' I said, and I knew where Healy was going. The money was never coming back if it had been wired to the Empress Islands, and Craw clearly knew that was where it had ended up. So why even bother asking me to try and recover it?

'You think she's holding back on something to do with the money?'

'Maybe. I haven't seen her for a long time,' Healy went on, 'but the one thing you could always say about Craw was that, when she was busy ending your career, she could at least look you in the eyes as she did it. Today felt different. We were in the cells and . . . she could hardly even make eye contact with me.'

I thought back to the conversation I'd had with her the day before.

She'd sounded scared.

'She spoke like Craw, she acted like Craw, she made my blood pressure go through the roof like Craw. But afterwards, I started to think . . .' Healy paused. 'I started to think she might be lying to us.'

27

At 3 a.m., unable to sleep, I grabbed my laptop.

Going to the Skyline's home page, I scrolled to the bottom and found an 'About Us' link. That took me to a staff listing, where there were photos and mini profiles of the executive team.

At the top were the Zinter brothers, photographed together, Asha on the right, Caleb on the left. They had the same red-brown hair, Asha just had less of it; Caleb had a beard, Asha was clean-shaven; both had dark brown eyes, the same nose, the same mouth, but Caleb was in better shape than his brother: Asha looked his fifty-one years; Caleb seemed younger.

I scrolled down some more. The photograph for the resort manager was just a black square, with 'Currently Recruiting' under it. Craw had said a new resort manager had just started, so the page hadn't been updated.

Underneath that was what I'd come for.

A photograph of Melanie Craw.

It had been seven years since I'd last seen her. I'd never known her with anything other than short blonde hair, but now it was long, tied back in a ponytail, and a honey-brown colour. She was older, obviously, but she'd aged well, and – although the corporate photo was only of her head and upper body – she looked in great shape.

Are those the only things that have changed about you?

I'd spent hours tossing and turning, replaying what Healy had said about her, his suspicions that she might have lied to us. I didn't know quite what I expected to find on the staff page of the Skyline's corporate website. Maybe it was more that I wanted to see Craw again. Maybe I thought, in her face, there might be some giveaway, some confirmation that she wasn't the person I'd known before.

But Craw wasn't the only thing keeping me awake.

I couldn't stop thinking about Tori Wolton, about who she really was and what she knew about the disappearance of Marc, Kyle and Clara. I kept thinking about the tyre track at the quarry, and about how Kyle had spent six days looking at the same true crime website.

By the time the sun came up, I was still awake.

I got to the Tube station just before 7 a.m. to find that there were delays on both lines because of signalling problems. For a moment, I thought about going by road, but it was rush hour and driving all the way up to Tori Wolton's flat in Angel would probably take twice as long, so I found a space at the end of a bench and waited it out.

'David?'

I looked up. A woman in her early twenties had appeared next to me. She was in a floral dress and a long, thin raincoat. She was also heavily pregnant.

It took a second for me to recognize her, because I'd never seen her in the flesh – in fact had only ever seen her in a photograph – and that was two nights ago on the website of a legal firm.

'Alice,' I said to her.

She seemed surprised. 'How did you know that?'

'I spoke to Colm Healy and he mentioned that you'd been at the Castle hearings on the day I was giving evidence there.' *And he also said you were asking questions about me.* 'You're with King and Parsons, right?'

'Yes. I've been there twelve months.'

163

I stood. 'Did you want to sit?'

'Oh, that's kind of you.'

She took my place at the end of the bench.

'Do you live around here then?' I asked.

'In Richmond, yes.'

'With Liam?'

'Yes. We're going to move somewhere less expensive when this little thing comes along, though.'

As she ran a hand across her bump, I took her in properly. Her face was markless, a sweep of perfectly smooth skin delicately enhanced with make-up. She must have been five-eight, maybe even taller, but she seemed demure, a little reticent in her movement, and it created an impression of someone who was physically smaller.

'So are you on your way to work?' I asked.

'Yes.' She looked at the train that was at the platform, its doors open. 'Well, I was before it all came to an abrupt halt here. Are you heading somewhere?'

'I am.'

'I mean, obviously.' She laughed a little nervously. 'That was a stupid question. I just meant . . .' A pause. 'I'm not sure what I meant.' She glanced at me and then away again, and as I eased us into a polite conversation about her becoming a mother, I started to see a pattern. It was subtle, but it was there: a fractional pause every time she tried to think of some new angle for conversation. And it wasn't down to the fact that we'd never spoken before. It was something else.

'I've never met a missing persons investigator before,' she said.

'Well, you can cross it off your bucket list now.'

She was wearing a bracelet with six daisies on it, and as she talked, she played with it, feeding the daisies back and forth on the loop. 'Do many of the people you look for turn up?'

'I try my best to make sure they do.'

'Right. Yours seems like such a fascinating job. When I saw you at the hearings . . .' She searched for what to say. 'Well, I went online after and read about some of the cases you've worked.'

'Don't believe everything you read.'

'That's embarrassing to admit, isn't it?' she said. 'Reading up about you like that. It makes me sound like a stalker.'

'Not really. It sounds like you were just doing your job.'

'Is there one case in particular that you remember?' Subtly, I could feel the mood change. But before I even had the chance to respond, she broke out into another smile. 'I was just interested. You've found so many missing people, I thought there might be a case that sticks out.'

I watched her, trying again to figure out what was going on here – but then, above us, the departure board had changed without either of us noticing, its readout listing the trains due in over the next five minutes.

Alice stood up. 'Well, anyway, I thought I'd say hello.'

'I'm glad you did. It was nice to meet you.'

I expected her to go.

But she didn't.

'Can I ask you a small favour, David? Can we keep this between us?'

'Keep what?'

'This . . .' She trailed off. 'This conversation.'

'Who would I tell?'

'Colm maybe. And he might tell Liam.'

I studied her. 'Was there something else you wanted to talk about?'

'I just . . .' She stopped. 'Is that okay? Please?'

'If that's what you want.'

'It is. And I appreciate it. Thank you.'

Her eyes skittered away from me again.

And then I watched her head back inside the carriage.

28

I was still thinking about the bizarre conversation I'd had with Alice as the train squealed into Angel station. As soon as I got to the surface, though, I cleared my head and reset. Whatever was going on with her wasn't my priority.

This was.

Heading left out of the station, I walked down to City Road and then double-backed along Colebrooke Row, following it all the way up to Regent's Canal. The flat was in the first street on the other side of the water, the middle property in a long row of elegant, four-storey townhouses. The second I entered the road, my internal alarm started blaring again. How did someone who had no financial history afford to rent a flat in a road like this?

Maybe the answers are inside.

Number twenty-four was halfway down the street.

The building had been divided into four flats. With my hands in my pockets, I started playing with the lockpicks I'd brought, eyeing the rest of the road, looking for movement, for faces at windows. This time of the morning, people were busy, getting ready for work, for the school run, but that didn't make me any more relaxed: none of the houses had porches, even overhangs; the front entrances were completely exposed, the doors sitting at the pavement edge.

I'd have to be quick.

I looked both ways – furtively checking windows again, and then the parking spaces either side of the street for signs of a green Mondeo.

No one was watching.

There were no cars I recognized.

I went to work on the door.

Entrances to flats were never as secure as houses. Landlords were often so focused on the security and condition of the properties *inside* the building, they forgot about the door at the front. I checked over my shoulder – left, right – and then heard a door somewhere else open behind me – children, a mother telling them off.

By then, I was already in.

I darted through, into the ground-floor hallway, and quickly pushed the door shut. Pausing, I stood there and listened to the family outside, making sure I hadn't raised their suspicions. The mother was still ripping into her kids.

To my left, on the wall, were four mail slots.

The first three were empty.

The slot for the top-floor flat was full.

I reached in and took out Tori Wolton's mail. It was junk. Reams of flyers, local community leaflets, and one letter from Islington Council that was simply addressed to 'The Homeowner'. At the bottom, I found a leaflet from the local Neighbourhood Watch group, which had a date printed at the top.

Wednesday 5 April.

Five weeks ago.

Putting the mail back in its slot, I moved up, passing the doors for the first- and second-floor flats. On the top floor, the flat Tori Wolton had rented was set back a little, the doorway at the end of a short corridor with a skylight in the ceiling. Some sun was escaping in, but mostly the glass was covered in a sea of moss and mould.

I stepped up to the door and knocked on it.

Silence from inside.

Getting out my picks again, I slid them into the lock and started to feel for the pins. It was marginally more secure than the one installed at the front, but not much.

In less than thirty seconds, I heard a click.

Slowly, the door inched back into the gloom of the flat.

29

I started in the kitchen, going through its drawers and cupboards. Based on the junk mail I'd found downstairs, it felt likely Tori Wolton had already moved out, and the kitchen seemed to confirm that: all that was left was what must have been provided by the landlord. There was no food in the fridge, nothing on the worktops. The surfaces were shining, the cupboards, the handles, even the lino. Given that Wolton's rental period didn't end for another three weeks – and she'd already been gone for five – it seemed likely that she was the one who'd cleaned up, not her landlord. It made me wonder if her landlord even knew she'd left early – after all, the less contact she had with people, the easier it was for her to maintain anonymity. Either way, it was clear she didn't want to risk leaving any trace of herself when someone finally entered.

I exited the kitchen and headed along the hallway.

The bedroom and living area were one room, separated by a three-quarters high dividing wall and – again – they'd been rigorously cleaned. There was a TV in the corner, inside a glass-fronted cabinet. In the same cabinet was a router and what looked like a printer.

I checked over the bathroom, and then the bedside cabinet. Both were empty. Back in the living room, I took a moment. She'd moved out of the flat early. Why?

My phone buzzed in my pocket.

It was Healy.

The Whaler stuff is in the shared drive. Heading out to interview
Ramis and Linkers. Let me know if you want to meet up later to discuss.

I went to the folder I'd set up and, as promised, he'd sent me everything.

It must have taken him hours.

Years back, when I'd first met Healy, he'd been impetuous and volatile, and while he'd been a skilled detective, he'd rarely had the patience for paperwork. Things had changed. His notes were detailed, and when I clicked through to the 1GB file of scans from the police file on Yanis's murder, I noticed it had been uploaded just after 3 a.m. If I'd harboured doubts about bringing him in, they were almost entirely allayed as I went through his efforts.

Almost, but not completely.

Despite everything, I did sometimes wonder where that older, more unpredictable Healy had gone; whether he really had been cast off for good – or just hidden somewhere deeper in the shadows.

The router blinked at me from the TV cabinet, and then my gaze settled on the printer for a second time. I realized a light was winking on the top of that too.

I moved across, opened the cabinet and edged the printer towards me. The screen on the front of it was flashing with an error message.

Paper jam.

I pushed the Options button, and then Current Job. On-screen now were the details for the last document printed out.

It had the filename 'UpperSt_Boxes.pdf'.

Upper Street was the road that snaked north through Angel and Islington, from Angel Tube Station all the way up to Highbury Corner – just ten minutes' walk away.

I googled 'Upper St Boxes'.

A mailbox company.

I started gently tugging the crinkled sheet out from inside the printer. There was hardly anything printed on it – just two lines of what looked like terms and conditions. Someone – presumably Tori Wolton – had printed out a document, grabbed the first page from the tray, but not realized that a few lines had carried over on to the second, which had got stuck in the machine.

And then I spotted something else.

It was so tiny, I'd missed it the first time. I smoothed the printout some more and then tilted it towards the window so that sunlight flooded the page – and at the top, faint grey and in minuscule five-point script, were three words and a number.

Wolton, Tori.

Box #5349.

Healy

London | *Now*

Healy got to Canary Wharf early.

Neil Linkers was waiting for him on a stool in the window of a Pret in Jubilee Place Mall. He was dressed in the uniform he wore as a security guard at Gaito Bank on South Colonnade, and looked like the job was crushing his soul. After buying them both coffees, Healy slid on to the stool next to Linkers and saw an echo of his own life in the young man's face: this was how Healy had looked in the weeks after Craw had fired him from the police – lost, hopeless.

Healy spent an hour listening to Linkers recount his memories from the night the Whaler vanished. He had good recall, and everything he remembered fitted with the interview he'd originally given Thames Valley Police. But at the end of it, Healy still didn't have any new information to get his teeth into.

'You ever see Ramis any more?'

'No,' Linkers said. 'We fell out of touch after he retired.'

'Do you think he could have had anything to do with this?'

Linkers frowned. 'What?'

'Ramis. He was down there by the cells the whole time.'

The question didn't seem to compute with Linkers, and Healy had found absolutely nothing in Ramis's own statement to the police to even remotely support the idea that he was lying. Ramis was a veteran detective of twenty-five years who by all accounts had done a very good job of running security at the casino during his time there. From what Healy could gather, he was liked, respected and credible.

But the Whaler had vanished from that cell somehow.

It wasn't magic.

And sometimes even credible witnesses lied.

Healy jumped on the Jubilee up to Wembley Park, and then changed to the Metropolitan and took it all the way to Chorley-wood. It felt like the journey went on forever.

Once he finally arrived, he exited the station and tried calling Gordon Ramis's mobile again, more out of hope than expectation. It went straight to voicemail. That was all Healy had got over the past two days, and although he'd left three messages for Ramis, none of them had elicited a response. There had been a landline number in the police file, but that had gone unanswered as well, so taking a train into the suburbs for an hour and door-stepping the former head of security felt like the only option that Healy had left.

He headed up some steps and cut through a copse of houses, emerging at the edge of Chorleywood Common. Ramis's house was an attractive end-of-terrace with a dainty porch and a flowering vine climbing up its sides.

Healy rang the doorbell.

Glancing through a bay window to his left, he spotted a TV, and it was on – so someone was definitely home. But when he couldn't see or hear any movement from inside, he rang the doorbell again and knocked twice.

This time, someone appeared, a silhouette beyond the glass.

The door opened a little way, revealing a woman in her late sixties, with short, white-grey hair. She had an apron on that had a photograph of a West Highland white terrier in the middle and the name *Archie*, with a heart for the dot above the *i*.

'Yes?'

'Mrs Ramis?'

'Shute.'

'I'm sorry?'

'My surname's Shute.'

'Oh. I was looking for the Ramis home.'

Healy stepped back, glancing along the row of houses.

'You've got the right place,' she said, a half-smile on her face, as if amused by Healy's confusion. 'I was an actress before I met Gordon, so I kept my maiden name.'

'An actress. Wow.'

She waved her hand. 'It's not as impressive as it sounds.'

'So is it Ms or Mrs Shute?'

'It's Lorna.'

'Ah, even better. I'm Colm.' He showed her his driving licence. 'I'm a . . .' He paused. *I'm a what exactly?* 'I used to be a detective down in London – at the moment I'm helping out, trying to locate a missing person.'

It wasn't exactly the truth, but it would do.

'A missing person? Oh, goodness.'

'Is your husband around at all?' Healy asked, glancing over her shoulder, into what he could see of the house. There was no indication that anyone else was home. And when his gaze came back to Lorna, Healy realized why.

Ah shite.

He knew grief when he saw it.

'Gordon died eight months ago.'

Now it made sense why calls to Ramis's phone kept going to voicemail. And Healy was willing to bet that the reason the mobile – *and* the voicemail – were still active was so that Lorna could call the number occasionally and listen to her husband's voice. It wasn't a stretch: Healy had done exactly the same thing after Leanne had died. It had taken him a year to cancel the contract, and then another year to deal with the pain of not hearing her.

'I'm very sorry for your loss, Lorna.'

'Thank you.' A shimmer in her eyes. 'You said someone is missing?'

'Yes. A man called Morgan Annerson.'

A blank.

'He was known in the media as "the Whaler".'

This time, there was something.

'Have you heard of the Whaler, Lorna?'

But he could already tell that she had.

'What have you heard about him?'

She swallowed, eyed Healy. 'Maybe you'd better come in.'

30

Upper Street Boxes was in a bank of shops opposite Islington Green.

As I entered the store, the guy working behind the counter glanced up. I gave him a smile and said good morning, looking confident as I strode past him, into a long row of mailboxes. I'd been worried that they might have been operated with cards or an app, but it looked like all of them used a physical key. It was a stroke of luck I was about to take full advantage of.

The further down I went, the more I began to realize that number 5349 was in a row of bigger units at the back. Not only that, but it was fractionally outside the range of the nearest CCTV camera and positioned in the furthest, gloomiest corner of the store, both of which had to have been a deliberate decision on Tori Wolton's part.

I dropped to my haunches.

Glancing behind me, double-checking I hadn't aroused any suspicion from the guy at the front, I set to work on the lock. It was more complicated than the ones that had been installed at Wolton's flat – a lever lock, rather than a straightforward pin tumbler. The first thing I had to establish was whether there was a 'curtain' inside, a device used in lever locks to prevent them being picked. If there was, I had a tool for it, but it would take me longer to get the box open, and I would risk drawing attention to myself.

I pushed in my regular pick and tension wrench.

There *was* a curtain.

I went to my coat pocket and grabbed the tool that I needed.

It was T-shaped, a little cumbersome. I took in my surroundings again, looking all the way along the corridor of boxes to the front counter: the same guy was sitting in exactly the same position at his desk, staring at his PC. I needed to take advantage of the fact that he appeared to be distracted, but that meant working fast – and the problem with lockpicking, especially in the hands of an amateur, was that it was pretty far from that.

My thoughts started racing.

Why would Wolton pay for a unit in this place? I could only really think of one reason: she didn't want anyone to intercept her post. That anonymity she craved was her weapon. I doubted her neighbours knew anything about her – just as her landlord didn't know she'd already moved out – but she would have been forced to show her face if anyone else received and signed for her mail. Or, of course, there could have been another reason entirely: she started paying for the box once she vacated the flat, knowing she'd never go back to the apartment.

But why move out of the flat early?

The lock clicked.

I withdrew the picks, pocketed them and pulled the door towards me. There was no mail inside, no letters, no bills.

Instead, the entire space was filled by a backpack.

Wolton wasn't using the mailbox for post.

She was using it as a hiding place.

Healy

Hertfordshire | *Now*

Healy waited in the living room while Lorna Shute made them tea.

Next to him, on the wall, were pictures of her and Ramis, and of the two of them with their kids – a boy and a girl – every photo charting the life of their family, from when the kids were small, to graduations and marriages.

Healy thought of Ciaran and Liam, and felt a sudden, piercing stab of jealousy. Why couldn't he have had this? Why couldn't he have had a family that loved him? Why didn't he have these memories?

He squeezed his eyes shut.

It would have been different if Craw hadn't sacked me. I wouldn't have spiralled. I could have got the boys back onside. I could have been a better –

'You said you *used* to be a detective?'

He opened his eyes, cleared his head.

'I'm retired,' he lied.

Lorna handed him a tea, shrugged off her apron and laid it on the sofa next to her. Healy could see the face of Archie the Westie again. He hadn't seen the dog anywhere, so he assumed Archie was someone else that Lorna had had to say goodbye to.

In his pocket, he felt his phone vibrating against his leg.

He ignored it.

'I've actually been hired by the Skyline to try and figure out what went on the night your husband arrested the Whaler.' He stopped, watching her reaction. She had her tea on her lap, her fingers at the curve of the handle, and she was gripping it so tightly her knuckles had blanched. 'Gordon was planning to retire, wasn't he?'

'Yes. It was his last week.' She glanced at a photograph of her husband. 'He enjoyed it at the Skyline, but he was looking forward to retirement. We both were. We'd been married forty-one years, had brought up two wonderful kids, had many lovely memories – but we wanted to travel, just the two of us. We were excited about being together, doing stuff we loved. I think, by the end, he'd just become tired of dragging himself out of bed in the middle of the night because there was some emergency at the casino.'

'Are you talking about the Whaler?'

'There were other emergencies down the years, but nothing quite like that one. No one had ever been killed at the Skyline before.'

'Did Gordon ever talk to you about it?'

'The murder? No, only that there had been a death at the casino – and then, a week later, the man responsible came back. That was it, really.'

Healy's phone buzzed again.

'Excuse me a second,' he said, taking it out.

It was Raker.

He was going to have to wait.

Pocketing the phone, he studied Lorna. It may have been a long time since he'd interviewed anyone, but Healy knew when someone was holding back on him.

'I just want the truth, Lorna.'

She nodded.

'You invited me in,' Healy said, more softly. 'Was there something you needed to say?'

She frowned. 'I've told you everything I know.'

'I don't think you have.'

That was her chance to come back at him, to tell him how dare he come into her home and accuse her. But she didn't.

'If you give me the truth, we can –'

'It's not fair.'

Healy eyed her. '"Not fair"?'

'We'd barely even started our retirement.' She tucked a strand of silver hair behind her ear, then reached forward and put her mug down. 'I only had him for four months. My Gordon, I mean. He'd only been retired four months . . .'

This wasn't the direction Healy had been expecting.

But let's see where it takes me.

'How did he die?'

'He had a heart attack, right out there.' She gestured through the patio doors, to the back garden. 'We were tidying up the garden for winter, and he . . . he simply . . .' She dabbed at her right eye with a tissue. 'He just keeled over. It was awful.'

Her head was tilted down so Healy was looking at the dome of her skull, at the whirl of her crown, but he could hear her start to sob, each one echoed in her shoulders. When she finally looked up, her expression had changed once again.

She still looked panicked, still looked scared.

But now she was angry too.

'They ruined everything,' she said.

'"They"?' Healy leaned forward. 'Who are "they", Lorna?'

This is it.

This is what she's been keeping back from me.

'We just . . .' She paused. 'We just couldn't get past it.'

'What was it you couldn't get past?'

'They said they would come back if we ever talked to anyone.'

Healy stiffened. 'Who did?'

She didn't answer.

'Lorna, it's okay. You're safe. You can tell me who –'

'No.' She shook her head. 'You could be working with them for all I know.'

'I'm not.'

She was trying to see if he was lying.

'I'm telling the truth,' Healy said. 'I can help you.'

'I don't know if I . . . I don't know . . .'

You've almost got her.

She's almost there.

And then he thought, *I'm not with the Met any more.*

I can do whatever it takes to get her to talk.

Reaching forward, across the coffee table that was between them, he took hold of her hand. She was surprised at first, looked like she might be about to pull away, and – for one horrible moment – Healy wondered if he'd just scorched any progress he might have made. But then she looked at him, and her eyes filled with tears, and her fingers slid in tight against his hand. 'It's eating me up . . .'

'What is, Lorna?'

'I lied,' she said, her voice breaking.

'About what happened at the casino?'

'Yes.'

'What did you lie about?'

Her head dropped again and she started to cry properly.

'Do you know how the Whaler disappeared?'

'Yes,' Lorna sobbed. 'Yes, I know everything.'

31

'I needed that,' Healy said, putting his coffee down and digging around in his jacket. We were sitting in a booth at the back of a coffee shop in Marylebone, rain tapping against the windows. He placed his notebook and his phone on the table. 'Sorry about not picking up earlier. I was deep in the weeds and about to get answers.'

'You texted to say the trip was worth it?'

He flipped the front of his notebook open and ran a hand across his shaved head, the red bristles crackling against his palm. When he leaned forward, his shirt fell away, and I could see past the V of his collar to the pink line at the centre of his chest. With Healy, not all scars were on the inside.

'Ramis is dead,' Healy said.

'What?'

'I talked to his widow.' He filled me in on his interview with Lorna Shute. 'She knows how the Whaler vanished from that cell. Want to take a guess as to how?'

'Did the Whaler have help?'

He frowned. 'How did you know that?'

I didn't say anything, just looked at Healy's notes.

I could feel his eyes on me.

'Are you going to tell me how you knew that already?'

'I'll explain in a second,' I said, 'but first I want you to take a look at something.' I got out my phone, went to my photos and selected a picture I'd taken earlier of Tori Wolton's mailbox. I swivelled the screen around so Healy could see clearly.

'What's this?' he said.

'It's a backpack.'

'I can see that. But why are you showing it to me?'

'It belongs to someone called Tori Wolton.'

He shrugged. 'Never heard of her.'

'It's likely a fake identity. But I got into her flat this morning and I found something in there that led me to this place.' I pointed to the screen. 'It's a mailbox company. That backpack was in one of their lockers.'

I swiped to the next picture on my phone.

'What's that?' Healy leaned in. 'Drugs?'

In the second photograph the backpack was fully open, revealing a series of shrink-wrapped packages, each the size of a mobile phone. I swiped to the next photograph: I'd taken the packages out and laid them on the floor beside one another. A few of them had been opened already – presumably by Wolton – the plastic wrapping torn, the contents exposed.

'It's cash,' I said. 'Thirty unopened ten-grand bricks, two half-used ones – and evidence of eight others already spent. She had four hundred grand in there.'

He shot me a look. 'Wait, what?'

'Four hundred grand to the penny.'

'The exact amount of money the Whaler stole from Anthony Yanis.'

'Correct. This was how I already knew the Whaler must have had help.'

'Because . . .' He stopped.

He knew, he just needed to hear me say it.

'Because I don't know how the hell it's possible, but my search for the Fowlers and your search for the Whaler, they're not two separate things – they're part of the same case.'

32

Healy was still staring at the photograph of the money.

'For most of today,' I said, 'I've been thinking about how Wolton may have had something to do with the Fowlers going missing. And now . . .' I studied the backpack. 'Look, don't get me wrong, the family may have gone willingly – that part's still not clear – but if we're assuming they didn't, taking them would have been impossible for one person to do. There were three of them in the dinghy. No way Tori Wolton overpowered three people on her own.'

'But if she *also* had help . . .'

'Right. It looks like the money the Whaler stole from Anthony Yanis is in a mailbox *belonging* to Tori Wolton. So, if they worked together at the Skyline, why couldn't they have worked together at the lake? And there's another reason that would make sense: remember you said the Whaler was never spotted once on CCTV in the lead-up to Yanis's murder and yet he knew the layout of all the cameras at the casino?'

Healy nodded.

'What if Wolton did the reconnaissance for him? No one was looking for her. She could have been coming in for weeks beforehand mapping the layout.'

I swiped to the next photo on my phone.

Off to the side of the shrink-wrapped bricks of cash were two other items. One was a plain A5 black card, with a silver embossed line in sans serif across the middle.

It said: *Guest #121 | Tori Wolton.*

The other was a gun.

'Money and weapons,' Healy muttered. 'This can't be good.'

'I don't know what that is,' I said, pinch-zooming in on the black card. 'It looks like some sort of invite, but there's nothing on the back and nothing else in the bag.' I glanced at his notes. 'Tell me exactly what Lorna said to you.'

'Never mind that. Do you think Craw knows the Whaler could be connected to the Fowler case?'

'I never mentioned the Fowlers by name to her.'

'So we'll just forget the fact that these cases – the search for that family, and Craw picking up the phone and asking you to track down the Whaler – *happened* to land in your lap at almost exactly the same time?' His gaze returned to my phone, to the backpack, to the cash. 'I know I've been out of the game for a while, but that's a coincidence so big you could write it on the side of a building.'

Healy was right: Sarah could have picked up the phone to me at any time during the last eight months; Craw had been at the casino for almost a year and had had even longer.

And yet they'd both contacted me inside the same week.

'Sarah Fowler won't know about any of this,' I said.

'You sure?'

'One hundred per cent.'

'And you said you never mentioned the Fowlers to Craw. So that means – what? That this whole thing's just a quirk of timing? That's what you're saying, right?' He shook his head. 'Come on, Raker. Craw's lying. I told you she was holding something back and now we've just found out why.'

'We don't know she's lying.'

'Why? Because she's Mrs High and Fucking Mighty?'

The caustic nature of his response stopped me.

'What does that mean?' I said.

'It means, where Craw's concerned, you're still thinking with your dick.'

'Don't talk shit, Healy. Craw and I are over. We've been over for years. A lot of the time, I don't even think we were anything in the first place.' I stopped, tried to calm myself. 'Do you *really* think Craw is holding back on us?'

'I said I did, didn't I?'

A couple at a nearby table glanced across at us.

I held up a hand, leaned into him and lowered my voice. 'Calm down. I'm just asking because I need you to be clear-headed. If you're not clear-headed, you can't be here.' I gave him a chance to come back at me. He didn't. 'You can talk about me and Craw, but it's *you* and her that have a problematic history. You promised me it wasn't an issue. So has it become an issue?'

'No.'

'Are you sure?'

'What, is there an echo in here? I'm sure.'

I leaned away from him again and, eventually, he looked down at the phone. I tried to get my thoughts into some sort of order, even as the residual worry about Healy – about whether I should have trusted him to go and see Craw for me – lingered. For now, though, that would have to wait.

'You said Lorna Shute told you exactly how the Whaler disappeared?'

He nodded. 'Yeah.'

'Start at the beginning and don't leave anything out.'

Healy

Lorna was sitting on the edge of the sofa, her knees together, her hands in her lap. 'Gordon got the call at about 2 a.m. I could see straight away that this was serious.'

'That was the call about the Whaler?' Healy asked.

She nodded. 'They'd arrested him at the casino.'

'So what happened after that?'

'About five minutes after he left, there was a knock at the door.'

Healy leaned forward.

'I figured Gordon must have forgotten something. So I didn't even think about it; didn't bother to check who it was. I took the chain off and just opened it.' The colour washed from her face. 'It wasn't Gordon.'

'Who was it?'

She glanced at Healy. He didn't move, didn't say anything, even though the adrenalin was flooding his system. 'She was in a balaclava.'

'It was a woman?'

'Yes. I could tell by her lips, the mascara at her eyes.'

'What else can you remember about her?'

'She was slim. Medium height. And strong. She grabbed me by the arm, put a hand on my mouth and I couldn't do a single thing to stop her. She dragged me back inside the house and, before I knew it, she had me face down in here . . .'

Her voice was starting to tremble as she talked.

'Did she speak to you at all?'

'Yes,' Lorna said. 'She got on top of me in here, and she leaned into my ear, and she said, "If you scream, I'll cut your throat."'

'Do you remember if she had an accent?'

Healy's leg had started vibrating, nervous energy coursing through him. Suddenly, he was back at the Met, inside an interview room, trying to get a witness to trust him, to talk, to take him through the case.

'I don't know,' Lorna said, frowning. 'Maybe.'

'A local one? London one? South-east?'

'No, I don't think so. She spoke very quietly and very quickly, but it didn't sound local to me. But I don't know . . . Everything was so confusing and I was so scared, I'm really not sure. All I could think was, "I don't want to die." I don't know how long she had me on the floor in here, but it felt like hours. My whole body hurt. I genuinely thought she was going to kill me. And then an alarm went off on her phone.'

'An alarm?'

'Yes. After that, she put me on to that sofa' – she pointed to the one Healy was on – 'and then told me she was going to make a call on *my* phone.'

'Did she say to who?'

'Yes,' Lorna said. 'To Gordon.'

After locking the Whaler inside the cell, Gordon Ramis told Linkers to get back up to the casino floor: 'Wait at the main doors for the cops and then bring them down.'

'Yes, boss,' Linkers said, and hurried off.

Ramis glanced at the cell again, picturing the killer they'd just secured inside, then headed into the kitchen opposite. Its bank of windows gave him a clear view of all four of the cells, and as he got the coffee machine going, he perched on a stool and got his phone out.

'Sir?'

He looked over at the locked cell. The voice was coming from inside. Ramis ignored it. The police would be here in a minute.

'Sir?'

Ramis glanced out at the cell again.

'Sir, are you there?'

He put his phone away, took a mouthful of coffee and then slid off the stool and headed back into the corridor. Pulling across the viewing hatch on the door, Ramis looked in at the cell. The Whaler was in the corner.

Something felt different.

That was the first thought Ramis had. But then, as he looked around the cell he thought, what could have possibly changed? Automatically, he checked that the door was still secure – which it was, which it was always going to be – and then his attention returned to the Whaler.

It's him, Ramis thought. He's what's different.

'What is it?' Ramis said, his tone less assured than he would have liked.

'I just wanted to say you should answer it.'

Ramis frowned. 'What? What the hell are you talking about?'

Suddenly, inside Ramis's jacket, his phone erupted into life. As he glanced at the Whaler, as he felt his mobile vibrate against his chest, his entire body went cold.

Taking an instinctive step back from the door, from the man inside it, Ramis reached into his jacket and retrieved his mobile.

'That'll be your wife,' the Whaler said.

'The woman in the balaclava, she handed me a piece of paper,' Lorna said, her eyes slowly filling with tears. 'On it there were things that I had to say to Gordon.'

'Lorna?' Ramis said, phone to his ear, looking into the cell at the Whaler.

'There's someone here, Gord.'

Ramis froze. 'What?'

'There's someone here with me.'

'Who?'

'They want me to give you some instructions or . . . or . . .'

Lorna went quiet. Ramis could hear her sobbing. The sound of his wife crying, the terror in her voice, hit him hard. He stepped up to the viewing hatch, looked at the Whaler, and banged his spare hand on the cell-door.

'What the hell's going on?' he spat into the cell.

The Whaler just stared at him, unmoved.

'Gordon?' Lorna said, her voice even smaller now.

'Are you hurt, sweetheart?'

'No. But she says she'll hurt me if you don't do what they want.'

Ramis's eyes returned to the cell. 'What does she want me to do?'

'Open the cell.'

Ramis looked in at the Whaler, the conflict tearing him apart. This guy had murdered someone. Stabbed them twenty-seven times. He'd written a message on the wall of the hotel room in his victim's blood. He was a psychopath. How could Ramis let him out? How the hell would he explain it?

'Lorna, I don't know if —'

Ramis was cut off by the sound of Lorna screaming.

'Lorna?'

'Open the cell.' A different, hushed female voice on the phone.

'Where's Lorna?' Ramis shouted.

'I'm here, Gord, I'm here,' his wife responded, back on the line. She sounded tearful, more frightened than ever. 'Please, Gord. Please. I'm scared. Just open it.'

Ramis gazed in at the Whaler.

For one bizarre moment, he could have sworn he looked almost apologetic, as if he felt sorry for Ramis.

But then the Whaler got to his feet.

Ramis stared down at the lock, at the mechanisms on the door. Somewhere at the back of his head, playing out like an old film, he could see the fallout from him opening the cell. He could picture the cops arriving,

Linkers with them, all of them staring into the empty room. He could see the act he'd have to put on to pretend he was as shocked as everyone else. He could see his world imploding – his career, his freedom even – as it came to light that he'd made the choice to let a murderer walk.

But none of it mattered right now.

All that mattered was Lorna.

He started unlocking the cell.

'Have you been down to see the cells?' Lorna asked.

'I went yesterday.'

'Gordon took me down there, right back at the start when he first got the job. The cells aren't the only secure part of the basement. There's another place – another locked-off area. It's right in the furthest corner, pretty much as far as you can go. Gordon told me he wasn't allowed to show me inside.'

'Why not?'

'I don't know,' Lorna said. 'But he called it "the Bunker".'

The Whaler stepped out of the cell.

For a split second, Ramis had the crazy idea of grabbing hold of this killer, of trying to threaten him in return. But then the Whaler moved again, stepping past Ramis, looking along the corridor in the direction Linkers had gone earlier. Ramis, still holding his phone to his ear, still listening to the soft sobs of his wife, watched as the Whaler straightened himself out and flipped up his hood. His face – handsome, sculpted – faded to shadow.

'Gordon?' Lorna said, her voice small on the line.

'Are you okay, Lorn?'

'I'm okay. But listen. I need to read this next part out to you.'

The Whaler watched.

'"This is almost over, Gordon. Your wife is going to be fine as long as you do two more easy things." ' Lorna paused. ' "One, you're going to keep your mouth shut. You're not going to tell anyone what happened tonight,

ever. When the police come down in a minute and you open the cell for them, you're going to tell them you don't know how this happened. You're going to pretend to be shocked. You're going to sit in interviews with them later on tonight and answer their questions, and you're going to make them believe you genuinely have no idea what went on. And in the weeks and months that follow, you and Lorna aren't going to say a word to anyone. Because if you do, I will come back and I will do to you what I did to Yanis." '

Ramis stared into the darkness of the hood.

' "Two," ' Lorna continued, ' "you're going to hand over your access card." '

'What? No, I can't just –'

' "You're going to hand over your access card," ' Lorna repeated, uncertainty and confusion written into every note in her voice. As if on cue, the Whaler extended his arm out to Ramis, palm facing up. As he did, his sleeve shifted and Ramis saw something tattooed on the underside of the guy's wrist.

A pair of wings.

And, under that, a number.

Reluctantly, Ramis went to the lanyard in his pocket. Inside a plastic sleeve was his pass. The key to the kingdom.

He placed it in the Whaler's hand.

' "When I'm done with the access card," ' Lorna said, ' "I will leave it outside the casino, in one of the flower beds. Again, I just want to remind you, Gordon: if you don't deny everything, if you don't lie through your teeth, if you try to fuck me over tonight, even once, I will . . . I . . ." '

Lorna stumbled over her words.

Ramis heard a sudden burst of movement.

'Lorna?' he said, desperation in his voice.

' "If you fuck me over even once," ' his wife said again, more unsteady now; she was crying again, ' "I'll cut Lorna's throat ear to ear and make you watch." '

Anger, panic, fear: it all rushed him at once.

The Whaler took another step forward.

' "Now," ' Lorna said, ' "what's the six-digit code for the Bunker?" '

33

As Healy returned to the table with more coffee, I swiped through another page of the Anthony Yanis case that he'd scanned for me.

'Is there any mention of the Bunker in here?'

Healy shook his head. 'No.'

'You never saw a locked-off area when you were down there?'

'Not one like Lorna described. We passed a lot of doors, but from what Lorna says, this Bunker area doesn't just have a card reader, it has a keypad that requires a six-digit code. I never saw anything like that. Wherever this place is – *whatever* it is – it must be as deep into that basement as it's possible to go.'

'And Lorna never discussed the Bunker with Ramis after that night?'

'No. I think a part of them believed that, if they talked about it, even between themselves, they'd jinx everything and the Whaler and the woman would come back.' Healy eyed his notes. 'At least we know one thing, though.'

'Why the Whaler returned to the Skyline a week after killing Yanis.'

I could see Healy was going back over the sequence of events, the same as I was: the Whaler returning to the casino seven days after butchering Yanis, deliberately looking into a camera, knowing the facial recognition tech would ID him; his arrest; and then his escape, with the help of Tori Wolton. The Whaler must have known how it would play out, because all of those acts were to facilitate his endgame: getting his hands on the access card that allowed Ramis, as head of security, entry to every part of the resort – including the Bunker.

'But what *is* the Bunker?' Healy said.

'And what's inside it?' I replied. 'You said there was no footage of the Whaler leaving the casino after he escaped that cell?'

'No.'

'There must be an exit inside or close to the Bunker, then.'

Healy nodded. 'That would make sense.'

The question was, how did all of this connect to the Fowlers? *And where else did these two cases intersect?* I couldn't think of a single other connection between Marc, Kyle and Clara, and Anthony Yanis, other than the money that the Whaler stole from him, with the help of a woman who may or may not have genuinely been Clara's friend.

I went back to the Yanis murder. The next page contained photographs from the crime scene. The opulence of the penthouse suite had been ruined. In the middle of the living area, a white carpet and coffee table were spattered with arterial spray.

I swiped again, and then again.

And then I paused.

I was looking at a picture of the wall behind Yanis. The body was out of focus in the foreground, though even slightly blurred the image was horrific. I knew he'd suffered twenty-seven knife wounds, but it looked like hundreds. Yet despite all this, my eye was drawn elsewhere, to the message – written in blood – on the wall.

Ephesians 5:13.

'This feels like a revenge killing,' Healy said.

I didn't disagree. It was frenzied, brutal.

'It also feels like an invitation,' I said. ' "All things become visible when exposed by the light." Why would you write that – *choose* that – if you weren't inviting someone to look deeper?'

'So you think the Whaler is trying to get us to look closer at Yanis?'

'Expose him to the light.' I shrugged. 'I don't know, maybe. And maybe once we've brought him into the light and we've seen what the Whaler wants us to see, we get some answers about the Fowlers.'

'Or maybe we don't.'

'Yeah, maybe we don't. But these cases *have* to be connected by something more than just the stolen money – and Yanis, and whatever Tori Wolton's role is in all of this, seems like a pretty good place to start.' I looked at the crime-scene photographs again. 'Did Thames Valley do a background on Yanis?'

'They did – it's towards the back – but it's mostly publicly available info. Born and educated in the States, made his money investing early in Retrigram, met a British girl, moved to the UK, stuck a ton of money into the Skyline when it looked like the Zinter brothers were going to get crushed by the banking crisis . . .' Healy went back a few pages in his notes. 'He lived in some mega-mansion outside York and he was basically a pro gambler. He'd come down to the Skyline three times a month, would fly out to Vegas and east to Macau at least eight times a year, normally more. Boozed, cheated. He sounds like a piece of shit, but I guess the rich can do whatever the hell they like.'

I swiped to the next page.

'So where does *he* fit in?'

I held up my phone so Healy could see the CCTV shot from the first night the Whaler appeared on the scene.

A multimillionaire like Anthony Yanis was going to be on a permanent state of high alert for frauds, charlatans and sharks. That was the nature of being wealthy. People constantly had angles. So what was it about the Whaler that was different in Yanis's eyes? Why did he drop his guard?

I looked at the Whaler again.

Morgan Annerson.

It occurred to me that this was the first time I'd properly laid eyes on him. The only photographs I'd seen of this killer were blurry CCTV shots from Google. This was different: a clear snapshot of a man who, five months later, would slaughter Yanis in a hotel suite. I centred him on-screen: mid-twenties, short black hair, dark eyes, light skin, tall and slim and very good-looking. In the darkest recesses of my head, I had the sudden sense that he might be familiar to me. Had I seen him somewhere before?

Unable to grasp it, I returned to the Fowlers. 'That true crime website Kyle was looking at still bothers me. It feels completely out of whack with what anyone knows about him. He showed zero interest in that area before or after.'

'You said there was some local case on there?'

'Yeah, a French kid called Pierre Decroix – he was at university in Exeter – who was found hanging from an apple tree. The suspicion was he was murdered. The orchard is about fifteen minutes from the Fowlers.'

'Any obvious connection between this French kid and Kyle – other than their proximity to one another?'

'Not that I've found so far.'

I thought about next moves, of trails we could follow from here. I had to keep the Fowlers in my sightline – they were my priority – but while we tried to dig out more defined connections between the Whaler, Tori Wolton, the murder of Anthony Yanis and the disappearance of the family, it was important to keep moving forward.

And there was one obvious place to start.

'We need to find out what's in that bunker,' I said.

34

On the way to the Tube, I called Sarah.

She was at the literary festival in Cardiff, but she ducked out of a talk she was listening to and found a quiet corner.

'Have you ever heard the name Morgan Annerson?' I asked.

'Anderson?'

'*Annerson.* Double n at the start.'

'No,' she said. 'No, that doesn't ring a bell.'

'Ever been to the Skyline?'

'Uh . . .' She seemed thrown by the change of direction.

'It's a casino and resort complex west of London.'

'Oh. I think I've read about it.'

'But you've never been?'

'No.'

'What about the rest of the family?'

'We didn't go up to London a lot.'

'Marc was never in the city for work?'

'I mean, yes, he was, but then he went all over the country for meetings. I don't ever remember him mentioning that place.'

'What about Kyle and Clara?'

'What, you mean did *they* ever visit a casino?'

'It's not something they would have done? There's a music venue there, a water park, shops.'

'No, that sort of thing really wasn't their scene.'

And now I was back to square one.

When we got to my house, I grabbed my car keys, and then – from the quiet of the kitchen – finally made the call to Melanie

Craw. As it connected, I watched Healy out in the garden, his head down, one hand subconsciously playing with his beard.

'Well, well, well,' Craw said, picking up. 'I thought you said you were too busy for the little people?' It was framed as a joke but didn't feel like one. 'Where's Dr Watson?'

'He's here.'

'Have you pulled rank on him now?'

'It's not like that,' I said, and remembered how Healy had spoken about Craw earlier. *Mrs High and Fucking Mighty*. I wondered again if I'd made a mistake asking Healy to go out and do the groundwork for me the day before. I'd sent him to the Skyline because I'd seen Craw's Whaler case as a side project, something that I could trust him with, something that I was intrigued by but that was a very distant second to me finding out what had happened to the Fowlers.

Twenty-four hours on, everything had changed.

'Have you ever heard of the Fowler family?' I asked her.

'Who?'

'Marc Fowler, his son, Kyle, and Kyle's girlfriend, Clara Dearton. They disappeared on Dartmoor eight months ago.'

'No, never heard of them.'

I listened for any sign that she might be lying to me. 'What about the name Tori Wolton? That ring any bells?'

'No. Where are you heading here, Raker?'

'The Fowlers are the family that I told you about the other day – the one I was down in Devon for. And I think Wolton might have taken them.'

'Okay. And?'

'And I'm back in London now, and I've just located a locker that Tori Wolton has been using – and in that locker she's storing a bag with four hundred grand in it.'

A beat. 'Wait, *what*?'

'So alarm bells are starting to go off at this point because

198

I'm wondering how it can be that two apparently different, completely unconnected disappearances land in my lap from two entirely different people within a couple of days of each other – and then turn out to be part of the same case.'

I paused, giving Craw a chance to respond.

She said nothing.

'Craw?'

'I don't know what to say,' she replied. 'Who hired you for the family?'

'Sarah Fowler. Marc's her husband, Kyle's her son.'

'Maybe there's something in her life that –'

'No.'

'So – what? – the suspicion automatically falls on me?'

'Did you know we might find that money?'

'What are you talking about?' Her voice had tightened.

'Tracking down the money should have been a wild goose chase. The same day the Whaler cashed in those chips, he transferred everything to an account in the Empress Islands. That's like firing it into a black hole. But then the cash miraculously turns up in this locker. So why ask me to try and locate it?'

'I asked you to try and locate the Whaler.'

'You asked me to do both – him *and* the money he stole.'

'We hoped you might find the money too.'

'"We"? As in, you and the Zinter brothers?'

'Yeah.'

'It's not even their money, it's Yanis's.'

'Yanis and his widow were friends of theirs.'

'But why do they care so much?'

'Because their friend was murdered, Raker – why do you think?'

'No, I mean about the money. They're billionaires. Four hundred grand is nothing to them. It's a drop in the ocean.'

'I don't know.'

'You didn't ask?'

'No, I didn't *ask*. Your bosses rock up to your workplace, they tell you that you have to do something, you go and do it.'

I rubbed at an eye, glancing out of the window.

Healy was looking in at me now.

'Is there anything else?' Craw said. 'I've got meetings.'

'We're coming in.'

'What?'

'We'll be at the Skyline in forty minutes.'

'To do what?'

'We want to see the Bunker.'

Silence.

'We'll be there in forty minutes,' I said again, and hung up.

35

We didn't talk much on our way out of London, although it was obvious we were both thinking about Melanie Craw. Healy was adamant she was lying, maybe even actively conspiring against us, but he had his reasons for leaning that way.

I was less sure.

She'd never been the easiest person to get along with, but the one thing I knew about Craw was that she was a straight arrow. As a single mother, as a daughter, as a cop, whether you agreed with her point of view or not, she always did what she thought was the right thing, and was always direct and conventional. Maybe too conventional at times, too unwilling to take risks. In the years I'd known her, she'd never bent the rules even once. But maybe she really *had* changed.

I just couldn't figure out why Craw – and, by extension, the Zinters – would make this search about tracking down the £400,000 as well as finding the Whaler. The cash wasn't theirs – and, even if it was, they could take the hit. I couldn't help but feel that, if they were asking me to find it, they knew the money *could* be found.

So either they weren't telling Craw everything, or she really did choose not to ask why. Or Healy was right: for whatever reason, she was deceiving us.

'You need to accept she's lying,' he said, as if reading my mind.

It was late afternoon and the traffic on the motorway had ground to a complete halt. Next to me, Healy was leafing through his notebook, going over the same things we'd already covered in the café, and again on the Tube out to Kew.

'I'll accept it if it turns out to be true.'

'You don't trust my judgement?'

'If I didn't trust your judgement, I wouldn't have sent you to the Skyline in the first place, would I?' I looked at him. He was staring out of the window now. 'All you ever knew her as was a cop. You didn't know her as a person.'

'She'd throw her own kids overboard to save herself.'

'She absolutely would not.'

'I'm *telling* you she would.'

I chose not to respond this time. There had been so many moments like this down the years: Healy with his blood up, raging about something that ultimately might not even matter; me having to talk him back either through negotiation or silence, and then worrying in the days afterwards that his ire might become a liability.

This time I chose silence.

'I forgot something,' Healy said after a while, tapping a finger on the corner of a page in his notebook. 'Something Lorna said.'

'What?'

'Ramis used to be a cop, so he was good at noticing things, small details. You know, things that might open up bigger leads in an investigation. Well, Lorna said he wrote some stuff down when he got home that night, after the Whaler escaped. They never ended up using it, never told anyone about it, because they were too shit-scared by the Whaler's threat, but Lorna dug out Ramis's notes for me. The Whaler had a tattoo on the underside of his wrist. Some wings and a number.'

'Did Ramis write down the number?'

'Yeah.' Healy took a pair of glasses from his inside pocket, put them on and brought the notes he'd made closer to him: '92366.'

'Any idea what it means?' I asked.

'No.'

He brought up Google on his phone. 'You put in a search for it, all you get back is shite like machine parts and catalogue numbers.' He tapped something else – and then stopped.

I saw a news story loading in.

'Wings,' he said softly, almost to himself.

'What?'

'Look at this news story. It's about a body they found in the US three years ago – in the 92366 zip code. It's some place out in the middle of nowhere called Wheaton.'

He turned the phone so I could see the headline.

POLICE APPEAL FOR WITNESSES
IN 'DESERT ANGEL' MURDER

I froze.

The car was moving but it felt like everything had stopped.

I've been focusing on the wrong thing.

I thought Kyle had gone back to *Evidence Bag* to look at the murder of the French student, even if I hadn't been able to figure out why.

But I was wrong.

That wasn't the entry in the top five he'd been looking at. It wasn't Bella in the Wych Elm, or the Smiley Face Murders, or the Ice Cream Shop Murders either.

It was the third entry on the list.

It was the skeleton they found in the Mojave.

It was the woman in the desert.

2020

Wheaton, California

It's February and the desert is cold.

There's snow on the peaks either side of Interstate 15, and in Wheaton – little more than a gas station, a truck stop and an ancient, long-shuttered Denny's – a yellow Chevy is making a right turn on to an old mining road. The road is just over three miles long and snakes across the Mojave in the direction of an abandoned copper mine. That's not where the Chevy is headed, though. The Chevy is headed beyond that, to the very end of the road, where there's a dust-blown parking lot at the beginning of the Clark Mountain trailhead. This early in the morning the sun is still coming up, so the mountain is little more than a silhouette – almost 8,000 feet of spires, all painted dark blue against the twilight.

Wheaton is three hours from Los Angeles and only fifteen minutes from the state line. The nearest town of any size is Primm, which isn't in California at all. And that's the direction that the Chevy has come from, because inside the vehicle are Will and Stacey Gomez, both twenty-nine, both residents of the city of Henderson, over sixty miles away. They left home at six this morning, crossing the desert in darkness for forty-five minutes, so they could get up to the Clark Mountain trailhead early. The forecast for this morning is fine, with cloud moving in mid-afternoon – and they want to be up and back before that happens. Both of them love winters on the mountains in this part of the world: the snow-kissed crests, the flawless blue skies.

The track up to the trailhead is the old mining road, so Will takes it slowly, the suspension of the Chevy creaking and popping as it bounces in and out of potholes.

They get about a mile up the track when Stacey stops singing along to the radio. Will doesn't notice immediately because he's concentrating on avoiding a series of deep fissures in the road, but then he glances across at his wife.

'What's up?' he asks.

She's looking at something.

'Stace?'

'Stop the car,' she says, without once taking her eyes off the window. 'Will,' she repeats. 'Stop the *car*.'

Will, confused, brings the car to a halt.

'What's going on?' he says, looking past her, trying to see what she's seeing. And it's not until she puts a finger to the glass, tapping a manicured nail against it, that he realizes what has got her attention: there's something in the middle of a ring of dense creosote bushes, about forty feet from the edge of the dirt track they're on.

'Can you see that?' Stacey asks.

And as Will leans closer, as they both stare through the fine layer of red dust coating the passenger window, it suddenly comes into focus.

It's an arm.

Three hours after the call comes in from Will and Stacey Gomez, Detective Gary Mailor pulls his Crown on to the mining road. He works at the sheriff's station in Barstow – just under ninety minutes away – and has had to make a hundred-mile drive along the interstate to get here. There's a satellite substation thirty-six miles from here, in Baker, but it's only staffed by deputies, so Mailor is the closest detective on duty today. That's the problem with San Bernardino County: it's over 20,000 square miles – the largest county on the entire planet – so, out here, he's learned there's no such thing as a local crime.

Two California Highway Patrol officers are waiting for him and, as he pulls his car up next to a yellow Chevy, he can see the CHP have cordoned off an area about forty feet from the mining road, where a halo of pale creosote bushes are growing.

Mailor switches off the engine but doesn't get out yet.

He's not a religious man, but before every case he's ever worked, he likes to take thirty seconds to himself – to close his eyes, to breathe, to find some measure of peace – because he knows what's coming next will just be noise and chaos.

When he's done, he gets out.

Mailor is forty-seven and has lived in Barstow his whole life. Before he joined the San Bernardino County Sheriff's Department, he was in the Marine Corps, stationed at the logistics base just east of the city. Sometimes, when he makes these journeys up and down the I-15, he thinks how little he knows of the world beyond the Mojave, because these journeys – the ninety-minute drives, the two-hour desert crossings – are often the furthest away from home he ever gets.

One of the CHP officers comes across to him as he puts on his jacket. Mailor always wears a jacket, even in the middle of summer, but he needs it today. The sun is out but the desert is still cool. The CHP officer introduces himself as Powell and launches into an account of what happened in the hours before Mailor arrived. Mailor is only half listening. Instead, he's looking beyond Powell to the couple who called it in, and then to the creosote bushes beyond them both. The buds are already showing, a ball of green-grey that will flower yellow in a couple of months and look beautiful when they do. But there's nothing beautiful here today.

Just noise and chaos, Mailor thinks.

He lets Powell finish, thanks him, and tells him to go down to the main road and make sure the coroner and forensic team don't miss the turn. The coroner was ten minutes behind Mailor, the forensic team about thirty minutes behind that.

The Gomezes are in their late twenties and are at the edge of the road holding hands. Stacey looks like she hasn't stopped crying for the past three hours, and Will has a thousand-yard stare that even Mailor's approach doesn't seem to disturb.

'Mr and Mrs Gomez?'

They look up.

'I'm Detective Mailor with the Sheriff's Department. I appreciate you being so patient this morning. I work down in Barstow, so it's taken me a while to get here.'

He offers them a smile, which they don't reciprocate.

'I'll be back shortly to ask you some questions,' he says softly, but he doesn't know how much they're taking in, so he carefully walk-slides down an incline, and moves out across the parched desert floor, the ground crazed like a cracked tile.

He stops at the cordon.

The first thing he notices is what she's wearing.

It's hard not to stare – hard for Mailor to look anywhere else except at her choice of clothes – because they seem so out of place here, so incongruous. But then he puts that to the back of his mind and concentrates on the rest of her.

She's on her front, looking towards him, although her eyes have long gone. Her face is sunken, little more than a skeleton now. Her hands are tied behind her back with rope, the rope still knotted in place, and her dress is torn along the bottom and at the shoulder. The insects have done their work, and the coyotes and ravens have picked at the bones, even carried one of them away. Mailor is no expert, but he's been to a lot of crime scenes in the desert, and seen a lot of dead bodies, and to him it looks like she's missing the radius on her left arm.

He steps under the cordon and then drops to his haunches five feet from the body, looking more closely at her face.

There's a bullet hole in her forehead.

He looks around, at the vast expanse of flat, dry land.

If the bullet's here, it's not close by.

Behind him, he hears the other CHP officer approaching. Mailor turns and can see from his name badge that he's called Koeman.

'The coroner's here,' Koeman says.

Mailor looks in the direction of the interstate, to the turn-off for the mining road. From where he is, crouched on the desert floor, all he can see is the white roof of an SUV and a plume of red dust swirling up the track behind it.

'Thanks,' he says. 'Can you do me a favour?'

Koeman nods.

'This is a through-and-through.' He points to the hole in the victim's skull. 'So I'm wondering if the slug is around here somewhere.'

'You want me to try and find it?'

'Yeah.'

But Koeman doesn't move.

'What is she supposed to be?' he says.

Mailor looks again at the woman, at her choice of clothes, and tries to make sense of it. The elegance of the white, knee-length dress – stained with blood and dirt, the hem of it torn – which must have been pristine when she first pulled it on. The wings, made from silver gauze and edged in white plastic, attached to the back of the dress. And then the halo – mostly wrecked – still clinging to the crown of her head.

'She's an angel,' Mailor says.

PART TWO

POLICE: Now this case is over and you look back at what's happened, is there anything you would have done differently?

RAKER: Of course.

POLICE: So you made mistakes?

RAKER: Are you saying you've never made a mistake?

POLICE: We're not talking about me.

RAKER: Look, you make the best decision you can in the pressure of that particular moment and you hope it'll be the right one.

POLICE: But sometimes it isn't?

RAKER: Why are you asking me this? You're a cop. You know how it works. Have *you* ever run a flawless case?

POLICE: No. But there's a difference between you and me.

RAKER: Yeah? And what's that?

POLICE: Unlike you, I've never got anyone killed.

4
The Bunker

36

Ahead of us, the towers of the Skyline emerged on the horizon.

I was still thinking about Kyle, about the line I could now draw from the list he'd been looking at on *Evidence Bag*, to the Desert Angel who was on that list; from the zip code and wings tattooed on the Whaler's skin, to the fact that the Whaler was almost certainly working with Tori Wolton; and then, finally, to Wolton herself, who was in possession of exactly the same amount of money that had been stolen from Anthony Yanis.

'Can you read me the full article?' I said to Healy.

' "San Bernardino County Sheriff's detectives are appealing for witnesses after the skeletal remains of a woman were found in desert just outside the small town of Wheaton, CA. She'd been shot in the back of the head." ' Healy paused, switched to Google Maps, put in a search for Wheaton, and I cast my mind back to the article on the Desert Angel in *Evidence Bag*. As far as I could remember, it hadn't specified a particular town, only talked about a woman being found in the Mojave and the outfit she'd been wearing. Healy started reading from Wikipedia: ' "Wheaton is an unincorporated community in San Bernardino County, California. It's situated on Interstate Fifteen in the south-east mountainous desert region at an elevation of 4,370 feet. It has a population of just twenty-eight and is located . . ."

He stopped.

'Is located where?' I said, glancing at him.

'Is located fifteen miles from the Nevada border.'

We looked out of the windscreen, towards the Skyline.

'So she was found – what? – an hour from Vegas?'

He checked Google Maps. 'Fifty-one minutes.'

'Is there any mention of Vegas in the story?'

Healy went back to the article, reading on. As he did, we passed under a huge sign, straddling all four lanes of the road, with WELCOME TO THE SKYLINE on it.

'"Sheriff's detective Gary Mailor,"' he said, reading off the screen again, '"who is leading the investigation, says they are confident they know who the woman is but are waiting for forensic confirmation. However, sources familiar with the case have told the *LA Times* that the woman has already been identified as Catalina Robbins, forty-three, who vanished in October after flying out to Las Vegas from the UK for a work conference."'

The Desert Angel was British.

I thought of Anthony Yanis, of how he'd visited Las Vegas at least eight times a year – and then how the Whaler had lain in wait for him back home in the UK.

All things become visible when exposed by the light.

'We've been searching for the Whaler's motivation in all of this, right?'

'Right,' Healy agreed.

'Why did he target Yanis? Why was the crime scene so vicious? You told me earlier that it felt like a revenge killing.'

'I mean, I could be wrong, but . . .' He shrugged. 'It reminds me of crime scenes I saw when I was a cop. That level of violence – it's anger, it's pain.'

'Does it say anything about the Desert Angel's family?'

Healy looked at me. 'You think the Whaler could be related to the Angel?'

'Well, the murder of someone you love is a pretty good reason for revenge. It's also a pretty good basis for the kind of fury we saw in Yanis's hotel suite.'

Healy searched the article. 'No, nothing about her family here.'

'Does it say whereabouts in the UK she was from?'

He searched again. 'Manchester.'

I took a second, trying to make the links. 'You said that Lorna Shute told you the woman who came to her house might have had an accent. What if it was Mancunian?'

'She'd be able to identify a northern accent, surely?'

'Not necessarily. Not everyone is good with accents. She was face down on the floor, confused, terrified for her life, unsure if she was ever going to make it out of that room alive – plus, she told you the woman spoke very quietly and very quickly, which may well have been a deliberate ploy to disguise her accent. Lorna had all of that going on and this woman was *also* busy making her read that prepared script down the phone to Ramis, so Lorna's attention was going to be entirely on that, not on trying to second-guess where her attacker was from. Are there any other details about Catalina Robbins's disappearance in that article?'

'No,' Healy said. 'Just that she was last seen at a Halloween fancy-dress party.'

'Google her and see if you can find any other stories.'

I entered the first car park, weaving my way past endless empty bays, trying to get closer to the casino. Even from half a mile away, the awning hanging over the main doors was bright as a star; large, quarter-scale skyscrapers – all different sizes and designs – were running above and either side of it, creating the impression of a big New York-like cityscape. But all I could think about was that a British woman had been killed and her body left to rot in desert outside Las Vegas.

Healy was still googling Catalina Robbins. As he did, I again cast my mind back to the article on *Evidence Bag*. The name Catalina Robbins rang a bell, which must have meant she'd been referenced in the article itself, and I remembered reading that she'd been clothed in a white dress, wings and halo when I'd first come across the list. There hadn't been much else – no mention of her being British, or her family, or her being in Vegas for work, or even of exactly how she went missing.

'Wait a second,' Healy said. He was on a new article now, scrolling through it. 'Listen to this. "The Halloween party that Robbins was last sighted at was in the Afrique."'

The Skyline's sister hotel in Las Vegas.

And the place Anthony Yanis liked to gamble in when he was there.

'"She was the mother of two children."'

I glanced at Healy. 'A son and a daughter?'

'Uh . . .' He looked again. 'Yeah.'

'Any pictures of them?'

'No, no pictures in this one.'

I paused, my thoughts racing, and then made the next, natural leap: 'Catalina Robbins was forty-three when she died. The Whaler would have been, say, twenty back then; Tori Wolton, around twenty-two. What if the Whaler and Tori Wolton are the Desert Angel's kids?'

'That's a big leap.'

'*Is* it?'

Healy looked at the story on his phone again and said nothing, because he knew the same as I did: this *had* to be what it looked like. On the inside of the Whaler's wrist was a tattoo that pointed directly towards Catalina Robbins – her costume, the zip code she was found in. And the night the Whaler had come back to the Skyline – a week after murdering Anthony Yanis – he'd sent a female accomplice to the Ramis house.

I pulled into a parking space and killed the engine.

Dean Martin was being piped out at full blast from the front of the casino. It was so deafening it was like I had the radio turned all the way up in the car.

'Why was Kyle so interested in the Desert Angel?' I said, as much to myself as to Healy. 'And why go back to that page for just six days? Why not after that time?'

'You think his digging around is the reason he was abducted?' Healy asked.

'He didn't disappear for another five months, but we have to consider it.'

'What about Marc and Clara? Were they just collateral damage?'

In the wrong place, on the wrong boat, at the wrong time.

Maybe that was the case for Marc.

But when it came to Clara, I kept thinking about how friendly Tori Wolton had got with her. The previous day, I'd considered the idea that she'd moved in on Clara in order to get closer to the Fowlers without ever having to expose herself to them directly. Now I wondered if it had been more focused than that.

Kyle was the real target – and Clara the perfect conduit.

Something else struck me too, something more tragic: Marc wasn't even supposed to *be* on that boat. He'd originally wanted to stay ashore, to try and help Sarah, to relieve her by taking Mable off her hands. But the dinghy was big, Clara's arm was in a sling and Kyle needed help rowing out, so Marc had been kind enough to agree.

And he never came back.

As all of that fitted into place, another thought returned to me: one that I didn't have an answer for, and that had been shadowing me since the very first time Sarah had picked up the phone and asked me to find her family. Even if I was right, how did they disappear in under a minute? I thought again about Sarah's tumour, and again about her insistence that she wasn't mistaken about the timings, wasn't confused, that her memories were unaffected by her illness.

I wanted to believe her because *she* believed it.

But, quietly, doubts had set in.

'Raker, look.'

I turned to Healy. He was holding his phone out to me, showing me a still from a CCTV camera outside the Afrique. Taxis were lined up to the left, people were flooding out on the right, and in the middle were some limos and hotel staff. Catalina Robbins had been circled for the purposes of the story, although I would have spotted her without it: among tens – perhaps hundreds – of other costumed partygoers, she was a beacon in her all-white dress and halo.

I studied Catalina's face, looking for similarities to the Whaler, to Tori Wolton, trying to confirm what I already suspected in my gut – that they were related – but the resolution wasn't good enough.

My gaze drifted out to other faces.

That was when I spotted him.

There were five people between them, countless others around them, and it looked like he might be talking to a couple who were exiting beside him – which was the perfect cover. When the cops had looked at this, he would just have been another anonymous face in the crowd.

But Healy and I knew differently.

Because, although he was talking to the couple, he wasn't looking at them. His head was turned in Catalina's direction – eyes on her, watching where she was going.

He'd been at the same party.

He'd been there the night she disappeared.

It was Anthony Yanis.

37

Healy led the way through the Skyline.

Everything was movement and noise: people at tables and slot machines; staff with trays full of drinks buzzing around the bars; tourists taking escalators off the gaming floor, up to huge mezzanine areas where there were more bars and more slot machines; and then the constant *ding ding ding* of the machines, the conversations, the laughter, the screams of excitement, the music, the lights.

As we walked, I called Craw.

It went straight to voicemail.

I texted her to tell her we were here.

The text remained unread.

I felt a flutter of disquiet. What if Healy was right? What if the straight-arrow version of Craw I remembered was no longer who she was?

What if she really *was* lying to us?

We'd arrived at a security door, *4D* marked at its centre. On the wall to the right was a card reader and an intercom.

As Healy pushed the buzzer, I took in the casino floor again.

People were everywhere – and so were CCTV cameras. I spotted three inside a couple of seconds, and then six more further out, eyes in the sky above the gaming floor. Some were trained on the tables, some on rows of slot machines. Above the security door we were waiting at was another camera.

'Yes?' A voice came over the intercom.

'We're here to see Craw,' Healy said.

A click and then silence.

They didn't even ask for a name.

We were both facing the door now, the camera above trained on us. In the very corner of the unit, to the left of the lens, a light was winking on and off.

The security door buzzed.

We watched it open, expecting Craw. Instead, we got a man in his thirties – huge, built like a heavyweight boxer, dressed in the casino security uniform with KERRILL on a name badge above his breast pocket. He looked between us both, then out at the gaming floor, as if we might have brought a team along with us.

'Melanie sends her apologies,' he said. He had an American accent. 'We have a room you can wait in, but she'll be a while.'

Healy and I looked at each other.

'Fine,' I said, and followed Kerrill through.

We took a flight of stairs down, and then were immediately in a long corridor full of doors. Some were open and, as we passed them, I could see they were offices – people at desks, on phone calls; whiteboards, filing cabinets. The deeper in we went, the harder it became to chart the route we were travelling, the changes in direction.

Everything looked exactly the same.

We arrived at a meeting room. It was small: a table with eight chairs around it, and a television screen on the wall that was playing a real-time feed from one of the casinos. The TV was edged with a frame to make it look like a window. At the end of the room was a sideboard with a jug of water and a coffee machine on it.

'Like I told you, she might be a while,' Kerrill explained again. 'But, in the meantime, she says help yourself to water or coffee.'

'While we wait for your boss to grace us with her presence, any chance you can turn the air con up?' Healy responded. 'It's like a bloody sauna in here.'

Kerrill left without saying anything.

Healy turned to me. *This seems normal to you?*

I glanced at the door, thinking for a moment, and when I turned to Healy again, he'd paused halfway to reaching for the jug of water.

Something had caught his attention.

'What's the matter?'

'Look what's been left here,' he said. He reached down and wriggled it out from under the jug, holding it up to me.

It was an envelope.

I took a step closer as Healy got out a penknife he kept on a keychain and scored the envelope along the top.

He peeled it open and looked inside.

'Raker,' he said. 'I think you'd better see this.'

38

Inside was a folded piece of lined paper and a plain white keycard.

I took the keycard out and opened the piece of paper fully. There were two things written on it. At the top were four words: *left, right, right, left.*

Under that it said: *17A93#.*

'Is that what I think it is?' Healy said.

I glanced around the room, looking for concealed cameras, immediately on edge. There were none that I could see, but it still felt too easy.

Like a trap.

'Raker?'

I opened the door of the meeting room and glanced either way along the corridor. It was empty, silent.

To the left, it was a dead end, but there was a right turn just before. Glancing at the piece of paper, I could see the first two instructions on the page. *Left, right.* Left out of the room we were in. Right into the turn.

'Talk to me, Raker.'

'Why would she leave us this?' I replied, holding up the note. 'Why would she leave us directions to the Bunker?'

And the six-digit code to get inside it.

Had Kerrill – the guy who'd walked us down here – known about this? Did *anyone* else know about this? Or had Craw wedged the envelope under the water jug – hidden it there, invited us to help ourselves to water and coffee – because it was only meant for us?

But why send us into the Bunker alone?

'Are we going?' Healy said.

It was still quiet outside, still empty.

I nodded. 'Just stay alert.'

We moved quickly, left out of the room and then right at the end. The next corridor we'd turned into was longer, an endless succession of doors, broken up with bright paintings and a few television screens, all of which were showing live feeds from different parts of the Skyline. Some of the doors were open as we passed them, including one for a surveillance suite, and then at the end we took a right, as instructed to on the piece of paper.

Four doors, two on either side.

And then one facing us.

The doors either side of us were stencilled with *Interview Suite #1* through to *#4*, but the one facing us was different.

It had a card reader next to it.

There was no keypad, so this wasn't the entrance to the Bunker – but I moved forward slowly anyway, aware of the fact that we had no clue about what was on the other side.

I ran the card through it.

The door buzzed and kicked back half an inch from the frame. Pushing at it, I watched it swing open to reveal another corridor. I was facing a wall now. The last turn we had to make was to our left, where – down the end – there was a red door. But when I checked to my right, there was a door down there too, this one grey with *Exit* stencilled on it and a pushbar along the middle.

I checked the red door again.

It had a keypad.

The Bunker.

Healy stepped past me and moved in the direction of the Bunker. But I went the other way, to my right, to the door marked *Exit*.

'What are you doing?' he asked.

'Satisfying my curiosity.'

I jammed in the pushbar and opened the exit door, revealing a set of concrete steps in a plain breezeblock-lined corridor. Taking the steps up, I emerged into a small underground car park. Six spaces, all vacant. The car park had one way in and out, secured with a floor-to-ceiling metal grate, and was at the bottom of a sloped ramp up to street level.

No one was getting in or out without a pass.

'Raker?'

Healy had arrived behind me.

'I guess we know why the Whaler was never caught on camera again after leaving the cell,' I said. We'd speculated that there must have been an exit inside the Bunker or close by – and here it was. 'Let's go.'

We returned to the red door.

As I approached it, I saw I'd missed another small branching corridor at the end, to the left of what we assumed was the Bunker. There was another TV screen down there and something stencilled on the wall, pointing away from us: an arrow.

Next to the arrow it said: *To the cells.*

I dragged my attention back to the Bunker door and then looked at the keypad. It had a simple digital display and a small lens. There were no other cameras dotted around that I could see.

Staring into the lens, I wondered if we were being watched – and if we were, by who – and then I swiped the card through the reader.

Somewhere inside the door, I heard a short buzz and a deep, resonant *clunk.* On the digital display, writing appeared: *Enter code.*

I punched in '17A93#'.

Another clunk.

And then, slowly, the door to the Bunker opened.

2019

Las Vegas, Nevada

Catalina Robbins tosses the sheets back and sits up in bed.

She checks her phone.

It's 4 a.m.

The curtains are slightly apart and a little light is drifting in through the gap, casting patterns across the ceiling. Catalina rolls her neck. Her whole body is stiff. It's from all the walking she did around the conference hall the previous day. And the jet lag. Jet lag always seems to hit her the hardest on the second night.

She looks at the clock again and wonders what her kids are doing right now. It's midday at home, and it's a Friday, so her son will be in school and her daughter will be at uni.

A smile traces her lips as she thinks of them.

She loves her kids so much.

She hates being away from them.

Hauling herself up, Catalina goes to the window and opens one of the curtains. Light washes in. She's on the fifteenth floor and from her room she can see up and down Las Vegas Boulevard: the Bellagio opposite, Paris to the right, the Cosmopolitan and the ARIA, and then even further down she spots New York-New York and the yellow-bronze facade of the Mandalay Bay.

The drums start.

Even though the windows in her hotel room are meant to be soundproofed, she can still hear them. Suppressed by the glass, they have a subdued, heartbeat-like rhythm. After thirty seconds, the animal noises begin – the roar of a lion, the sounds of monkeys, hyenas, elephants, birds. Against the cacophony of calls, cries and warbles, the waterfalls at the front of the resort erupt into life and tumble over their precipices, into the river below, which snakes across the entrance to the casino. They've got a jungle down there as well: Catalina read in the in-flight magazine on the way over that the owners of the Afrique planted something like 380,000 square feet of trees when it was built. From the fifteenth floor, it looks impressive, a sweep of green among a sprawl of concrete and neon.

Las Vegas is so ridiculous. It's her first time in the city and it feels like she's landed on another planet. It's not just the scale of it, the noise, the lights, the sheer excess, it's the fact that all of it is in the middle of the desert, hundreds of miles from anywhere. Catalina grew up in Oldham and has spent most of her life living and working in Manchester, so the nearest thing she's seen to this at home is Blackpool, and that's a bit like comparing a seafront kebab to a Michelin-star steak.

From the middle of the jungle, a thin spear of light erupts out, shooting into the night sky. It's coming from the entrance to the Lost City, situated right in the middle of the jungle, where a gold-plated staircase descends into the basement restaurant. The whole thing's built under thatch and has massive video screens showing off 360-degree views of African savannah. It's also open twenty-four hours.

As that thought comes to her, Catalina realizes she's hungry. She starts getting dressed.

Even at four thirty in the morning, the Lost City is busy.

A waiter takes Catalina to a booth, and despite the African theme, the menu is pure American. She orders a three-egg omelette and some rye toast and, after the waiter has brought over some coffee, she pulls her laptop out and starts going through work emails.

'The early bird catches the worm.' There's a guy seated in the next booth, facing her. He's midway through a plate of steak and eggs, using the tines of his fork to gesture to her laptop. 'I really hope they're paying you overtime.'

Catalina smiles politely. 'I should be so lucky.'

The man's big – overweight, actually – and has a thick mop of swept-back hair and a forehead beaded with sweat. In the pocket of his white linen shirt – the material almost translucent – are what look like casino chips.

'You're British,' he says.

'I am.'

'I live in the UK too.'

She looks up. 'You do?'

'Yeah. Just outside York. I'm originally from LA but then I met a girl from Leeds and the next minute . . .' He waved the fork around as if to say, *We fell in love and what can you do?* 'She didn't like LA so we moved to England. I've been there ever since.'

'Cool. York's a nice spot.'

'It is. So you're out here for work, huh?'

'Yep.'

'Which means you're back and forth to the Convention Center then?'

'Was that just a lucky guess or are you stalking me?'

The man laughs. 'It was just a guess. In my experience, people come to Vegas for three things: to lose money, to have sex without their partners knowing, or to attend a convention. You definitely don't look stupid enough to lose money. And I'm a gentleman, so I ignored the second thing and went straight for the third.'

'Well, it was a good guess.'

'You're at the tech show?'

'Yeah.'

'You're the next Zuckerberg, is that what you're saying?'

'Ha. Not quite. I don't do the technical stuff.'

'Oh. So you're the power behind the throne.'

'Head of PR.'

'So *definitely* the power behind the throne, then.'

Despite herself, Catalina is finding herself warming to the man. She doesn't think he's attractive, but he has an easy way about him, and she gets the impression that he's probably a good laugh.

'So what's the name of your company?' he asks.

'Golden Goose.'

'Shit, really? The *Collector* guys?'

Catalina fails to hide her surprise. Golden Goose are well known within the tech sector, but not so much on the outside. Their app, *Collector*, was the best-selling mobile game in Europe the year before.

'You've heard of us?' she says.

'Sure. You're in Salford, right? Media City?'

'That's right, yeah.'

'How's Brian doing?'

'Wait, are you saying you know Brian Lance?'

'I've met him a couple of times, yeah.'

Catalina eyes the man. 'Are you serious?'

'Yeah. Your CEO's a smart guy. Is he out here with you as well?'

'He is, yes. And Kevin, our creative lead.'

'Kevin Dunlop?'

Catalina laughs. 'All right, now you're starting to scare me. I'm really sorry if I should know who you are, but I'm drawing a blank here. Please don't tell Brian.'

'It'll be our little secret.' The man chuckles. 'Basically, I like to invest in clever start-ups, which is one of the reasons I talked to Brian and Kevin when they were developing *Collector*. We didn't end up going forward with anything, but I told them to keep in touch. I don't like making a big deal about what I do, even though – very obviously – this is a face that no person should ever forget.' He flutters his eyelids. 'My name's Anthony Yanis.'

'Oh shit.' Catalina burns with embarrassment. 'Shit, I'm sorry.'

'What have you got to be sorry about?'

'One of the original investors in Retrigram?'

'See? You do know who I am.'

'I feel like, as head of PR at an app development company, it's kind of a crime that I don't know your face.'

'It really isn't. I prefer it that way.'

The waiter brings over Catalina's meal, refills her coffee, and after he's gone, she says, 'Well, I'm Catalina. Cat.'

'It's lovely to meet you, Cat,' Yanis says, and raises his coffee cup. 'You know, you, Brian and Kevin should come to this Halloween party at the Congo tonight.' He obviously sees Catalina go blank at the name. 'It's the nightclub here.'

Catalina feels like she's about twenty years past nightclubs and fancy-dress parties, and she's pretty sure Anthony Yanis is too, given he's probably got a decade on her. But she knows what Brian will say if she goes back to him and tells him that she happened to chat to a billionaire investor over breakfast, and Yanis invited them to an event, and she said they couldn't make it.

So Catalina says, 'That sounds fun.'

'Cool,' Yanis replies. 'I'll put your names on the door. Any problems, just get them to call me. It all kicks off at ten.'

Catalina groans on the inside. Ten p.m. She's usually in bed by then.

'Great,' she says. 'I guess I'd better go and find a costume.'

39

The two of us stood there, watching the door to the Bunker arc away from us, its hinges groaning as it did – and then, inside, lighting kicked in.

Another corridor.

Its left-hand wall was covered in photographs, each one in a different type of frame and a different size. On the right, halfway along, was a bathroom; ahead of us was a living room. I could see walnut floorboards in there. Sofas. A fireplace. I hadn't known what to expect, what the Bunker would be or why the Whaler would want to get inside. But I hadn't considered it might be this.

An apartment.

Behind me, quietly, Healy said, 'Someone *lives* here?'

I took a step forward, my shoes sinking into a thick pile carpet, and pointed at the photographs on the wall. If somebody was living here, they hadn't been back for a while. There was dust all over the frames, cobwebs everywhere.

Almost every single space on the left-hand wall was filled with portraits. Most of the pictures seemed like they'd been taken by professional photographers, and in every photograph was a face I recognized – bands, singers, actors, comedians, sports and TV stars. But no matter who it was at the centre of the photo, the same two men were always alongside them.

Caleb and Asha Zinter.

I moved from one picture to the next. The Skyline opened in December 2008 and these went all the way back to the beginning. I saw actors who'd been dead for years, bands that had split up more than a decade ago, but it was possible to see the passage of time simply by looking at the brothers' faces.

'Look,' I said, and pointed to a photograph immediately to my left. It was hanging next to a shot of the brothers with the lead singer of one of the world's biggest bands, the three of them onstage – inside the Skyline's cavernous concert hall – during what must have been a rehearsal. This time, the Zinters had company.

Anthony Yanis.

I looked for other photographs of Yanis and found three. Two were of the brothers and Yanis posing for a shot with someone famous. The third was a framed photograph of a group of young men in their early twenties. I stepped in closer, but the clue was in a banner above their heads: *Graduating Class of 1994.*

At the front of the group were Caleb and Asha Zinter.

In the second row was Yanis.

They'd been in the same year at the California Institute of Technology. It must have been where they'd first met. The Zinters' father, Paul, had been back in Vegas, running four casinos, five or six years out from selling the lot of them and building the Afrique.

I took a picture of the graduation photo, then realized that there was a space on the wall right beside it where another photograph had once hung. Judging by the faded yellow square it had left on the wall, it had been about the same size as the graduation photograph.

It was the only empty space.

I moved down to the bathroom. It was extravagant, the fixtures and fittings finished in gold leaf, a huge mirror on the wall sending repeating images of me off into infinity. It would have been impressive if it hadn't been covered in dust. The tap on the bath was leaking too, a series of brown rings forming on the base of the tub.

'I don't get it.' Healy was standing in the doorway to the living area. He looked back at me. '*This* is what Craw is acting shifty about?'

We moved further in.

The living area was furnished beautifully, the walls covered in more frames – signed memorabilia, signed film posters, large canvases of singers and bands playing at the Skyline. In the middle was a huge, stylish sunken lounge containing the sofas I'd seen, laid out in an L-shape, chairs set around an oak table, an elegant dual-sided fireplace, a bar area and a big projector screen. It was like an ultra-modern five-star hotel suite – except one covered in dust and cobwebs.

'What the hell is going on, Raker?'

'I don't know,' I said. 'This must have been where the celebrities stayed when they visited the Skyline. They need that extra layer of security, away from the public. They need their own entrance in their own private car park so they can arrive and leave unseen.'

All of that made sense. What didn't make sense was Craw. Why hide that envelope for us? Why conceal the keycard and the code inside?

'That's *it*?' Healy said. 'The Bunker is just some room where celebrity arseholes can pretend they're better than everyone else?'

'Maybe Craw wanted us to see how the Whaler escaped the casino that night without being seen,' I said, frustrated, and spun around to check the hallway we'd come in through, making sure no one had trailed us without us realizing.

I stopped dead.

It was on the wall behind us, either side of – and above – the door connecting the living area to the hallway. Neither of us had noticed it on our way into the Bunker because we'd been moving forward, our attention fixed on what lay ahead – not behind.

'Healy.'

He glanced at me, saw where I was looking, and twisted around.

His face dropped. 'Fuck me.'

Healy started edging closer, his footsteps careful, as if the wall itself were somehow alive. I watched him go, my thoughts humming, trying to put the pieces together, as he began scratching a fingernail against the wall, concentrating on one part of it. When he was done with that, he moved to the next part, and then the next.

'It doesn't come off,' he said.

'I imagine that's the point.'

I glanced at the hallway connecting this room to the main door of the Bunker, then to the cobwebbed photos, the dust, the sense this place had gone months without use. Except it hadn't been months.

It had been sealed up for an entire year.

From the day after the Whaler got in.

And the reason the Zinters had done that was still scrawled across the wall of the Bunker – across wallpaper, memorabilia and photos – in permanent black paint.

Another message.

Another promise.

1 down 2 to go

40

'Here,' Healy said. 'There's more.'

I dragged my gaze from the message and followed his eye-line. On a patch of dusty skirting board, directly underneath the *g* of *go*, something else had been added in tiny letters, scratched into the wood.

Micah 6:12.

Healy immediately went to his phone, and, as he did, I ran a finger along the inscription. It had been made with something fine, precise – the very end of a blade, or perhaps a compass point. I looked around the Bunker, making sure that there weren't any other messages.

'My phone signal's shite in here,' Healy muttered. 'Okay, got it.'

'What's the quote?'

'"For the rich men thereof are full of violence . . ."' Healy stopped, glanced in my direction. He dragged his attention back to his phone screen. '"The inhabitants of this city have spoken lies and their tongue is deceitful in their mouth."'

The Zinter brothers – and Yanis – were the rich men and we were in their city. It couldn't have been much clearer.

One down. Two to go.

'So the Whaler's going after the Zinter brothers next?' Healy said.

That was certainly what it sounded like.

'All we know for sure,' I responded, 'is that we have Yanis on video the night Catalina Robbins disappeared, following her out of the Afrique – which is owned by the Zinters. Maybe the brothers were involved in her death, or maybe they helped cover it up.' I gestured to the Whaler's message. 'He obviously thinks so.'

'What was the point of going to all this trouble, though? The Whaler could have just got on a flight to Vegas, bought a gun, waited outside the Afrique and put one in the back of the Zinters' heads. Job done.'

'And then gone to prison.'

'But you get my meaning. Here' – he pointed to the writing on the wall – 'he's telling them he's coming. The element of surprise is gone. I mean, I get that he shits them up by doing this, proving he can go anywhere and do anything he wants, but . . .'

'Maybe there was a second reason he came here,' I said.

I took the steps down into the sunken lounge. My thoughts were racing, my gaze scanning the room for anything that might give us a clue. What other reason could there be for the Whaler to need to get inside here? At the back of the sunken lounge, there was a sideboard under the projection screen I'd seen earlier. I checked it over: empty fridges at both ends and empty drawers too.

'There's nothing else here,' Healy said.

I glanced back along the hallway, down towards the Bunker door, wondering what we might have overlooked on the way in.

That was when something caught my eye.

The missing photograph frame.

I'd seen it earlier but now, at a distance, its absence from the wall seemed even more pronounced. Why was that photo missing? When had it been taken? Was I putting two and two together and making five – or could the Whaler have removed it? Could that have been another reason for him to have got inside here? What could possibly have been so important about the photograph if he had?

'Raker.'

I looked at Healy. On top of the sideboard was a monitor showing the CCTV feed from the camera embedded in the keypad outside. On-screen, we could see all the way along the corridor to the door marked *Exit* that had taken us up to the car park.

Healy's gaze was locked on it.

In the corridor outside the Bunker, a door was opening.

Someone was coming.

She emerged, looked left – in the direction of the Bunker – then right to the door marked *Exit* that ascended into the secure car park.

Craw.

'What the hell is she doing?' Healy said.

'She knows we can see her.'

She lingered for a moment longer, looking directly into the keypad camera this time – and when she finally moved, she headed to the car park and up the stairs.

'Stay here,' I said.

'What?'

'Do another search. See if we've missed anything.'

He glanced at the image on the monitor. 'This could be a trap, Raker.'

'Well, we're about to find out.'

41

At the top of the stairs, Craw had left the door open.

The car park was still empty, the security gate still down. It was almost dark outside, which made it even darker here, below street level.

It took me a second to find Craw: she was in the gloom between two pillars, one side of her painted by a lamp, the other wrapped in shadow.

She had a black dress on.

From what I could see of her, she was made up: blusher, eyeshadow, lipstick, all things I'd never seen her wear during the years we'd known each other.

'We've got a cocktail party up on the top floor,' she said by way of explanation. Her voice echoed softly off the walls of the garage. 'Where's Healy?'

'In the Bunker,' I said. 'What's going on, Craw?'

Edging out of the shadows a little, she watched me for a moment, then looked past me to the stairs we'd come up. She was nervous.

'I haven't got much time. Kerrill's in a meeting – but not for long.'

'Kerrill?' I frowned. 'The guy who came to get us?'

'I made an excuse and told him I had to go to the toilet.'

'Aren't you his boss?'

'No. He doesn't work for the Skyline.'

'So who does he work for?'

'He works directly for Caleb Zinter.'

I felt something cold drag its way down my spine.

'We've got ten minutes,' Craw said quietly, rapidly. 'You're meant to be in that meeting room and you need to get back there. So this has to be quick.'

'Were you listening to us in that room?'

'What do you mean?'

'I mean, is the room bugged?'

'No. That room's clean.'

'So what's going –'

'*Raker.* Just listen, okay?'

She took a breath.

'Okay, so when I started working here ten months ago, Caleb and Asha flew out from Vegas to be here for my first few days. We went through the job, the team, things they wanted, and then Caleb took me to the Bunker and showed me the message on the wall in there. He said, because of what happened to Yanis here, they wanted their security beefed up whenever they were in London. They'd done it out in Vegas, out in Macau and the Red Phoenix too.'

'Why didn't you mention any of this before?'

'I never had the chance to. Look, I need you to *listen*, okay? According to Caleb, the Whaler was this complete psycho – some stalker-come-killer-come-nutjob – that had been hounding the Zinter family for years. Caleb said the Whaler was trying to blackmail Asha and him, had sent them threatening letters and emails, had been spotted watching their ex-wives and Asha's daughter in Vegas and out in LA. For whatever reason, this guy was obsessed, and when he killed Yanis and, a week later, got inside the Bunker – it was an earthquake. Caleb said they'd already reported the stalking to the cops back home, given them the letters too, and he put me in touch with a detective at Las Vegas Metro who confirmed it all. But Yanis getting murdered, then the Whaler getting into the Bunker – that was next level.'

Her eyes flicked to the stairs.

'I don't know, though . . . my Spidey sense was going the whole time he was telling me this. Something just didn't feel right. I ignored it for a while because this was the big new job that I'd been waiting for: the salary they were paying was insane, huge pension, amazing benefits – I wanted to make a success of it. And the Zinters themselves . . . I liked them. There's no point in pretending I didn't. I've met Caleb five or six times in the flesh, billions of times on Zoom, and we've always got on. Asha is quieter, a little awkward sometimes, but he's nice too. They've always been great bosses. Until a month or so ago, we had a resort manager here, but the Zinters always told me to just go direct to them if I ever needed anything. They'd been goo–'

'Wait a second, there's no resort manager here?'

'No.'

'You told me on the phone that a new resort manager had just started, wanted to make a good impression, and that all of this – this search for the Whaler – had come from the Zinters via him. That's not true?'

She shook her head. 'No.'

Which explained why, when I'd been on the Skyline's corporate website and had looked at the photos of the Zinter brothers and Craw, the resort manager role was just a black box with a line saying: *Currently recruiting.*

'Why would you lie about it?'

'Because Kerrill told me to. That's why he's here. That's why the brothers sent him over from Vegas and why they're not recruiting a new manager until this is all sorted. Everyone here thinks Kerrill's just another security grunt – but he isn't. He's worked with Caleb for years. He's his eyes and ears on the ground. He's listening in on things he shouldn't be, he's reading emails, he's pulling internet activity. His one focus is locating the Whaler before he resurfaces and comes for the Zinters again. *Kerrill's* the one beefing up their security now, not me.'

'So he's doing *your* job as well the resort manager's? Why?'

'Because Caleb doesn't trust me any more.'

'Yeah, but why?'

'Because I couldn't let things go.' She halted, glanced at me, her face pale, her expression so lucid it was hard to even look at her. She was absolutely terrified. 'On the surface, the Zinters are good guys. That's the side of them they show the world. But, deep down, they're utterly ruthless – especially Caleb.'

'Has he threatened you?'

'Yes. I'm only alive right now because they still need me for one more thing.'

'And what's that?'

'You.'

42

'Me?' I stared at Craw. 'What are you talking about?'

'I knew in my gut something wasn't right from the second Caleb took me inside the Bunker. The whole story about the Whaler being some psycho who was stalking them and had finally got to Yanis . . . I mean, it happens. I've seen it. I dealt with crazy every single day I was a police officer, so I know what obsession is. But it just didn't feel right. It didn't feel like they were telling me everything.' She shook her head. 'Instinctively, something just didn't add up, and although I didn't know what it was, I couldn't let it go. I denied it, pretended to forget it – but it was always there.'

She fell back into the shadows a little, as if she didn't want me to see her any more.

'Two weeks back, Kerrill flies in out of the blue. I don't know the guy from Adam, but he seems okay. He tells me, before we recruit a new resort manager, he's been sent by the Zinters to do a top-line review of the Skyline. I ask him what he means, and he tells me it's nothing to worry about, that he won't be treading on my toes, and that he did the same in Macau at the Red Phoenix. He's just going to look at the numbers and make sure it's all healthy.'

Her eyes were distant, replaying everything.

'That night, I called Macau,' she said, 'spoke to the manager there. He'd never even heard of Kerrill. No one there knew this fucking guy. And so suddenly, all those same instincts from ten months ago – the ones I buried when Caleb showed me around the Bunker in my first few days here – they all came flooding back, and there was just no way I could push them down for a second time.' She made a sound, almost a sigh. 'So I started doing some digging on the Zinters and Yanis.'

'Yeah, but where do I fit in?'

She held up a hand to me. *I'm almost there.*

'Ten days ago, I hired this guy to do some work for me in Vegas. When I was with Police Scotland, we did this cultural exchange thing where a bunch of senior officers from the States came over to Glasgow to see how we did things here, then we did the same thing in return. In LA, I met this ex-detective who I got on with . . .' She blinked. It had clearly been more than just *got on with.* 'We kept in touch, so I called him, and offered to pay him to drive up to Vegas and ask some questions for me on the QT. I didn't tell him everything, just enough. So he arrives there, and he starts asking around, and eventually he finds out that this cop at Las Vegas Metro who Caleb mentioned – the one he put me in contact with, who was backing up their story about the Whaler being some obsessed stalker – is four months away from retirement. And, once he calls it a day, guess what's next for him?'

'Is he going to work for the Zinters?'

'Bingo. An advisory role on triple his salary as a cop.'

'So he's in their pocket?'

'That would be the assumption. It reads like them rewarding him for a career spent saying what they want him to say – like, the Whaler is a stalker. And so my guy out there, he digs a bit deeper into this cop's history and he finds something.'

'What?'

'This cop – his name is Theroux – was involved in a case back in the day. The incident happened in California, but it ended up having a Vegas thread to it.'

'What was the incident?'

'Initially, it was a disappearance in Vegas but, after that, it became a –'

'Murder. Are you talking about the Desert Angel?'

She frowned. 'What?'

'The Desert Angel case? Catalina Robbins?'

'No. I don't know what that is.'

I felt thrown.

'So what murder are you talking about?'

'Mur*ders*,' Craw replied. 'It wasn't one. It was three.'

2008

Los Angeles, California

Casey Ryker pulls up outside the Joneses' house at 11 a.m.

It's an unseasonably hot day at the end of March, almost seventy degrees already, and it's only going to get hotter once the smog clears.

She heads to the front porch. The screen has been pulled shut, but the door is open and Casey can see all the way through to the kitchen. Mrs Jones is in there clearing away breakfast plates. Next to her, Florida's seven-year-old sister, Miriam, is on a stool at the island, eating cereal while playing with a Nintendo DS.

'Knock knock,' Casey says, and pulls back the screen door.

'Coming!' Florida shouts in response from somewhere upstairs.

In the kitchen, Mrs Jones swivels round, already smiling. Wiping her hands on her apron, she comes through to the hallway, big frame swaying, and wraps Casey in her arms. '*Hola mi vida, cómo estás?*'

Mrs Jones is from Ciudad Juárez, but left Mexico with her parents when she was three. Florida's dad was born in England but has been in the States forever.

Casey hugs Mrs Jones back. 'I'm good, Mrs J. How are you?'

Mrs Jones releases Casey and looks her up and down. 'What is it with you girls? You're all too skinny. I keep saying the same to Florida.'

'All those hours in the gym, Mrs J.'

Mrs Jones laughs, then gently touches Casey on the top of her arm. 'How's your mom doing, sweetheart?'

Casey shrugs. 'Up and down, I guess.'

'She'll come right.'

Casey nods, even though both of them know she won't come right, because she's never come right any of the other times she's relapsed. Casey's dad passed on three years ago, and now her mom isn't even pretending to be clean.

Unexpectedly, Mrs Jones brings Casey in for a second, longer hug.

Casey doesn't resist. She's twenty-one, but a part of her still craves this contact because, upsetting as it is to acknowledge, Mrs Jones has shown her more affection in moments like this than her own mom has shown her in two decades. Casey savours it – Mrs Jones's substance, her heft, her tenderness – and then Florida appears at the top of the stairs, suitcase in hand, and says, 'Mami, you're gonna suffocate her.'

Mrs Jones lets go of Casey.

'You weren't suffocating me, Mrs J.'

Casey smiles again – a smile Mrs Jones returns – and in that moment Casey realizes how much she loves it here, how warm this house feels, and as she goes to the stairs to help Florida with the case, she feels jealous at what Florida has.

It isn't the first time.

The feeling is still there as Casey noses her shitbox of a Buick up Lindley Avenue and along Nordhoff towards North Hills, where Ryan lives with his mom.

'Casey Fantasey,' Ryan sing-songs after dumping his suitcase in the trunk and climbing into the back of the car. He shuffles between the seats and plants a kiss on Casey's cheek. He's wearing blusher and painted his nails red, white and blue.

'You know it's not the 4th of July yet, right?' Casey says.

'Well, someone round here has to make an effort,' he replies, looking at Casey's joggers and Florida's yoga pants, his expression deadpan. 'We're supposed to be arriving in style, and you two rock up looking like you're off to a PTA meeting.'

'Hey,' Casey says, 'these are my best joggers.'

'Oh, honey,' Ryan says, as if he feels sorry for her. It's his expression that does it. They all burst into laughter.

They head north towards Santa Clarita.

Ryan does most of the talking and spends the first part of the journey discussing a guy his mom has started dating who has a prominent mole on his face. Ryan's dad died of a brain aneurysm when Ryan was only six, so Casey and he often bond about their fragmented childhoods, although Ryan's situation is a work of art compared to Casey's. Whenever the two of them talk, Florida tends to just sit there and listen – because what else is she going to do? Her childhood has been perfect. She's got nothing to contribute.

Casey glances at Florida. As she does, that same acerbic voice at the back of Casey's head resurfaces: *You'll never understand what it's like for Ryan and me.*

'I'm so happy we all get to do this,' Florida says, and grabs Casey's hand on the steering wheel. 'This is going to be amazing.'

A stab of guilt spears Casey between the ribs.

What the hell is wrong with me? she thinks.

Ryan starts talking again, perched between their seats, and it helps Casey forget the turbulence of her thoughts. She looks at Florida again, smiles back and squeezes her friend's hand in return, and then the women listen to Ryan as he begins telling them another story. Soon, they're all roaring with laughter.

As they get on to Interstate 15, the laughter dies down and is replaced by the three of them singing at the top of their voices to a mixtape Florida has made for the Buick's old cassette player. By the time they close in on Primm, the music has finished and they've descended into a comfortable silence built on fifteen years of friendship.

On the outskirts of Las Vegas, the excitement starts to build again.

'How far up the strip are we?' Florida asks.

'In the middle,' Ryan responds.

They pass the *Welcome to Las Vegas* sign.

Tourists are gathered underneath it, striking poses. It's starting to get dark and, ahead of them, the city is coming alive.

'Vegas, baby!' Ryan squeals, and Casey turns the radio on and all the way up until it's so loud it makes the Buick's dashboard shake, and all three of them are either singing loudly or collapsing into fits of giggles.

In this moment, everything is perfect.

And then they see it up ahead, a huge temple-like structure, painted patterns all over it, with immense concrete lion heads on either side. They see huge waterfalls next to those, and a fake jungle out front with a river snaking through it.

And, finally, they see the colossal name of the place, towering above everything, its letters lit in dazzling green and gold.

The Afrique.

43

'The three of them were old school friends,' Craw said. 'Casey, Florida and Ryan.'

In the shadows of the car park, neither of us moved.

'This happened fifteen years ago. March 2008.'

Eleven years before Catalina Robbins was murdered.

'They'd driven up from LA to Vegas for spring break,' Craw continued. 'They'd been planning it for months. Then, on the second night, they disappeared. Four days after that, their bodies were discovered 270 miles away, back in LA. Guess where they stayed when they were in Vegas?'

'The Afrique?'

'Correct.'

Just like the Desert Angel.

'Cops in LA asked Las Vegas Metro to speak to the security team at the Afrique about pulling some film. The request landed on Theroux's desk. He pulled the footage and sent it out to LA. He seemed to be fully cooperative. But then detectives at the LAPD noticed the timecodes were all screwy. The date was fine, but the clock kept resetting to zero – and there were these almost-imperceptible series of jumps on the film. They called Theroux about it, and he said it was down to a software issue at the Afrique, and the jumps were a technical glitch with the system.'

'Which sounds like bullshit.'

'It was. They weren't jumps, they were cuts.'

'Something had been removed from the film.'

'Or some*one*.'

Someone like the Zinters or Anthony Yanis.

'What did the LAPD do?'

'They subpoenaed the Afrique and had them pull the footage straight off the servers – but once they got it back to the lab, it was the same. The LAPD's theory was always that the original footage had been overwritten with the edited version. But they could never prove it. The Zinters, like Theroux, acted all frustrated, they told the cops in LA they'd get to the bottom of it – but, you know . . .'

'They didn't,' I said.

'The suspicion at the LAPD was always that these kids had been captured on video talking to the person – or people – who ended up killing them. And, through interviews, LA detectives managed to come up with a description of a man who *was* seen with Casey Ryker in the hours before she vanished. So the LAPD put together a composite sketch of this suspect and released the composite to the public.'

'No one could ID him?'

'No. Zero bites. But the composite was the absolute spitting image of Anthony Yanis – it's just so obvious now. At the time, though, they couldn't match a face to a name. It didn't help that the cops were looking in Nevada and California for the killer, when in reality he was five thousand miles away, all tucked up in his Yorkshire castle.'

'So where do the Zinters fit in?'

'They're involved.'

'But you don't have the evidence to prove it?'

'No. But they're involved.'

I gave myself a moment – thinking, turning it all over.

'Why would Yanis and the Zinters dump the three bodies in LA?'

'Distance from the crime.'

'That's a lot of distance,' I said. 'It's a big risk putting three bodies in the back of a car and driving four hours.' But then I paused. Most of those 270 miles were desert highway. Maybe it wouldn't have been that much of a risk at all. In fact, maybe it was smart as hell. If one or all of them had done the drive at night, they would have been reducing the risks of traffic stops and random police patrols pulling them over. And by leaving the bodies in California, it created confusion and turned the whole thing into a cross-jurisdictional nightmare. 'Where were the three bodies found?' I asked.

'Some concrete basin where storm debris collects. Florida's body was down by the water, Casey and Ryan were among some trees. It felt chaotic, apparently. Cops wondered if the killer might have got spooked.'

'Someone saw him?'

'Or he messed up somehow. My guy out in LA says the debris basin is on a slope, so Florida could have accidentally rolled away from the treeline and ended up by the water. Maybe our killer panicked after that and cut his losses.'

'How were they killed?'

'They'd all had their hands tied behind them. And they'd all been shot in the head.'

Just like the Desert Angel.

'Casey's injuries were more severe, though,' Craw went on. 'She'd been roughed up before she was killed.'

'Any idea why she was treated differently?'

'From the sounds of things, Casey was tough. Her mum was a drug addict and her dad had died three years before, so she'd been forged that way. If these kids were going down, *she* was going to be the one that was putting up a fight.'

But there was something else in her face.

'There's more?'

'The kids were all found shoeless and had all these scratches and bruises up their legs. It looked like they'd been running through bush or scrub.'

'They'd escaped?'

'Or were deliberately set free.'

'Why?'

'For sport.' Craw grimaced. 'The same type of bullet was used on all of them. Hunting rounds.'

Something soured in my stomach.

Maybe that was the real reason the men had dumped the bodies in California: Nevada was mostly open desert. In California, there were mountains and forests. They could set the kids free and track them like game. And when they were done, they could leave the three of them hundreds of miles from the place they were last seen in.

'You've really never heard of the Desert Angel?' I asked.

Craw shook her head. 'No. Who is that?'

I told her what I knew about Catalina Robbins and then went to my phone and found the picture I needed. 'Look,' I said. On-screen was the CCTV image of Catalina leaving the Afrique. 'In the crowd behind her. To the right, about five people back.'

Instantly, her face collapsed. 'Yanis.'

'There's another thing. Catalina was mostly a skeleton when she was found, but her hands had been tied behind her back and she was shot in the head.'

We paused briefly, letting everything wash over us. Catalina had been dumped in the desert, not in California. But her wrists had been bound and she'd been killed the same way, just like the three friends eleven years before. *So maybe the cops in LA had been right.* Maybe Yanis or the brothers had been spooked at the debris basin – maybe someone *had* been coming – which was why they hadn't risked going back to California with Catalina. Instead, they chose the vast, lonely expanse of the Mojave.

'What I don't understand is why these cases haven't been connected,' I said as Craw handed me back my phone.

253

'I don't know either,' she said. 'But I can tell you from experience that two different cases, with the best part of eleven years and three hundred miles between them – that's exactly the sort of thing that *does* get missed. I think the bigger point here is that the Zinters and Yanis are the prime suspects.'

Yanis could have been doing this for years.

All of them could have been.

They could have killed others.

'So are you going to tell me where I fit in?' I said.

Craw glanced at her watch. It was obvious she needed to go. 'My guy out in LA sent all the info he gathered to my inbox. Literally, five minutes after it drops, Kerrill pitches up and says he wants to talk.'

'Kerrill's got access to your work emails?'

'Work emails, company phone, my laptop – by the time I realized, it was too late.'

'What did he say?'

'He said, "I'm going to be straight with you, Melanie. You've been digging into things that don't really concern you and that's become a problem. So why don't we press reset and start again? How does one hundred grand sound?"'

'He tried to pay you hush money?'

'Yes.'

'Did you take it?'

She didn't answer.

'You *took* it?'

'Yes, I took it,' she said, her voice taut.

'Why?'

'Because if I didn't . . .' She stopped. 'If I didn't, he said he'd kill my kids.'

44

The temperature seemed to drop.

'I turned down the cash at first,' Craw said, voice small. 'But then he just changed. It was like a light going out. I don't scare easily . . .'

But Kerrill scared me.

'He grabbed me here' – her throat – 'and I could barely breathe. I thought my neck was going to snap. He leans in and says, "Take the money or I'll kill your daughters and make you watch."' A flicker in her face. 'So I took the money.'

It was just five words.

But they were as painful to her as any she'd ever spoken.

'That was last week,' she said. 'I thought, "It's not going to get any worse than this. It can't." Then, three days ago, he comes up to me and he begins asking about you.'

'What was he asking?'

'He'd found out about our history – all sides of it. He wanted to know who you were, what you were like. And then he said he wanted me to call you and ask you to look for the Whaler.'

'But you don't know why?'

'Because he knows you're good. Because you know me. Because I told him you always trusted me to do the right thing.' Her voice started to tremor. 'I'm sorry, Raker. I was just so scared for my girls.'

'He must have asked you to call me because of the Fowlers.'

'What?'

'The Fowlers, the Whaler, Yanis – it's all part of the same

case, and the Zinters know it.' I paused, my head nothing but noise. 'What I don't get is why risk it?'

'What do you mean?'

'I mean, whoever the brothers ended up hiring – whether it was me or someone else – things were always likely to end here: someone goes and digs deep enough and suddenly what the brothers and Yanis have done gets exposed.'

'The risk is worth the reward.'

'They want to find the Whaler that much?'

'They've been trying to find him ever since he offed Yanis in that hotel suite – and they've constantly failed. And as long as he's out there, and any potential accomplices too, he's a threat to them.'

One down. Two to go.

'And when I find him,' I said, 'they're going to kill him?'

'Yes.'

'And what happens to me?'

This time, Craw just blinked.

You find the location of the Whaler for them, they move in on him, and then once he's in the ground – and Tori Wolton too – there's a third grave right next to them.

'Are they going to kill Healy too?'

Her lack of response was confirmation.

Me. Healy.

We already knew too much.

'I'm trying not to let it happen to either of you.' There was a hitch in Craw's voice, but then she looked me in the eye – fierce, resolute. 'I just needed time to think, to formulate a plan. Why do you think I'm here, putting my daughters' lives in danger? Why do you think I left that security card for you? Why do you think I told you to try and recover that four hundred grand?'

'Because you didn't think we'd find it.'

'Exactly. I *never* thought you'd find that money. I thought it was long gone. It was the whole reason I told you to try and find it in the first place – because I knew it wouldn't sit right with you. I knew it wouldn't make sense to you to go after it. Like you said, four hundred grand's a drop in the ocean to the Zinters and the cash wasn't even theirs in the first place. They never even mentioned the money. It was just me trying to warn you. I was trying to tell you, "None of this is what it seems."'

And she was right.

Going after the money had never made sense to me.

'I need to go,' she said. 'Kerrill's been on a security call with Macau and I need to get back before it ends. I'm going to tell him I don't want to see you, and then he's going to come to the office and tell you we can't meet. You're going to act pissed off, mouth a few objections, then leave the casino.'

She opened her clutch bag.

Reaching a hand in, she removed something.

It was a flash drive.

'This is everything my guy out in LA gathered on that triple murder. I don't know if there's anything here, but . . .' She glanced at the stairs. 'I hope there is.'

She reached into her clutch bag again and took out something else. In her hands was an invitation. 'I need to get to this cocktail party,' she said, unfolding it.

'Wait a second.' I put a hand to her arm, stopping her.

'What?'

'That invite. Can I see it?'

She handed it to me.

I took it, examining the front. It was expensive black card, A5, and had a silver embossed line in sans serif in the centre.

The line said: *Guest #005 | Melanie Craw.*

I'd seen an invitation like this before.

It had been in Tori Wolton's mailbox.

Guest #121 | Tori Wolton.

'Who's attending this party?'

'Who's attending it?' she said. 'What, you want a list of two hundred names?'

'Are the Zinters coming?'

'Yeah. How did you know that?'

'Are they here now?'

'No. They just landed. They'll be here in fifty minutes. Why?' I handed her back the invitation.

'Because the woman who I think took the Fowlers is on the guest list.'

'*What?*'

'And if she's got an invite,' I said, 'I'm betting the Whaler's got one too.'

Healy

Healy finished searching the rest of the Bunker and returned to the living area, checking the monitor on top of the sideboard. He'd watched Raker disappear up the stairs and out of view, and he'd been gone well over ten minutes now.

What if it really *had* been a trap?

But then, as he looked at the sideboard again, something occurred to him. He swivelled the monitor away from him so he could see where the wires at the back snaked out.

They led over the rear edge of the sideboard.

Going to one end of it, Healy attempted to shuffle the sideboard out from the wall. The whole thing weighed a ton. Eventually, though, he got it far enough away to look behind it. The gap was full of dust, cobwebs, detritus, but Healy ignored that and concentrated on what he could see: the wires led to a removable plastic panel on the wall. He reached over and took off the panel.

A decoder-shaped hard drive blinked at him from inside.

He leaned closer.

The hard drive had a VCR-style control panel on it, including a button marked MENU. When he pushed it, the feed from the keypad camera vanished from the monitor and was replaced by a basic-looking options menu. At the very top was a sub-menu marked SAVED FILES.

He selected it.

A waterfall of folders loaded, the dates on them in reverse

chronological order. It was saved footage from the camera, going back a year. That meant all the footage from the previous May was still saved on the hard drive.

He went to Saturday 21 May last year.

The night the Whaler got into the Bunker.

Pushing Play, Healy watched as the monitor returned a now-familiar, near-fisheye view from the keypad camera into the corridor outside. The camera must have been motion-activated because for the first few seconds the screen was just black – but then, suddenly, it snapped into life.

The door to the car-park stairs had set it off.

It was being opened by someone.

The door stopped halfway, the person beyond it still not visible. As Healy kept his gaze fixed on the image, he thought of the EMI transmitter the Whaler had concealed on himself the night he was arrested. The fact that the CCTV units out on the casino floor hadn't been affected in the same way as the video from the cells must have meant the transmitter could be manually turned on and off: the Whaler needed the cameras on the floor to work in order for the facial recognition tech to capture him at the blackjack table; but once he got to the cells, he didn't want anyone to know how he escaped. And, right now, as Healy watched the half-open door, there was no sign of the transmitter at work here either. No static. No ghosting of the image.

The door opened all the way out.

Wait a second.

It took a moment for Healy to process what he was seeing: a shadow-figure at the bottom of the stairs, a can of black paint in one hand.

And then, slowly, the person beyond the door came into the light.

45

I re-entered the Bunker. 'Healy, we have to go.'

He was sitting with his back to me at the sideboard.

'*Healy.*'

He turned and I told him about the cocktail party. 'It's full of investors, millionaires, private equity firms – all the sort of people the Zinters need to fund an expansion they're planning for the Skyline. The brothers landed at some private airfield down in Surrey an hour ago.'

'They're *here*?'

'They will be. I think Tori Wolton is coming too. And if she's coming, the Whaler's coming. And if they're coming together, they're coming to end this.'

We both looked at the message on the wall.

One down.

Two to go.

'So what are you telling me?' Healy said. 'The Whaler and Wolton are just going to off the Zinter brothers in front of a room full of witnesses?'

'No, they'll be smarter than that – but this is the moment they've been waiting for. The Zinters have increased their security measures since Yanis was killed. The brothers aren't as easy to get at any more. But at this party, investors aren't going to get into bed with them if Caleb and Asha are surrounded by a bunch of security grunts. That'll just unsettle people and make the Zinters look vulnerable. The brothers need to have conversations, shake hands, let people get close to them, and they need their security teams to keep their distance – otherwise they're not going to get the money they need. So I don't know how the Whaler and Wolton got on the guest list, or what identity the Whaler is even going to use, but I know two things. The Zinters have no idea who Tori Wolton is – to them, she's just another name to bleed for cash. And she and the Whaler aren't coming for the cocktails.'

'So what's our plan?'

'First, we need to go back to that meeting room. I'll explain everything Craw told me on the way. And then, after Kerrill kicks us out, we're going to collect two spare invitations from the front desk. Craw said she'll leave them there for us.'

'And this?' Healy said, waving a hand at himself – his jeans, his trainers. 'We're going to a cocktail party, not Burger King.'

'They've got a suit-hire place off reception.'

He nodded, but then turned back to the monitor on the sideboard, and now I took in what he'd done while I'd been with Craw.

'What have you been doing?' I asked.

'I need to show you something.' He edged the monitor around to face me. 'And you're not going to like it.'

2019

Las Vegas, Nevada

Catalina gets back to the hotel room just after 5 p.m.

She's exhausted.

The conference hall was packed. They did back-to-back demos of *Collector 2.0* from nine until three, and then she sat in on ninety minutes of interviews, as tech mags and newspapers fired questions at Brian and Kevin. She had to force herself to stay awake, and that involved mainlining coffee all afternoon.

Even if she'd fallen asleep, though, Catalina is pretty sure she would have remained firmly in Brian's good books. He told her she was a genius for getting a conversation up and running with Anthony Yanis, so the three of them came home via the Fashion Show shopping mall, where they managed to pick up costumes.

Catalina is going to the Halloween party as an angel.

She collapses on to the bed, armed with a sub from a deli in the foyer, and tears into the sandwich. As she eats, she checks her messages and sees she's got replies from both her kids. Even her son has actually replied to Catalina's earlier text asking how school had been. Teenagers normally keep to a fairly rigid routine of two- or three-word replies – or no replies at all.

She smiles to herself as she reads it.

> **School was boring but football
> was good. I scored a goal**

She knows they're not going to be up now – it's after 1 a.m. at home – but she replies to her son first, then her daughter.

To her surprise, the message she sends to her daughter immediately switches to two blue ticks and she gets a response:

Love the Vegas photos Mum! We miss you too.
You can call me if you like x

Catalina doesn't need a second invitation. Even as her daughter appears on-screen, Catalina still feels like she's a million miles away from them. It's pretty much always been the three of them – Catalina's ex cheated on her during her second pregnancy, and as far as her children are concerned, they don't have a dad any more.

'Hey, Mum.'

'Hey, honey. You're up late. Can't you sleep?'

'It's this assignment. It has to be in tomorrow and I've still got a couple of things to do on it.' She sighs. 'This Master's is absolutely kicking my arse.'

Catalina worries about her kids all the time, but she worries especially about her daughter. She's an army reservist, a life choice that Catalina strongly suspects was made more out of curiosity than desire, and – for all sorts of reasons – can probably be traced back to a lack of a father figure growing up. Although her daughter only goes to reservist training once a week and at weekends – and has only ever been away once with the army, to a training camp in Kenya – Catalina worries that one day she'll come home and say she wants to make the switch to the regular army. It was why Catalina was so happy when she wanted to do a Master's after graduating in Psychology, because it would keep her at home and steer her further away from the military. But now Catalina just worries about the Master's instead. It's in Applied Psychology, and basically seems to involve creating endless, hyper-complicated models that map how humans think in order to predict their behaviour. Her daughter's textbooks are like reading Mandarin and her workload is getting more and more insane.

'You'll get there, honey,' she says, because if she says what she really thinks, her daughter will probably close up on her. 'Make sure you rest too, though, okay?'

She can almost hear the smile in her daughter's voice as the response comes back: 'All right, Mum. Don't worry. Once this is done, I'll chill. For a day.'

Catalina feels another surge of love for her daughter: she's smart, and funny, sweet and kind. She's so proud of her.

'And your brother?' she asks. 'I heard he scored a goal earlier.'

'Yeah, he did. I think I even spotted a smile on his face.'

'Aw, my Benny,' Catalina says. 'Has he been good for you and your gran?'

'Yeah, he's been fine. You know what he's like. You don't get a lot out of him in the mornings, but he warms up in the evenings. Another reason I've got to try and finish this assignment is because he wants me to take him out at the weekend.'

'He does?'

'He wants to go walking on the moors.'

Catalina laughs. 'What's he like?'

'Why can't he just play videogames like a normal boy?'

'Because he *isn't* a normal boy,' Catalina laughs. She aches to see them again. 'You two are just so perfect.'

'Thanks, Mum. I'd better go. We're looking forward to having you home.'

'I'm looking forward to getting home. Don't work all night. Even soon-to-be-famous psychologists need sleep sometimes.'

Her daughter laughs. 'I love you, Mum.'

Catalina's heart swells. 'I love you too, Tori.'

46

Reaching down behind the sideboard, he unpaused the image. It was the view from the keypad camera, into the corridor beyond the Bunker.

The timecode showed 03:09 a.m.

And the date was Saturday 21 May 2022.

'This is the night the Whaler got inside?'

'Yeah,' Healy said. 'Watch.'

For fifteen seconds, nothing happened, and then – on the right, out of shot – the shadow of someone approaching. They were coming from the direction of the cells, forming on the wall as an outline, the fractured image of them reflected in a TV that was piping out a live feed from one of the gaming floors.

The screen started to fill with static.

Within seconds, it had obscured any view of the Whaler we might have had. The EMI device he'd used at the cells had obviously still been switched on at this point.

I glanced at Healy. 'I don't understand what you want me to see.'

Healy leaned in and pressed Rewind. The video went back ten minutes – beyond the point at which we'd started – and then the monitor went dark.

'Just tell me what's going on, Hea–'

'Wait,' he said, cutting me off.

Almost as soon as he said it, the monitor sprang into life again. The keypad camera was motion-activated, and it took me a moment to realize what it had reacted *to*. The first movement was small, just the *Exit* door shifting an inch away from its frame. With a second movement, it opened to the half-way point.

I leaned in closer.

This wasn't the Whaler, because he'd come from the right, from the direction of the cells, ten minutes *after* this.

So was it Tori Wolton?

The door moved for a third time and opened all the way out.

She remained a silhouette for a moment, paused there at the bottom of the stairs, one hand slightly ahead so that the can of black paint she had in her hands was just on the edge of the light.

Something at the back of my head pulsed.

This isn't what you think.

Finally, she stepped all the way out of the shadows.

Almost as soon as she did, she retreated again. She was in the light for less than a second. She'd peered to her left, down the corridor in the direction of where she must have known the Whaler would be coming from – the cells – and then she'd stepped back, letting the dark swallow her whole again. But that split second was all I needed.

I knew who she was.

I'd spent the last week searching for her.

It was Clara.

47

'What the hell's going on, Raker?'

The entire room felt like it had fallen away. I could barely hear Healy. I could barely tear my eyes from the screen.

'*Raker?*'

I tried to think, tried to make everything we'd learned and figured out over the last few days fit into place. This must have been the reason Clara had so few friends and lived such a small, contained life: because all of it was a construct, a life she had built from scratch over the last year and made absolutely watertight. Her friends, her work, her background, they were all either deliberately and carefully assembled, her friendships – even the ten months she'd spent in a relationship with Kyle – cynically built, so that, to outsiders like me, they would all look real – or they were stolen. I suspected, if I dug down deeper, I'd discover that the actual Clara Dearton was a real person, genuinely orphaned as a child. But, like Morgan Annerson and – I was increasingly certain – Tori Wolton, the real Clara Dearton was dead, her life and identity simply a space for another person to fit into and shelter inside.

'Clara must have been the instigator,' I said softly, almost to myself.

'What?'

'On the lake that day. She must have instigated that last trip out on the boat. It must have been her suggestion to Kyle, because she knew the Whaler had come down that track and was waiting for them.'

Had Clara's rotator cuff even been injured? Had she used the sling to conceal a weapon? Was all of this connected to what Kyle had been looking at on *Evidence Bag*? Had he found out something that he shouldn't have? I had answers for so little, it was almost overwhelming. The only thing that seemed certain now was that we must have been right about Marc: he was simply unlucky, tragically so. He wasn't even supposed to have *been* on that boat.

'Are we going?' Healy said.

I couldn't tear my eyes away from the monitor, the frozen image of Clara captured for a split second, looking out from the doorway.

'Press Play,' I said.

'What?'

'Just press Play.'

Healy did as I asked.

On-screen, Clara retreated into the shadows.

'She doesn't reappear again?' I asked.

'No. She waits in the dark for the Whaler to arrive, presumably because she knows the EMI will do its thing once he does. After that, if she's there, she's static.'

Healy fast-forwarded it to 03:09.

'Nine minutes past three in the morning,' he said. 'You'll see the Whaler's shadow appear right about . . .'

The timecode ticked over.

'. . . now.'

Adrenalin coursed through my blood as I rewatched the same section again – the shadow that formed as the Whaler closed in on the Bunker; the interference that began as he did. But, before the static kicked in fully, I saw something.

Something I'd missed before.

'Go back fifteen seconds,' I said.

He did as I asked and played the same section again.

'Stop when I tell you.' I leaned into the monitor, watching as

269

the footage played out a third time. 'Ready?' The shadow of the Whaler formed on the wall again; static started to spread across the video. '*Now.*'

Healy hit Pause.

I got as close as I could to the screen. 'Look,' I said, and tapped the monitor – but not the shadow, not the static, not the corridor itself.

I pointed to the TV that had been hung on the wall *in* the corridor.

'I've seen these TVs all over the basement,' I said. 'They show feeds from the resort to make it feel as if there are windows down here.'

'So?'

'Every so often, the feed changes.'

'So? So what?'

'So, look,' I said, and tapped the TV on-screen. 'It's between feeds right now. It's literally making the switch from one to the other in this second here.'

That was when Healy understood.

As the TV made the switch between feeds, its screen went black.

And in the black of the screen was a reflection.

'It's him,' Healy muttered.

We could see the Whaler in the TV.

He wasn't in control of this moment, this second of capture, because he didn't realize he was being recorded.

This was the most candid view we'd ever had of him.

And in it, I could finally see the truth.

'Wait,' Healy said, frowning. 'We already know what this prick looks like. Why does it help that we can see his reflection?'

'Because his reflection exposes his trick.'

'What? What are you talking about?'

'He's been completely caught off guard.' I tapped the image

of the Whaler on-screen. 'Look at the way he's walking now. Look at the way he's tucking his hair behind his ear, even though it's short. It's habit. It's muscle memory. *This* is where Tori Wolton fits in.'

Healy, the frown still carved into his brow, turned to the monitor again.

And then, a second later, his face dropped.

'Holy shit.'

'That's a wig,' I said, 'those are contact lenses, those clothes are deliberately male-looking. All of it – every part of the Whaler as we know him – has been a lie.'

But it was a lie everyone had fallen for.

'The Whaler isn't a man,' I said. 'It's a woman.'

5
The Party

48

We tidied up the Bunker and hurried back to the meeting room.

It was Healy who broke the silence: 'How did we miss it? How did we never realize the Whaler was a . . .' He trailed off, as if he still couldn't believe it.

'Because Tori Wolton has been controlling the narrative, start to finish,' I said. 'She stayed just out of sight, or sat in the right position, or used the ideal route – other than for a split second on the video we just saw, where she hadn't thought she'd be seen. She wore a baseball cap to hide her face. Maybe she altered her voice, I don't know. But if she ever let the cameras see her, it was because she *wanted* them to see her. She's smart, organized. Every part of this – right down to the use of the EMI device – has been about hiding in plain sight.'

I checked my watch.

In twenty minutes, the Zinters would be here.

Come on, Kerrill.

Come and tell us Craw isn't available.

'That was why no one could ever find the Whaler,' Healy said.

'Yeah. He butchers Anthony Yanis, then he completely vanishes off the radar. A week later, he appears out of nowhere again, comes back in here, writes his message on the wall and – *boom* – he's gone a second time. No one has a clue how he does it – not the Zinters, not the cops. Twelve months later, they still haven't located him. The Zinters have zero leads, the cops have a cold case.'

'Because everyone's looking for a man.'

I nodded. 'Right.'

'But surely Yanis knew the Whaler was a woman?'

'There's a lot at play here – but yes, he must have done.' I tried to pull all the pieces together in my head. 'This afternoon, you had a picture of the Whaler the night that he was arrested and taken down to the cells. It was the first time I'd seen him – and yet, straight away, I thought there was something familiar about him. It was because somewhere, at the back of my mind – despite how well disguised she was as a man – I must have matched the Whaler to the face I'd seen on Tori Wolton's driving licence.' I paused, frustrated with myself. 'At least that explains why every man who met the Whaler talked about how attractive he was.'

'But what about Yanis? He knew she was a woman, he knew the truth, so – what? – he just played pretend?'

'I think so, yeah. When it was just the two of them, it would have been too hard for her to hide. She must have allowed Yanis to see the truth about herself, and then persuaded him not to tell anyone, to keep their relationship – or the *fiction* that was their relationship – under wraps. Maybe she spun him some kind of story, a reason why he needed to keep her sex, who she *really* was, a secret. Maybe she said her life was in danger if he told people the truth, I don't know. Craw mentioned to you that Yanis liked younger women, and Wolton was ticking that box – she was almost thirty *years* younger – so because Yanis only ever thought with his dick and Wolton is objectively beautiful – and way out of his league – he must have been happy enough to play ball with her deception. In public he helped her maintain the fiction that she was a man, just a platonic friend of his; in private he got to see the real her – or what he thought was the real her. And Yanis keeping her secret from everyone, even the Zinters? Well, that wasn't going to bother him either. It sounds like he kept plenty of secrets about plenty of things. And the whole time, over the five months they knew each other, she was slowly gaining his trust, just waiting for the right moment to move in for the kill.'

The door to the office opened.

Kerrill looked between us and then at the room, as if searching for something that was out of place.

'Is Craw coming?' I said, playing the part.

'No. She's not going to make it. Something else has come up.'

I did what Craw asked me to do and ranted and raved for a while, but Kerrill showed zero reaction. He wasn't threatened by me or Healy.

Two minutes later, he was walking us out.

49

We got to the security door we'd come in through.

The second we stepped beyond it, out on to the casino floor, Kerrill pushed the door shut and a cacophony of noise, light and movement washed in.

'Let's go,' I said.

We headed back through the Empire State casino, through the Shard and the Chrysler, and made a beeline to the vast reception in the foyer.

Craw had followed through on her promise and left two invites at the front desk for us: they were generic, just a number on the front rather than specific names. They were presumably for last-minute attendees who weren't on the guest list that had been sent out six months ago.

Next, we took a flight of stairs up to the suit-hire place.

We chose our suits, then I left Healy with my credit card and told him to come and find me once he was done. Ten floors above us, the party was already in full swing, and, according to Craw, the Zinters were due to arrive any minute. The desire to be there was like an itch in my skin.

But there was something I needed to do first.

I took the stairs down to the foyer, and then a second flight to a floor below it. It was a bland, low-lit corridor with tinted floor-to-ceiling glass on the left.

Behind the glass was the business centre.

Making sure no one could see my screen, I slid in at one of the computers there and slotted in the flash drive that Craw had given me. On it was the work her investigator out in LA had compiled on the murders of Casey Ryker, Florida Jones and Ryan Ling. While the machine dealt with the drive, I loaded Google and searched for 'Catalina Robbins'. It fed in some of the stories that Healy had read aloud in the car on the way here, plus some others that he hadn't got around to looking at.

I skipped anything we'd seen before and went straight to the stories we hadn't had the time to check before getting to the Skyline.

The first was in *USA Today*. I skim-read it, looked at the accompanying photographs, backed out and went to the next link, then the next. I worked through them all as quickly as possible. I knew the details already about the day Catalina was found – or enough of them, at least – and was searching for something else.

On page two of the Google results, I found it.

It was a link to an article in the *Manchester Evening News*. When I clicked on it, it loaded a story that had run seven days after Catalina's initial disappearance, and featured an appeal from her family back home in the UK for information about her whereabouts. Halfway down was what I'd been searching all the other stories for.

A photo.

They were sitting on a sofa in Catalina's house in Oldham – where they'd grown up – Catalina's mother in the middle, with her arms around two children. It was hard to look at: the worry, the lack of sleep, the panic, the fear – all of it was written into their faces like ink. In the American stories, it had mentioned Catalina having two kids, a son and a daughter, but there hadn't been any pictures.

Now I had one.

The boy was fifteen. He would be eighteen or nineteen now, much more mature, possibly very different physically. In the shot, he was still gangly, awkward-looking, his black hair a mop, his face pockmarked with acne.

I looked at the daughter.

Originally, Healy and I had speculated that the Whaler and Tori Wolton might be a son and daughter – a brother and sister – working together to avenge the death of their mother. But that was when we'd thought the Whaler was a man.

Instead we were dealing with two women.

And only one of them was Catalina Robbins's child.

Hello, Tori.

She was three years younger, but it was her. Blonde hair, the same high cheekbones, the pearlescent blue eyes, the button nose. Even in grief, even in the perpetual suffering that must have plagued her and her family during those first few weeks after the disappearance, Tori was striking.

Underneath the picture was a caption.

Catalina's children, Victoria, 22, and
Benjamin, 15, with Catalina's mother, Lilly, 74.

So her real name was Victoria. That must have been why she'd chosen to steal the identity of a Tori. After all, it was easier to live a lie when it was mostly built on truth.

With one last look at Victoria Robbins, I closed the web browser and returned to the desktop.

As I did, Healy entered the room and came around the bank of computers to where I was sitting. 'Have you found them?'

'I've found Tori.'

'Is it like we thought?'

'Yeah, she's definitely Catalina's daughter.'

'What about Clara?'

The icon for a flash drive called 'CRFJRL' was now waiting.

Casey Ryker. Florida Jones. Ryan Ling.

I opened the PDF. It ran to eighty-seven scanned pages, a mix of notes that Craw's friend in the States had typed out for her, and photocopies of pages from the original murder book the LAPD had put together. I moved through it at speed, knowing I could go back to it in more detail later on if I needed to.

There were very few photos in the scans that Craw's investigator in the States had sent. Mostly it was just typewritten pages.

Even so, less than a minute later, I'd found something.

'Look,' I said, zooming in on a paragraph. 'Here.'

Healy leaned closer. 'Florida Jones had a younger sister.'

'"Her name was Miriam",' I said, repeating what was written in the report. '"Their dad was from England and their mother from Mexico."'

We glanced at each other. Clara was olive-skinned, dark-haired and dark-eyed. And if Miriam Jones had been seven when Florida was killed, fifteen years on she'd be twenty-two – exactly the same age as Clara.

'The age, the physical description of Miriam here – Latina, black hair, brown eyes, five-six – it's a match for her. Plus, there's something else.'

'Lorna Shute,' Healy said, as if he were reading my mind.

'She said the woman that came to her house might have had an accent. What if the accent was American?'

'She doesn't know what an American accent sounds like?'

'Maybe she wasn't processing that level of detail when she was face down on the floor of her living room, absolutely terrified for her life, being forced to read out that script to her husband for reasons she didn't fully understand. And even when the woman in the balaclava *did* speak to her, it was only three or four whispered words here and there.'

'And the rest of the time?' Healy said. 'When Clara-stroke-Miriam was with the Fowlers? When she was working? What, she just put on an English accent?'

'Her dad was English, so she would have grown up listening to him. She would likely have spent time with – or talking to – English relatives. Maybe she'd even been fully *ingrained* in British culture through her dad.'

And then a memory flared.

Something Clara's book-club friend had said that had surprised me. *Clara had a wicked sense of humour. She was really good at impressions.* I remembered the friend talking about Clara's uncanny *Fargo* impersonation.

'Or maybe she was just a really good mimic,' I said, explaining what the friend had told me.

The question was, if we were right, if Victoria Robbins and Miriam Jones were two daughters of victims in connected cases, how did they get drawn into each other's orbits from opposite sides of the world?

And at what stage did they make a pact to exact revenge on the three men they thought were responsible for the murders of their mother and sister?

One down.

Two to go.

'Let's get to that party,' I said.

Irvine, California

Polite applause fills the auditorium.

Pete Tomer leans forward at the lectern, thanks everyone for coming, then heads towards the steps at the side of the stage. His knees and hips are hurting from standing so long, so he's a little slow descending, and he's careful too. Tomer is nothing if not realistic about his age, and although his son, Billy, still jokes that he's 'rocking it' at seventy, it only takes one misplaced foot, one turn of an ankle, to end up in the ER. Tomer hates being old. But he hates feeling old even more.

As he heads up the side of the auditorium, occasionally being stopped by a keen student with a question, he sees someone emerge from the back row. At first, the person is a shadow, half-hidden beneath the glare of the stage lamps – but as they come further out into the light, Tomer realizes it's not another student. It's someone older. More than that, Tomer feels like he knows him.

But if I did, I knew him a long time ago.

'Pete?'

Tomer takes the man's hand, shaking it. 'Hey.'

'It's me.' A smile. 'Darnell.'

It's the smile that gets Tomer there a fraction of a second before the name – and then everything comes flooding back.

Darnell Savage.

Tomer can't even take a guess at how long it's been. They met socially for a while after Tomer left the Sheriff's Department, but then slowly, over time, they lost touch.

'Wow,' he says. 'Darnell, man. What's it been? Twenty years?'

'It's got to be.' Darnell looks around the auditorium. Students are filing out, passing them. Tomer moves out of their way. 'I saw that you were doing a talk at UCI, but I didn't realize you'd be so damn popular.'

Tomer laughs. 'Most of these kids have been dragged here against their will, believe me. You ever meet a detective called Joline Kader back in the day?'

'The name rings a bell.'

'She taught here for a long time after she left the force, and we kind of kept in touch, and she ended up persuading me to come in and bore the kids on the Criminology courses about the bad old days.' He's joking, but it's basically the truth. Part of the degree deals with the history of law enforcement, and the staff here like the perspective Tomer brings on what investigations were like before the wheel was invented. 'Other than this it's just yoga, coffee mornings and constant hip pain.'

'You enjoying it? Apart from the hip pain, obviously.'

'Retirement has its moments. So what are you up to these days?'

'I've actually started doing some private work. The kids are all grown up now, and I was just sitting around at home watching daytime TV, so I thought, "What the hell?" I got my licence about four years ago.' Darnell shrugs. 'It's a lot of waiting around in parking lots as husbands and wives do things they're not telling their husbands and wives about – but it keeps me busy.'

'I can't believe your kids are all grown up now.'

'I know. Billy too. How's he doing?'

'He's good,' Tomer says. 'He's married and living up in Thousand Oaks.'

'Has he got kids?'

'Yeah. They've just had their first.'

'So you're a grandpa?'

'I am. A very proud one. Time goes by so fast.'

Darnell doesn't respond and, briefly, Tomer sees something pass his face. He wonders what it is and whether it's something to do with Darnell's kids.

'So I refuse to believe you came all the way down here for a lecture.'

'No.' Darnell pauses, a frown still lingering on his face.

'And now I know you didn't,' Tomer says.

'I got cancer.'

It's such a bolt from the blue, it takes Tomer a split second to properly deal with what he's heard. 'Oh, Darnell.' He stops. 'Man, I'm so sorry.'

Darnell's eyes are still on the stage, his fingers working a thread on his coat – and in that moment Tomer sees what else he's carrying, what he hasn't said yet.

'Oh no,' Tomer says softly.

'Yeah.' *It's terminal.*

'How long have you got?'

A shrug. 'A couple of months.'

'Shit. I'm so sorry, Darnell.'

'It's okay,' he says, a tremor in his voice, 'but it's the reason I came here today. Before things really go south, I need to speak to you about a case we had.'

'A case?'

'Yeah. It was back in 1993.' A beat. 'You remember Wilma Steski?'

Steski.

It takes a second for the surname to land, for Tomer to raid his memories of the time he spent with Darnell. But then he gets there, and as he does he flinches.

'Yeah,' Darnell says quietly. 'Yeah, that's her.'

Tomer pictures that day as they went up into the mountains – the snow flickering across the windshield on the journey up; the bitter cold as they both got out of the car; the unpaved parking lot, with the barrier on the bend and the ravine beyond – and the body they found there.

Wilma.

Her hands tied behind her.

Her legs scratched and bruised.

The hunting round in the back of her head.

'Like I say, I've only got a couple of months left,' Darnell says, 'so before I go . . .' He stops. 'Before I go, I've got to tell you something, Pete.'

'Tell me something?'

'It's about Wilma.'

Darnell stops playing with the thread on his coat.

'I've got a confession to make.'

50

The doors of the elevator opened.

Healy and I looked at each other – a deep breath – and then moved out, into a long corridor. Right at the very end, two brawny security staff were stationed either side of a glamorous woman in a long, flowing ball gown, who was checking invites. Behind them was a doorway into a massive multi-room, multi-level conference space, which looked more like the vestibule of a vast country estate, a string quartet playing Schubert in front of a grand staircase.

'Good evening, gentlemen,' the woman in the ball gown said as we reached the doors and handed over our invites. 'Could I take your names?'

'Alex Murphy,' I replied, and then pointed to Healy. 'Bob Morton.'

She wrote them at the bottom of a printed list of guests. 'And what company are you with?'

'OCP.'

'Thank you,' she said. 'Could I take a contact number?'

This must have been so the Zinters knew who to try and chase for investment. I reeled off a fake number and then the security guards began patting us down.

I looked again at the people gathered in the foyer and wondered how much of this security was for them and how much of it was for the Zinters. The brothers knew that somewhere – even if it wasn't here – the Whaler was lying in wait for them.

They just didn't know he was actually here tonight.

Or that he wasn't even a man.

'Have a pleasant evening,' one of the guards said, and we moved past them and into the party.

'Alex Murphy and Bob Morton?' Healy said under his breath. 'Where did you pluck that shite from?'

'*RoboCop.*'

He smiled, and then a waiter came past with a tray and offered us champagne. We both declined and I took in our surroundings.

The place was even bigger than I'd thought. In front of us, the grand staircase spiralled up to an L-shaped mezzanine where guests had gathered at a floor-to-ceiling window. Out of the window was a spectacular view of the skyscrapers at the Skyline's front. To my left were some doors into another big room. This one had been done up like a study, with beautiful art deco flourishes. The room to my right was bigger still – the same art deco design, the same glass roof with views of the same skyscrapers, but much wider and built in three tiers, stair-cases everywhere, creating a flow from one level to the next. If the other side was like a study, this was more like an enormous drawing room, with enough floor space to hold corporate parties and conferences but designed in a way that made it feel strangely intimate, even with all the people in it. Right at the back of the bottom tier was a long bar and a view out across the roof of the Skyline's shopping mall.

'Let's split up,' I said, pointing Healy towards the study. 'Text me if you see anything.'

I moved through the crowds, searching the room for any faces I recognized. The Zinters hadn't arrived yet – or, if they had, they were in the study, where Healy was headed. There was no sign of Tori Wolton or Clara.

That's not their names.

Their names are Victoria Robbins and Miriam Jones.

I was finding it hard to make the adjustment. I'd spent so

long knowing them by their aliases that their actual names made them feel less real to me somehow.

I couldn't stop thinking about Marc and Kyle too.

What had Clara – *Miriam* – working with Tori meant for the other two? I tried not to dwell on it – not because I didn't want the answers but because I needed to stay focused – and moved deeper into the room. My progress slowed, the crowds congealing around me. The multiple staircases didn't help. In front of me and at my periphery, guests were moving up and down constantly, and it became almost impossible to keep track of them.

I got all the way down to the bar, and – finding a space at the counter – rested an elbow against it, so I was still half facing the room, and ordered a beer. As I waited, I texted Healy to ask if he had eyes on anyone. He replied almost instantly:

Nothing

I looked out at the room again, going from face to face, and for the first time I felt a murmur of doubt. Had I called this wrong somehow? Was it possible the invite I'd found in the mailbox – with Tori Wolton's name on it – *wasn't* part of her and Clara's plan to get to the Zinters? Or perhaps it was a plan that they'd abandoned for being too risky? After all, there were over two hundred people here.

One of the bar staff put a beer down next to me on the counter. I picked it up, took a sip and then noticed something: a security monitor was in the corner of the bar, tucked under the countertop, its feed showing the whole room from a camera above my head. As I watched it, my phone buzzed a second time.

They're here

51

The Zinter brothers entered the foyer.

They greeted a crowd of people at the entrance and then moved into the drawing-room area, where I was, already in conversation with a group of grey-haired men in their fifties.

Both of the brothers were in tuxedos.

Caleb was slim, fit, tanned, and had come armed with a dazzling smile and an everyman way that put people instantly at ease. He oozed charisma, and the further in he got, the more people gravitated towards him. Asha followed in his wake – bigger, and much less youthful – but while he was obviously the more introverted of the two, when he talked to people, they seemed to listen. As the brothers worked the first part of the room, shaking hands and starting conversations, their dynamic began to become more evident: one of them was the entertainer and the front man; the other was the custodian and the brains.

They diverged, heading off in different directions.

I adjusted my position at the bar, worried about being spotted by them, and tried to keep an eye on them both. But as the word spread about the Zinters' arrival, more people started shifting towards the middle tier, where Caleb was, and towards the corner of the top tier, where Asha had gone. After a while, it became harder to track the brothers among the crowds.

Healy texted again.

What am I missing?

I replied to tell him, 'Nothing so far,' and then asked if there was any sign of Tori or Clara on his side. It didn't take him long to respond:

No. Where the hell are they?

I told him to come through to my side.

When I looked up again, Caleb had come even closer to me – maybe only fifty feet away now – and was at my level, which meant it was harder to see him among the crowds. I looked out, across the rest of the room, trying to pinpoint faces that might be turned Caleb's or Asha's way – watching them, tracking them.

But I couldn't see anyone suspicious.

Healy entered the tiered drawing room, pausing at the main doors and taking everything in. He spotted Asha first – still on the top tier – and then, after he located me at the bar at the bottom, his attention shifted to Caleb. From where I was, I could hear that Caleb was telling a story about a gambler at their casino out in Macau. Everyone was laughing.

I searched the rest of the room again – and then something caught my eye on the monitor tucked under the bar. There was a problem with it.

I leaned in.

The CCTV feed.

It was slowly disintegrating into a snowstorm of static.

Shit.

I grabbed my phone, needing to warn Healy.

The Whaler is here RIGHT NOW

And then I froze.

From out of nowhere – before I could hit Send – a hand had closed around mine. It crunched my fingers against my mobile, instantly stopping me from using it.

Someone was reaching in from behind me.

They'd been behind the bar and, although I'd looked at the bar staff, I realized now that I hadn't looked anywhere close enough.

I'd missed someone.

I followed the hand that was on mine, back to the male bartender, dressed in a white shirt and blue tie, who had hold of me. His head was completely shaved and his chin was covered in a thick, black beard. He was bigger than the photos I'd seen of him, his skin more tanned, his face more mature.

But it was him.

It really is him.

Kyle.

Healy

The Skyline | *Now*

Wait, where was Raker?

Healy couldn't see him any more.

He glanced at Asha Zinter, who was talking to a member of security now, and then further down to where Caleb was. He was holding court on the bottom tier – telling some sort of story, his teeth ridiculously white, everyone laughing.

Sidestepping to his left, Healy tried to get a better angle on the end of the bar. There were so many people in here now. He hated crowds at the best of times, but he hated them even more when they were made up entirely of rich, entitled arseholes.

Where the hell are you, Raker?

He checked his phone, the messages the two of them had been sending each other moments ago. Briefly, three dots appeared and then vanished.

Had Raker been trying to send him a text?

He moved even further left, stopping at the bottom of a staircase which wound up to a mezzanine level – and, as he did, he breathed a sigh of relief.

He had a clearer view of the bar now and could see Raker was still there, at the end of it – but it looked like he was talking to someone. Healy couldn't see who.

'You spotted anything?'

Healy turned round.

Craw.

She was a few feet behind him, checking her messages.

To anyone watching, it wouldn't look like they were having a conversation at all.

'I was just keeping an eye on your pals from Vegas,' Healy replied.

He could almost feel her bristle.

'They're not my pals.'

'Sorry, I meant business partners.'

'They're not that either.'

'The one hundred grand you took from them says otherwise.'

'Fuck you, Healy.'

Healy zeroed in on Raker again. Something was going on, but he couldn't quite get a sense of what. Who was he talking to down there?

Grabbing his phone from his pocket, he sent Raker a text:

You ok?

Healy watched his screen, but the text remained unread.

Eyes still on Raker, he thought of the hush money Craw had taken from Kerrill, and said, 'So what are you going to do with your new-found wealth?'

Silence from behind him.

'Still deciding, then, I guess.'

'Why are you such a prick?'

He turned a little, automatically reacting, looking across his shoulder at her. 'I don't know. I guess when people screw you over, it tends to make you that way.'

'I didn't screw you over.'

'You ruined my life.' He faced the room again. 'You know what the irony of all this is? You fired me from the Met because I was trying to do right by my girl. And now here we are, all these years down the line, and you're busy taking money from the heinous fucking people who run this place in order to protect your *own* kids.'

'Me firing you had nothing to do with your girl.'

He glanced back at her. 'It had *everything* to do with her.'

'No, it didn't.'

'I was trying to find the bastard who killed her.'

'You've remembered it wrong.'

'No, I haven't. I was trying to find him and all you did was get in my way.'

'You've remembered it all *wrong*, Healy,' Craw repeated. 'You weren't even on my team when you were searching for Leanne. When you and Raker were running around the Dead Tracks all those years back, searching those woods for the guy who took her, I hadn't even been transferred to your station then.'

Healy frowned. 'No, that's not –'

'It's right. I arrived a year after Leanne died, a year after the Met arrested the piece of shit who killed her, and the reason I sacked you had nothing to do with you trying to find her murderer. He was already in prison by the time I arrived at the station. Over the last eleven years, your brain has rewritten history.'

'No, you're messing with my –'

'I fired you because you broke the law. You were trying to find a way to smuggle a *knife* into prison. You were trying to get inside a room, alone with Leanne's killer, because you had some insane fucking plan to cut his throat.'

Healy flinched, her words landing like a flurry of punches.

'That's the reason I had to fire you, Healy.'

He denied it for a moment longer.

But then images flooded him like punctures of light. Everything that had happened to him over the last decade – the depression, being minutes from suicide, his heart attack, disappearing into the hinterland of his faked death – all of it had impaired his memories and disrupted his recall.

Craw *did* start the year after Leanne died.

It was suddenly so clear to him.

He pressed himself against the wall, his legs almost buckling from under him. Craw wasn't part of the team at the Met that had tried to stop him – and Raker – from going into the Dead Tracks, to the place they knew Leanne had been taken.

Craw wasn't there when Healy found his daughter.

When I shattered.

She only emerged after, when he started thinking about revenge, about ending the life of the man who'd taken Leanne from him; when he'd used old friends in the Met, even used Raker – without them ever realizing – because he thought they could unwittingly get him inside the prison and closer to his daughter's killer.

I lied to them.

I lied to myself.

And I pushed all of it down.

He pressed himself even harder against the wall, his heart hammering, scared now that he might black out, and then glanced over his shoulder at Craw again.

She was gone.

And when he looked out at the room, searching it for the Zinters – realizing he'd lost track of where they were and what they were doing – a new wave of panic tremored through his chest.

The brothers had vanished.

52

He let go of my hand and inched away from me.

I still couldn't believe it was him.

There was a column at the end of the bar, behind which some big crates of beer and wine had been stored, and the moment he stepped back behind it, he was obscured from view.

Another waiter came in, heading to a box of champagne on the far side. As he started opening it up, Kyle busied himself by emptying beer bottles off trays into recycling bins. Once the waiter was gone again, he instantly turned back to me, his face changing – getting harder, more heated – and I realized how outdated all the photos I'd had of him were. It had only been eight months since he'd vanished, but eight months ago he'd still been a boy – fresh-faced, callow.

He wasn't that any more.

'You're not messing this up for us,' he said.

I looked at the monitor under the bar, saw the static again.

Us.

My phone buzzed against my closed palm. I had two new messages from Healy. In the first one he was asking if I was okay.

The second was more stark:

I don't know where the Zinters are

'You're not going to use that phone,' Kyle said, taking a half-step closer to me, still partially hidden from the rest of the room, behind the crates. 'You're not going to stop us.'

I looked for Healy and found him instantly. When we made

eye contact, he seemed relieved, his question obvious: *What the hell's going on?*

I searched for Tori and Clara, couldn't see them and then glanced at the monitor for a second time. The static was starting to clear.

'Did you hear me?' Kyle hissed.

I tried to put the fact that it was Kyle in front of me – here, *now*; that he was actively working with the two women – to the back of my mind. For now, that wasn't what mattered. What mattered was stopping more people from dying.

'Kyle, where are Tori and Clara?'

He just stared at me.

I looked out at the room, searching – but I knew, simply based on the fact that the monitor had returned to normal, that if they'd been here, they were gone now.

I quickly started typing a message to Healy.

Tori and Clara were here and

'Don't press Send,' Kyle said, interrupting me.

I glanced at him. 'Kyle, *listen* to me: you don't want to do this.'

'No.' He was different now, disconcertingly calm. 'No, you don't understand. Even if you send that text, you're going to be wasting your time.'

I edged closer to him. 'What are you talking about?'

'I'm talking about that.'

He gestured to the beer bottle on the counter next to me. The one I'd been drinking from.

'What the hell have you done?'

'It's simple,' he said. 'I've drugged you.'

53

My blood was thumping, heart racing.

I felt like it was working already.

'In three minutes, you're going to start looking like you're drunk,' he said. 'You'll barely be able to stand up at the bar. And because you'll end up making such a scene, security will come down here and you'll be escorted out.'

'You've made a mistake.'

'No, I haven't.'

'When security come for me, they're not going to escort me out, Kyle. They're going to go through my pockets and find my notebook, through the messages on my phone, and the Zinters are going to realize I already know too much. And then they're going to put me in the back of a car, take me somewhere quiet and kill me.'

He stared at me. 'What?'

'Where are Tori and Clara?'

'Kill you? What are you talking about?'

'I don't have time to explain. Where are Tori and Clara?'

He shifted his weight, eyeing me as if he was trying to work out whether I was being genuine or not. In that moment, I suddenly saw the echo of the kid he was: only just nineteen. And much as he'd changed in eight months, that kid was scared.

'Kyle,' I said softly, 'did Tori and Clara tell you to drug me?'

His eyes flicked from me over to what he could see of the party. I did the same, looking again at the faces surrounding us. Were they still here? Was he searching for them?

'Kyle. Please. This is important.'

As he dragged his gaze back, I saw something flash up on his smartwatch. He kept his attention focused on me, deliberately, but then his watch flashed a second time with a notification.

'Is that them?'

Kyle didn't respond.

I looked out again. Had they been here the whole time?

'Kyle,' I said, turning back to him just as he'd finished glancing at the message. 'You don't know what you're involved in –'

'Don't patronize me. I know what I'm involved in. I *chose* this.'

I took a breath, held up a hand to him, trying to restore the calm that I didn't feel in any part of me. I was panicking now, finding it hard to concentrate.

'People are going to die, Kyle.'

'No.'

'They are.'

'No, they're not.'

'They *are.*'

Again, he eyed me, as if searching my face for a lie. I couldn't decide if he genuinely believed the women *weren't* going to murder the Zinters – or if he was playing some elaborate game with me.

I studied him again. *This doesn't feel like a game.*

'This isn't you.'

'You don't know anything about me,' he said, through his teeth.

'I know enough.'

He shook his head. 'No, you –'

'I know your mum and sister miss you desperately.'

The mention of Sarah and Mable hit him like a train.

A second later, one of the waiters walked past us, going to the crates to grab some wine. Kyle made it look like he was working – but instead all he was doing was staring down at multiple reflections of himself in the glass of the bottles.

The other waiter left.

I looked at my watch.

A minute and a half had been eaten up already.

Kyle glanced at me and then away again. And, as he did, he said something, almost out of the corner of his mouth, both his hands still on the crate.

'What did you say?'

His eyes went to me again. 'How is she?'

'Your mum?' I shrugged. 'She's broken.'

His mouth flattened into a line, as if he didn't care.

But he did.

He cared too much – and this was how I could get at him. 'She's sick, Kyle.'

'What?' He straightened. 'What are you talk–'

'Your mum's sick,' I repeated, and although I didn't want to use Sarah's illness as a weapon, I suddenly realized the power it had to pull down his defences.

'What are you talking about?'

'She has a brain tumour.'

His whole face – his entire body – crumpled.

'What?'

He looked like he might be about to break down completely – and I began to realize just how much stress he was under, exactly *how* much he was wavering.

'What?' he said again. 'What are you talking about?'

'Your mum has a brain tumour.'

'No. No, you're talking shit.'

'I'm not. She was diagnosed before you even disappeared, she just didn't tell you. Those were the fights you used to hear between her and Marc.'

He tried to speak, tried to say something.

'They were fighting about money. Marc wanted to fly her to Singapore to get an op, your mum didn't want to because it would have cost a quarter of million to do it.'

'That's not . . .' He paused. 'It can't be.'

His mind was going at a thousand miles per hour now, a cascade of questions, a deluge of guilt and fear and horror.

I moved in for the kill.

'Kyle, listen to me very carefully.' I stopped, waiting for him to lift his head, to look at me. It took an age. I tried not to hurry him, to push him, because this moment was pivotal – but the whole time I was counting down.

Thirty seconds left.

'If you don't want to spend the rest of your mum's life talking to her from prison, then you need to tell me where Tori and Clara are.'

He shook his head.

'You do, Kyle. You need to tell me where they are, so I can tell my friend over there, and he can make sure no one has to die tonight.' I held up my phone – Healy's message thread open – and stepped even closer. 'I know what the Zinters did to Tori's mum and Clara's sister. I get it. I know what Anthony Yanis did.'

He looked at me blankly.

He doesn't know who Yanis is.

I logged it and moved on: 'I know exactly the type of men the Zinters are, Kyle, because I've spent my life hunting people just like them. But if they're dead, we don't find out the truth about what they've done. If they're dead, no one wins.'

'That's not what they're going to –'

'Whatever Tori and Clara have told you isn't the whole truth. You shouldn't be a part of this. This isn't your fight.'

'It is.'

'It isn't. Where are they?'

I glanced at my watch.

Five seconds.

'Kyle, where are they?'

Four. Three. Two.

I looked out at the floor, at the faces around me, at Healy.

One.

Time was up.

Except I didn't feel any different.

I glanced at Kyle again – and this time he was just staring at me, his eyes wet, his skin pale.

'I lied,' he said.

My heart rate was slowing, not increasing.

I didn't feel sick, didn't feel woozy.

'You lied about drugging me?'

He nodded.

'Why?'

His entire body was perfectly still, as if he was in shock.

'Kyle,' I said. 'Why did you lie to me?'

He held up his watch. 'They told me to.'

'But why?'

'Because they needed me to delay you.'

54

It had all been a sleight of hand. The security monitor, Kyle's reappearance, the fake drug – it was all to force my attention away from them, from the fact that they'd been in the room and had moved in on the Zinters.

And now the brothers were gone.

I reached forward and grabbed Kyle's arm.

'What are you doing?' he said.

'You're coming with me.' I yanked him out from behind the crates and dragged him forward. He tried to shake me off, but then I pulled him in close, before any of the other guests could notice. 'Listen to me.'

'I'm not listening to –'

'*Listen* to me. Tori and Clara, they've been planning this for a long time. You might *think* you're as much a part of this as they are, you might have got into this because you love Clara, and you think she loves you too. Maybe she does, but they haven't told you the whole truth.'

'They have.'

'They *haven't*. You didn't even know who Anthony Yanis was.'

'What?'

'Did you? You've never heard of him.'

'So? So what?'

'What do you think it is you're doing here?'

'I don't have to –'

'Why are you involved in this?'

He stared at me. 'To help them get answers.'

'Who, Tori and Clara?'

'You don't understand what –'

'This isn't some noble search for answers, Kyle, it's revenge. Pure and simple. They haven't told you about Yanis, I'm guessing they haven't told you the plan is to kill the Zinters, which means there's going to be other stuff they haven't told you about as well. You think you're here – what? – helping Clara? Helping the girl you fell in love with? Is that it? What did you think was going to happen once Tori and Clara got the brothers?'

He was rattled, panicked.

'*Kyle.*'

'I can't tell you . . . I just . . . This is . . .' He faded out.

'A year ago, Tori butchered Anthony Yanis in the penthouse upstairs.'

'*What?*'

'And I can guarantee that Clara knew about it. She may even have helped plan it, I don't know. What I can tell you for certain is that Tori stabbed Anthony Yanis twenty-seven times and wrote a message on the wall in his blood.'

His expression fell away.

'You're not the same as them, Kyle. You're just a kid from the sticks who misses his home. You're in way too deep here. I know it, you know it. And if you think for a single second that they're coming back for you if you get caught, think again.'

'I'm not going to get caugh–'

'*Enough.* Maybe you got into this because you wanted to help Clara, because she told you about the men who murdered her sister – but you need to forget about that now. You're not good at this. You're not cold-blooded enough. You *are* going to get caught, and I'll tell you what Tori and Clara will do when that happens. They will slip on some other identity and they will disappear – and it'll be you who's doing the time, watching your mum die while you eat prison food.'

His face drained to the colour of ash.

'So, again,' I said, 'what is it you think you're involved in here?'

He shook his head.

'They're going to kill the Zinter brothers tonight, Kyle. Is that what you signed up for? *Is* it? Talk to me.'

He shook his head a second time.

Frustrated, I dragged him forward, leading us back up to where Healy was. Even as he saw Kyle – even as he recognized the boy whose photos I'd shown him over the last couple of days – it took him a second to fully grasp who I was with.

'What the hell . . . ?' he muttered, looking between us.

'Where are the Zinters?' I said to Kyle.

He seemed so young again, so completely out of his depth.

'Where are the *Zinters*, Kyle?'

'One of the security team came to get them.'

Next to me, I saw Healy flinch.

'Healy?'

'Someone from security was talking to Asha,' he said.

'When?'

'Like, ten minutes ago.'

'Why didn't you *text* me?'

'It just, uh . . . Craw. I was talking to Craw.'

It was too late to worry about it now, so I pushed Kyle again: 'Why did someone from the security team come to get Asha?'

'They took a call,' Kyle said. 'It was about Asha's daughter.'

'What about her?'

I could see Healy edging closer, his eyes glued to Kyle.

'They've been told she's been rushed into hospital back home in LA.'

I studied Kyle. 'But – what? – that's a lie?'

'Yes.'

I quickly put two and two together. 'Was the caller Clara?'

'Yes.'

And this time she hadn't needed to put on an accent. Her actual accent was the perfect cover for a call purporting to be from the States.

'And then?'

'Clara pretended there had been an attempted kidnapping, that Asha's daughter had managed to get away but was badly injured.' And I saw the rest before Kyle even got a chance to confirm it: Kerrill's new policy – and his beefing up of the brothers' protection at the Skyline – meant security would circle the wagons instantly in order to guard Caleb and Asha from harm. They'd need to establish whether the attempted kidnapping was a random event or part of some coordinated takedown of the Zinters – and that meant moving the brothers somewhere safe.

Or somewhere that was supposed to be safe.

'Are the brothers in the Bunker now?'

A hint of surprise in Kyle's face.

'Is that where they are, Kyle?'

'Yes.'

'How are Tori and Clara going to get to the brothers in the Bunker if Caleb and Asha are holed up in there with a security team?'

'There won't *be* a security team down there.'

'Why not?'

'Look around you. The security teams are still here.'

I glanced out at the room. He was right. Security staff were dotted throughout, scanning the party, apparently unconcerned that the Zinters had left. Although now I could see a couple of them getting twitchy. One was talking into an earpiece.

'You need to tell me what the hell's going on, Kyle.'

'The member of security that was talking to Asha, the one that *he* saw' – Kyle gestured to Healy – 'she was the one who's been assigned to shadow the brothers while they're in London. She's also the only one that even knows there *was* a call.'

She.

'Wait, are you talking about *Tori*?'

'Yes.'

'*Tori's* on the Zinters' security team?'

'Yes. Everyone thinks that she's an ex-soldier called Lucy Stenson. The casino hired her three months ago. That's why, when she told the other staff here that she was taking the brothers out to deal with a private matter, they trusted her.'

'And now Tori has the Zinters in the Bunker.'

'Yes.'

'And they genuinely have no idea who she is?'

'No,' Kyle said, shaking his head. 'But they're about to find out.'

Irvine, California

There's a Starbucks in a building adjacent to the Department for Criminology, Law and Society, but Darnell tells Pete Tomer he'd prefer to talk somewhere quieter.

They walk out to Tomer's Bronco – Darnell's battered GMC parked further down – and then Tomer follows Darnell down Route 73 towards Laguna Hills. As he drives, he thinks of Wilma Steski again, of that morning in the mountains almost thirty years ago. He thinks of the hunt for the killer and the constant dead ends he and Darnell hit, until Tomer left the Sheriff's Department to take the job at Glendale PD. Now he feels guilty that he didn't even bother picking up the phone to Darnell to check in. Tomer would think of Wilma often, and especially Wilma's parents – their grief, their unanswered questions – in the time after he left. He would think of how their only child had been taken from them. But that was all it ever was.

Just passing thoughts.

I let her down.

They wind their way to the Pacific Ridge trailhead in Crystal Cove State Park. It's a beautiful spot, a ruffle of blue-grey chaparral hills to the north, more to the south, the Pacific beyond that, all of it lit by the warm sunlight of mid-May.

A brightly painted RV is parked up in a space just along from where Darnell pulls in, a sign outside saying JAMIE'S JAVA. 'I dated a woman in Newport Beach for a while,' Darnell explains. 'She was nuts, but she introduced me to this place.'

There are some picnic tables in the shade on the other side of the street, so Darnell asks Tomer how he takes his coffee and tells him to grab a seat. Tomer sits, watches Darnell queuing, still trying to work out what's going on, and then Darnell brings their coffees over.

He perches himself at the picnic table and the bench creaks under his weight. 'Thank you for coming.' He stares at Tomer, as if he's trying to articulate his thoughts. 'You were one of the best people I ever worked with, Pete. You saw cases the same way I did. I think I understood you. You definitely understood me.'

Tomer doesn't know what to say.

'I hope I'm not speaking out of turn,' he continues, 'but one of the things I felt we shared was . . . I don't know. It was, like, we couldn't let things go. I mean, I worked a ton of cases in my time, and I can still remember a whole bunch about all of them – and even the ones I don't remember as well, I can remember a little.'

'I think you have too high an opinion of me.'

Darnell frowns.

'Wilma Steski . . .' Tomer stops. 'I should have done more.'

'After you left, she wasn't your fight.'

'A case like that – it's everyone's fight.'

Darnell just nods. 'I found out I had cancer smack-dab in the middle of Covid. Everything was locked down, so I was having to go into hospital on my own. Sometimes my kids would drop me off and wait out in the parking lot and we'd video-call each other – but they had jobs, school, so they couldn't be there all the time. Without them, I'd read, or listen to music, or watch a movie on my iPad. But then I was down in the basement at home one day, trying to find something, and – out of the blue – I stumbled across all the notebooks I had from when I was a detective at the LASD. I'd kept them all. It just felt wrong to get rid of all that history, all those people I tried to get answers for. So, I started taking the notebooks into the hospital with me, and reading through them while I was getting chemo. I think a part of me just wanted to recapture some of those moments – the buzz I used to get when I broke a case – because the treatment was relentless, and I felt like shit the whole time, and if I let it, the cancer would infect every single thought I had.'

Tomer waits, a breeze rolling in off the hills, stirring the trees.

'Even once the chemo was done, the whole world was still locked down. And I couldn't go anywhere, anyway, because my immune system was shot. So I stayed at home and picked up Wilma's case again.'

'Why hers?'

'It was the only one I ever failed to solve.' The pain shimmers. 'And when I started digging down into it, spending whole days on the internet, making calls to cops I'd known – getting them to pull strings for me, getting them to send me files and evidence – I began to realize something. The case had changed.'

'What do you mean?'

'I mean, back in 1993, we thought Wilma was just a one-off murder. But she wasn't. I connected her to the killing of three college friends in 2008, and then to the death of a British woman in Las Vegas in 2019.'

'What?'

'Wilma was the start – but she wasn't the end.'

Tomer has to take a second to fully understand what he's being told. 'Wait, you think this is the work of a *serial killer?*'

'I see them more as hunters.'

'"Them?"' Tomer frowns. 'There's more than one?'

'I think there's three of them.'

'Holy shit, Darnell. Have you told anyone?'

He shakes his head. 'No.'

'Why not?'

'Have you talked to any cops lately? Since lockdown, all they have is backlog. They're understaffed, overstretched and there's no money to reopen cold cases anyway. Plus, every cop I know has clearance targets they're never going to reach, so which detective out there do you think will be happy adding five new bodies to their slate, one of which is nearly thirty years old? No, I haven't taken this to the cops. After doing all this work on joining the dots, I knew if I took it to the LAPD, or the LASD, or San Bernardino County, or Las Vegas Metro – *any* of them – it would get dumped in a filing cabinet and forgotten about, or they wouldn't take a look in the first place.'

'They would if we're talking about a serial –'

'It would get forgotten, Pete. Believe me. And even if some cop somewhere thought there was something in what I'd found, it's a cross-jurisdictional nightmare – different forces, different counties, different states, across three *decades*. These cases, they're basically the most unappealing bowl of shit a cop could wish for.'

'Give it to me, then,' Tomer says. 'I'll work it.'

'It's been worked, Pete. It's already been worked.'

Tomer drops his head, trying to get level with Darnell's eye-line. 'What do you mean, "it's already been worked"? Are you saying you *did* pass it on to someone?'

Darnell looks up at him.

And then, finally, he nods.

He takes Tomer back eight months, to the September before.

Darnell's in a coffee shop in Studio City. It's on Ventura Boulevard, so it's always noisy, especially at the tables and chairs out front.

He orders a black coffee and checks the time.

He's ten minutes early.

Darnell looks around him.

California dropped all its restrictions two months ago, but there are a few people at tables nearby still wearing masks, and when a couple arrive after him and see the only vacant table is very close to where Darnell is sitting, they leave. Darnell isn't offended. No one knows other people's lives. Earlier in the year, he would have been the same, because although he'd finished his chemo, his doctors told him it could take up to nine months for his immune system to fully recover, and he wouldn't have risked being close to anyone who might put him back in hospital.

But that was before.

This is now.

As of four weeks ago, there's no longer any point in worrying about his lack of immunity, or whether catching Covid might make him seriously ill, or even finish him off entirely. Because four weeks ago he went to the clinic for his six-monthly check-up and, an hour later, he returned to his car a dead man.

The cancer was back.

And this time it's not going away.

He gets out his phone, goes to his calendar and swipes his way into next year, into May 2022 – the month he will decide to drive out to Irvine to meet Pete Tomer at the university – into June, and then to July. He's marked up July 3.

Maybe he'll see it, or maybe he won't.

But the oncologist said he had nine months.

July 3 is when his nine months are up.

As he stares at the date, as he feels the familiar twist of fear coiling in the pit of his stomach, he spots movement in the coffee shop, out of the corner of his eye.

He looks up.

He sees them before they see him.

He takes them in for the first time, assessing them, and then one makes eye contact with him, raises her hand – a gesture he returns – and comes across to the table, just as the waitress brings out Darnell's coffee.

They sit, order coffees for themselves.

Once the waitress has left again, Darnell holds out a hand to the youngest of the two women and says, 'It's nice to finally meet you.'

Miriam Jones smiles. 'You too.'

Darnell glances at the other woman.

'And you must be Tori,' he says.

55

We headed down to the elevators.

'What happened that day at the quarry?' I said to Kyle quietly, not wanting to be overheard.

'I don't want to talk about it.'

'You're not going to have a choice before long. You either talk to me or you talk to the police.'

The elevator doors pinged open.

We moved inside and, as soon as the doors closed again, I caught Kyle looking at Healy, as if he'd only just realized he was coming with us.

I introduced them and hit the button for the bottom floor.

'So when did Clara tell you who she was and what she and Tori were planning?'

'I don't want to talk about it,' he said again.

I thought of how Kyle had blanked on me when I'd mentioned Anthony Yanis. 'They've been lying to you, Kyle.'

He flashed me a look that tried to tell me he knew everything; that the two women had shared every single part of their plan, their history, their lives.

But it was all artifice.

They hadn't.

He was starting to realize that now.

Whatever had been going on between Kyle and Clara prior to them vanishing, it had been real. Or, at least, it had been real on Kyle's side. The question was whether it had been as real for Clara – and if it wasn't, why she and Tori had let him in.

'What did you think you were getting involved in?'

Again, no response.

'If you don't talk to me, I can't help you.'

'I don't *want* your fucking help!' he spat.

I felt a fizz of frustration, but there was only so much I could do right now. If I was going to get him to talk, I needed to get him somewhere less stressful.

The doors opened into the main foyer.

'Let's go,' I said, tugging on Kyle's arm.

'Do you even know your way around the basement?'

'No. Do you?'

He shook his head. 'No.'

'Then we need another way in,' I said, and headed to the main doors.

There was a storm outside. Rain lashed down as we made our way around the front of the Skyline, following a covered, neon-drenched walkway towards the side of the property. It went on and on, the building unfurling in the darkness endlessly.

'Where the hell are we going?' I heard one of them shout from behind me, but it was hard to be sure whether it was Kyle or Healy because the rain was so loud.

I got to the end and looked along the eastern flank of the building. More light. More entrances. Hundreds of windows. Music being piped out of speakers hidden in flowerbeds. And then a sign, 100 feet down, low lit and with no writing on it – just an arrow pointing left, in towards the Skyline.

'I need to know something before we go any further,' I said to Kyle, having to raise my voice to be heard above the storm. 'What happened to Marc?'

He shook his head. 'I'm not talking about this.'

'Is he dead?'

He shook his head again.

But, this time, I glimpsed the truth.

He couldn't hide it.

I could see the hurt, the pain. Marc was gone and his death had been a residual trauma that had waged war in Kyle's conscience ever since.

'What happened at the quarry, Kyle?'

He tried to make his face a blank.

'How did he end up dead?'

He blinked, then again, his eyes slowly filling with tears. Looking away, he furtively wiped them and dragged a breath in. It was all an attempt to hide just how much Marc had mattered to him; to pretend that all that he cared about was completing whatever it was the women had made him believe he was a part of.

But Kyle wasn't a zealot.

He wasn't bonded to this revenge mission by the blood that had been spilled at that debris basin in LA, and eleven years later, out in the Nevada desert.

He was just a kid.

He was a kid that had loved Marc.

'Did Tori kill him?'

A flicker.

'Where's his body, Kyle?'

'I don't want to –'

'It's too late. There's no turning back. Where's his body?'

'They didn't, uh . . .' He stopped himself.

'They didn't tell you?'

It was something else they'd kept back from him.

'Why did it have to happen the way it did at the quarry?' I asked. 'Why did you and Clara have to disappear like that?'

'You don't understand!' he shouted, the words instantly lost in the rain.

I thought about Sarah, about what the news was going to do to her. She was already teetering, barely coping with the shadow of her illness, the demands of a two-year-old and the looming financial disaster that was her house.

And now her husband was dead.

'Why would you get involved in something like this?'

'You don't understand.'

'*Help* me understand.'

'No. *No.*'

'What did the women say they needed you for? There must have been a reason they let you in?'

Silence.

I looked along the edge of the building again, to the arrow pointing left, and then checked my watch. We'd been gone from the party for over fifteen minutes. If Kerrill and the rest of his security team weren't already getting twitchy about Caleb and Asha's continued absence from the party – or the absence of the woman who'd been assigned to look after them – they were about to.

Moving off, I heard wet footsteps slapping behind me, as Kyle and then Healy fell into place. We hurried down to where the sign was.

Once I got there, I stopped.

It was pointing to a sloped concrete ramp that angled off the road and took vehicles down to a floor-to-ceiling metal gate built under street level.

'What are you doing?' Kyle asked me.

I took out the keycard that Craw had left for Healy and me when we'd first got to the meeting room.

There was a card reader on the wall next to the metal gate.

Beyond that was a private car park.

It was the one that connected to the Bunker.

56

The gate rattled up on its runners, its noise disguised by the rain.

The car park was no longer empty.

There was a white van parked in it.

It was next to the spot where Craw had been standing earlier. Its front faced us, the hazards blinking, their muted orange light illuminating the concrete walls. There was no one inside and, beyond the windscreen, we could see all the way through to where the back doors were open.

I glanced at Kyle. 'Is this theirs?'

He nodded.

So Tori and Clara were still here.

My gaze switched to the stairs at the back on the right that descended into the corridor with the Bunker in it – and then looked over my shoulder at Kyle.

'Are you okay?' I said to him.

He'd reached out for the wall next to him, had started to look pale even in the subdued light of the down ramp.

Healy noticed too: 'What's the matter, kid?'

'Nothing.'

Was this some game? Another attempt to trick us?

I glanced at the van, at the stairs.

What game would it be?

'Stay here,' I said to Kyle.

He frowned. 'What?'

'I don't want you coming with us.'

'*Why?*'

'Because I don't trust you, Kyle.'

He looked unsteady, as if everything he'd done and been a part of was suddenly washing over him. What I'd told him about Sarah – about her illness – seemed to have broken the spell.

Seemed to.

But I couldn't be absolutely sure.

Healy and I went around the van and looked into the back. There was rope inside and a black hood.

There was also a backpack.

'Is that the one that was in the mailbox?' Healy asked.

'Yeah.' I unzipped it. It was still full of the cash that Tori Wolton had stolen from Anthony Yanis.

'Raker.'

I looked up, following Healy's gaze, through the van, out of the windscreen, to where Kyle was standing. Kyle's head had dropped, his chin almost pressed to his chest, and he was taking small half-steps back, like he was cowering.

Or retreating.

I spun around in the other direction.

At the top of the steps down to the Bunker was Caleb Zinter.

His nose was busted, blood spattered down the white shirt he was wearing and all over his jacket. His hands had been tied behind him and he had a square of silver duct tape over his mouth. He looked between me and Healy and then started pleading with us for help, his eyes widening, his breath coming faster, a wet, pulpy mix of sounds.

That was when I saw who was on the stairwell behind him.

'No one needs to get hurt,' a voice said.

It was female.

A Mancunian accent.

'We're just going to take what we need and go.'

And then, very slowly, Tori came into the light.

57

She was dressed like a member of security but had discarded the jacket somewhere and pulled on a body warmer and a beanie. And without make-up, with the small black beanie covering most of her hair – which she'd now dyed auburn – she'd once again started to look like the Whaler.

Many names. Many identities.

She glanced to her left, out across the parking garage to where Kyle was, and I saw Kyle retreat again, almost into the rain.

Then her attention switched back to me.

Moving in behind Caleb, she put her fingers to his neck – blood on her hands – and edged him forward.

He stiffened as she did.

She had a gun.

The end of the barrel was pressed into the base of his spine, and as she shifted him out from the staircase, she moved in an arc around us, so he was always in front of her. She stopped ten feet away, Caleb still obscuring her, only Healy and me between her, her hostage and the back of the van.

Out of the corner of my eye: more movement.

Clara.

She emerged at the top of the steps in a black knee-length dress, her hair in a ponytail. She had a thin jacket on, an invite poking out of it.

It was the one I'd seen inside the mailbox in Angel.

As Clara took another step, I saw she was holding a roll of silver duct tape.

'Where's Asha?' I said to them, glancing at the blood on Tori's hands. Caleb reacted, short, sharp jets of air rushing out of his nose.

Tori silenced him instantly, pressing the gun into his back, so his stomach distended, his whole body curving.

She put her mouth to his ear. 'Stop.'

He went quiet.

'Get out of our way,' she said to me.

I held up a hand. 'I know what the Zinters did. I know what they did to your mother, to Clar—' I stopped myself. 'To Miriam's sister. But if you murder both the brothers, the world doesn't get to hear what —'

'You don't know what you're talking about.'

'What about the other families?' I said. I gestured to Clara. She was hard to see, her clothes merging with the dark. 'It wasn't just Florida in that debris basin —'

'There are no families left. Everyone's gone. The only people who can get any kind of justice for the victims are standing right here.'

Caleb started to make a series of desperate sounds.

'Shut up,' she hissed.

'Tori,' I said. 'You aren't —'

'Don't call me Tori, don't call me anything. We're not friends.' She stared at me. 'I know who you are. I know what you do. You seem like a good man, and there's not many of those around. But if you don't get out of the way, I'll put a bullet in you. And I think you know I mean it.'

I stabbed a man twenty-seven times.

I splashed his blood all over the walls.

I'm not bluffing.

'Why is Kyle here?' I asked her.

She ignored me, shunted Caleb forward.

'Why disappear at the quarry like that?'

Edging closer to us, to the van, only the top of her head and her eyes visible above his shoulder, she glanced at me.

'Tori, just help me understand what's going on here.'

'Get the hell out of my way.'

She pointed the gun towards us.

We moved away from the doors, around to the side of the van, and then she told us to head into the open space between the vehicle and the stairs.

I turned to Clara. 'Why choose the lake to disappear from?'

She didn't even look at me, just kept her gaze fixed on Tori.

'You could have done it anywhere. You and Kyle could have just walked out the front door and vanished, and Marc would still be alive. At the lake, you –'

'*Shut the fuck up!*' Tori screamed.

I turned back to her, her voice still echoing off the walls of the car park.

'If you say one more word,' she said, aiming the gun at me from the side of Caleb's head, 'I swear to you, I will . . .'

But then she stopped.

Something else had caught her attention. She was staring beyond me and Healy, her eyes trained on the stairs behind us, leading down to the Bunker.

I turned again in Clara's direction.

She appeared to be levitating in the darkness, her arms trapped at her side, the toe ends of her black heels barely touching the polished concrete of the floor.

Around her neck was an arm.

Kerrill.

'Drop the gun,' he said to Tori, 'or I break her neck.'

58

Kerrill shifted forward, Clara against him.

He was so strong, so big, she could barely move, both her hands on his arm, trying to loosen the grip he had on her neck. She couldn't even feel the floor now, so it was like being at the end of a noose. Kerrill – his eyes on Tori – increased the pressure, showing instantly how easy it would be for him to crush Clara's larynx.

'Drop the gun,' he said.

Tori didn't move.

'Did you hear me? I said drop the –'

She put a hand to Caleb's shoulder and pushed down, forcing him on to his knees in front of her. 'How about this instead?' she said calmly. 'You let her go and I don't put a bullet in the back of your boss's head.'

She placed the gun against Caleb's skull.

'I mean, don't get me wrong, there would be a certain poetic irony in killing him like this. After all' – she leaned forward, to Caleb's ear, and hissed the rest – 'this is exactly what you did to my mum, you piece of shit.' She righted herself, looked at Kerrill. 'But I've got other plans for Caleb – and they don't involve you screwing everything up. So put her down, big boy.'

'I'm not going to do that.'

'Put her down.'

He watched her, his eyes narrowing. 'Who are you *really*?'

He hadn't quite put it together yet. All he was focused on right now was that, whatever this woman had claimed to be in order to get herself a job on the Zinters' security team, it was a lie. But, as he continued to stare at her, I saw something else: a tiny spark of recognition that was about to become a flame. He would have seen the image of the Whaler. It was a face he knew intimately. He just couldn't yet see past the bigger lie to the truth buried beneath: that the Whaler was a woman.

'Put her down,' Tori said again.

'Listen to me,' Kerrill responded. 'There are no good choices for you here. All you've got are . . .' He trailed off.

He'd finally got there.

Tori cocked the gun. 'Put her down.'

He was still staring at her in disbelief.

'Put her down.'

'You devious little bitch,' he mumbled.

'Put her *down.*'

It took Kerrill a moment to find his equilibrium, and then his face hardened. 'I've got fifteen men out looking for Caleb and Asha. In five minutes, it's going to be you against an army. It's over.'

For the first time Tori seemed to doubt herself. *An army.* The gun wobbled slightly in her hand.

Kerrill picked up on it.

'Drop it,' he said.

She tore her eyes away from Clara, from Kerrill, then looked towards the open metal gate. At first I thought she was searching for Kyle in the shadows there.

But she wasn't.

As the rain came down outside – a raucous, relentless downpour – she was starting to realize that there was no way to get Clara back without giving Caleb to Kerrill. Her plans had gone south.

She didn't have a way out.

Footsteps slapped against the stairs and a second security guard appeared from behind Kerrill. 'Asha's in the Bunker,' the

325

guard said, his voice panicked. But then he stopped, saw what else was going on, and his face blanched.

'Stay back,' Kerrill responded, without looking.

Tori was still watching the exit, listening to the rain, eyes focused on the flow of water as it cascaded down the ramp and into a drain at the bottom.

'Hey!' Kerrill said. 'Are you listening to me?'

Tori still didn't turn back to face him.

'Are you *listening* to me?' Kerrill shouted.

And as she finally dragged her attention back to us, her eyes first going to me and then to Kerrill, I saw everything I needed to know.

She'd been playing out all the angles in her head.

And now she'd made a decision.

It was like a charge in the air.

Instinctively, I took a half-step back, tugging at Healy and inching him away with me. Kerrill noticed it too – tensing, straightening, filling out – seeming to want to make himself more solid, even bigger, as if he was trying to intimidate her.

A look passed between Tori and Clara.

A tiny movement of the eyes.

And then Clara did the opposite to Kerrill – she shrank, almost as if she was bracing herself – and in that split second, I could see everything.

The depth of their friendship.

The strength of their bond.

And how far they would go to save it.

Tori pulled the trigger.

2022

Irvine, California

Pete Tomer listens as Darnell explains who the two women were who turned up to the coffee shop on Ventura Boulevard the September before.

'So Miriam's the sister of Florida Jones?'

'Yes,' Darnell says.

'And Tori is the daughter of Catalina Robbins?'

'Yes.'

'How the hell did you work it all out?'

'Because once I found the similarities in the three cases, I started trying to get in touch with the families. Except none of them are around any more.'

'No one?'

'Miriam and Tori – they're basically the only people left with any familial connection to these murders.'

'But doesn't Tori Robbins live in England?'

'Yes.'

'So she flew out to LA just to meet you in that café?'

'Yes.'

Tomer studies Darnell, sensing that he's not quite telling him everything, but he decides to stay quiet and just watch.

'Tori's mom was found out in the desert in February 2020,' Darnell says, 'only a few weeks before the world locked down. She's not all that different from me.'

'Who, Tori?'

'Yes.' Darnell looks up. 'We both spent lockdown thinking

about death. I was thinking about mine, and – when I wasn't doing that – I was thinking about these murders. She was thinking about her mom. She was thinking about how the person she loved most in the world had been taken from her, and how her mom's body had lain out in that desert for four months, unclaimed. Any forensic evidence that might have been there – anything this cop, Mailor, could have used – was either tainted or completely destroyed. Her mom was five thousand miles away, on the other side of the world, and Tori couldn't do a damn thing about it. And the longer it went on, the longer she went without answers or hope, the more it did something else to her. It made her really fucking angry.'

Tomer angles his head, trying to get a read on Darnell.

'I wanted her and Miriam to meet,' Darnell says, 'because they were the only two people left who cared about these murders being solved. So I introduced them over Zoom and the two of them . . . they just clicked. Shared trauma forges an intense bond, I suppose, but it was more than that. They were like these kindred spirits. And so as soon as they turned up at that coffee shop, I could see how much I'd missed.'

'Missed?'

'I'd assumed they'd only talked that once, when I'd first introduced them on Zoom. But they hadn't. From the second I saw them in the flesh, it was obvious they were completely comfortable with each other, that they knew exactly what the other one was thinking. They must have talked for hours without me, because they'd already formed this kind of . . .' He pauses. 'Sisterhood.'

There's something hidden in the word.

Something big.

Darnell is looking down at the table as he says, 'I thought I was doing something good, Pete. I thought, "At least before I go, I'll finally be able to show these girls the truth about what happened to the people they loved." I never thought what I was doing – the evidence I'd gathered – might change them.'

'What do you mean, "change them"?'

'I mean, Tori was an army reservist, so she was trained, she was disciplined, and she was also crazy friggin' smart – she's got a Master's in Psychology, although you didn't need to know that to know she was clever. You could just see it in her eyes. But, at the end of the day, these girls, they were still just kids. Early to mid-twenties, not much in the way of life experience. Miriam had been working on the front desk in a Marriott since she was eighteen. She wasn't in the game. She wasn't some hardcore criminal. Neither of them was. I didn't think they were capable of . . .' He stops, raises his eyes to Tomer's, and they're so full of pain and remorse. 'I thought, at worst, they'd take the information I gave them – the casework I'd done, the answers I'd found – and get some closure from it. At best, after I was gone, they might start hassling some of these police departments, and maybe a way down the line, they might even find a cop somewhere who had the time to look into it all.'

'So you gave them your casework?'

'Yes. This big zip file. I showed them all the things the victims shared – the way their hands were tied, the way they'd been hunted, the round that killed them, and how all of them, even Wilma, had some sort of connection to Vegas. Catalina was on a work trip there. Casey, Florida and Ryan were in the city for the weekend. Wilma had been in Vegas with some friends just before her death. These men, whether they dumped the body in the desert, like they did with Catalina, or they drove them back to LA and dumped them there, like they did with the three friends, or they just came to LA to do the deed, like with Wilma – it was all obfuscation. It was to throw investigators off the scent. Vegas was the real hunting ground.'

329

'And you know who the men are?'

'Yes. I think I've ID'd all three of them.'

'How?'

'I found some surveillance video buried in a historical archive in Las Vegas. It's of Florida, Ryan and Casey getting into a car with the three men. It's taken from a street camera outside the Afrique.'

'But that doesn't mean these men are —'

'That's the last time any of the friends were seen alive. Literally, the last time. Plus, eyewitnesses who saw the three of them in the casino before they vanished gave a physical description of a male who was seen talking to Casey at one of the slot machines. The artist's sketch is an almost exact match for Anthony Yanis. He's one of the men in that car. There's other things too. You remember when we first started working the Wilma Steski murder, we talked to the boys in her class at college?'

'Sure. She went to the California Institute of Technology, right?'

'Right. Well, guess who else was at Caltech when she was?'

Tomer glances at Darnell. 'This Anthony Yanis guy?'

'Bingo. In fact, not just Yanis. The other two guys in that car with him are brothers. Caleb and Asha Zinter. You heard of them?'

'No.'

'The Afrique is theirs.'

'They own it?'

'Yeah. Well, they were at Caltech too. None of them was on the same course as Wilma, but they were in the same year as her.'

'Shit.'

Darnell goes to his cellphone and then turns it around so Tomer can see the screen. It's another still from a surveillance video. 'This is taken outside the Afrique the last time Catalina Robbins was seen alive. She was leaving a Halloween party.'

'So?'

'So, look,' Darnell says and places a finger over a face in the crowd behind Catalina. 'That's Anthony Yanis. The motherfucker's following her.'

Tomer stares at the image, unsure what to even say.

'So, no,' Darnell says, 'I haven't got a slam-dunk piece of evidence that shows an abduction, or them taking these kids out to the woods to hunt them down. But is it just coincidence that Casey, Florida and Ryan never came back to the hotel after getting in that car? Is it coincidence that Yanis is following Catalina the night she disappeared and got dumped in the desert? Is it coincidence that all three of these men were at the same university – in the same *year* – as Wilma Steski?'

Tomer is still staring at the phone, his mind going at a thousand miles per hour. 'Can't you take all of this to one of the original detectives?'

'The guy who worked Casey's, Florida's and Ryan's murders – Sanders – left the force in 2014.'

'What about the cop who looked into Catalina Robbins?'

'Mailor? He had a stroke last year.' Darnell shrugged. 'It's like I keep telling you: the families are all gone, any cops who might have cared are retired or most of the way to the grave – it's just me and these girls.'

Tomer tries to think, tries to clear his head.

But Darnell starts talking again: 'So I gave Tori and Miriam the work. I gave them the names, I gave them pictures and profiles of the men, I gave them the whole case I'd built because I thought one day – maybe some time in the future after I'm gone, maybe when things have calmed down and some cop somewhere has two damn minutes to spare – the girls might get some justice for their families. Or, you know, maybe Tori and Miriam could become champions for these murders – get to know the cases, then take it all to the press; guilt the cops into reopening it that way. But before any of that, primarily, I just wanted them to have some answers. That's all. Just some answers. Some closure.'

'But?'

Darnell does something else on his cellphone and places it on the picnic table so Tomer can read off the screen. It's a newspaper headline.

'I thought,' Darnell starts to say, then flounders. 'I thought, because you and I looked at our cases the same back in the day – because we held on to these victims in the way we did – that you might understand what I was trying to do. I kept thinking, "I need to confess to someone, to tell them what I did" – and every time I told myself that, I thought of you, Pete. All of this, it was just . . .' He stops, and then he repeats himself: 'I was just trying to help. I was just trying to get them some closure.'

Tomer picks up Darnell's cellphone. On-screen is the website for a British newspaper. The article has yesterday's date. He looks at the headline.

BILLIONAIRE BUTCHERED AT LONDON SUPERCASINO

Under that is a photo of the victim.

It's Anthony Yanis.

'This happened yesterday,' Darnell says, gesturing to Yanis, his voice giving way. 'I gave those girls this case because I wanted to go to my maker having helped them get some kind of justice for Wilma, for their families. But now I'm sitting here with you, Pete . . .' He swallowed. 'I'm sitting here because I need to confess something.'

Tomer is still staring at the photo of Yanis.

A caption underneath says he was stabbed twenty-seven times.

'Now I realize I did something much, much worse than help them.'

Finally, Tomer brings his eyes up to Darnell's.

'What I really did was light a fire in both of them.' Darnell can't hold Tomer's gaze. 'What I really did was turn two young women into killers.'

59

The sound of the gunshot ripped through the car park – and then Caleb Zinter's body slumped forward and hit the floor.

For a second, no one moved.

We all just stared – stunned – at what was left of his head. And as time stood still, I thought about what Tori had said, about how she'd still had plans for Caleb – but, whatever those plans had been, she'd destroyed them in order to get her friend back. This was more than a partnership, more even than a friendship.

To the two of them, this was everything.

Blood began running out from under Caleb – and, as it did, everything snapped back into focus.

Tori was advancing on Kerrill.

It took a second longer for everyone else to react – and, by the time we did, Tori was already halfway across the car park, gun up in front of her.

Another look passed between her and Clara.

Clara knew instantly what to do.

She clamped her jaw on to Kerrill's arm, her mouth snapping shut on the skin between the crease of his elbow and the middle of his forearm.

'Fuck!' he yelled, her teeth tearing at his skin.

He sucked in a breath, the shock and the pain obvious – and then the force of his grip lessened just a fraction.

It was all Clara needed.

She dropped slightly in his arms, slipping down towards his stomach – and as she dropped, she ducked her head.

She knew what was coming.

Too late, Kerrill – his top half now exposed – did too.

Tori fired twice.

One went into Kerrill's shoulder and – as Kerrill clutched it desperately, Clara now a heap on the floor – the other went into his throat.

It happened so fast, it was just a blur of movement and blood. Kerrill's body dropped back towards the steps, towards the security guard frozen there.

Tori grabbed Clara by the hand and yanked her forward.

Kerrill's body tumbled down the steps.

I couldn't see him; I only heard his fall.

The other security guard cowered, hands up in front of his face, but – when he saw Tori wasn't going to shoot him – he made a break down the steps.

The door to the basement opened and slammed shut.

'Tori,' I said quietly, gently. 'Tori, you need to –'

'I don't need to do *anything*!' she screamed back. She looked like she was trying to clear her head. 'Are you okay?' she said to Clara.

Clara nodded and got to her feet.

Tori glanced towards Kyle at the exit gate, who was partly obscured by the dark. I tried to interpret the look in her eyes, but it was gone as quickly as it had arrived.

She looked at Clara again, then at Caleb. 'Get his phone.'

Clara hurried over and dropped to her haunches next to the body. As she started digging through Caleb's pockets, I saw Tori wobble, just a fraction.

The shock was hitting her.

'Tori, you can't keep running.'

'I'm not running,' she said. 'Running is what cowards do.'

Clara stood, Caleb's phone in her hand.

She gave it to Tori, who pocketed it without taking her eyes off me. 'I've never run.' She prodded Caleb's prone body, then held up her hand and showed me the blood on it, which must have belonged to Asha. 'They were all running from *me*.' But now her voice was unexpectedly muted.

She seemed almost mournful.

The Zinters and Anthony Yanis were dead, the men who'd cost her and Clara their family, their childhoods, the people they loved. Maybe it hadn't gone down in the way they'd planned, but they'd done it. In a purely technical sense, it was over.

Except it would never really be over.

Perhaps when they'd been deep in it – when the anger and the grief was at its worst and most intense – the women had been so focused on the endgame, they hadn't ever stopped to think about the chaos the two of them had wrought. But, over time, it would land, and it would land hard. The Zinter brothers and Yanis were one thing, perhaps Kerrill as well – but Marc was another. That was going to haunt them, especially Clara. The Fowlers, the loving family unit who'd let her in – whether she'd been playing a game or not – was about to be torn apart again. And the two of them were responsible. They'd done to Sarah what had been done to them.

'Get in the van,' she said to Clara.

Clara did as she was told – the dynamic between the women stark – and as she crossed the parking garage, she spotted Kyle for the first time.

He stepped out of the shadows, the rain jagging behind him.

What lay between them was suddenly so lucid: Clara – *Miriam* – had genuinely cared for Kyle. Maybe she hadn't been honest with him, but I recognized regret when I saw it. She mouthed the words *I'm sorry*, and then got into the passenger side.

'No one else was supposed to get hurt,' Tori said, watching Clara, her voice so hushed I could barely hear her above the storm. Her exhaustion was plain. This had been a long road, a plan that they'd worked on and refined over and over again, until they had it down pat.

And it had still gone wrong.

'I just wanted him to admit what he did.' She glanced at the body of Caleb Zinter, face down on the concrete, his blood like a crimson oil slick. 'That was why I was taking him. I was going to put him on video and get him to confess, and then I'd put it with all the other stuff we've got and send it to the pre–' She stopped herself, realizing the words were spilling out of her involuntarily.

'Send it to the press?' I said, finishing her sentence.

She didn't reply.

The other stuff. It must have been some kind of evidence package: a road map of all the things the men had done, with Caleb's video confession as the cherry on top. And on whatever desk it landed, there wouldn't have been a trace of Tori or Clara in it.

'Once he confessed, you were going to kill him?' I asked. In her face, I saw the answer straight away: *Of course I was going to kill him – just like he killed my mother.* 'So what's the point of sending everything to the press?'

She frowned.

'No one's going to prison for what was done to your mum, Tori. You murdered Yanis. You've murdered both the brothers. Whether the world knows what they did or not, no one will answer for these crimes. You've just made sure of that.'

'What do you think would have happened if they all ended up in prison? They'd have lived out the rest of their days in comfort. Rich people – rich *men* – always land on their feet. Money greases the wheels of everything – and those pricks had more money than God – so why do you think prison would be any different?'

'But they're not –'

337

'Shut up,' she said. 'Just shut up. You don't get it, do you? I want to destroy them. That's why I wanted his confession, why I'm going to send every single piece of evidence I've ever collected over the last two years to the media. I'm going to ruin the Zinter name.' Her eyes dropped to Caleb again. 'And then I was going to kill him. As long as he was breathing, he could still lawyer up, or brief his friends in the media for favourable stories about how he'd been stitched up, or falsely accused. If he's dead, he doesn't have a voice. *I* am the voice. This wasn't supposed to happen – not like this – but I'm still going to tear down their empire, piece by piece.'

I took a step towards her.

'Don't.'

She'd noticed immediately, even though her gaze was still on Caleb.

'I wanted him to confess,' she went on, absolutely still, 'but I wanted him to understand too. I wanted it to be the last thing he *ever* understood. I wanted him to see the damage he'd done to us, to our families, in our *faces* as he talked into that lens. But it was never supposed to be like this . . .' She glanced at the steps, at the dark of the stairwell Kerrill had fallen into; maybe she was thinking of Marc as well. Maybe she was even thinking about Sarah, and Kyle.

'Tori, what happened that day at the quarry?'

Her eyes were still on the stairs.

'Why there? Why do it like you did?'

Nothing again.

'How did you pull it off?'

I wasn't getting through to her.

'Did you remove a photo from the wall in the Bunker?'

This time there was a minor flinch.

'You did, didn't you?'

Healy looked at me, confused. We hadn't had the chance to

338

talk about it, about my theory that it may have been another reason she'd got into the Bunker that night.

To add it to the package of evidence.

'What was the photo of?' I asked.

Behind me, Kyle started coughing.

Tori looked, and then so did I.

'I was never sure if I could trust him,' she said, meaning Kyle, and then she glanced at Clara, who was leaning forward, her hands gripping the dashboard, watching Kyle too. 'But she was smitten. Having him involved made her happier, better, which is why I agreed to bring him in.' Clara couldn't hear us from inside the van. 'Kyle was useful in that respect, and I needed an extra pair of eyes at the party tonight – it was a three-person job – so that worked out well too. But we never told him everything. He was too naive; never fierce enough. He wouldn't have been able to handle the truth. So we told him we were here tonight to get these men's confessions. That was all. He thought we'd just hand them over to the police once we were done and then go home to our lives like nothing had ever happened.'

Kyle started coughing again, more violently this time. He was doubled over, one hand on the wall for support – pale, sallow, struggling.

'I agreed to bring him in because of her – but allowing him off the leash tonight was always going to be a disaster.' She shrugged. 'Earlier on, when I messaged him, telling him to pretend he'd laced your drink, that was just a version of something I'd already done to him.'

I looked at her. 'What?'

'I knew we'd gone as far with him as we could.'

'You've *drugged* him?'

He was struggling to stay upright – coughing, retching.

'I took out an insurance policy,' she said. 'I haven't told Clara.

I mean, I didn't *want* to do it – I genuinely mean it: no one else was supposed to get hurt – but I had to. This was always going to be where he left us. We can't carry the weight of him from here – and I can't have him spilling his guts about the little he knows.'

'What did you give him?'

'I spiked his drink before the party.'

'*Tori*, what sedative did you give him?'

'No, it isn't a sedative,' she said matter-of-factly, all signs of shock gone, the steel, the ruthlessness, back in her face. 'It's poison.'

60

Tori moved to the rear of the van.

'You *poisoned* him?'

She slammed one of the back doors shut.

Kyle was on his haunches, one hand on the ground, one arm across his stomach – moaning, swaying, retching.

'Tori, what did you give him?'

She slammed the other door closed.

'Digoxin,' she said.

I didn't know much about poisons, but I knew that digoxin came from the foxglove plant and that it was slow-acting. The toxic effects sometimes didn't kick in until two hours after ingestion. There was an antidote – but to get that, Kyle needed a hospital.

'I know you think I'm as bad as they are,' she said, and glanced at Caleb's body. 'I'm not. I'm not like them.'

'I need to call an ambulance for Ky–'

'He's on Dartmoor.'

I stopped, took an automatic step closer. 'What?'

'He's on Dartmoor,' she repeated.

'Who is?'

But I knew.

Deep down, I knew, and a hush settled around us.

'You mean Marc?'

They must have buried him where they killed him.

'He's near Fernworthy Reservoir,' she said.

That was in the middle of Dartmoor, maybe five miles from the quarry where all of this had begun for me.

'There's a forest there, on the southern side of the water.' She was speaking so softly, I was struggling to hear her. 'It's got wooden barriers that separate the trees from the road, and about halfway along the reservoir is a white gate. It's the only one. You'll know you've almost reached it when you see the phone box.' She paused. 'That death, what we had to do to him . . .' She was staring into space. 'I never wanted it. He was a good person. He didn't deserve that ending.'

'So, if you didn't have to do it, why *did* you?'

'Things happened at the quarry that weren't supposed to.'

'Like what?'

She dropped the gun to her side.

'Like what, Tori?'

Nothing.

'Didn't you realize Marc was going to be in that boat?'

I thought about how Marc had wanted to stay behind; how he was only there because his stepson had asked him to help them row out. So what did that mean? That the plan for that day – to disappear at the quarry – was something *else* Kyle had been kept out of the loop about? He surely wouldn't have asked for Marc's help otherwise.

When Tori didn't reply a third time, I glanced at Healy. 'Call an ambulance.'

'No,' Tori responded, raising the gun.

'You can't let him die.'

'I can't let him talk.' But her voice was barely a whisper and she was staring at the gun as if she didn't even recognize it now. 'I meant what I told you before,' she said, hovering at the back of the van, her face blinking orange in the glow from the hazard lights. 'I admire what you do. I get that you had to try and stop us. I get that you want answers.'

'Sarah Fowler is grieving like you are.'

'I know.'

'Give me something that I can give *her*.'

'One day I will.'

And then she vanished behind the van.

I moved towards it, towards the passenger side, the engine starting up – and then Clara buzzed the window down.

She'd been passed the gun.

I stopped, watched as both the women looked out at me, their faces showing no pleasure, no enjoyment. There were tears in Clara's eyes.

'Tori –'

She hit the accelerator.

The van whipped past Kyle, on to the ramp.

I followed it, Healy behind me, running to the bottom of the slope and looking up – the rain lashing down, the night illuminated for a second as a fork of lightning spiked across the sky – and, as we got there, the van pulled out on to the road.

That was when I heard the squeal of tyres.

But not from the women's vehicle.

From the vehicle that smashed into the side of it.

61

It seemed to come out of nowhere.

One second Tori was pulling out on to the road, the next, a jet-black Land Rover – *Security* written on its door – careered out of the night and crunched into the side of the van.

The noise was colossal: a screaming tear of metal; the shattering of windows as the women's van tilted; and then the right-hand side left the road entirely and toppled over once and then again, on to its roof. As it did, the Land Rover spun out, swerving on the wet tarmac, and hit a concrete wall, headlights shattering, the bonnet crunching inwards.

Healy said something from behind me – I couldn't hear what, only the horror in his voice – and then I turned to him. He'd already called for an ambulance. 'Just get a load of paramedics here now,' he barked into the phone, and hung up.

'You need to go and search the Bunker,' I told him.

'What?' Healy looked out at the smoking vehicles. '*Now?*'

'We need to make sure we haven't missed anything.'

'What would we have missed?'

'I don't know. Maybe something to do with Asha.'

'*Asha?*' Healy eyed me like I was losing it. 'He's dead, Raker. She had his *blood* all over her hands and just admitted to killing him.'

'So why would Tori have killed him but tried to take Caleb with her?'

'Who gives a shit?' Healy said, and gestured up the ramp, to the car crash, to the sound of a horn – shrieking, constant – punching through the rainstorm now.

'It feels like we've missed something.'

'We haven't missed anything.'

'Just do it, Healy.'

He rolled his eyes and then hurried off to the stairs.

I glanced at Kyle. He was lying on the ground a few feet from me, knees up to his chest, moaning softly. He was semi-conscious now.

Fighting against the wind, I rushed up the ramp, glancing at the Land Rover. I had no choice but to prioritize, so I went to the passenger side of the van. The vehicle was on its roof, the damage along one flank – the passenger side – where the impact had been. The door had concaved, crumpling inwards, way past the end of the dashboard – and Clara was bent around it.

It looked like her hip might be broken, I suspected her ribs were too, and one leg was wedged between the buckled door and the dashboard. She was hanging in place, secured by the seatbelt, her dark hair falling downwards in tangled, vertical lines. There was blood running from her nose and cuts on her face.

I reached in and felt for a pulse.

It was faint, and it was getting fainter.

I got down on my hands and knees and looked all the way through the cab. Tori was unconscious too, hanging in place by her seatbelt, and had a deep gash on her brow, where her face must have whipped forward and hit the wheel.

Otherwise, I couldn't see any other injuries.

Getting down on my front, I shuffled in through the broken window, positioning myself under Clara, and tried to release her seatbelt. It was jammed. I tried again, pushing harder. It still didn't release.

Now there was something else.

I could smell petrol.

I looked through the front – the windscreen punctured, the

display built into the dashboard cracked – and out to the engine. The bonnet had completely concertinaed, the left-hand edge releasing thick clouds of steam into the night. And as the wind stirred, the smell of petrol got stronger.

But not just petrol.

Engine oil.

Brake fluid.

All it would need was a spark from a severed cable and the whole van would go up in flames. I needed to get the women out before it became a fireball.

I jabbed at Clara's belt release again.

Nothing.

Come on.

Again. Again.

This time, it popped.

Clara dropped down on to me. She stirred briefly, moaning softly, and as her body lay against mine, I could feel her ribs moving.

At least two were broken.

I shifted around her, trying to get a better angle on her leg, and moved to the middle of the cab. Next to me, Tori was still hanging down, lights out.

Turning back to Clara, I used my new angle to see all the way along her body, from her shoulder to her legs. One of her legs was outside the van now, her foot in a puddle. The other was bent under her, like she was kneeling.

I stopped, an acrid stench drifting in.

Smoke.

I glanced between the seats – along the bed of the van, to the back doors. Both of them were still closed, but they both had small glass panels in them.

Through the glass, I could see fire.

The petrol tank had caught light.

As quickly as I could, I awkwardly slid my legs around either side of Clara, so her head was on my stomach and my hands were under her arms, and I started pulling.

I needed to release her leg.

And I need to do it now.

When I pulled, everything below her left knee stayed put. I tried again, and again, my back against Tori, her head knocking against mine as I yanked from the centre of the van.

You're going to break her leg, I thought.

But what choice did I have?

In a couple of minutes, it wouldn't matter if her leg was broken or not, because all that would be left of her was ash.

The glass in the back doors imploded inwards.

Flames reached in, licking at the doors and the roof, at the side panels. I tried not to look, tried not to lose focus, just pulled again and again.

Even from here, I could feel the heat.

The stench of smoke.

Come on, Clara.

Gritting my teeth, I hauled her towards me, pouring every single ounce of strength I had into the movement – and I heard something pop. She instantly came loose, her leg – the angle of it abnormal – floundering out of the space between the dashboard and the door.

I'd dislocated her knee.

There had been no reaction from her at all.

I glanced at the fire, getting closer, hotter, and then quickly checked her neck for a pulse. This time, I couldn't feel one. I tried her wrist. Nothing.

Shit.

I dragged myself out of the driver's side, under Tori's hanging body, and then turned, grabbed Clara's arms and pulled her all the way through. Once she was on the tarmac, I scooped her up and staggered across to a grass bank, well clear of the vehicle, where I set her down.

I felt for a pulse again.

Was there one?

My chest was thumping, I was exhausted. I wasn't sure if it was her heart I felt against my fingers or my own.

In the distance: sirens.

Forget it.

Just get Tori out.

I hurried back to the van – directly to the driver's side – flames ripping out of the petrol tank and consuming the back half of the vehicle.

Dropping to my knees, I reached in for Tori.

Except the driver's seat was empty.

Tori had vanished.

62

Where the hell was Tori?

It had taken me less than a minute to haul Clara free of the vehicle and get her to a safe distance.

But less than a minute was all Tori had needed.

I got down on to my knees, checking the cab a second time. She really was gone.

But as I thought about retreating – conscious of the fire, the intensity of the heat, the smoke, the fact that the van could go off like a bomb any minute – my gaze switched to something I'd glimpsed as I'd been pulling Clara out.

The display on the dashboard.

The engine was running, so it was still on – and although the screen itself was cracked along one side, an idea hit me.

I reached in and tapped NAVIGATION, then GPS.

Something spat – a red-hot spark singeing the sleeve of my jacket.

I had thirty seconds.

Less.

I looked at the screen. No address had been put in, no route set. I pressed on PREVIOUS JOURNEYS, feeling the heat on my neck, my hands. I was sweating, rivers of it running down my back, from my hairline.

More sparks.

One hit my face, burning my jaw. I tried to ignore it as the display brought up the last time the GPS had been used.

The answer was eight weeks ago.

It was the *only* time it had been used.

Scrambling around in my pocket, I got out my phone, tapped Camera and quickly took a picture of the postcode on-screen. A second later, I was shuffling out.

The fire ripped into the front of the van, the flames seeming to reach out for me, into the night, into the spaces I'd occupied only seconds before. Peeling myself up off the rain-soaked tarmac, I hurried across the road, to the Land Rover the security team had been driving.

The driver was dead. I knew it straight away. The airbag was inflated but his neck was bent at an unnatural angle, the apex of his spine protruding horribly under the skin. On the passenger seat, the other guy's face was resting on the airbag. I hurried around, yanking open the door, and released him from his belt.

He flopped into my arms.

I felt for a pulse as I dragged him away, and again as I put him on to the grass bank that Clara was lying on. It looked like his leg was broken and his jaw had shattered.

But he was alive.

I wondered if the collision had been deliberate on the part of the Land Rover, an attempt to stop the van getting away.

If it was, the cost had been high.

Going to Clara again, I checked her jacket pockets, looking for Caleb Zinter's phone – and then I remembered that she'd given it to Tori in the car park.

I glanced at the van, a raging beacon in the darkness, people inside the resort – in the casinos, in their hotel rooms – gazing out at it.

The sirens were louder than the storm now, police cars leading the charge. Somewhere beyond them I could see two ambulances.

I got to my feet and sprinted back across to Kyle.

'Kyle?'

Nothing.

'*Kyle?*'

No sound, no movement.

I grabbed his wrist, put my fingers against it.

I could barely feel anything.

'Don't die on me, Kyle.'

And as the police appeared, their lights washing across the concrete and neon, I went to my phone and looked at the photo I'd taken, at the postcode I'd found on the GPS in the van.

OL3 7NN.

OL. *Oldham.*

The town Tori had grown up in.

PART THREE

01:59:03

POLICE: You gave us a statement at the
   scene a few nights back. A lot of
   things were going on there – fires
   to put out – so, when we finish up,
   I want to go over some of that stuff
   again, to make sure we have it down
   right. But, before I do that, I
   want to talk to you about what
   happened tonight, a few hours ago.
   I want to talk about what you found
   at that postcode. You said the house
   there had some sort of basement?
RAKER: Yes.
POLICE: And there was a ladder down to it?
RAKER: Yes.
POLICE: And what happened after you
   found the ladder?
RAKER: We obviously started to climb
   down.
POLICE: 'We' being you and Mr Healy?
RAKER: Correct.
POLICE: Did you have any idea where the
   ladder led?
RAKER: No.

POLICE: What were you feeling as you climbed down?

RAKER: Scared. Terrified, actually.

POLICE: You and Healy knew she was going to be down there?

RAKER: Not for sure.

POLICE: And when you got down there – what then?

RAKER: That was when we found the other bodies.

6
The Postcode

63

Clara didn't survive the trip to the hospital.

Three of her ribs had snapped in the crash, and one had pierced her aorta. She'd been dying from the moment the Land Rover had smashed into her side of the van, crushing the door against her and catastrophically twisting her body.

It was hard to say if Kyle was going to be any luckier.

He made it to hospital, where he was quickly administered Digifab, a digoxin antidote. That should have resulted in a full recovery.

Instead he went into cardiac arrest.

What the doctors had no idea of at the time, because Kyle was completely unaware of it himself, was that he had arrythmia. And as the digoxin had gone to work on him, causing the extreme stomach pain, nausea and dizziness I'd seen him experiencing at the Skyline, it had also gone to work on his irregular heartbeat. The Digifab had barely had a chance to hit his system when his heart stopped pumping blood to the rest of his body. Doctors had to shock him twice to bring him back. So, when Sarah arrived in London in the hours after and got the first look at her missing son in eight months, Kyle was unconscious.

I found all of that out second hand, from the police.

I was taken from the Skyline to a station in Slough by two detectives called Bakhash and Clarkson. At midnight, as they booked me in, they were still trying to work out what was going on, and who was responsible for what. So they read me my rights, made me hand in my property – including my phone and watch – and I called a solicitor. After that they led me to a holding cell and, when I asked about Kyle and Clara, that was when they told me one was dead and one was fighting for his life.

As I waited to be interviewed, I thought of Kyle, Clara, and Marc – and then of Healy, as I had done ever since leaving the casino. I hadn't seen him again after he'd gone to look in the Bunker. Did that mean anything? Or had the police just told him to stay put down there as they'd poured into the Skyline? And when I wasn't thinking about any of that, I was thinking about the postcode I'd found on the GPS. Oldham was where Tori had been brought up, where her mum Catalina had come from – and it was where Tori's brother was from too.

Benjamin.

In everything that had gone on, he'd become almost an afterthought. I'd seen a picture of him with Tori and their grandmother in the *Manchester Evening News*, but that and what was in the article was basically all I knew about him. He'd been fifteen at the time of his mother's death, which would have made him eighteen or nineteen now. Did he have any idea what his sister was up to? Was he the reason she'd recently driven to the Oldham postcode? I didn't know, but Benjamin Robbins was a loose thread and that thread needed pulling.

At one in the morning, my solicitor came to talk to me, going over everything that was likely to come up, and then I was transferred from the cell to an interview suite and the same two cops – Bakhash and Clarkson – returned to fire questions at me and expand on the statement I'd given at the Skyline.

Bakhash was a tall, square-jawed DI in his fifties, his black hair closely cropped, his beard speckled grey. Clarkson was smaller, in her thirties and more serious, her pale face set in monochrome except for the blue of her eyes.

I told them everything – almost.

The only thing I left out was breaking into the flat in Angel.

The rest I handed over, even the postcode, because it would have been dangerous to hold it back. The postcode might have been the difference between capturing Tori and her vanishing into the ether again – and as much as I wanted the answers from Tori, for myself as well as for Sarah, it would have been irresponsible to say nothing.

After a while, I got the clear sense that they weren't going to charge me with anything – and a couple of hours into the interview they seemed to confirm as much. I asked if I could call Sarah, and Bakhash lent me a phone and sat in as I did. It was just after three in the morning but I knew, given everything that was going on, Sarah wouldn't be asleep. I decided to video-call her, so I could actually see her and look her in the face as we talked.

'The doctors say he's serious but stable,' she sobbed to me. I didn't like the fact that it had been the cops who'd given Sarah the news about Kyle and not me, but there was no way I could have prevented it. It made it even harder to listen to her pain, harder still to see it playing out, to hear the confusion in her voice. 'I just . . .' She stopped as Mable wandered into shot, rubbing her eyes. 'You're meant to be asleep in the chair, sweetheart.'

'Hey, Mable,' I said, gently.

Mable didn't respond.

Sarah hauled her daughter up, trying to keep her voice buoyant for a two-year-old who didn't understand any of this. In the background, out of focus, I could see the vague outline of Kyle on a hospital bed. Mable rubbed her eyes again.

She was exhausted.

They both were.

Mable glanced into her mum's phone from the safety of Sarah's shoulder, and then – after examining me for a moment – held out her arm. There was a toy watch on her wrist, a small digital readout embedded in a pink butterfly.

'Wow,' I said. 'What a cool watch.'

'It's a special watch, isn't it, Mabe?' Sarah responded.

Mable nodded.

'What's so special about it?' Sarah asked her.

Mable shrank a little against her mum, shy again.

'Come on, you can tell David.'

Mable shook her head.

'You can speak to people through it, can't you?'

Another nod.

'Who can you speak to?'

Mable eyed me, then said something that sounded like, 'Daddy.'

Something fluttered in Sarah's face.

'Daddy, that's right.' She was blinking faster now. 'And who else?'

'Kyle.'

'Kyle can hear you even though he's asleep, can't he?'

Mable nodded.

'And who else?'

'Clara.'

Mable pronounced it something close to *Cara*, although it came out as a single syllable. Sarah just looked at me, her eyes filling with tears.

'Wow,' I said to Mable. 'That's amazing.'

I looked at Sarah again. She was staring at the top of Mable's head now, neck muscles taut, desperately trying to stop herself from crying.

'I just don't understand anything,' she said softly.

'I know.'

She glanced over her shoulder at Kyle. 'What happened to him?'

'I'm still trying to figure some of that out.'

'I mean, where has he *been* for eight months?'

I wanted to explain it to her – the pull to do that was immense – but trying to help her see clearly while she was at her son's bedside, praying he would wake up, wasn't the time. It wasn't just because she was overwhelmed, it was because my understanding of exactly what had happened to Kyle since his disappearance, and how he, Tori and Clara had come together and operated, was still murky. I had a lot of answers, but not enough, and I didn't want to return to Sarah with anything less than the complete truth.

Clara was dead, so she wasn't going to fill in the blanks for me, and Kyle was in an induced coma.

So there was only thing left to do.

Find Tori Robbins.

64

Just before 5 a.m., Bakhash and Clarkson returned.

Bakhash sat down and spread out some paperwork in front of him.

'I wanted to pick your brains.'

I looked between them, trying to take a guess at where this new direction was about to go, but both of their expressions were blank.

'Not without my solicitor,' I said.

Bakhash nodded, as if he'd been expecting that response. 'I was hoping maybe we could talk before we let you go, just the three of us.' He tilted his head slightly, then pointed to the recording equipment in a unit fixed to the table. 'The tape's not on. This would be totally off the record. Just an exchange of ideas.'

He stared at me, something going on behind his eyes. It could have been a classic cop's tactic – prolonging the silence, making it uncomfortable – but it didn't feel like it.

'We're not charging you with anything, David. You're a smart guy, so you've guessed that already.' He leafed through some of the paperwork. 'I had to tick the official boxes, go through the checklist first. You understand. But there are still some serious gaps in our knowledge. Things that, in the first hours of an investigation like this, should already be crystal clear to us. And right now, I don't have the time or inclination to dance around the PACE Act. We've got an investigation here that's not just cross-jurisdictional but cross-continental, thanks to the crimes you say took place in Las Vegas and LA – and I can't spend my first days navigating this shitshow with one hand tied behind my back.'

Still I waited, trying to figure out where this was heading.

'The Robbins family have never owned a house in that post-code you gave us,' he said. 'Tori never lived there. Catalina never lived there. We've just had confirmation down the line from the GMP. That OL3 7NN postcode – that isn't even the town of Oldham itself, it's an area to the east. It's Saddleworth Moor.'

I didn't know that area of the country well, but I knew Saddleworth Moor was at the north-western tip of the Peak District, and was more elevated and wilder than the rest of the national park. It was also where Ian Brady and Myra Hindley had buried the bodies of at least three children in the early 1960s.

'The cops up there didn't find anything?'

'That area is ninety-nine per cent moorland – and the parts that aren't are farms. The GMP asked around at the farms. No Tori. No nothing.'

I paused, thinking. 'Was the van a rental?'

'You're thinking, if it was a rental, someone else could have put that postcode into the satnav on a previous hire?'

Although, even as Bakhash said it, I realized what a coincidence that would have been – that a random person, shortly before Tori rented the van, happened to have put in an Oldham postcode.

'It was a rental, yeah,' Bakhash said. 'She used the Tori Wolton ID, because I guess she knew – if anyone like us went looking – that identity would go nowhere. However, she *did* buy the green Mondeo you saw tailing you down in Devon – she picked it up for cash last November from a second-hand dealer in Southwark.'

I wondered if Clara had ever driven it.

It would have explained why I'd spotted someone watching me that day. I doubted Tori would have made the same mistake.

'There's something else,' Bakhash said. His attention dropped to the paperwork. 'Something we found out while we were looking into that postcode.'

'What?'

'It's to do with Tori's brother.'

I leaned a little closer. 'What about him?'

Bakhash glanced at Clarkson.

She glanced at him.

'He seems to have vanished too.'

65

Bakhash turned some of the pages around on the table, allowing me to see.

'He has a bank account,' he said, indicating a printed statement. 'That hasn't been touched since the end of August last year, and there's almost nothing in it anyway. Forty-seven pounds. He had a job stacking shelves at Tesco for a while before that, but the boss there told us that Benjamin stopped turning up for work around the same time he last touched his bank account. He had a phone contract with Three, but it was pay as you go – and guess when he last topped that up?'

'August last year.'

'Correct.'

'Is the grandmother still around?'

'No. She died two years ago.'

'So what happened to Catalina Robbins's house?'

'Tori sold it a year and a half ago. She appears to have funnelled the money through the same bank account she originally stuck Anthony Yanis's cash in: the one in the Empress Islands, under the name Morgan Annerson. Unfortunately, unless the money from that house sale *also* turns up in a rucksack inside a mailbox, we've got no real idea where that cash is being spent, or what on, or how much is left.'

'Surely Benjamin would have been a beneficiary in Catalina's will? Why's he only got forty-seven pounds in his bank account when he should have been entitled to half the proceeds from that house sale?'

'We're digging into it, but at the moment it's unclear whether this is Tori somehow, and for whatever reason, stealing her brother's half of the inheritance – or if that Morgan Annerson bank account is actually one they *both* have access to.'

Authorities here, given everything that had come to light, would go the legal route, and begin applying to have the account's assets frozen and revealed. But that would take time – months, maybe longer – and if Tori was smart, and she was, she'd have already moved her money somewhere else entirely.

For now, the bigger issue was tracking down Tori, and then maybe we could work out why no one could find her brother. Perhaps his apparent disappearance had nothing to do with his sister's crimes at the Skyline – but the timing was suspect.

'So, basically,' Bakhash said, 'I don't understand the relevance of that postcode you found, I can't find Tori, and now I can't find her brother.'

'The postcode's a lead,' I said, sounding more certain than I felt.

'And you know that how?'

'I trust my instincts.'

'Well, whether you're right or you're wrong, how do we find Tori?'

'I just told you – that postcode.'

'There's nothing *there*, Raker.'

'It's right next to the town she and her brother are from. It's the area they grew up in. I'm telling you, that postcode was on the satnav for a reason.'

'Did she ever mention Oldham to you?'

'No.'

'Did she ever mention her brother to you?'

'No. But it's not like we stood there and had a relaxed chat last night. She was pointing a gun at my face.'

Clarkson spoke up now: 'What do you think happened at that quarry?'

It was the only thing she'd said for hours. I looked at her, her expression giving nothing away.

'I don't know,' I said. 'I think we're only going to know that part for sure once Kyle wakes up – or if we find Tori.'

'And Kyle?' she asked. 'Why did they involve him?'

'I asked him – and them – that question myself, over and over.'

'And?'

'And they wouldn't tell me.'

'So it sounds like you don't know much.'

'I can speculate if you'd prefer that.'

She just shrugged.

'Tori said moving in on the Zinter brothers was a three-person job. She needed an extra pair of eyes. So there was a practical element to it. But she also said something else . . .' I paused, trying to remember her exact words. ' "I was never sure if I could trust him, but it made her happier, better." She was talking about Kyle and Clara.'

'So she brought him on board for Clara's benefit?'

'Maybe to keep her focused, yeah. I mean, from everything I've seen and heard, Kyle was deeply in love with her, so if she was even close to feeling the same way, she was probably thinking as much – if not more – about Kyle as she was about the Zinters and Yanis.'

'Then it would make even less sense to bring him on board,' Clarkson said. 'All Tori's doing then is distracting Clara from the job at hand.'

'Or focusing her. With Kyle close by, she doesn't have to be pining for him the whole time. She can just concentrate on the work.'

Clarkson stared at me, her expression neutral.

'Look,' I said, 'I don't know for sure. None of us will until Tori's arrested. All I know is that bringing Kyle in meant Tori

369

had an extra pair of eyes at the Skyline last night. From what she said, I think she just saw him as a short-term solution.'

'But she didn't tell Clara that?'

'Tori said she was done with Kyle after tonight. She didn't trust him and she didn't want him – in her words – "spilling his guts". That's why she poisoned him and didn't tell Clara. And if she didn't tell Clara that, there were probably other things she didn't tell her too.' It hit me then just how many layers there were, even in the Tori-Clara-Kyle axis. Just lies upon lies upon lies.

Clarkson told Bakhash she was going to check on something, and – with a last look at me – she exited the interview room.

Bakhash waited for the door to click shut.

'I think we're done here, David.'

'Where's Healy?'

Bakhash stood up. 'We just need to keep him in a little longer.'

But he didn't look at me this time, just gathered up his paperwork and went to the door. And, despite how open he appeared to have been, as much as he'd shared since returning to the room, it was like he couldn't wait to get out now.

It was like he didn't want to talk to me about Healy.

66

In the silence of the interview room, I cast my mind back to the night before.

I'd sent Healy to the Bunker because I'd wanted to know if there was anything we'd missed that could explain why Tori had taken Caleb with her but not Asha.

I hadn't seen him since.

So why would Bakhash keep something back about Healy?

I'd barely even asked myself the question when the door to the room opened again, and Clarkson appeared in the gap. 'Do you need the toilet before you go?'

'No.'

She checked the corridor. 'Good. Then let me show you the way.'

'I said I'm fine.'

'I'll show you the way.' She stared at me, blinking.

She opened the door even further.

Hesitant, I stepped out from behind the table. She backed away, into the corridor, checking both directions again. I passed her, into the empty hallway.

'Follow me,' she said.

She didn't wait for a response. We went all the way to the end, past every door, to where the male and female toilets were. Checking over her shoulder, making sure no one was watching, she pushed open the door for the gents.

It squealed back on its hinges.

Inside was a single cubicle and one basin. Built into the far wall was a high, frosted glass window, with security bars in front of it.

Standing under that was Healy.

Clarkson shoved me in, glanced along the corridor again, and then stepped inside. Pushing the door shut behind her, she slid the bolt across.

I glanced at Healy, relieved to see him. 'You okay?'

'I'm good. You?'

'Fine.' I looked at Clarkson. 'What the hell's going on?'

'We've only got a couple of minutes.'

'Then you'd better –'

'Shut up,' she interrupted. 'Just shut up a minute and let me think.' She took a moment, and then her gaze fell on Healy. 'Raker doesn't know.'

Healy frowned. 'You haven't *told* him?'

I looked between them both. 'Told me what?'

Healy

The Skyline | *Last Night*

Healy looked back, over his shoulder, to the car-park steps.

At the bottom of the stairwell, Kerrill was on his back. His neck was broken from the fall, his head turned the wrong way, his lifeless eyes staring at Healy.

Most of his throat was missing.

Healy dragged his attention away.

In front of him, the Bunker was open.

He passed into the hallway full of photographs, glancing up at the empty space on the wall that Raker had mentioned to Tori. Slowing his pace, he stopped in the doorway to the living area, looking around, trying to get a sense of whether anything was different from when he and Raker had left.

The message was still on the wall. Everything was still covered in dust. The only thing that had changed in the hour since they were here was in the centre of the sunken lounge.

That was where Asha Zinter was.

He was tied to a chair and there was blood on his face and shaved head. His wrists were behind him, duct-taped to the legs of the chair, and his head was all the way forward, his chin against his chest.

There was a second chair next to him.

It was empty now, but it must have been where Caleb had been sitting.

Healy moved in closer, looking at the blood on Asha's scalp,

373

hunting for the source of it. Wherever the cut was, it wasn't on his head.

He tilted Asha, checking around his gut.

No bullet holes.

No knife wounds.

No bruising.

He glanced at the blood on Asha's head for a second time and then began to realize that it had dried in a familiar pattern. A circular shape at the centre. Five lines coming off it.

Is that a handprint?

Healy thought of Tori.

She'd come up to the car park with blood on her hands.

Caleb's nose had been busted, broken, the blood from it staining the white of his shirt. But, apart from that, he'd had no injuries, there was no sense he'd been attacked. Seemingly, all the women had done to Asha was grab hold of his head – but for what reason?

To move him?

Healy glanced at the empty chair.

Or to force him to look at Caleb?

'Help me.'

Healy's heart hit his throat.

He stumbled away – still on his haunches – falling on to his backside. *Shit. He's still alive.* Asha raised his head, saliva at his lips.

His eyes filled with tears.

His throat tremored.

And then, sobbing, he said, 'I'm not who you think I am.'

67

I stared at Healy. 'He's *alive*?'

'Yeah.' He nodded. 'The women had given him a mild dose of sedative. He was dopey but he was conscious.'

'What has he said?' I asked Clarkson.

'He's fully lawyered up and has spent the last nine hours *no-commenting* our officers. At the moment, short of his name, he's offered nothing.'

'Why wouldn't you tell me this before?' I said to her.

'We needed to get your stories down and figure out what was what. Not that we've got very far. Any idea what "I'm not who you think I am" means?'

I shook my head, turned to Healy. 'You?'

'No.'

'Did he say anything else?'

'No. Other than that, he just kept asking for help.'

I let the new information wash over me. 'Maybe he's just in denial. I watched them for a while at that party last night and Caleb was smooth, confident; he had this magnetic quality that drew people to him. Asha wasn't like that. He was quieter, more circumspect. He looked like he operated in his brother's shadow, and without the protection of that shadow, maybe he's trying to save his skin, trying to pretend that he's not as culpable as Caleb and Yanis.'

'What if he *isn't* as culpable?' Clarkson said. We both looked at her. 'We've been talking to the head of security at the Skyline . . . uh . . .'

'Melanie Craw.'

'Craw, right. She says she passed on to you a PDF that an investigator over in LA put together for her – about the murder of the three kids in Vegas.'

'Casey, Florida and Ryan. Right.'

'Did you look at the PDF she gave you?'

'Very briefly. Craw handed me the flash drive about two seconds before I realized the Zinter brothers were going to be at that party.'

Clarkson went to her pocket and started going through her phone. As I watched her, I said, 'Why are you here? Where's Bakhash?'

'He's busy with the super and the DCI for the next ten minutes.' She looked up at us, something new in her expression. 'Our DCI came across from the Met.'

It was only seven words, but it was enough.

The Met hated both of us – Healy, because a long time ago he'd sided with me, and not them, in the search for his missing daughter; me, because I'd never lived a day as a cop, yet I spent my life solving cold cases they'd given up on. Perhaps more than that, though, it was because I'd exposed endemic police corruption on a case a long time ago, and what I'd found had not only stunted careers at the Met, it had ended them entirely. People were demoted, sacked, and they were plastered all over the papers. And a few of the officers who remained had never forgotten. My work back then hadn't led to a culture shift. All it had done was create more committed enemies.

'So what are you saying?' I asked her. 'Your DCI is coming after us?'

'He thinks you're not telling us the truth,' Clarkson said.

'Then why are we being let go?'

'Because there's no evidence against you – yet.' She glanced at her phone. 'We can't hold you if we don't have anything – but he'll make us work until we find something we can use against you both.'

Healy shook his head. 'This petty shite when everything else is going on?'

Clarkson tossed the phone across the room to me. I caught it and looked at the screen. It was a picture from the PDF Craw had given me, one I'd moved quickly past in the brief moments I'd spent with the document: a CCTV shot, taken from a street camera outside the Afrique. In the bottom corner was a date stamp: 29 March 2008.

The day the three friends disappeared.

Even if they hadn't been circled, I still would have spotted them all.

But it wasn't Casey, Florida and Ryan I was looking at.

It was who they were with.

2008

Las Vegas, Nevada

The three of them are in a room at the back of the Afrique.

They can't see the Strip – that's on the opposite side of the casino – only the vast, flat roof of a parking garage and the sprawl of east Las Vegas as it unravels across the desert floor to the mountains.

Casey wakes at 2 p.m.

She's the first one up.

The previous night – their first night in Vegas – they hadn't got in until five. They'd gone out to the Strip to find a place to eat, then found a bar, then another, and when they finally got back to the Afrique, they'd gone straight to Kilimanjaro – the main casino – and had spent two hours feeding one-dollar bills into the slots.

This is the first time the three of them have got together properly in over six months. At high school, they'd been inseparable, but then Florida had gone to UCLA, Ryan had headed off to community college, and Casey had got a job at a Gap in Northridge, and it became harder to align their lives. It doesn't feel like it's been six months, though, and it's already been so much fun.

Even the hangover is worth it, Casey thinks.

The bright desert sun is streaming through the slatted blinds at the window, but it hasn't woken either of the other two yet. Florida is asleep on the opposite side of the king-size bed, her vest top rolled up under her where she's been fidgeting in the

378

night, and Ryan is face down on the sleeper couch, snoring softly.

Casey pads through to the bathroom.

She washes her face, then downs a couple of glasses of water and an Advil, and as she heads back through to the bedroom, she starts to realize how hungry she is. Grabbing a pair of pants and a hoody, she runs a brush through her hair and then leaves Florida and Ryan and heads to the elevator.

From the foyer, she follows a long walkway – built to resemble a rope bridge crossing a swollen jungle river – and ends up in a diner. It's busy, but there's some room on one side, and Casey goes in, sits down and orders some pancakes.

Her cellphone buzzes.

It's Florida.

> Where are you? You ok? x

Casey replies, explaining that everything's cool, and says:

> Why don't you come and join me?
> I'm having pancakes! x

Florida responds straight away:

> Will do! Just need to call home first x

Casey stares at Florida's reply and somewhere, deep in her gut, she feels the same pang of jealousy that she felt the day before at the Joneses' house. It's so petty, so embarrassing that she keeps feeling this way about her best friend, but Casey can't help it. She just stares at Florida's reply and imagines her calling her mom, her dad and her sister – she thinks of how good it felt to be hugged by Mrs Jones, and how much better that hug must feel when your mom is actually a part of your life – and the jealousy doesn't vanish, it just festers. Casey puts the phone away before she texts something she regrets, and the waitress brings across her pancakes.

She wolfs down the meal, pays, and then heads into the nearest casino. She finds five bucks in her hoody and feeds one of the bills into the machine.

Someone takes the stool next to hers.

She doesn't look at him until a couple of minutes in, when his slot blares out a condolence message. When she does, he rolls his eyes and says, 'What is it they say about the house always wins?'

'I think it's "the house always wins",' Casey replies.

Casey feeds another dollar bill in. She can feel the guy's eyes on her.

'I think I saw you last night.'

She taps the Play button. 'Yeah?'

'Yeah. You were in the Congo Lounge, right?'

This time, she looks at him, taking him in properly. He's decent-enough looking for an older guy, although he's carrying too much weight.

'Yeah,' she says, 'that was us.'

'You and your friends looked like you were having a good time. You up in Vegas for the weekend?'

'Yeah.'

'Let me guess: last night was your first night?'

She eyes him again. 'What are you, psychic?'

'No.' He laughs. 'But when you come to Vegas as often as I do, you tend to see the same patterns repeating. First night is always the biggest night.'

Her gaze is still on him, taking him in. She never lets the real Casey be seen – the one that's vulnerable and horribly insecure – only the version of her that's hard, no-nonsense and fearless, so as she stares at the man, she expects him to wither. That's what men always do when she shows them their usual bullshit

380

isn't going to work on her. Instead, he smiles again, as if he's seen right through the facade.

'So why are you in Vegas,' she says, 'apart from trying to hit on girls half your age?'

'Is that what I'm doing?'

A moment later, one of the Afrique staff – a big bull in a black suit – appears out of nowhere, and says to the man, 'Can I get you something to drink?'

'Yeah, I'll take a bourbon on the rocks.'

The bull heads off. As Casey watches him go, she glances again at the man on the stool. He's smartly dressed – name brands, Rolex – and has one of the new cellphones from Apple tucked into the breast pocket of his shirt. Casey read somewhere that they cost almost six hundred bucks.

'So you've got a personal butler?' she says to him.

The man follows her eyeline out across the casino to where the giant in the black suit is. 'You mean Kerrill?' he says. 'No. I just have friends in high places.'

'Meaning what?'

He turns to properly face her. 'I know the owners.'

'The owners of what?'

The man smiles, and then sees she's serious. 'This,' he says, gesturing to the slots, to the casino.

'You know the owners of the Afrique?'

'Yeah, they're my best friends.'

She looks for the lie. 'You serious?'

'Yeah, why wouldn't I be?'

'Because men are full of shit.'

He laughs yet again.

'Your best friends are genuinely the owners of the Afrique?' she repeats, but much more slowly, as if he's hard of hearing. 'No bullshit?'

'No bullshit,' the man echoes, and crosses himself. 'I mean,

I would have offered to get you a drink as well – but I didn't want to get accused of anything.'

She looks past him to the bar, where his drink is being made. 'Would you like something?' he asks.

She hesitates for a second, but then says, 'Sure.'

He turns on the stool and holds up two fingers to Kerrill.

'I'm Anthony, by the way,' the man says.

Casey is excited when she gets back to the room.

Ryan is awake, sprawled on the sleeper couch, in a towel, his hair wet, and has an eye mask on. He peels it up off his face when Casey enters, and growls, 'It's your fault my head feels like this,' before snapping the mask back.

'Where's Flo?' Casey asks.

Ryan jabs a thumb at the balcony. Casey steers her way across the room and looks through the sliding doors. Florida is on her cell, looking towards the mountains. The air conditioning is on, and the doors are closed, so Casey can't hear exactly what Florida is saying, but she can hear she's talking to her seven-year-old sister.

'. . . a bit like Disneyland, but for adults,' she's saying to Miriam. 'When you're a little older, I'll bring you here.' Florida pauses and then bursts out laughing. 'Yeah, okay, I promise we can do that. But don't tell Mom you said that, okay?' She stops a second time, her face alight. The sisters absolutely adore each other.

Something tightens in the pit of Casey's stomach.

'We're going out in a couple of hours,' she says to Ryan.

Ryan peels his face mask up. 'What?'

'I met a guy down in the bar. He's best friends with the owners of the Afrique; these two brothers – the Zinters. One of them's got this crazy-ass home out in the desert. There's going to be a party there tonight.'

He groans. 'But I'm hanging out of my ass here.'

'Don't be a baby. We came here to party, didn't we?'

A smile on Ryan's face.

'Didn't we?'

'We did,' he says.

'Then get your party heels on.'

Ryan takes his eye mask off and hauls himself to his feet. 'Urgh, I feel like someone took a dump in my mouth.' He glances to the balcony where, over the sound of the air con, they can hear Florida laughing again. 'Flo said she wanted to have a steadier night tonight. Maybe have dinner and see a show and –'

'Fuck that,' Casey says, more sharply than she intended.

Ryan studies her.

'What?' she says.

'You been down there doing lines of coke or something?'

'What are you talking about?'

'You seem on edge.'

'I'm fine. I just want to go out, that's all.'

'I'm just saying, Flo probably won't be up for it.'

'Then we vote her down, don't we?'

Ryan narrows his eyes, trying to get a read on Casey, but Casey knows he'll never see the truth: that, right now, she doesn't give a shit what Florida wants.

Florida has everything she wants already.

Tonight, they're doing what makes Casey happy.

And that means being downstairs at 6 p.m. – in the pick-up area at the front of the Afrique – and riding an SUV out into the desert with Anthony Yanis and the Zinter brothers.

68

I looked at the CCTV shot. The three friends were off to the left of the pick-up area, outside the front of the casino, next to a very expensive jet-black SUV. Casey Ryker was already in the back seat; Florida and Ryan seemed as if they were about to get in.

Casey was sharing a joke with the driver.

The driver was Caleb Zinter.

Next to him, on the passenger side, was Anthony Yanis, smiling, arms resting on his belly, checking his mobile phone.

And then, beyond the SUV, half facing his brother and his best friend – and the three passengers – was Asha.

The shot had been taken long distance, by a public camera, because the Afrique – or, more specifically, the Zinters and their watchdog, Kerrill – were never going to allow investigators access to the unedited surveillance footage from the casino.

But there was nothing they could do about this shot.

The street camera didn't belong to them.

'I spoke to Craw,' Clarkson said, 'who put me in touch with her investigator out in the States. He says this footage is in some historical archive in Vegas that maps out how the city changes over time. What's interesting is that this video was uploaded to the archive in 2008 and only one other person – apart from him – has ever looked at it in the past fifteen years. It was another ex-cop. His name was Darnell Savage.'

'Never heard of him.'

'Google tells me he was the lead detective on a murder back in 1993. A young woman called Wilma Steski. I googled her too. She was found in the LA mountains – her hands had been tied behind her, and she'd been killed with a hunting round.'

Something crawled under my skin.

'That sounds just like the murders you described to Bakhash and me, right?' Clarkson prompted. 'The three friends? Catalina Robbins?'

I stared at the CCTV shot of the men.

How many more did you kill?

'This Darnell Savage,' Healy said, 'have you tried calling him?'

'He's dead.'

'Are there any other pictures of them like this one?' I asked.

'No, just that. But what do you see there?'

Healy leaned in, looking at the picture over my shoulder, and then I pinch-zoomed in on Asha, behind the SUV.

I stared at him, at his stance.

That half-turn.

'Is he even going with them?' Healy asked, echoing my thoughts.

'I don't know,' Clarkson replied, although from her tone it sounded as though we'd just picked out exactly the thing she'd wanted us to. 'Maybe. Or maybe he's heading back *into* the casino. It's hard to tell from the way he's standing. The angle he's at is ambiguous enough to be interpreted either way. Tori and Clara clearly thought he was about to get into that car.'

I looked up. 'But?'

'But what if he wasn't?'

I'm not who you think I am.

'What, are you suggesting Asha knows absolutely nothing about what his brother and Yanis were up to?' I paused, looking at her, but the more I turned things over in my head, the more I could see the angle. *I'm not who you think I am.*

I'm not a murderer.

She gestured for me to throw back her phone. Once she'd

put it away, she glanced at her watch. 'Adnan – I mean, DI Bakhash – will be done in two minutes, so you two need to be back where we left you by then.'

'Bakhash knows you're here?'

'Yes. This was just as much his idea as mine.'

'So, *again*, why are you telling us all of this?'

She rolled her shoulders, as if readying herself. 'As long as Asha doesn't talk, we've got nothing. Clara's dead, Kyle's in a coma, Tori's on the lam. We have no Caleb, no Kerrill, and Yanis has been in the ground for a year. When we have a grey area, inept police officers – who have consistently failed upwards – start trying to shape unanswered questions into something that fits their agenda.' She let us fill in the blanks. That was what their DCI was busy doing right now. 'They start saying, "Maybe Healy and Raker know something. Maybe the reason Asha isn't talking to us is because he's in cahoots with the two of them. Maybe this is some plan they've concocted."'

She'd become animated in a way I hadn't seen all night, and now the absolute antipathy she felt for her DCI was stark in her face. But then she calmed herself, the glacier blue of her eyes not leaving ours. 'Bakhash did some digging on you two. I did as well. I read about what happened in that forest.'

Healy flinched at the mention of *forest*.

And even though it was thirteen years ago, even though it should have felt like another lifetime, the memories came flooding back to me too, fully formed, full colour: Healy and me in the forest known as the Dead Tracks; inside the darkness of the place Leanne had been left in; her killer, a psychopath the press had nicknamed Dr Glass; and then the cops who'd followed us into those woods, the way they'd tried to stop us, and the corruption they'd been trying to hide.

I looked at Healy.

He was frozen.

We were rooted in his worst memory.

'Our DCI,' Clarkson said, 'he used to know some of the guys who worked out in east London on that case. He says they were good men, proud cops, and you destroyed their lives when you went public with what you found out. But me and Bakhash, we know that's bullshit. We know which side of the fence to come down on here.'

I nodded at her; a silent thank you.

'This case needs to be run by Bakhash, not by the DCI, not by anyone who isn't interested in getting to the truth. But, in order for that to happen, we need something. We need a lead, a break, a witness, *something*. And that's where you two come in. You don't have to deal with the politics and the bullshit and the hierarchy. You can just go and do the right thing.'

'And what's that?'

She looked between us. 'Finish what you started.'

69

I drove Healy as far as Kew, then dropped him outside the Tube station.

'I want to be on the road by nine tomorrow.'

He nodded and got out of the car.

'You can stay at mine if it's easier than going back to Lewisham.'

'It's fine,' he said. 'I want to get a change of clothes.' He stood at the open door, looking in at me. 'It's a long way to go for nothing.'

'Tori had that postcode in her satnav for a reason.'

'The cops say otherwise.'

'When did we start believing cops?'

I smiled, he returned it, then he pushed the door shut. As I watched him head to the Tube, I thought about the prospect of driving 215 miles in the morning for absolutely no reward; to an area in which there was nothing except a few farms and a swathe of wild, empty moorland.

It was a risk.

But I couldn't shake the feeling that something had been missed.

I was making dinner when Healy called me.

'You got the news on?' he said.

I did, but not in the kitchen. I headed through to the living room, where I'd left BBC News running. They were reporting live from Dartmoor.

As I saw the pictures, my heart sank.

The body was exactly where Tori Robbins had said she'd put it.

I stopped making dinner, my appetite gone, and just watched, flicking between news channels, refreshing my laptop, waiting for definite confirmation it was him.

There were no updates for hours.

But then – very slowly – tiny snippets of information began filtering out from sources in the forest, and pretty soon the online news website *FeedMe* had broken the story based on what an insider on the case had told them.

The body was Marc's.

It wasn't a surprise, but a little part of me collapsed anyway.

I tried calling Sarah at the hospital, but the call went straight to her voicemail, and the way she sounded on the recorded message – the happiness in her voice, in the version of her that had existed before all of this – just added to the sadness I felt for her, my feeling of helplessness. Nothing I could say would make it better for her.

But I left her a message anyway, telling her how sorry I was.

Afterwards, I thought of Kyle in the coma, of the person at the party who looked like a man but was still very much a boy. I thought about all the questions I would have for him, about the relationship he'd had with the girl he'd known, at least for some of the time they were together, as Clara Dearton.

He needed to wake up.

He needed to get better.

Without him, the circle would never fully close on this case, and Sarah might never recover.

Her husband was gone.

She couldn't lose her son too.

70

Of all the things that the newspapers, TV channels and websites reported the next morning, of all the things that stuck with me in the feeding frenzy that followed the discovery of Marc's body, it was seven words in a report on LBC that got to me the most. I was listening to it as I got ready for the drive up to Oldham.

Fowler was still wearing a life jacket.

It stopped me dead, as if someone had put a hand to my chest.

For some reason, I couldn't shake the imagery of it, or the story that it told. Eight months after he'd done something good for the stepson he loved like his own, eight months after picking up that oar, eight months after being buried in a forest on Dartmoor, the only part of him that was still intact was the one part of him that should never have been there in the first place.

He'd never wanted to go out on that lake.

But he'd gone all the same.

And now the life jacket was all that was left of him.

At eight thirty the next morning, someone rang the doorbell.

I expected it to be Healy, but as I headed downstairs, I could see the distorted shape of a woman in the frosted glass, motionless, waiting.

I opened the front door.

It took me a split second to match a name to a face, because – even though it had only been a matter of days since I'd bumped into her at the station in Kew – my head was so full of noise, I couldn't quite place her, here on my doorstep.

'Alice-Leigh,' I said.

Liam Healy's girlfriend.

She touched a hand to her swollen belly, and then glanced out into the road, as if looking for someone. I thought about our first meeting, and how weird it had been at the end when she'd asked me not to tell anyone about it.

'This is a surprise.'

'I know. I'm sorry to turn up so early – and at your home too.' She stopped. 'I just took a chance on you being here, I guess.'

Her hair was tied back into a plait, revealing that same unblemished face, her slight frame hidden beneath the raincoat and a summer dress with flowers on the breast. She pulled the raincoat tighter, taking a step back.

'I wanted to, um . . .' A pause. 'I wanted to tell you something.'

'Tell *me* something?'

'Yes.'

As I waited, I tried to imagine what she could possibly need to tell me. I didn't even know her; I'd only met her for the very first time, in passing, at a Tube station. And then I remembered what Healy had mentioned a few days ago, when he'd been to meet Ciaran and Liam: Alice had been asking questions about me.

'Is this to do with the Castle hearings?' I asked, making the obvious leap. She was part of the legal team collating testimony there; I'd given evidence.

'No,' she said. 'No, it's nothing to do with that.'

I waited again.

'There's something I need to kind of, uh . . .' A beat. 'There's something I need to admit to you. I've been thinking about how to say this for days now, and then this morning I saw all the stories about what happened at the casino, and I saw you were mentioned, and I was reading about the Fowler family, and it reminded me that I should have . . . I should have . . .'

I stepped closer. 'Should have what?'

She'd fallen silent again.

'Is this something to do with the Fowlers?'

She began doing what she'd done the first time we'd talked: she started playing with her bracelet, six daisies on it, her fingers feeding the daisies up and down the loop of the band.

'Alice?'

Still she played with her bracelet.

'Look, Alice, I'm about to head out. In fact, your future father-in-law is going to be here in ten minutes.' I smiled at her, using it as a way to get her to tell me what she was doing here, to coax out whatever this was – but, instead, the mention of Healy seemed to spook her. 'What's going on?'

She looked at me.

'Is it to do with Colm?'

Nothing.

'Is it to do with what happened at the Skyline?'

She shook her head, as if that was the furthest thing this could ever have been about. 'I need to go,' she said.

'Why don't you just tell me what's on your mind?'

But she'd already started walking away, telling me that she'd get my number and give me a call in the next couple of days. And as she headed back towards the front gate, as I tried to understand what was going on and why she would come all the way out here at eight thirty in the morning, something she'd said reignited at the back of my head: *I saw all the stories about what happened at the casino, and I saw you were mentioned, and I was reading about the Fowler family, and it reminded me that I should have . . . I should have . . .*

She should have told me something.

But what?

And what if it *was* to do with the Fowler case?

7
The Brother

71

We arrived in the north-west just after one thirty.

The weather was awful, rain sheeting down, a dense mist cresting the apex of Saddleworth Moor so that, as we ascended out of the villages to the west of it, it was like being on a plane, taking off into clouds.

At the top, I drove along the only road that bisected the moorland, but it was hopeless, the fog too thick. Healy checked his phone for the forecast.

'It's due to clear at about five,' he said.

We'd have to come back.

Before giving up, we drove to the three farms located within the postcode area and asked about Tori. We showed photos of her, surreptitiously took a look around the properties, searching for hiding places, for reasons why any of the farmers might conceal a fugitive. We found nothing.

After that, we descended back into a village on the western edge of the moors and found a table at the window of a café.

As we ordered, I thought again about mentioning Alice-Leigh to Healy, and her visit to my house – but I decided against it because I couldn't figure out where she belonged in all of this, or why she'd been acting so strangely. Maybe, in thinking she might know something about my case, I'd been trying to make a puzzle piece I didn't understand fit with one I did. But she clearly had something she needed to say – and even if it seemed more likely it had to do with Liam, or the Healy family as a whole, if I told Healy that, I knew his focus would slip.

His family were an open wound.

And, right now, I needed his head in the game.

The rain stopped just before five.

Just as we were heading back to the car – the sun finally puncturing the thick clouds – my phone started ringing.

It was an unknown number.

'Give me a second,' I said to Healy and hit Answer. 'David Raker.'

'Mr Raker . . .'

A male voice.

American.

The line was quiet, distant.

'Mr Raker,' he said again, 'my name's Pete Tomer.'

Now

Irvine, California

Pete Tomer leaves home early and is at UCI by seven thirty.

He still needs to make some tweaks to the lecture he's giving to a bunch of second-year Criminology students, and although he's done pretty much the same presentation for nearly four years now, he always tries to make subtle, interesting changes to the template, as much for his own sanity as the kids'.

After parking up, he heads across Aldrich Park, the heat of the day already simmering, and takes a table outside a Starbucks on the science campus.

He orders a coffee and a muffin, then picks at the muffin as he navigates his way back through the PowerPoint. Gradually, the campus becomes busier, students emerging into the light of day, folders tucked under arms, laptop bags slung over shoulders. About an hour in, just as Tomer finishes preparing the lecture, he sees a student making a beeline for him.

'Good morning,' the girl says.

'Good morning. It's Ella, right?'

'That's right,' Ella responds, and glances at Tomer's laptop. 'Sorry, I didn't mean to interrupt you. I just saw you here and suddenly remembered the lecture you gave last semester – about that case you had.'

'Which case was that?' Tomer asks. 'I had a lot of them.'

Ella frowns, as if silently admonishing herself for the slip-up. 'I was thinking about that one you had back in – I think it was 1993?'

'Wilma Steski.'

'She was the girl you and your partner found in the LA mountains?'

'Right. What about her?'

'Oh.' Ella seems temporarily thrown. 'Oh, I'm guessing you haven't seen, then.'

Tomer frowns. 'Seen what?'

'It's all over the news this morning,' Ella says. 'An investigator in London has just found out who killed her.'

72

We headed back up on to the moors as I talked with Pete Tomer.

I had a number on my website that redirected calls to my mobile – and now he was calling from a Starbucks at UC Irvine, where he'd spent half an hour looking at news reports from the Skyline.

'So the Wilma Steski case was yours?' I asked him as we ascended into wild moorland, the grass glistening from the rain – browns darker, greens more lush.

'Until I left the Sheriff's Department, yeah.'

'But your partner kept working it?'

'Darnell worked it until it couldn't be worked any more.'

'Darnell Savage?'

'Yeah. Have you heard of him?'

I explained to Tomer about how Craw's investigator in the US had found the CCTV footage of Casey, Florida and Ryan getting into a car with Yanis and the Zinter brothers in the hours before the three of them disappeared; and how the only other person to dig into that historical archive and look at that footage in the last fifteen years had been Darnell Savage.

Healy made notes as Tomer talked and I continued the drive up, keeping my eyes on the road and the elevated sweep of Saddleworth Moor.

'So if Darnell connected the murders,' I said, 'and he was convinced that the Zinter brothers and Yanis were responsible, why didn't he take it to the cops?'

'A few reasons. He was dying for one, and I don't think he wanted to spend the last few months of his life driving back and forward to police stations, or lawyer's offices, or being dragged to depositions. But the evidence was circumstantial too. He had the surveillance footage of the Zinters and Yanis getting into the car with the three friends. He had Yanis in a crowd behind Catalina Robbins as she left that Halloween party. And he had the fact that the men were at Caltech with Wilma Steski at the time she was murdered. But he didn't have a slam dunk. Plus, this was just after lockdown and police forces were struggling to cope – cutbacks, a surge in crime rates, ever more impossible clearance targets.'

'So no one would want five extra cold cases on their plate,' Healy said.

'Exactly. Plus, even if he *was* thinking about doing it – about handing all his work over to the cops – the women killing Anthony Yanis changed everything.'

'Why?' I asked.

'He handed Tori and Clara what he'd compiled, expecting them to use it as a jumping-off point. I think he had the notion that they'd be champions for all those victims – that they'd familiarize themselves with the cases, and then go out to the press, crank up the pressure, *force* the cops to reopen all those investigations. Instead of that, his work acted like a stick of dynamite. It blew everything up. He handed that file over to them and they used it to turn the tables on the men. Suddenly, the Zinters and Yanis weren't doing the hunting any more – it was Tori and Clara. Darnell was the one that brought them together. He was the one that started it.'

'What stopped you going to the cops yourself?'

Tomer didn't respond to start with. Then, quietly, he said, 'I guess I wanted to see how it all played out.'

'What do you mean?'

But almost as soon as I'd asked the question, I saw the answer hidden in the silence of his response. The women had taken their revenge on Yanis. It made sense that the Zinter brothers would be next. And Tomer wasn't about to stop them.

'You work enough cases,' he said, his voice more hushed now, more soulful, 'it builds up in you. This feeling of . . .' A long pause. 'Helplessness. You do what you can, you solve what you can, but sometimes these assholes deserve what's coming.'

Healy glanced at me, me at him, and I knew, from our shared history, that he identified with what Tomer had said, with the choice that Tomer had made to let it all play out. Healy had caught many killers – including the one that took his own daughter's life – but the fact that they went on living, breathing, ageing, *experiencing*, had been profoundly hard for him to deal with. As a cop, as any kind of investigator, you were supposed to make your peace with it, to crave justice and to promote due process. But investigators like Tomer and Healy were only human. They spent their working lives dealing with right and wrong, good and evil, and sometimes the lines between those things blurred, and sometimes you were okay with that.

'Those men,' Tomer said. 'They reaped what they sowed.'

73

We drove up and back over Saddleworth Moor as the evening crept in.

At first, I assumed it was going to be unhelpful, the dwindling light making it more difficult to see anything. Instead, as the sun began bleeding across the hills, the sky bruising, lights started coming on in properties adjacent to us.

The farms we'd been to.

The car park at a reservoir in the valley to the south.

And a light, about half a mile off the road, to the north of us.

'What the hell are you doing?' Healy said, as I yanked the car into a lay-by.

'What's that?'

I was pointing up a track that rose gently towards an escarpment of grey rock and fir trees. It was closed off by a metal gate, PRIVATE LAND printed on a sign across the middle. We'd been past it several times already and had seen nothing there – just an undulating series of sloped fields running up to the rock face. Beyond the top of the escarpment was a mobile-phone mast. But now, with the day beginning to fade, I could see a speck of light among the fir trees, right under the shadow of the bluff. In the wind, as the trees moved very gently, it drifted in and out of view – pale, almost ethereal.

'You see it?' I asked Healy.

He nodded.

'Let's check it out.'

I parked the car and we climbed over the gate. As the wind stirred, the fir trees up ahead swayed in time, and the pinprick of light that we'd seen from the road became larger. It was a square with a black line along the middle.

A window.

Immediately, I led us away from the track, into the grass that ran adjacent to it, growing long among a sprawl of trees. The sun was starting to dip behind the spine of the escarpment, three-quarters of it gone already, and anything on this side of the ridge had become shadowed and difficult to make out.

We couldn't see in through the window.

But it didn't mean someone couldn't see out.

The ground suddenly rose sharply, obscuring the window for a moment, so I moved back on to the track. The hill we were on crested about twenty-five feet ahead of us. I could see a roof now and the gritstone escarpment behind it, as well as the point of the mobile-phone mast on the other side of the vast curtain of rock. But, as I heard Healy behind me, his shoes making a muted scuff on the gravel, the window finally came back into view.

It was part of a stone cottage.

The building was dilapidated, the roof tiles slipping or gone entirely, the other windows at the front simply black holes – no glass, no frames, just mouths full of shadows. The cottage looked like it hadn't been occupied for years.

Except I knew that wasn't true, because the light we'd seen from the road was coming from a television. I could see it through a window on the side.

And that wasn't the only reason I knew someone was here.

The other reason was parked ten feet away.

It was a green Mondeo.

74

Healy moved level with me, seeing the car.

The registration plates had been changed, presumably to prevent it from pinging ANPR cameras on the way up here. We looked from the car to the house.

Next to the window was a side door. There was one at the front too with a white sticker on it. I couldn't read anything from where I was, but it wasn't hard to imagine that whatever was printed on it was a warning.

This cottage had been condemned.

'There must be a door at the back,' Healy whispered.

Beneath the vertical face of the escarpment, the rear of the cottage was entirely wrapped in darkness.

'I'll go,' he said.

'You sure?'

He nodded.

'Just be careful.'

I watched him head off along the front of the house, veering away from it to start with so that he could use a dip at the side of the track as cover from the front windows. He looked back as he got to the far end of the cottage, then he was gone.

I hurried to the side door.

Placing a hand on the peeled, warped wood, I inched down the handle and eased the door back into the gloom of the cottage. As it started to creak, I stopped it and slipped through the gap, into a hallway. It ran left to right, doors at either end.

For a moment, all I could hear was the wind, the soft whine of it as it funnelled through the cracks and fissures of the house.

But then, slowly, another sound faded in.

A hum.

What *was* that?

Moving right, I headed down to the end. It was a former bedroom. An old bed frame sat in the middle of a flagstone floor, a fireplace in the corner. I backed out and returned to the hallway, going the other way, to where the second door was. At the entrance, I peered inside.

A living room.

The television I'd seen was on a table, pulled out into the middle of the room, and, because the set was facing in my direction, because it was so bright against the shadows everywhere else, it was hard to see what was beyond it.

To my left was the front of the house – the door with the notice on it and two broken windows.

On the opposite wall to me was another door – it must have led to the back of the property, where Healy was coming in from.

To my right was the kitchen.

I looked inside it. On a near-collapsed worktop sat a compact diesel generator, the source of the humming sound I'd heard. It had been smothered in towels to reduce the noise it was making. The lead for an extension cable was plugged into it and snaked away, back into the living room.

Next to the generator was a mobile phone.

The decision to encamp here was smart: the cottage wasn't only abandoned, it was right next to a mast – which meant the signal would be near perfect. Not that it made much difference for the moment: the SIM card had been removed and was lying next to the phone.

I double-checked the living room again, eyeing the doorway on the opposite side, through which Healy would be coming – and then the darkness in the corner, beyond the TV.

I couldn't see a thing there.

That half of the living room was just an abyss.

Taking out my own mobile phone, I used the glow of the screen and cast it towards the corner of the living room, as best I could. It didn't carry far, didn't reveal much, but it didn't look like anyone was there.

At least as far as I can tell.

I thought of Healy again, of what he might have found – *who* he might have found – then stepped back into the kitchen and tapped the screen of the phone next to the generator.

An image formed in the murk of the room.

It was a Las Vegas Raiders badge.

I checked again for signs of anyone coming, anyone watching me, and then swiped up on the phone screen, expecting the security to kick in.

It didn't.

It just immediately unlocked.

I went to Settings to see who the phone belonged to, even though I already had a strong suspicion – and the Apple ID confirmed it.

It was Caleb's.

I remembered Clara going through his pockets at the Skyline.

I scrolled quickly through Caleb's text messages, his Whats-Apps, his emails, his most recent calls, looking for anything that felt anomalous, but something was obvious straight away: this wasn't his work phone, this was his personal phone. Almost all his messages were from family and friends about things unrelated to work. There were some calls from the Skyline, as well as some texts from people who clearly worked there, but the messages were personal in nature, not professional. Everything else – all the other numbers that had called him – were American.

All of them except one.

It was a forty-nine-second call from an 01749 area code. The number had only dialled Caleb once, and when I googled the geographical area on my own phone I saw it was Somerset, south-east of the Mendips.

A noise.

I inched out into the living room, gazing into the shadows beyond the television, then to the door opposite which led deeper into the cottage. Now all I could hear was the hum of the generator and the moan of the wind.

I shuffled forward, my pulse quickening, moving closer to the TV. It had been paused on a near-white image, which was why it was so bright. As I reached the table it was on, I tried to see what lay behind it.

It was too dark.

I used the dull light from my phone screen again, directing it into the shadows as I edged around the table.

And then I stopped.

In the corner of the room, I could see faces.

Healy

Healy peered along the back of the cottage.

There was a small, narrow garden wedged between the rear of the house and the face of the escarpment, the grass overgrown and awash with weeds.

No glass in any of the windows back here.

And no door.

He tensed as he edged forward, looking in through the first window, past some jagged glass left in the frame, to what appeared to be a bedroom.

It was empty.

At the gap the back door had once occupied, he stopped, glass crunching under his feet, and then leaned in through the open space.

A hallway led away from him to the front of the house. There were two doors on his left and none on his right. The second door on his left, at the other end of the hallway, must have gone through to the living room, where Healy assumed Raker was. The first door, closest to him, led into another short corridor.

He stepped all the way into the house, one of the floorboards creaking underfoot, and paused. In the silence now he could hear a soft hum.

Was it coming from the living room?

He looked again through the first door on his left.

There was an empty room at the end of the corridor, which

didn't seem as if it was accessible from anywhere else but here – and that meant Raker wouldn't know about it, because it was built behind the living room.

Healy inched through the first door.

He glanced over his shoulder, the cottage almost entirely dark, what was left of the sun, whatever light remained above the escarpment, gone from the house. Halfway down the corridor, he had no choice but to remove his phone, holding it up, using the screen to illuminate what lay ahead.

He reached the empty room at the end.

But it wasn't completely empty.

On the floor, in the middle, was a sleeping bag. Next to that was a backpack. He crouched next to the backpack and unzipped it.

The first thing he saw was a wash bag.

He opened it. It was full of deodorant, creams, make-up, hairspray – and, as he went through them, he noticed something.

Every item was under 100ml.

Travel-sized.

Tori was getting ready to flee the country.

75

The faces looked out at me.

They were photographs, part of a pinboard that had been propped on the thick, scarred stone mantelpiece above the fireplace.

It wasn't just photographs – it was notes, torn maps with locations circled, lists, photocopies. I tried to make some order of it but, in the half-light, it was hard. I brought my phone further up, thought about switching to the torch function, rather than just using the light from the screen. But, as I looked at the broken windows, at the moors that had almost faded from existence outside, it felt too much of a risk.

I didn't know if Tori was inside or outside, or even here at all.

And, until I did, I didn't want to give myself away.

I turned back to the mantelpiece, took another step closer and raised my phone again. There was a photograph of Wilma Steski; one of Casey Ryker, Florida Jones and Ryan Ling; and another of Catalina Robbins, in the centre, as if she were the sun, the rest of them the planets.

I spotted a cut-out magazine article, with a corporate shot of Caleb Zinter at the top. Below that was a photo of Anthony Yanis. It was a selfie, but not taken by him. It had been taken by the person he'd known as Morgan Annerson.

Tori.

She was putting on a smile, her face touching Yanis's. Judging by the reflection in a mirror behind them, they were in a bed-room somewhere, alone.

Sometimes photos lied, but this one said so much.

Yanis had completely fallen for her. It was there, in his eyes, all the explanation I ever needed about exactly how good Tori was, and how completely she'd dismantled Yanis's defences. She was stunning; in this shot, taken away from prying eyes in the privacy of the bedroom, there was no disguise, which seemed to confirm what Healy and I had first speculated: that Yanis had known Tori was a woman all along – and that whatever story she'd spun him, whatever reason she'd given him for keeping that information to himself, he'd gone along with. He believed whatever they had was real.

I looked at the rest of the board.

There were a few faces I didn't recognize, other articles and cuttings that didn't make sense, but one thing was immediately obvious: there was no Asha anywhere. I recalled Clarkson's theory about Asha not having any knowledge of what was going on – and then shifted my focus to another photograph in the bottom right.

It was still in its frame and leaning against the pinboard.

This is it.

This was the one Tori must have gone back for, the photo that she'd removed from the Skyline. I recognized the frame instantly: it was identical to one that was still hanging on the wall of the Bunker. That one had been a Caltech graduation photo of the Zinter brothers and Yanis. This one was a group of forty or so students at some kind of university ball – but it was Caltech again. I could see its name on a banner – and, at the front, I spotted a young Caleb Zinter. Next to him was Anthony Yanis.

Wilma Steski was in the front row too.

She was among a group of boys, elegant in a ball gown, smiling.

I felt something stir as I looked at the photograph, as if I'd seen something else in it, but then my attention switched again, this time to the edge of the fireplace.

411

Leaning against it was a video camera on a tripod.

The tripod was at a slant, its legs set together, but the camera was still attached to the top, leads plugged into the side. When I followed their path along the floor, I saw they connected to the back of the TV. The leads were composites, the camera was old, the television could have been even older.

It was all analogue.

Whatever was on the camera was deliberately being kept offline.

I reached over and pulled out the screen on the side of the camera. Rotating it towards me, I saw the same white image on its screen that was also on the TV. In a timecode at the bottom, the video had been paused at 00:00:07.

A noise from behind me.

I looked across the living room; to the smashed and broken windows, to the front door.

The same noise again.

I turned further, looking to the door that led out to the back of the house: the entrance Healy should have come through.

Where the hell was he?

The noise came a third time.

Wait, was it coming from *inside* the living room?

I felt a cool finger trace the ridge of my spine.

How could it be coming from the living room? There was nothing in here that could be making the noise I was hearing. Because the noise I was hearing . . .

I stopped, my blood thumping.

The noise I was hearing was a whimper.

76

I swung my phone around, trying to figure out what was going on.

The noise sounded like it was coming from inside here – but there were no hiding places left. I'd been into every corner of the room now.

Healy.

What if it was coming from the back of the house?

I passed from the living room to the hallway, looking for any sign of him, keeping my phone low, not wanting to cast too much light ahead of me. I didn't know what might be waiting for me out here. I didn't know where Tori was.

All I knew was that Healy hadn't come through yet.

And he should have come through ages ago.

The hallway ran down to a space where the back entrance had once been – now just a peeling frame – and, on the right-hand wall, adjacent to it, was a door. That appeared to lead into another corridor running parallel to the living room.

Was that where he'd gone?

'Healy?' I whispered.

The shadows seemed longer here, thicker, and there was sound coming from everywhere now: the hum of the generator, the moan of the wind, the creak of the cottage as its old bones shifted.

And then the whimper again.

I turned, confused. It *definitely* sounded like it was coming from the living room. Retreating, inching back inside, I stopped, listened.

It came again.

Again.

I took in the TV, the table it was on, the kitchen on the far side.

And then I glanced at the fireplace.

The same faces emerged from the dark, pinned to the board on its mantelpiece. But as I edged closer, my gaze dropped to the neck of the chimney itself.

It was six feet wide.

I didn't know how far it went back.

But it was big enough to hide in.

I felt a prickle in my scalp.

'Hello?' I whispered.

The whimper again – but movement now too.

Three feet from the chimney, I finally started to see it. A shape. Two feet away, it became even clearer: I could see feet, the bottom part of four chair legs.

Whoever it was had been covered by a black sheet.

They were facing me, placed far enough back to fit into the neck of the chimney, and now – as they could feel me getting closer, knowing and hearing that I wasn't Tori – their feet started to move, desperate to try and get my attention.

'It's okay,' I said softly, getting down on to my haunches and placing my phone on the floor next to me, light facing up. It was hard to get an idea of whether it was a man or a woman, even whether it was an adult or a kid, but – using the light – I reached forward, grabbed hold of the black sheet and slowly pulled it towards me.

It fell away.

I stared into the darkness under the mantelpiece.

'Marc?'

Healy

The Cottage | *Now*

Healy set the wash bag down and looked inside the backpack again.

There was an iPad.

It was in a pocket at the back. Taking it out, he pushed the Home button. The screen lit up. It was fully charged.

It was also brand new.

There were no third-party apps on it, and it hadn't been synced up to any other devices. It looked like it had literally just come out of the box.

He glanced at the wash bag again.

If she was making her escape and fleeing the country, the iPad made sense now. She was going to dump all her existing tech so she could switch to something new that wasn't going to leave a trail.

There was one last thing inside the bag.

A zip-up wallet.

He lifted it out. It had two pouches: one had a Spanish passport in it; the other contained a folded piece of paper.

Healy looked at the passport.

The photo was of Tori Robbins, but she'd changed her appearance yet again. Her hair was jet black and past her shoulders. Her skin was tanned.

The name in the passport reflected that.

Talia Gomez.

Born in Madrid in February 1995.

He unfolded the piece of paper. It was a printed copy of an e-ticket for a British Airways flight, taking off in two days' time.

Heathrow to Windhoek.

Namibia.

He glanced at the iPad, at the passport. Healy didn't know a damn thing about Namibia – but he could take a guess at why Tori had chosen it as a place to head.

There was no extradition treaty with the UK.

Click.

Healy went to swivel, to see what had made the noise – but he'd barely shifted before a hand clamped on to the back of his neck and stopped him.

'Ssshhhh,' a voice said from behind him.

77

In the shadows of the chimney, a terrified face looked out.

'Marc?' I said again, still stunned.

His eyes went past me to the door, as if he were waiting for someone to appear, and then – when he looked at me again – he began to make pleading sounds through the duct tape over his mouth.

Help me, he was trying to say.

Please help me.

My gaze switched back to the framed photograph stolen from the Bunker, taken at Caltech when Caleb Zinter and Anthony Yanis were in their late teens or early twenties. Earlier, there had been something about it that had made me stop, something I hadn't been able to get at.

Now I understood what.

As I took a half-step closer to it, I remembered what Sarah had told me, right back at the start: *He was offered this huge university scholarship when he was eighteen. There was no way his parents could have afforded to send him to uni otherwise.*

The scholarship had been to Caltech.

He was in the second row, directly behind Caleb and Yanis but mostly hidden by the kid in front of him, which was how I'd missed him the first time. He was saying something to Caleb, whispering in his ear, making Caleb and Yanis laugh.

For a second I couldn't rip my eyes away from the younger version of him, and then I glanced out into the dark, towards the kitchen, towards Caleb's phone.

The 01749 area code.

Could it have been Marc calling Caleb?

I looked at Marc, at the duct tape on his mouth, his eyes wide and pleading with me to free him. When I didn't, they started to fill with tears.

I hesitated, trying desperately to thread everything together.

He was almost convulsing now, straining at his binds.

I thought about what I knew – the media reports that Marc was dead, that the cops had pulled his skeletal remains out of a grave last night on Dartmoor; Tori willingly giving up the location to me at the Skyline – and I realized that at no point did I actually ever hear her *talk* about Marc being dead. She talked around it the whole time, and so did Kyle. Whenever I asked him about Marc, he kept repeating the same thing: he didn't want to speak about it. When I'd asked him straight if Marc was dead, he'd shaken his head. I thought it had been because he was grieving the stepdad he'd loved and didn't want to discuss it. But he was being honest with me.

No, he was saying, *Marc isn't dead.*

Marc lurched again, his eyes on the door behind me. I told him to calm down and dropped to my haunches, peeling the duct tape away from his mouth.

He let out a long, rasping breath, and then he was talking: 'Oh shit, oh shit' – fast, scared –'please help me, please help me.'

'Calm down,' I said.

'She's going to kill us if you don't –'

'Marc, calm down.'

But now he was looking past me again.

And the colour had drained from his face.

I turned. Healy was standing in the doorway, his hands up.

Behind him, half concealed by the darkness, was someone else, a cut on her forehead from the car crash.

She had a gun at Healy's neck.

'Step away from him,' Tori said.

78

Healy stumbled forward, pushed by Tori.

She was all in black, hard to see, her face a pale moon against the night. 'It looks like I picked the wrong time to go and check the perimeter,' she said. 'I step out for ten minutes and suddenly the cavalry arrives.'

She moved even closer to Healy.

I looked at Marc again, at everything on the mantelpiece above him.

'So I guess now you know why I went back,' Tori said, seeing where my eyeline had landed.

I stared at the framed photo, leaning against the pinboard.

'That picture there is basically the only one I could find that shows all of them at Caltech together. I mean, look at them: Marc whispering in Caleb's ear, telling his little joke; Caleb and Yanis laughing like it's the funniest thing they've ever heard. Thick as thieves.' She took another step so that she was hidden behind Healy, who she'd now forced to face me. 'Yanis told me about the picture one night when he was pawing me. I'd asked him about his university friends. He said he didn't have many photos from those days, but the Zinters had one on the wall downstairs. You could get him to tell you anything when he had the horn.'

'She's got it all wrong,' Marc said, looking at me.

'No, I haven't.'

'I was friends with them, yes,' he sobbed, eyes on me. He looked genuinely terrified. 'But I never hurt anyone. I never had any idea what they were doing. I swear I didn't. All these things she says I've done, I swear I haven't –'

'Shut up,' Tori spat.

'If what she's been telling me is right,' Marc moaned, 'if Caleb and Anthony were killing people, I had no idea. I swear I didn't. I never killed anyone. I never hurt –'

'*Shut up.*'

Silence.

The wind gently whistled through the house.

I had so many questions, I didn't know where to start.

'They were at Caltech together,' I said to Tori, as if saying it aloud might help me see more clearly. 'And – what? – this photo is why you think Marc was involved?'

'I wasn't,' Marc sobbed. 'I wasn't involved in any of –'

'*Oh,*' Tori said, cutting him off but talking to me. 'What, he couldn't have been involved because he seems like such a stand-up guy? Because he's a daddy? Because he lived in England and all of this happened in the States?' She looked at Marc. 'That was the whole point, wasn't it, Marc? Sating your appetite in the US and vanishing back here, so the cops were busy scrabbling around in the dark on the wrong side of the Atlantic? He and his mate Yanis had the same idea where that was concerned. England was their hiding place.'

'No.' Marc shook his head. 'No, that's not true.'

'I'm not sure this photograph is proof of anything, Tori.'

'That's what I've been trying to tell her,' Marc responded, his voice giving way. 'Yes, they were my friends, but I never had any idea that they were –'

'Marc, Caleb and Yanis used to go hunting at Big Bear Lake.' Tori cut him off again. 'Yanis told me. When they were at Caltech, they'd leave Asha back in LA with all his Physics friends and the three of them would drive up to the lake.'

'So what are you saying? Asha really *didn't* know what was going on?'

'No.'

'You don't think he knew anything?'

'No.'

I'm not who you think I am.

It wasn't just Asha saying, *I'm not a murderer.*

It was him realizing who his brother really was.

'These three would go up to the lake and they'd shoot jack-rabbits, deer, wild pigs, black bears. But, after a while, I guess animals just weren't cutting it any more.'

Memories returned to me: on the second day of the case, when I'd parked in the Fowlers' garage, I'd seen two air rifles in a rack on the wall in there; later, in one of the videos I'd watched of the family, Marc and Kyle were laughing about Marc finishing way out in front in a game of laser tag. Did any of it mean anything? Did it mean he was a skilled marksman and highly proficient with weapons?

I glanced at the pinboard.

The face of Wilma Steski stared back.

Marc had begun shaking his head. 'She's lying. I mean, yes, we went hunting together. I enjoyed shooting. But not people.' His eyes filled with tears. 'Not people.'

'I'm not lying,' Tori replied, a shape built from shadows behind Healy. 'Yanis never confessed to the murders, but he'd unwittingly give me information – little things that helped me fill gaps in my knowledge, like those hunting trips, like the weapons they used when they got there, like the bullets they'd shoot. That was when you first started using those .270 Winchester rounds, wasn't it, Marc?'

'I don't know what you're talking –'

'Yanis told me that was your round of choice, so don't lie. You three started out using those bullets on animals – and then, in 1993, you used them on Wilma Steski.'

'*No!*'

'That was why I had to stay with Yanis for five months,' Tori said to me. 'I hated that fucking slob. Whenever he touched me, I felt like I was going to puke.'

'But he didn't ever tell his friends the truth about you?'

'No.'

'Why not?'

'I made up a story about how I was escaping an abusive ex; that the Morgan Annerson name, the more masculine appearance I maintained in public, was just a way to keep me safe from him. I told Yanis he couldn't tell anyone, and if he did, I'd leave him. I played the part. I looked good for him in private, young and pristine, just how he liked it; I even told him my real name was Tori, so he'd think I *really* trusted him, and to see if the name clicked with him. But it never did. It wasn't hard to fool him. He became absolutely obsessed with me, which was another reason it was so easy to get him talking. But those five months . . .' Her eyes went off, into the darkness. 'They were the longest five months of my life, just waiting for the moments when I could get him talking about Caleb, about Marc, about the three of them together, and I could add it to what I already knew.'

'So that Caltech photograph isn't your only evidence?'

'No. I have what Yanis told me – and what other people have said as well.'

I paused, thinking of Pete Tomer.

'Do you mean Darnell Savage?'

She seemed surprised – even impressed – that I knew who Darnell was. 'Yes,' she said. 'But Darnell made a mistake. *He* thought it was Caleb, Yanis and *Asha* who were the hunters, because he found that CCTV video of the Zinter brothers and Yanis in a car with Casey, Florida and Ryan. But Asha wasn't getting into that car.'

I thought of Asha's half-turn in the photo that Clarkson had showed us at the police station. 'He was heading back inside the casino,' I said.

'Yes,' Tori replied. 'The other two were waiting there for Marc. He was on his way out. He was the third hunter. I mean, don't get me wrong, I thought it was Asha too to start with – but then I moved in on Yanis, and I started getting close to him, and he began to talk about his past, and I realized Asha was always on the outside. When Yanis talked, it was him, Caleb and Marc – never Asha. He was friends with Asha, but he called Asha boring, a robot. So that was when I started looking into Marc, and then one of the witness statements Darnell dug up suddenly made sense. Darnell couldn't make it fit when he thought it was the brothers and Yanis.'

'What statement are you talking about?'

'Just before the three friends went missing, a witness said they heard a man with a British accent talking to Yanis and Caleb outside the Afrique. Darnell thought this British guy was irrelevant. So did the original cops who worked the case. So did I for a long time.' She paused, eyes flicking to Marc. 'But now I can see the truth.'

'That doesn't prove *anything!*' Marc shouted, his voice breaking up. Saliva bubbled at his lips. He turned to me. 'I'm not denying I spent time with them. I'm not. They were old university friends. I'd go out there for aerospace exhibitions. I was at Nellis Air Force Base because I worked with the US military as part of my job. I was in LA because that's where Lockheed Martin are. What was I going to do? Fly to Vegas or out to LA and *not* pick up the phone to them?' He glanced from me to Tori, then back to me. 'I'm not the same as them. I swear to you I'm not. They were my friends, but I swear on my daughter's life I had no idea that they killed anyone.' A fresh wave of tears.

I looked at Tori.

She just watched him with an expression that was difficult to read. I turned to Healy, and I saw the same questions in his face that must have been in mine.

What the hell is going on?
Who do we trust?
What happens next?

'Wilma Steski went to Vegas a couple of weekends before she was murdered,' Tori said, her gaze still locked on Marc. Her voice was quieter all of a sudden, but there was a sharper edge to it now. 'Can you guess who went with her?'

'So what?' Marc said. '*Most* of us in that photo went to Vegas for the weekend. There were forty people on that trip. What about everyone *else*?' He near-screamed the last part. 'I barely even knew Wilma. Why is it me that's the prime susp–'

'That was where you and your mates hatched your plan to take her up into the mountains, wasn't it, Marc? Set her free? Hunt her down like the animals you used to pick off at Big Bear Lake?'

Marc started shaking his head, muttering, 'No, no, no.'

'But you didn't want to give her too much of a chance, did you? You didn't want her to actually get *away* from you? So you tied her hands behind her and took her shoes.'

Still shaking his head: 'No.'

I looked at the pinboard. There was a lot on it, but it still seemed so disparate: a collection of things that didn't quite connect up.

'Do you still have Darnell's casework?' I asked her.

'No. It was in the glovebox in the van.'

And all that was left of the van was a burnt shell.

'And the video camera?' I pointed to it. 'What's on it?'

'Just some test footage I took outside to make sure the camera worked,' she said. I glanced at the TV screen: I realized now that the paused image wasn't just white, it was clouds. 'Later, I was going to put him in front of it.'

She was going to get a confession from Marc.

'Obviously, the original aim was to get both him *and* Caleb in

424

front of the camera,' she went on, as if reading my mind. 'But that got messed up at the Skyline.'

'And after you got their confessions?'

But we all knew what came after, even Marc, and as he saw the gun move at Tori's side, he began trying to free himself from his binds – scared, desperate.

Tears streamed down his face.

'I don't want to die. *Please*. I'm innocent. I just want my family –'

'He's very good,' Tori said, talking over him. 'Isn't he?'

I stared at Marc.

If this really was a lie, it was close to perfect.

'What happened at the quarry?' I said.

They both looked at me now.

But it was Tori who responded: 'A lot. Too much.' She stopped again, her gaze distant, the memories of that day lucidly playing out in her eyes. After a moment she shivered out of it and said, 'I don't know if it might be better to tell it in reverse.'

I frowned. 'What do you mean?'

'I mean, aren't you wondering why he's here? Aren't you wondering where he's been for the last eight months?'

I glanced at Marc while trying to interpret the subtext in Tori's question. And then I got there: 'He escaped at the quarry.'

She nodded. 'Very good.'

'You, Clara and Kyle tried to abduct him at the lake, but he got away.'

'Close enough.'

'Tell me the rest, then.'

'Like I say, it might be better in reverse.'

'I don't want to do it in reverse, Tori, I want to –'

'I don't give a shit what you want,' she said, a razor's edge to her voice now. 'You're not in control here.'

I swallowed, eyed her, then looked towards the kitchen.

Caleb's phone.

'Marc escaped from you at the quarry – and then he hid out in Somerset.'

A half-smile. 'Very good again.'

'That was the 01749 number that called Caleb?'

She nodded. 'That's where this murdering piece of shit has been squirrelled away for the last eight months. I knew he and Caleb would have got in touch – that's why I wanted Miriam to get Caleb's phone. I didn't realize he had two – one work, one personal. But we lucked out. Miriam picked the right one when she went through his pockets.' A pause. It was the first time she'd said her friend's name aloud since we'd got here and, briefly, it seemed to unbalance her. 'All I needed was one solitary lead,' she said softly. 'And that one call from the number down in Somerset was it.'

'So you didn't know where Marc was until you found that number?'

'No.'

'She doesn't know what she's talking about,' Marc sobbed to me.

Tori's eyes narrowed. 'You *were* hiding out there, weren't you?'

'Yes. But I was hiding from *you*.'

'I found out it was a payphone and went straight from the Skyline down to Somerset,' Tori said, killing any follow-up I might have been hoping to ask Marc. 'It didn't take long searching the village before I discovered the house he was staying in. So I watched for a while and then I grabbed him, and then drove him up here. We arrived a couple of hours ago.' She looked around the cottage. 'Miriam and I have been using this place since we left the flat in Angel. We did all our prep there, but we wanted somewhere new for the final few weeks; somewhere that we could abandon quickly if we had to and not leave

426

a trace. I knew this place would be here. I used to come with Mum when we were kids. It's been empty for years. On my days off from the security gig at the Skyline, I'd drive up here and we'd work on everything together.'

I looked at Marc, tears on his face.

'So, yeah, he's been hiding out in Somerset for eight months,' she said, 'hoping that his mate Caleb, or one of Caleb's lackies, would hunt me down and take me off the board before I could find him.' She looked at Marc. 'I guess the plan after I was dead was to re-emerge from hiding?' He shook his head like she was crazy. 'Go home to your wife with some pack of lies and play pretend again?'

'She's delusional,' Marc said.

'Why did you tell me Marc was dead?' I asked Tori.

'Because I needed to buy myself some time in order to locate him, get to wherever he was, and then bring him all the way up here. By telling you he was in that grave, and then you telling the cops, I knew they'd all flood down to Dartmoor and I'd have the space and time to grab Marc and do what I needed to get done. And then, a few days from now, when the cops finally got the forensics back and they realized that it *wasn't* Marc's skeleton in that grave, I'd already be long gone.'

I thought of the news reports I'd seen the previous night, the sources that had said it was Marc. And something else came together: '*You* were the source. You called *FeedMe* and told them it was Marc's body.'

She shrugged. 'They might be on the internet, but they're still a tabloid. They've got no ethics. All they care about is page impressions. You only need one journalist to be willing to run with an unverified source – one that's more desperate for an exclusive than the facts – and the rest follow. Like I say, the lie wouldn't have stood up for very long – in a few days, it would have all fallen apart. But a few days was all I needed.'

'So who's *really* in that grave?'

She didn't answer this time.

I remembered what Tori had said in the car park. *That death, what we had to do to him . . . I never wanted it. He was a good person. He didn't deserve that ending.* She'd made us believe she was talking about Marc, even though she never mentioned him by name.

But she was talking about someone else.

'Is it Benjamin?'

A tremor seemed to pass across the room. I couldn't see her completely in the dark, but I could see enough. Something had altered. I could see an agonized twist of pain on her face.

'It's your brother buried in that grave, isn't it, Tori?'

I took a step and she instantly put the gun to Healy's head.

He flinched, straightened.

'Don't,' she said to me.

I held up a hand. 'How did Benjamin die?'

'I know,' Marc said quietly.

I glanced across my shoulder at him.

'I know,' he said again. 'I know because I was *there*.'

'What are you talking about?'

'It happened at the quarry.'

I looked between Marc and Tori.

But, this time, she said nothing.

'It's the reason she won't tell you straight what happened at the lake,' Marc said, tears running down his cheeks. 'It's the reason she's spouting all this crap about telling the story in reverse. She's trying to delay, trying to confuse you, because she doesn't want you to know the truth about what happened.'

'And what's the truth?'

Marc blinked more tears away. 'She murdered her own brother.'

79

I stared at Tori. 'Is he right?'

She didn't deny it; didn't say anything at all.

'*Listen* to me,' Marc said, pushing forward so hard on the chair, the legs shifted an inch. '*Please,* just listen to me. Yes, that was me who made the call to Caleb. Yes, I was hiding from her. She made it clear when she tried to kidnap me – before I escaped from them all at the quarry – that she was going to murder me. She thought I was involved in these killings. What else was I supposed to do?'

'You could have gone to the police,' I said.

'The *police?*' He looked at me like I was crazy. 'What good have the police been in all of this? Do you seriously think they would have protected me? The same people who've spent the last year thinking Anthony's killer was a *man?*' He gestured to Tori, his lip trembling, his eyes wet. 'No, if I went home, I would have put Sarah at risk. I would have put my little girl at risk. I hid to *protect* them both, to protect myself, and I called Caleb because I wanted to know if it was true. I just wanted to hear him say it. After everything Tori accused me of at the lake that day, I wanted to ask if he and Anthony really *did* kill Tori's mum and Clara's sister. I wanted to know –'

'Enough,' Tori said.

'I called him once,' Marc continued, still looking at me, 'to ask him if it was true. *Once.* And then I didn't speak to him again. I mean, it's right there on his phone. You can see I'm not lying –'

'*Enough.*' Tori pointed the gun at him.

Marc was breathing hard, his shoulders rising and falling.

429

As the wind picked up again, rattling the roof tiles above us, I genuinely had no idea what the truth was any more.

There were holes in both their stories.

Things that didn't make sense.

All I could do was focus in on what I knew for sure – and that was that, of the two of them, Tori was the only confirmed killer. I'd seen her pull the trigger myself.

She might even have killed her own brother.

I couldn't say what Marc was.

He started crying again, trying to stem the flow of tears by brushing a cheek against his shoulder. He was a wreck – or seemed it.

Again, I went back to what I knew for sure.

He'd confronted Sarah's ex at the builders' yard and had been aggressive and threatening – but there had been obvious reasons for that. Otherwise, there was nothing in his life that even remotely suggested the kind of cruelty and sadism that had been inflicted on Wilma, the three friends and Catalina Robbins.

In fact, everything Tori had accused him of, every way in which she'd tried to pin him to these murders, he appeared to have a rational explanation for. Even hiding from her in the aftermath of whatever happened at the quarry, extreme as it was, fitted the image of the man that Sarah had described to me. He'd been protecting them.

And then something caught my eye.

Healy's left hand was in his pocket. He had moved it there without anyone noticing. What the hell was he doing? I glanced at Tori again, who didn't seem to have clocked it.

Yet.

'What's the plan here?' I said, trying to keep her attention on me, pointing at the pinboard, the video camera; at Marc, at myself. 'Why are you telling us all of this?'

'You want to know, don't you?'

'Yeah, but are you just going to let us walk away after you're done?'

She didn't respond.

'Or are you going to kill us?'

Again, nothing.

'Tori, I don't know what's –'

'*Healy?*'

We all stopped. From somewhere else, there was a different voice, saying Healy's name.

'*Healy?*'

The four of us looked at each other.

It was a female; distant, muted.

Tori understood what was happening a second before I did: she locked her arm around Healy's neck, yanked him back towards her, and put the gun to the side of his head.

'Take it out,' she said to him.

He nodded, best as he could, and drew his left hand out of his pocket.

'Slowly.'

He was holding his phone.

The screen was illuminated.

It was in the middle of a call.

Tori grabbed it from him, looked at who was on the line and then instantly ended the conversation. She threw the handset against the wall. The case shattered, the screen splintering, but she made sure it was dead by grinding it into the flagstone floor with her boot – teeth gritted, stamping on it repeatedly.

'You stupid *prick*,' she spat, and trapped Healy in a standing headlock again, her mouth at his ear. 'Is Clarkson a cop?'

Healy's eyes stayed on mine, his hands on her arm.

'Is Clarkson a *cop?*'

'Yes,' he wheezed.

431

'*Shit*. How long have you had her on the line?'

He tried to swallow. 'Long enough.'

She released Healy and he staggered forward a little, holding his throat, but I kept my gaze fixed on Tori in the shadows behind him.

I didn't know if Healy's move had made it better or worse for us.

She was furious.

But now she was against the clock.

She glanced at the pinboard, at the camera on the tripod. I could see the intensity of her thoughts, the intelligence behind her eyes, the swirl of information that she was dealing with and making order of.

But then she seemed to relax, fill out.

She looked at me. 'Okay, Clarkson probably has our location now, thanks to your pal here. So let's assume they're on their way. The GMP's average response time is sixteen and a half minutes. Up here, it'll be longer. Twenty, twenty-two.'

I felt a slow, creeping dread slither through me.

Was this it? Had Healy forced her into doing something drastic now? Was she about to pull the trigger? I looked at Marc, who looked at me, and he seemed to sense something big was coming too because he looked terrified again.

'Tori,' I said. 'Tori, listen. We can –'

'I don't want to cut it too fine.'

I frowned. 'What?'

'So let's say we've got ten minutes.'

'What do you mean? Ten minutes to do what?'

'To talk about it.'

She checked her watch again.

And then, finally, she said, 'To talk about what happened at the quarry . . .'

80

I felt completely thrown. The clock was running down, the cops were on their way and yet she wanted to talk about the quarry.

I wanted to talk about it too.

I wanted to know *everything*.

But why wasn't she making a break for it?

She did something to her watch, and then – as she turned her wrist – I saw she'd started a ten-minute countdown.

'I guess I should begin with Kyle,' she said. 'He was never part of the plan. Or, not to the degree he ended up being involved. He and Miriam, they just . . .' She searched for the right word. 'Clicked. I didn't expect that. I mean, she was twenty-two, four years older than him. I didn't think it would last. But Miriam said he was so kind, so sweet. He listened to her, cared for her, was mature, intelligent. The more she talked about him, the more alarm bells went off – but I told her it was fine in the short term, because it added colour to the life of Clara Dearton. I'd sent her to Devon to get to know him as a friend. I wanted her to be someone who would pass in and out of his life, but would let us get familiar with the Fowlers.'

'You're deranged,' Marc muttered, again wiping an eye on his shoulder.

I didn't even know what to say.

I still didn't understand what she was doing.

'I told Miriam that at some point she was going to have to drop Kyle and walk away, and she said that she understood. But knowing it and doing it – they were two different things. And she didn't just start falling for Kyle, she started falling for the whole family. It was clouding her judgement. I mean, even him' – she pointed at Marc – 'she started to like. I could see it. She was telling herself not to, but at the same time she was allowing herself to get seduced by the pretend version of himself that he put on for everyone. And I knew why she fell for it. I'm not stupid.'

Tori looked at me. *It was like having a family again.*

She felt wanted.

She felt loved.

'In the end, she'd built up such an attachment to the family that I could really only see one way out. That was why I brought Kyle on-board.'

She checked her watch.

I glanced at mine.

Ninety seconds had passed already.

When I turned back to Tori, her eyes were on Marc. 'I needed to change the dynamic. I needed Kyle to look at Marc differently, to know the truth about who his stepdad was. Because if I did that, it would unbalance him, shatter the illusion of who Marc was – and if Kyle was seeing clearly, it'd be a hard reset for Miriam too.'

'So what did you do to prove to Kyle who Marc was?'

'That.' She gestured to the pinboard. 'We showed him all the work Darnell had compiled for us. We helped him join the dots between the murders and Marc.'

'You sold him a lie,' Marc moaned.

'We showed him the truth.'

'It's not the truth. It's your *version* of the truth.'

'You don't know what your –'

'He's my *boy*.'

'He isn't *your* boy.'

'I love him,' Marc said, 'and he loved me, and you tried to

destroy every good thing – every good memory – he and I had together.'

Marc dropped his head – disconsolate, exhausted.

I saw Healy watching him, still the same question on his face. *What was real here?*

'But you said there weren't any photos of Marc in Darnell's casework?'

'No,' Tori responded.

'And you said Darnell dismissed the man with the British accent who was seen talking to the three friends as irrelevant.'

'Only because he couldn't make it fit the evidence he had. Like I told you, he thought the three hunters were Caleb, Yanis and Asha. I believed that too until I got Yanis talking. But it was Marc. He was British. He had all that history with Caleb and Yanis. He was at Caltech with them, he was in the same year as Wilma Steski, he went hunting with Caleb and Yanis, used the same *rounds* that were found in the victims. We had enough to show Kyle we were right.'

But *were* they right?

I didn't know any more, because none of those things were smoking guns. The only photograph that even showed Marc in the same room as Caleb and Yanis was a faded shot from thirty years ago. I started to wonder if one of the major reasons Kyle agreed to come on-board, to work with the women, wasn't Tori's evidence, such as it was, but Clara herself: her history, her story, her pain. Kyle was deeply in love for the first time – and that first love didn't just consume, often it blinded.

'When did Kyle first get involved?' I asked.

'In the April.'

Five months before the quarry. That must have been just before Kyle had gone searching on *Evidence Bag* for stories about Tori's mum.

'He was curious,' Tori said. 'But we quickly put a stop to that.

If he wanted answers, he came to us. We kept everything offline.'

That explained why Kyle's time on *Evidence Bag* had only lasted six days.

She looked at Marc. 'But even though we told him the truth about Marc, I could still see the battle raging in him.'

'What do you mean?'

'I mean, even though he was infatuated with Miriam, Kyle still had so many moments when he didn't believe Marc was the man we'd described. They'd sit down to dinner together in the evening, or the two of them would watch the football, or they'd go out for a run, and Kyle would be all over the place again. That was why I told you I never really trusted him. I brought him on to help Miriam focus, and that part worked. She didn't have to keep what we were doing secret from Kyle any more, which made her happier, and in turn made her better. But Kyle . . .' She took a breath. 'It was exhausting. I kept having to get Miriam to tell him about her family. *Remind* him. She'd sit there, almost every single day, telling him about how, when those men killed Florida, they destroyed Miriam's life. She'd tell him how her dad got on the booze, her mum the painkillers; how they lost their jobs, lost their house . . .' Her voice began to tremor, the suffering of the Joneses her own suffering too. 'Miriam's mum ended up drowning in the bathtub. Her dad wrapped his car around a lamp post. You can trace both of those things back to him.'

As she looked at Marc again, I said, 'But Kyle didn't even know about Yanis. When I told him about you killing Yanis at the Skyline, he blanked.'

She nodded. 'We gave him the edited highlights from Darnell's casework, ignored Yanis and kept his attention on Caleb and Marc. It was hard enough to keep him focused on Marc, on what we needed to do. If we'd talked about what we'd done to

Yanis at the Skyline, Kyle would have freaked out. So we told him enough to make him feel like he was looped in – but not everything. Like I said, I realized early on that, if Kyle was close, Miriam was focused. We were too far down the line for me to abandon her – not that I wanted to do that. She was like a sister to me. But with Kyle there, I had the best version of her, the one that was sharp and organized. She wasn't with me on the night that Yanis died – she wanted to be, but we just couldn't make it work without risking it all. But she set it all up for me. She was in the Skyline for weeks before I first went and introduced myself to Yanis. She was a brilliant organizer. She mapped out every casino floor inside there, every camera, so I knew exactly where I was going before I ever stepped foot in there. She did all this research for me on Yanis, on Caleb, on Marc. We were a perfect team. She was the arrow; I was the arrowhead.' *She was the planner; I was the executor.* 'Kyle was always too soft. He was already up and down about Marc the whole bloody time – imagine if I'd then pulled him aside and told him that I'd killed Yanis.'

'But he wasn't too soft to abandon his family.'

'We told him, once we'd done what we needed to do, that he could go back. We would give him a story to tell about why he'd been missing.'

'Which was a lie.'

She just looked at me. If she'd had any intention of letting Kyle return home, she wouldn't have poisoned him the night before.

'You didn't tell him you were going to kill Caleb and Marc, did you?'

'No,' she said.

'So what did he think the endgame was?'

'That we were going to get the confessions from the men and then hand them over to the police. He bought into it,

437

because it was what Miriam said was going to happen. Whatever she said to him, he believed.' She glanced at Marc, his eyes red, his body slumped. 'I do think, deep down, a part of him wanted to see the real Marc. He wanted to see the monster. He wanted to see whether his stepdad could really be that man.'

'And the killing came easy to you?' I asked.

She searched my face for judgement, for revulsion at all the lives she'd taken. But I wasn't asking the question to bait her. I genuinely wanted to know.

She glanced at her watch again.

I did the same.

Five minutes left.

'No,' she said, her voice calm despite the ticking clock. 'It didn't come easy. In the moment with Yanis, I let it all out. This was one of the men who took my mum from me; one of the men who destroyed all those other families too. I had so much rage. But, afterwards, I was a mess. The gravity of what I'd done began to crush me. And in those moments, I would read newspaper stories online about Mum, about how she was just dumped in the desert like she meant nothing to anyone . . .' Her voice trembled for the first time. 'Sometimes I'd think, "What's wrong with me?" And then I'd read about my mum, and about all the other people these fucking animals killed, and I'd think, "There's nothing wrong with me. What I'm doing is right. It's just." I wasn't going to let those men go to jail. That would be too good for them.'

Marc shook his head again. His spirit suddenly seemed broken. Tori had a gun; he was tied to a chair. There was no way out.

Not unless I can stop her pulling that trigger.

'Tell me about the quarry,' I said.

'I *am* telling you.'

'No, not the build-up, the actual day. How did you make all of it happen inside sixty seconds?'

438

She shrugged. 'We didn't.'

'What?'

'We'd been testing sedatives for weeks – dosages, how long they lasted, all of that. Miriam dropped enough into Sarah's drink before they headed out on that boat to put her under for around thirty minutes. Once they got to the shore where I was waiting, Miriam went back around to where Sarah was and set Sarah's watch back, while Kyle and I dealt with him.' She glanced at Marc and I remembered how Marc had talked about escaping from the quarry. Now all I needed to know was how it had gone down. 'Miriam stayed with Sarah, kept an eye on Mable – and then, a few minutes before Sarah was due to wake up, she headed back around to us. By the time she got back to us . . .' She stopped, glanced at Marc again, at me. *By the time she got back to us, it had all gone to shit. Marc had escaped.* 'Anyway, that's why, when Sarah finally woke up, it looked like only a minute had passed.'

A time change and a tiny amount of sedative was all it had taken to have three people disappear into thin air – to fool Sarah, and park rangers, and the cops.

And me.

'I knew about Sarah's tumour,' Tori said. 'Kyle and Miriam didn't – I didn't tell them, because I knew it would mess with their heads in the run-up to the lake – but I knew. We got hold of her phone through Kyle because I wanted to know more about her, and I read her messages and texts. Buried in her emails were a couple from the hospital.'

She paused, looked at me, a flash of guilt.

'You knew the sixty-seconds thing would play into the police's fears about Sarah possibly being sick,' I said. 'How it might have affected her judgement and memory.'

'Yes.'

Marc's face hardened. 'She was *sick*. How could you do that to her?'

439

Tori just looked at him, unmoved.

'But at some point later on she must have noticed her watch was half an hour out?' I said. *And if she had, why hadn't she ever mentioned that detail to me?*

Tori shook her head. 'Miriam told me that Sarah always took her watch off at night and left it downstairs, in the kitchen, next to her purse. The same routine, every evening. That was where the whole idea started. So, after she got back from the lake, I got into the house while she and Mable were sleeping and altered the time back.'

Again, it was so simple.

They would have just used Kyle's front-door key.

They didn't even have to break in.

'Mable could have drowned while Sarah was unconscious.' I kept my voice even, non-threatening. 'She was wandering around at the shore by herself for –'

'Miriam was watching her.'

'Not the whole time.'

'She was *fine.*'

'So why take Marc at the quarry?' I said. 'Why make it so elaborate?'

'It wasn't elaborate, it was simple. Or supposed to be. We did it at the lake because he loved that place and his guard would be completely down – but mostly because there would be no cameras and no witnesses. We could get him off the boat and away from the quarry and no one would ever see a thing. Plus, like I said, the impossibility of it all, that tiny amount of time that Sarah claimed she was asleep for, it would all help play into . . .' She stopped again. *Into Sarah's illness.* 'It was going to be so clean.' Her voice was hushed, the regret woven into it. *Going* to be so clean. But it hadn't been.

Marc had escaped.

Something had gone wrong.

She sidestepped out from behind Healy. 'You want to know what my endgame is? Do you want to know why I'm standing here and explaining all of this to you – basically confessing? It's because there was barely enough time to get everything done *before* you arrived here – and there definitely isn't now. You finding me so soon, this stunt your mate here pulled with the phone call, I don't have the time to put it all together now. I wanted the media to have everything. I wanted to send it to them properly ordered, easy to follow, logical. I wanted it watertight.'

She checked her watch.

Two minutes.

And as I looked at her – as her eyes returned to mine – something she'd just said sank in: *I don't have the time to put it all together now.*

'Healy and I are the replacement for the evidence you were going to send out.'

Something moved in her expression.

Confirmation.

I looked outside, searching the darkness for any sign of the cops. 'When the cops arrive, *we're* going to be the ones that fill in the gaps for them. All the stuff you were going to use is here. But instead of you writing a letter to the media that explains it all, and sending it out with the evidence, *we're* going to be your letter.'

A hint of a smile on her face.

'But you haven't told us everything,' I said.

'What haven't I told you?'

'You haven't told us the exact details of how it went down.' I took a tiny step closer to her. 'You haven't told us why you killed Benjamin.'

Another minor movement in her face.

'And even if you do, this isn't enough,' I said, pointing to the pinboard. 'You know that, right? This is circumstantial. It doesn't prove that Marc killed anyone. It doesn't prove that –'

'All I ask is that you remember what I've told you. It's important that you tell people the truth. As my gran used to say, "Do not forget to do good and to share with others." Hebrews 13:16.' The corners of her mouth turned up. 'I loved her deeply, but she could be a bit much sometimes. Anyway, I don't think she – or Jesus – were ever big fans of revenge.'

She came around the table, to the television.

Marc started to panic behind me, thinking this was it, the end, the last bullet for the last of the hunters.

But then Tori went to the video camera instead.

She took it into the centre of the room, and – kicking out the legs with her foot – set the tripod down. 'If you try to follow me, I'll kill you,' she said.

As she let go of the tripod, her sleeve crept up her arm – and, for the first time, I saw the ink on her wrist: a pair of angel's wings and a zip code.

And then, with one last look at us, she moved through the door, returning to the darkness of the hallway that would take her to the back room and her things.

And, after that, we never saw Victoria Robbins again.

81

I told Healy to cut Marc loose with his penknife.

Marc began thanking us, over and over, almost on the verge of tears again.

But I was only half listening.

I was too busy staring at the pinboard, at the photos, the cuttings, the Post-it notes in handwriting I was struggling to read and that only appeared to tell a part of what might have gone on. It all felt so disconnected. There was a single photograph of Marc, nothing about Benjamin Robbins at all, and a bunch of people and places that didn't seem relevant to anything Tori had talked about.

And I still had no clue whether Marc was guilty or not.

He lifted himself out of the chair, his bones clicking stiffly, and wiped his eyes. Rubbing his wrists where they'd been bound with duct tape, he looked at us and cowered. He seemed genuinely terrified, and I had the same thought that I'd had earlier on: *If this is a lie, it's as good as any I've ever seen.* There was no hint of deception in his face, no sense that this was an act.

'Thank you.' His eyes flicked out to the room. 'I don't know who you are, or why you're here, but thank you.'

'Sarah hired me to find you.'

At the mention of Sarah, tears filled his eyes again. 'Is she okay? I've tried to keep an eye on her from afar. I even took a train down there once, stood outside the house and watched her in the kitchen.' He looked broken. 'I miss them so much.'

Again, I couldn't detect a lie.

If there is one.

'What are you thinking?' Healy said to me.

My eyes strayed back to the pinboard. 'Tori was smart. I mean, *seriously* smart. But all of this . . .' I pointed to the board. 'This is a mess.'

'She said we were the ones who were going to fill in the gaps.'

I nodded. 'But she hasn't given us enough of the picture. We can't join the dots on this stuff. I mean, what does this have to do with anything?' I tapped a cutting from a business magazine. It was a profile of a woman called Rina Trego, who – according to a caption – was the owner of a small chain of restaurants in Birmingham. 'Or this.' I singled out a screenshot from a GOV.UK page where a vehicle search had been made for a Renault Kangoo. I looked at the other things that were dotted around: pictures of jewellery; a satellite map of a Scottish village called Comty; a hotel room from Booking.com; printouts from Google Street View.

'Would it be possible for me to go to the toilet?'

We looked at Marc.

'You can come with me if you don't trust me. I just . . .' He swallowed. 'I've been here hours and I'm . . .' Now he looked embarrassed. 'I'm desperate.'

'I'll take him,' Healy said, and looked at Marc. 'I walk you out, you take a piss, you zip up, we come back. If you try anything, I'll stick this penknife in your throat. Clear?'

'Clear,' Marc echoed, his voice small.

As they left, I heard sirens cutting across the wind for the first time. I glanced out of the windows and into the darkness of the moors.

A tiny blink of blue light had pierced the night.

I switched my attention back to the pinboard – but, instead, my gaze stopped on something else.

The video camera.

Tori had moved it, set it down in the middle of the room . . . and done nothing. It was still connected to the TV, still paused on the same white screen.

I hurried across to it and pressed Play.

On the TV, the white screen came to life.

The camera panned down from the clouds it had been paused on to the outside of the cottage during the day. Wind crackled in its microphone.

This was the test footage Tori had been talking about.

I turned up the volume. On-screen, in a jagged shard of glass in one of the windows, I glimpsed her reflection. She was in a hoody, leggings, holding the camera at her shoulder. There was no date on the footage, but this must have been recent – maybe one of her days off from the Skyline.

She passed into the cottage.

The wind stopped battering the microphone as she headed into the room I was in now. Clara was at the table. She was sitting down, a laptop open in front of her, and looked across her shoulder at Tori, smiling. 'What are you doing with that?'

'Making sure it works,' Tori responded.

Tori began to zoom in on Clara. 'Are you ready for your close-up, darling?' she said in a posh accent. 'This is your big moment.'

Clara started laughing.

Tori did too, the camera shaking against her, and for a fraction of a second, these weren't two killers, they were two friends – two young women who'd spent more of their lives as children than as adults – laughing about something stupid.

'You're going to be famous,' Tori said.

Clara was still laughing. 'I don't want to be fam–'

The video cut to black.

I took a step closer, trying to work out why Tori would switch off the camera in the middle of Clara saying something.

But then I realized the camera hadn't stopped.

Whatever this was now, it had been recorded *over* the test footage of Tori and Clara. I listened, could hear talking on the video, but it was very muffled.

And then the screen lightened.

The picture focused.

And everything changed.

82

Tori had been standing in front of the lens.

It was why it had been black.

But as she stepped away, everything became clearer.

She was in the living room of the cottage. It was daytime but her surroundings were shadowed. As she took another step forward, I saw her left hand trailing slightly, as if she'd just reached behind herself for something and was trying to disguise having done so.

The control panel on the camera.

She'd covertly pressed Record on it.

In the footage, the video camera was still on the tripod, and the tripod was leaning diagonally against the mantelpiece. It wasn't supposed to be on. It wasn't supposed to be recording. It was why the picture was at a slant.

She took a third step, a fourth.

'I just loved my family so much,' Tori said.

Beyond her, the living room was dark and she'd stopped this side of the table, her back to the camera. The TV was off.

'My mum brought us up without any help,' she said. 'Our dad pissed off as soon as Ben was born. He never wanted me, not really, but he definitely didn't want a second. It turned out to be the best thing he ever did. It forged the three of us.'

She leaned forward, put her hands on the table.

'Ben was a good kid, a good little brother. He was funny, such a gentle soul. Like, every year he'd pick Mum flowers from the garden and bring them in for her birthday. It was just this silly tradition we had, but it was . . . it was . . .'

It was everything.

Who was she talking to?

'And then Mum was taken from us, and – after that – Covid hit. Being locked down like that, it was like a pressure cooker. Every day, I felt more powerless, got angrier. And when I couldn't get any angrier, I got focused, thinking about what I was going to do with that anger. That was why it felt like fate when Darnell Savage called me. He put me in touch with Miriam, and the two of us . . .' She'd half turned now; I could see her eyes glistening. 'We were kindred spirits, Mim and me. We knew what we needed to do.'

Out of the corner of my eye, I saw more blue lights against the darkness of the moors; the snatched wail of a siren caught on the wind.

On-screen, Tori had started talking again: 'Ben was the same. I mean, you think *I* was close to Mum . . . He was a teenager, so he never would have admitted it, but Mum was his sun and his stars. So when Miriam and I started to plan everything out, I thought, "I can channel his anger into this." He was seventeen by then, he'd filled out, become strong. We were alone one night, we'd had a few drinks, we were upset because my gran had just died, and I said to him, "What would you do if the person who killed Mum was here now?" And everything about him changed.' She clicked her fingers. 'Just like that. This *rage*. So I introduced him to Miriam on Zoom – who was already pretending to be Clara by then and living down in Devon – and I told him we'd been working together for months and that we were going to move in on Yanis. After that, I took Ben down to London with us.'

It struck me again how organized the two women had been; how efficiently they'd folded all their fury and heartache into their mission.

But who the hell is she confessing this to?

'Unfortunately, he started drinking,' she said quietly. 'I stopped being able to trust him. I started to realize that I *couldn't* let him get involved in all of this because he was too volatile, too unreliable. I think that was another reason why I let Kyle join us eventually. He gave us that physical advantage if we needed it, he was the third person I knew we might eventually require in order to get at Caleb, but he was quiet, and he was steady. He was the total opposite of Ben. Ben just wouldn't focus at all.'

'You stupid fucking bitch.'

A whisper from the night.

I tensed, edged closer to the TV.

'I brought Ben with us to the quarry that day,' Tori said, as if she hadn't even heard the voice, 'because I wanted him to see. I couldn't take him with me when I got rid of Yanis at the Skyline, but I could take him with me to the quarry. I just told him to sit in the car and watch. That was all he was supposed to do.' She shifted slightly to the left, turning her face even more. It was like she was subtly opening herself up, allowing the camera to see beyond her, into the shadows. 'I wanted him to see one of the men who murdered Mum up close.' And then she moved again.

Another half-step.

Another.

And although her movements were only small, although it looked like she was simply changing position at the table, what she was really doing was allowing the camera a full view of what was in front of her.

'And what do you think your brother made of it all after I cut his throat?' The second voice again. It was much more familiar this time. 'Were you glad you brought him with you? Was it worth

449

it? You really are a fucking child. You all were. You thought you were so clever, but now look at you. One's dead, one's in a coma, and your brother is in a grave.'

'You destroyed my family.'

And then his face came out of the shadows – into the grey light cast by a nearby window – and Marc Fowler, expressionless, unemotional, said, 'So what?'

83

I stared at him, at this new version of him, transfixed by the way he looked.

His expression was a complete void.

He leaned further forward, pushing against the duct tape that secured him to the chair he was on, and said something else – but this time it was too quiet for me to pick up.

'Do you admit you murdered her?' Tori said. Even through the old speakers at the back of the TV set, unrefined as they were, I could hear the tautness of her voice. And now everything that had come before this moment – her standing inside this cottage and answering my questions; her using us as a proxy to fill in the gaps that remained – made sense. We only needed some of the answers.

The rest were on here.

Out of the old speakers on the TV, as Marc's voice got a little louder, I realized what he was saying. He was repeating the same thing, whispering it – putting on a southern accent, toying with her.

'Run, Catalina, run.'

'So you admit it?' Tori asked again.

She needed him to say it.

She needed it on tape.

He glanced beyond her. For one terrible second I thought he'd figured out he was being recorded. But then his focus switched back to her.

'Yes,' he said simply.

'It was your bullet that killed her?'

'It was,' he said, leaning back on the chair, half of him vanishing into the night. 'I was always the best hunter. Anthony had the gift of the gab, so would be the one who kicked things off when we decided to switch it up.' *Switch it up*. From animals to humans. 'He was the one who first chatted with your mum, with Casey Ryker too; he was the one who spoke to Wilma Steski the most. He was my blood brother, but he was a fat bastard – too much food, too much booze. So he was never going to make the kill shot. And Caleb . . . Cay was good. It was usually between us. But I was better.'

He looked at Tori, studied her from the shadows.

She was absolutely still.

'We set the three friends loose in the Angeles National Forest. I shot Casey Ryker. She was a firecracker, a tough cookie. The hardest one to kill. Cay, he did Florida and Ryan. Once they were all dead, we put them in the back of a truck and dumped them at the debris basin. Before that, in '93, with Wilma – we let Ant have her. He got lucky more than anything. Cay and I, we circled her, forced her around towards him, made it easy for him.' Marc made her wait. 'And your mum . . .' Another pause, prolonging the pain.

Tori took the bait. 'What about her?'

Her voice gave way.

Marc picked up on it instantly, like a scent. 'We put her in the back of Caleb's truck and drove her up an old mining track, into the high desert. There are trees up there, it's elevated, but they're not as thick. It wasn't as much fun as when we set Casey, Florida and Ryan loose. That was a real challenge. Your mum . . .' He shrugged. 'She was a good runner. Fit. Lovely little body, actually. But, out in the desert, it's just easier to track game. So the chase didn't last long.'

'You're a monster,' Tori said quietly.

'I guess that makes two of us.'

'We're not the same.'

'Anthony and Caleb would say otherwise.'

'They got what they deserved.'

'And is that what I'm going to get too? You going to stick a knife in me twenty-seven times and then plaster a Bible quote over the wall in my blood?'

She didn't respond.

'You should never have taken your brother to the quarry,' Marc said. 'You know that, right? If you'd left him out of this, he'd still be alive. You're the reason he died.'

She said nothing.

'He was "just supposed to watch from the car", you say. Basic error. Never bring anyone in you don't trust one hundred per cent of the time. I mean, I remember that day like it only just happened. Clara pulling that little pistol out of her sling, telling me to row over to where you'd parked at the shore. The expression on Kyle's face . . .' He trailed off, blinked. Despite everything, I caught the first real moment of vulnerability: he genuinely loved Kyle, loved Sarah, loved Mable too. So much of what he'd done was psychopathic, so perhaps his love for them was irreparably flawed, a love that ultimately served his own purposes and not theirs – but whatever it was, whatever he felt for them, it was real to him. 'That look on Kyle's face, that was when it brought it home to me – even more than Clara pointing the gun. I could see how much she'd fucked with his head. When he looked at me, it was like he was looking at a stranger . . .'

'We told him the truth about you.'

'The things you do for love,' he said, as if he hadn't even heard her, as if he was still trapped in the memory of how Kyle had looked at him. His gaze switched back to Tori. 'The second we got to the shore – when Clara passed you the gun and then ran off to mess with Sarah's watch – I knew your brother was the weak point. Inside that car, gripping the wheel, like a bull ready to charge. I thought, "If he comes at me, I can use it." And that was what he did. He stormed out of that car, shouting, swearing, waving his knife around. I knew you didn't have control; Kyle didn't know what the hell to do either. I mean, you obviously didn't even know your brother had *brought* that knife. So when he got to me it was easy to spin him around. He was way too angry, had zero control. It was easy to get the knife, easy to put it to his throat, easy to get you to drop the gun. I should have taken your car – but I didn't think about it in that moment. There was too much going on. All I was thinking was, "I need to create a diversion so I can get away."' He paused. 'So that was why I cut your brother's throat.'

Now she wobbled.

It was subtle, maybe not even visible to Marc, but I could see it. She pressed the front of her thigh against the edge of the table, using it to support her weight.

'When I was running, the last thing I saw was you trying to get your brother into the car. There was so much blood. You must have known you couldn't save him?'

'He was my brother.'

'You had to try, I guess,' Marc responded, as if Tori had said nothing. 'Why did you bury him in that grave on Dartmoor?'

She remained quiet, but the answer seemed obvious: Ben was dying, and even if in the panic of the moment she'd been thinking about driving him to a hospital, she knew the truth. With his throat cut, her brother would be dead long before she ever got him to a doctor – and being at a hospital meant questions.

She'd never get a shot at Caleb.

She'd never get a second chance with Marc.

Her brother's death would have been for nothing.

'Ben couldn't swim,' Tori said. 'He never learned. In the

run-up to that day, I thought, "I need everything to go perfectly. I don't want to leave *anything* to chance. So I put a life
jacket on him – on both of us – just to be sure. I went through
all the worst-case scenarios in my planning – everything – right
down to you fighting back, dragging us into water, trying to
drown us. I didn't want to leave a single thing to chance. But . . .'
She stopped. 'But I had a blind spot.'

'He was your blind spot.'

Silence – profound, weighted with everything that had
happened.

'I don't know what your plan is,' Marc said. He looked out at
the room but still didn't seem to notice the camera. 'Was it to
make me confess? You know I'll deny it all, right? You know
that, when it comes down to it, I've got a good explanation
for everything? The problem *you've* got is that now everyone
knows who you really are. Tori Robbins's picture is already
all over the media. The public know what you look like. The
public know you're a killer. That's called a *position of weakness*.
Me? All anyone knows about me is that I'm a loving husband
and father, a respected work colleague, and there's absolutely
nothing in my past that even remotely points towards the version of me you're trying to sell them. And whether you kill me
or you don't, all anyone will know after this is that you and your
friends tried to abduct me eight months ago because you
thought I was – what? – a *serial killer*? It won't stack up. You're
going to look like the hunter here, not me. I mean, I was hiding
down in Somerset because I was just so scared of you.'

'You *were* scared of me.'

'Don't flatter yourself. I was only supposed to be down there
for a few weeks. Caleb was all talk as usual. "I got my best man
on it. Sit tight." He had a burner I used to call him on – except
for that one time when I'd been stewing, getting angrier and
angrier that Cay *still* hadn't found you, and I just didn't think.

I slipped up and called him on his personal phone. I'd been sitting there for *months* at that point, waiting for Kerrill to find Clara, you and Kyle.' As he said Kyle's name, his voice gave way a fraction. And it happened again as he started talking about Sarah, and about Mable: 'That day when I went back to Totnes and sat outside the house, just watching Sarah, I saw her and Mabe jump in the car and I thought, "Fuck it," and got inside. I just wanted to be . . .' The bravado was gone.

I just wanted to be closer to them.

'I saw she'd hired Raker; saw notes about it on her laptop, internet searches. I said to Caleb, "We can use this. Raker's good. If anyone can find Kyle, Clara and Tori, it'll be him – and if he finds you lot, we can find out who this Whaler was who killed Anthony."' He smiled at her, humourlessly. 'We knew you must have been a team, that the Whaler must have been a *part* of your team, but we honestly never realized that you and he were the same person. It seems insane now, but we just never put two and two together. Anthony being so hung up on you . . .' He looked Tori up and down, taking in her face, her body. 'I mean, I get it. Who wouldn't want a piece of you? But him not telling us he had a new girlfriend, keeping you secret like that, that's why we're here now. If he'd stopped thinking about his dick for one second and told us, you'd be dead. I would have put the bullet in you myself.'

'You've always underestimated me,' Tori said in response.

Now something felt different. If I could feel it just watching, Marc would have definitely felt it there in the room.

'You called me a child earlier,' she said. 'If I was a child, you'd have got to me before I got to you. If I was a child, I wouldn't have survived as long as I have, found a guy to do my IDs for me, another to get me a gun and teach me how to disappear in plain sight. If I was a child, I wouldn't have walked into the heart of the Skyline and got a job right under your

456

noses.' The anger in her was raw and unmistakable. 'I wouldn't have had you and your friends fooled about whether I was even a man or a woman. And there's something else that I don't think I would have been able to do . . .'

She was making him wait this time.

'This thing – the reason you're here – it's not just about Wilma, and Casey, and Ryan, and Florida, and Catalina' – every name said slowly, emphasized, as if being etched forever into stone – 'it's also about something else. It's about something even your friends Anthony and Caleb don't know about.'

And then there it was in his face.

Shock.

Panic.

What has she found out about him?

'I spent the best part of two years planning and executing all of this. I made it my life's work getting to know Yanis, and Caleb, and you – and when I started on you, I began finding things that didn't add up. Whenever Miriam – sorry, *Clara* – was at your house, she'd go through your drawers and take photos of bank statements and credit-card receipts. She'd go into your computer and look around for me. So, because I'm *not* a child, because neither of us were, that was how we found Rina Trego.'

Rina Trego.

I remembered the picture from the business magazine, the article profiling her small chain of restaurants.

'That was how I found Isabelle McLeish.'

McLeish. A Scottish name.

The satellite picture of the Scottish village called Comty.

'That was how I found Alyssa Venables, who's never actually turned up, but whose necklace was found outside the hotel she was staying in at Birmingham NEC.'

The hotel room and the jewellery pictures on the board.

457

'That was how I found out about your secret car, the one you keep stored in a garage in Plymouth that Sarah doesn't know about, that *no one* knows about.'

The Renault Kangoo.

'That was how I found out that you didn't just kill in the US, when you were there having fun with your pals *Ant* and *Cay*. You did it here. I think you might have been doing it here since you came back from Caltech in the mid-nineties. I think you do it when you go away to work conferences, like at the NEC, or when you have to go and see customers, like you do up in Comty in Scotland. I mean, you don't shit in your own back-yard, right? And no one else has a clue, do they, Marc? Even Anthony and Caleb. This has always been your own little private thing.' She took a step closer, moving to the other side of the table but not obscuring him from the camera. 'So if I was a child, how would I have figured out you've raped and killed seven women?'

84

I froze. *Seven women. Seven more victims.*

And now the game was up.

It was all over Marc's face.

For the first time, the best liar I'd ever seen didn't have a lie good enough. And I finally realized why Tori hadn't killed him, like she'd killed Yanis and Caleb.

She wanted the seven other victims to have a voice.

She wanted to give their families closure.

And the only way to do that was if the cops forced Marc to talk.

Suddenly, like a switch snapping on, the room filled in around me, the specks I'd seen against the darkness now fully formed police cars, their sirens wailing, blue light washing across the moorland. They couldn't be more than a mile away.

But where the hell is Healy?

I checked my watch.

He and Marc had been gone way too long.

Pausing the video camera, I hurried across to the door that led out to the back of the house. Wind whispered past me, carried into the cottage.

In the hallway, there was no movement.

'Healy?'

My heart started to thump in my chest. What the hell had I done? I'd sent him into the dark with a serial killer.

I darted along the hallway, quickening my pace.

Halfway down, I saw a shard of broken glass on the floor. I pulled down the sleeve of my jacket and scooped it up, gripping the sides with the fabric.

'Healy?'

Sirens, getting louder.

I stopped at the back entrance – at what had once been the rear door – and looked along the corridor, into the bedroom that Tori had been sleeping in.

I said his name again.

Nothing.

Outside, the wind hit me hard, funnelled along the back of the house by the wall of the escarpment.

Blue light everywhere now, painting the moors.

'Healy?'

My voice was being drowned out by the sirens.

I got to the side of the house and looked out across the hills, down to the main road. There were three police cars at the gate. A fourth wasn't far behind.

That was when I saw him.

I saw both of them.

Marc was lying in a patch of long grass to the side of the track as it began to ascend sharply from the cottage. He was face down, the grass moving around him. Blood leaked from his hairline. I saw more blood on a rock, embedded in the dirt close by. When I felt for a pulse, one faintly tapped back against my fingers.

Five feet from Marc lay Healy.

He was face up, eyes closed, not moving.

His jacket was torn – showing the struggle they'd had – and there was blood all over his stomach. It looked like he might have landed on his arm too, bent it under him, broken it. It was twisted from the elbow at an impossible angle.

'Healy?'

I whipped open his jacket, trying to get a better look at the blood.

Had he been stabbed?

460

'Get away from him!'

An officer rushed out of the first car to arrive, sprinting across to me, telling me to identify myself, repeatedly screaming at me to get away from the bodies.

And as I staggered back, as I collapsed on to the grass, as I told the cops my name, I shouted that we needed an ambulance.

So many secrets.

So much pain.

I didn't want there to be any more.

02:23:11

POLICE: So that was how Mr Healy got
  injured?
RAKER: Yes. How is he?
POLICE: I don't know. I can try and find
  out for you.
RAKER: Can you at least tell me if he's
  alive?
POLICE: I can't.
RAKER: Why not?
POLICE: Because I don't know for sure that
  he is.

8
The Tethers

85

A week later, Benjamin Robbins was buried in a cemetery just outside Oldham, next to his mother and his grandmother. Police stationed undercover officers at the scene, posing as mourners, hoping that Tori might make an appearance, but she was never going to show. Wherever she was, she would know about the funeral, would be reading about it. And I imagined that, quietly, in the corner of whatever room she was in, in whatever country she'd escaped to, she was grieving profoundly for the brother she lost. She hadn't killed him, but taking him to the quarry, trying to feed his anger and sense of injustice, sharing her act of revenge, led Ben to the final moments of his life.

It was one of the many reasons I felt conflicted about her.

On some level, Marc had been right: the two of them were – at the very least – a partial reflection of each other. It wasn't just that they were both killers, it was the fact that the murders they'd committed were so calculated and so brutal. Tori had stabbed a man twenty-seven times before daubing a message on the wall in his blood, and ruthlessly executed two more. A week in, the police were still trying to work out what exactly Marc had done, when, and to whom. But as they used more of the information Tori had gathered, it became clear how cruel and relentless Marc was.

He'd existed below the radar for thirty years, had kept an entire swathe of his life from his wife and children, from his parents, from anyone who'd ever known him. He'd bought cars second-hand and registered them to false addresses, and had applied for credit cards in false names. Just like in the US, where the crimes were connected because they had the same MO, in the UK, Marc established another pattern: he would kill on work trips or when he attended conferences, which was one of the ways in which Tori had linked him to unsolved crimes that had happened nearby. Often, it turned out, he would stay on an extra couple of days, telling Sarah that was how long the events lasted, when the truth was, some of the meetings were just a few hours. He'd scope out the victim and the places they inhabited multiple times, constructing the blueprint for the kill across repeat visits to the same place until he was satisfied the planning phase was complete. And, in some ways, that too was an echo of what Tori and Clara did as they'd prepared to move in on Anthony Yanis.

So Tori was a killer, one who had ended three lives. But, unlike with Marc, a part of me – perhaps a part that I didn't really want to acknowledge – still felt some sympathy for her.

I tried to tell myself it wasn't right.

But that didn't make the feeling any less real.

The police in the UK alerted Interpol, who in turn coordinated a manhunt for Tori, starting in Namibia. But I knew, instinctively, that she wouldn't have headed to Windhoek. That plan had gone out of the window the second Healy had found her passport and ticket in the other room of the cottage. She'd gone somewhere else, invented a new life somewhere different, and she was never going to come up for air.

The name Victoria Robbins was history.

And so was the girl from Oldham who'd once inhabited it.

86

Tori's wish to bring down the Zinter empire never materialized.

As it was always going to be, once he was cleared by the police and it became obvious that Asha had no knowledge of his brother's crimes, there was almost no impact on the casinos at all. Asha went on TV, apologized for his brother's actions – and, from the little I knew about him, did so sincerely – and confirmed he knew nothing about the activities of the men who'd been his friends since university. He also said he was founding a college fund in the memory of his brother's victims.

When I spoke to Sarah in the days after, she said he'd been in touch with her personally, and offered to fly her, Kyle and Mable out to his holiday home in the Swiss Alps to aid Kyle's recovery, and to help them get away from the glare of the media spotlight at home. It was a decent gesture, one that Sarah took up after Kyle awoke from the coma and was eventually released from hospital. She called me the day after they arrived and told me it was amazing, a beautiful, catered chalet halfway up a mountain. She said they'd settled in and were enjoying some time together, and that she was grateful not to be in a house where the memories of her husband – and the questions she had about him – weren't written into its walls; where every TV channel carried his face, and every website his name. Asha flew them out to a place where all of that felt a million miles away. And a day later, he did something even better: he offered to pay for the operation Sarah needed in Singapore. It wouldn't help Sarah forget, but it would help her start again, healthy, with the children she loved.

'Can I ask you something?' she said at the end of one of the calls we had, just before she was due to fly out for her op. 'Actually, I don't even know if it's a question, really.' She paused for a long time. 'He's contacted me. He wants us to see him.'

She'd stopped referring to her husband by his name, a show of fortitude that she'd managed to sustain throughout the time we'd been talking on the phone. But now her voice became soft.

'What do you think you're going to do?' I asked.

'What do *you* think I should do?'

'That's really only a decision you can make, Sarah.'

I got the sense that a large part of her desperately wanted to see him, not just because he was her husband and, despite the crimes he was accused of, had appeared to love her, but because she wanted to see if she'd missed something. She'd spent a decade with him, had seen him treat Kyle like a son, love Mable, love her, had been willing to sell everything they'd ever owned to get her to Singapore for the operation. She wanted to see if that person was still there, if he was real – and if he was, how she'd missed the other version of Marc hidden inside him.

The police had decided not to pursue charges against Kyle, concentrating their time instead on Marc, on Caleb and Yanis, on coordinating an investigation across two continents and tracking down Tori. In exchange, Kyle sat in his hospital bed and gave them everything he knew. And so Sarah had had no choice but to sit alongside him and listen. She'd listened to her son talk about Marc, about the stranger she'd shared a house with, a bed with, a family with, and had never seen a hint of, and all it did was raise more questions. That was why, in the end, I knew she'd go to see him.

She needed answers.

She needed to look him in the eye.

I'd always thought that the Marc who'd gone to that builders' yard to confront Daryl Beaumont had been an aberration, an abnormality formed by pressure, and love, and emotion.

But it wasn't.

That side of Marc had been there all along.

And, while she would soon start to get better, and while her son had returned to her broken but fixable, Sarah still needed to see the stranger she'd been married to before she could fully and completely begin the next stage of her life.

87

Around the same time as Ben's funeral, Pete Tomer video-called me.

There had been a memorial service for Casey Ryker, Florida Jones and Ryan Ling out in LA and he'd gone along. He said it was well attended, and while he was there, he met Gary Mailor, the detective from Barstow, a town in the middle of the Mojave Desert, who had worked Catalina Robbins's case, and Calvin Sanders, the ex-LAPD Robbery and Homicide detective who had been the lead at the debris basin.

'Mailor's in a pretty bad way,' Tomer said. 'He had a stroke a couple of years back, so he was there with a nurse. But I managed to understand some of what he was saying. He told me, even after he got sick, he still kept Catalina's photograph tacked up on a wall at home. He said, with his nurse's help, he'd been going back to the case once a month for the last three years. So the fact that these killers have finally been identified because of you . . .' He paused. 'Basically, he and Sanders wanted me to pass on their thanks.'

'I appreciate it,' I said, 'but I'm not really sure I deserve it.'

'Why?'

'I don't know. I feel like I'm a guest turning up to a party ten years late. There's no close family left.'

'You mean out here?'

'Yeah. Casey's dad died years back, her mother basically abandoned her, both of Wilma Steski's parents are long gone; Florida's family imploded, and Ryan's mum is dead too. Whoever was there at that service today, it means something to them, but it doesn't mean everything; not like with family.'

'None of that's your fault.'

'I know.'

'We can control a lot of things, but we can't control time. People get older. They die. And, anyway, maybe this was supposed to be the way it got solved. Maybe it was the *only* way it was ever going to get solved.'

'What do you mean?'

'I don't know. Maybe I'm just losing it in my old age, but . . .' He stopped. 'Look, I worked Wilma's case thirty years ago; you've been working yours now – and despite us being on opposite sides of the world, both those investigations turned out to be at either end of the same trail. What are the chances?'

I studied him on-screen. 'Are you talking about destiny?'

'No.' He laughed. 'I don't believe in that shit.'

'Coincidence?'

'There *are* no coincidences – come on, that's the first rule of police work.' But then his smile dropped away. 'I don't know what I'm trying to say, really. Maybe that, sometimes in life, the ties that bind, they bind for a reason.'

He'd landed on something I'd been thinking about for a while – not just on this case, but on some of the other cases I'd worked down the years. How, despite decades and distance, there were tethers binding us to people we didn't know and hadn't met yet, but who eventually, inescapably, we'd be drawn towards.

Maybe there was something to the idea.

Or maybe it was less baroque: something more like luck, or chance, that ended up bringing a case like this to its close.

Neither of us could ever really know for sure.

But if those tethers did exist, if they bound us to people in

471

our lives that would eventually matter, and through those rela-
tionships we could find endings and perhaps a measure of peace
for those who were hurting, I wanted to believe in them.

Life was so traumatic.

There was so much heartbreak, so much pain.

I wanted to believe in something better.

88

Healy was released from hospital the day after the events at the cottage.

He called me as he headed to the Tube, recalling how it had gone down on the moors: Marc had tried to make a break for it; Healy had grabbed him; the two of them had lost their footing on the sloped track and, as they'd collapsed, Healy had landed on his arm and broken it instantly; Marc had scooped up a shard of loose granite, stabbed it into Healy's stomach; and Healy had responded – powered by adrenalin – kicking Marc's legs out from under him. That was when Marc had fallen and knocked himself out. Shortly after, Healy had blacked out from the pain himself.

Following that phone call, I saw very little of him for a week.

The stomach injury looked bad, but doctors said it wasn't serious – so stitched up and with his arm in plaster, Healy returned to his job as a security guard, because it was a zero-hours contract and if he didn't turn up, he didn't get paid. In the hours either side of that, we were in and out of the same police station – giving Bakhash, Clarkson and a visiting detective from Manchester multiple accounts of what went on – but we rarely passed each other and my calls to him went unanswered.

Knowing Healy, he just wanted some space.

One night, after getting back from another interview at the station in Slough, I decided to call Melanie Craw to see how she was doing.

'I'm worried,' she said.

'Why, what's the matter?'

'The cops haven't asked me about that money.'

The hush money.

The one hundred grand she took from Caleb.

'But you told them about it?'

She didn't reply.

'You didn't tell the police about it?'

'If I tell them, it's over.'

'What are you talking about?'

'Use your head, Raker. I built my whole career – even *this* career – on being a straight arrow. Anyone who's ever known me will tell you that I held myself to exactly the same standards I expected from the people who worked for me. So if I sit there and tell the cops I took a hundred grand from Caleb Zinter, what do you think is going to happen? My reputation will be destroyed. And all I *am* is my reputation.'

'That's not true –'

'It *is* true. You don't get it. I'm a woman. Men can do all the shit they want and people forgive them. But a woman? It'll be Armageddon.'

'Maybe they don't know about the money.'

'The cops?' She stopped. 'Yeah, maybe not.'

'They must have been through the Zinters' accounts.'

'You'd have thought so.'

'So perhaps Caleb, or Kerrill, or whoever it was that wired you that money, disguised it as something else. Is it hidden at your end too?'

'I was careful, yeah.'

'Then if the cops haven't mentioned it already, they probably don't know.'

I was still tired, physically and emotionally drained from the case, so – after the call with Craw – I went to bed and spent a while texting Rebekah Murphy, a woman who had hired me the previous year to find her mother. At the end of that search,

474

there had been a flicker of something between us, something I hadn't felt for a long time, and we'd texted and video-called often in the time since. The problem was, she lived in New York, had roots there, two young daughters, so as much as we'd got on, I knew we were both frightened to address the one big problem we had.

She was 3,500 miles away from me.

I went to bed that night thinking again about the conversation I'd had with Pete Tomer, about the connective tissue that shaped our lives, wondering whether – somehow, as difficult as it was for both of us to see right now – Rebekah and I might be able to overcome the physical distance between us.

She made me happy.

She made my life better, even from the other side of an ocean.

Ours was a tether that I hoped would endure.

89

The next morning, my phone woke me out of a dead sleep.

Daylight was pouring in.

Groggy, I grabbed the mobile off the bedside table. 'Hello?'

'You up?' It was Healy.

'What time is it?'

'Nine thirty.'

I pulled the phone away from my ear, double-checking, not quite believing it could be so late. I'd been out for almost eleven straight hours.

'I'm outside,' Healy said.

I looked along the landing and down the stairs to where Healy's silhouette rippled in the frosted glass panel of the front door.

'Okay, give me a sec.'

Pulling on some trousers and a T-shirt, I headed down and let him in. 'You look like shite,' he muttered as he moved past me – arm in a sling, wincing a little from his stomach injury – and headed to the kitchen.

I put some coffee on. 'You been to Siberia or something?'

'What?'

'I left you about ten voicemails.'

'Yeah, sorry.' He shrugged. 'Been trying to work, then there's all these bloody interviews at the station, and then juggling all this stuff with Liam and Ciaran . . .'

'Any progress?'

'With the boys? I'm seeing them again next week.'

'That's something, right?'

'Yeah,' Healy said, simply.

I poured us both a coffee – but, as I pushed his mug across the worktop towards him, I stopped.

There was something in his face.

'What?' I said.

'You see the news this morning?'

'No. You woke me up, remember?'

He just nodded.

'Are you going to make me pull it out of you?'

'They arrested Craw.'

I frowned. 'What?'

'She didn't tell them about that money she took.'

I thought back to the conversation I'd had with her the night before. She'd been right. It would destroy her reputation, it would set light to her career, and – because society was still so skewed – she *would* be judged more harshly, even though she'd taken the money to protect her girls.

But then something else popped into my head.

How did the police know what the money was for? How did they know it was a bribe if Craw had never told them? It could just have been a huge bonus. Asha couldn't have told the cops the truth, because he was totally out of the loop on what Caleb and Kerrill were doing.

And then I looked at Healy again.

And, this time, my heart sank.

'Oh shit, Healy.'

He didn't say anything.

'*You* told them?'

He shrugged again.

'What the hell were you thinking?'

'What was *I* thinking?' He was immediately incredulous. 'Have you forgotten what she did? She torched my career. She sacked me from the Met –'

477

'Because you were trying to kill a *prisoner*.'

'He wasn't just a "prisoner".'

'Whether you like it or not, Glass was a pris–'

'Don't ever say his name. Don't ever say his fucking name in front of me.' His face flushed, the rage he felt for his daughter's killer still burning all these years later. 'Craw ruined me. Being a cop was all I knew. She took that away. She destroyed my life, she destroyed my family, she destroyed everything. *She's* the reason I have to sit there and be a punching bag for my sons.'

'That isn't down to her.'

'If she hadn't sacked me, I wouldn't have spiralled.'

'You can't put all of that on her.'

'Why not?'

I rubbed at an eye. 'Healy, listen to me. She's not the reason –'

The doorbell rang.

We both looked along the hallway.

I closed my eyes, tried to regain my composure, and then – with one last, lingering look at Healy – went to the door and opened it.

'Hi, David.'

It was Alice-Leigh.

She leaned slightly to her left, looking back along the hallway to where Healy was standing, staring at her, confused as to why his son's girlfriend was at my door.

'Ah, good,' she said. 'You're both here.'

'Alice?' Healy responded, confused.

But she didn't react to him.

Instead, her eyes were back on mine.

'I've finally come to tell you the truth,' she said.

90

I led her through to the kitchen, offering her a seat at the table.

Healy smiled at Alice – pretending that it wasn't a surprise that she'd just turned up out of the blue – and asked her how she was feeling.

'Heavy,' she said.

She gently rubbed her belly.

'I hope my son has been looking after you?'

'He has. Liam's a good man.'

Healy agreed, but the truth was he didn't really know if Liam was a good man or not.

'What's going on, Alice?' I asked her gently.

She cleared her throat. One hand went to her bracelet, same as it had done the other times I'd met her, and she started playing with the six daisies on it.

'This is, um . . .' She stopped, looked between us. 'I've been trying to figure out how to, uh . . . how to . . .' Again she stopped. 'I've been trying to figure out how to say what I need to say to you both for months now, but I don't know . . .' Slowly, her gaze landed on Healy. 'Do you know how Liam and I met?'

Healy pushed out another smile, but it was a facade, just like before. He had absolutely no idea. He'd seen his son once in eight years.

'I'm not sure he ever mentioned it.'

'We met in a pub. This real dive of a place.'

'That sounds like Liam.'

'I just, uh . . .' Alice started to nervously scratch the back of her hand. 'I just love Liam so much.'

'I know you do, sweetheart,' Healy said.

But it was clear we didn't get what she was trying to say, because she started shaking her head. 'I just wanted to see what all of you were like. That's all. It was just curiosity. I didn't think it would go any further. I just wanted to talk to each of you, nothing more. But then I went into that pub. Liam was the first of you that I sought out, because I'd found out that pub was where he drank, and we started talking, and the next thing I knew we were suddenly going out on dates. I fell in love with him so quickly, so *hard*, and I knew it wasn't right, because he had no idea what my original motive was for being in that pub. But now we're bound to one another. I'm having a baby with him, and I just . . .' She sank in her seat. 'I swear, I just wanted to see what your family was like. Liam. Ciaran. Gemma. You.'

She looked at Healy.

'What are you talking about?' he asked.

It came out sharply.

'It's okay, Alice,' I said, stepping in, maintaining the same tone, the same volume. She'd gone back to playing with her bracelet, to sliding the six daisies up and down the band. 'I think you need to tell us what's happening here.'

It took a long time for her to look up again.

'I haven't told Liam,' she said. 'I don't know how to.'

'Told him what?'

'About my past.'

I leaned closer. 'What about your past?'

Her finger strayed back to the bracelet again, and as I looked at it more closely I saw there was something engraved on the band – tiny, almost imperceptible.

She saw me looking and held up her hand, letting me see.

The engraving was one word.

RIP.

'I was born guilty,' she said. 'My whole life has been tarnished by him. I always think I can escape what he did, the shadow it cast across me, but I never can. That was why I wanted to become a lawyer. It's why I got this band. This band's a reminder of who I am, who I'll always be, and I'm just so sorry.' She looked at Healy. 'I'm so sorry for what he did. I'm so sorry I sought you all out. If I'd never done that, if I'd never gone to that pub, I never would have fallen in love with your son . . .' She started to cry. 'I'm so sorry I fell in love with Liam.'

Healy looked at me, completely thrown.

But I was already a step ahead.

I was already seeing the tethers.

Somewhere in the shadows of my thoughts, a memory surfaced: me, in an interview room, thirteen years ago, in the aftermath of another case.

Six daisies on a band.

Six bodies buried in the dark.

And as I began to realize who Alice-Leigh was, I looked at Healy, confusion on his face, and I thought of Liam and Ciaran, and I remembered Gemma – Healy's ex-wife – and the pain and grief that had shattered their lives when Leanne died.

And I looked at Alice again.

And I looked at her swollen belly.

And I realized, for all of them, the pain was only just beginning.

POLICE: This is the resumption of the
    interview with David Raker about the
    events at Hark's Hill Woods, aka
    'the Dead Tracks'. Today's date is
    25 October 2011. So, David, just to
    go back to what happened when you
    found Glass's hiding place. You and
    Healy climbed into that manhole
    cover, down the ladder, and into the
    place where he kept his victims?

RAKER: Yes, as I've told you repeatedly
    for the past two hours and forty
    minutes.

POLICE: And that was the place where Colm
    Healy got injured?

RAKER: Yes.

POLICE: And it was where you found the six
    bodies?

RAKER: Yes.

POLICE: Including Colm Healy's daughter,
    Leanne?

RAKER: Yes.

POLICE: And you think all of them were
    killed by Dr Glass?

RAKER: I don't think. I know. You
do too.

POLICE: And Glass, he had a wife and
child, correct?

RAKER: Yes. They're both dead.

POLICE: We did some digging around and
we've found out that you're right –
he did have a wife and child, and
they *are* both dead. But we discovered
something else.

RAKER: What?

POLICE: Glass had a second child with
another woman.

RAKER: What?

POLICE: This was almost a decade back.
We think he killed the mother. He
made it look like a suicide. The
child has been in social care since
aged two.

RAKER: How old's the kid?

POLICE: She's nine now.

RAKER: It's a girl?

POLICE: Yes.

RAKER: Is she okay?

POLICE: She's fine. I guess her problems
aren't going to come now, they're
going to come when she's older, and
she realizes her father is a
psychopath who murdered six people
and is going to be spending the rest
of his life behind bars.

RAKER: Have you met her?

POLICE: The girl? No. We sent a
    specialist team around to speak to
    her. They said she's a sweet kid.
RAKER: What's her name?
POLICE: Her name's Alice.

Author's Note

As with all my books, my hope is that *The Missing Family* can be read as a standalone novel without any prior knowledge of the David Raker series. However, if you are interested in filling in some background on the origins of the Dr Glass story – particularly in preparation for the next Raker novel – *The Dead Tracks* is a good place to start. *Vanished*, which follows directly on from *The Dead Tracks*, is also useful for explaining why Healy's relationship with Melanie Craw is so complicated and how he got fired from the Met. If you decide not to read either, it won't affect your enjoyment or understanding of what comes next in the series, it's just a useful way to shed light on how exactly we ended up here.

Two other quick things . . . As eagle-eyed procedural experts will have already noted, I've altered and adapted some real-life police practices – particularly with regard to investigations and interviews – in *The Missing Family*. This has purely been done to keep you turning those pages. And, of course, the Skyline, the Afrique and the Red Phoenix are all fictional casinos but based very closely on the supercasinos Las Vegas has become known for. If anyone is interested in finding out about the origins of these mega-resorts, may I suggest Peter Earley's brilliant book, *Supercasino: Inside the New Las Vegas.*

Acknowledgements

As always, a huge thank you to everyone at Michael Joseph – and Penguin as a whole – who do such an incredible job of ensuring my books end up in the hands (and ears – thank you to the Penguin audio team!) of readers like you. An extra special thank you to my wonderful publisher and editor, Maxine Hitchcock, as well as to Emma Plater and particularly Clare Bowron, who both helped knock this story into shape. Oh, and thank you to Caroline Pretty too, my eagle-eyed copyeditor and skilled unraveller of terrible timelines. Finally, huge thanks to the amazing team behind the scenes who do such a brilliant job for me, but who I rarely get the chance to say thank you to personally: Kallie Townsend, Ciara Berry, Mubarak Elmubarak, Hattie Evans, Beatrix McIntyre, Jon Kennedy Becci Livingstone, Helen Eka, Stella Newing, James Keyte, Christina Ellicott, Laura Garrod, Kelly Mason, Hannah Padgham, Emily Harvey, Richard Rowlands and Akua Akowuah.

Thank you to everyone at Darley Anderson, including Jade Kavanagh, Mary Darby, Georgia Fuller and Rosanna Bellingham, as well as Sheila David at Catapult. And, of course, all the thanks and then a whole lot more to the queen herself, Camilla Bolton – my agent, my friend, and one of my very favourite people.

To Lorna Shute (and to Rob Allen who put her forward), the winner of the 2023 Clic Sargent Young People vs Cancer auction: thank you. I hope you liked your namesake in the book – and the mention of Archie the Westie!

Thank you to Chris Ewan, Claire Douglas and Gilly Macmillan for sharing the pain, lovely lunches and tons of laughs.

To my family, both here and in South Africa – Boxie, Di, Delme, Kim, Declan, Nathan, Josh, Lucy, Rich, Hannah, Sam, Jo, Barry – thank you for all of your love and support. It means so much. But an extra special shout-out to my mum and dad. You're the best. Always have been, always will be.

Thank you to the two women who are unlucky enough to share a house with me: my daughter, Erin, who absolutely *promises* to read my books in her gap year (don't put any money on it), and my wife, Sharlé, who steadies the ship mid-manuscript when I'm having a moment and who also doubles-up as the world's greatest continuity expert.

And, of course, thank you to you, my wonderful readers, without whom none of this is possible. Thank you for buying my books, talking about them, recommending them and reviewing them. Your support never, ever gets taken for granted.